SOMEONE AT A DISTANCE

by

DOROTHY WHIPPLE

with a new preface by

NINA BAWDEN

PERSEPHONE BOOKS
LONDON

Published by Persephone Books Ltd 1999

Reprinted as a Persephone Classic
in 2008, 2011 and 2018

First published by John Murray 1953

© 1968 Judith Eldergill

Preface © Nina Bawden 1999

Typeset in ITC Baskerville by Keystroke,
High Street, Tettenhall, Wolverhampton

Printed and bound in Germany by
GGP Media GmbH, Poessneck

ISBN 978 1 906462 00 0

Persephone Books Ltd
59 Lamb's Conduit Street
London WC1N 3NB
020 7242 9292

www.persephonebooks.co.uk

PREFACE

The writing of fiction is a dreadful trade. Critical assessment can be capricious, publishers uncertain; good books perish, bad ones thrive; worldwide best sellers can sink without trace. Dorothy Whipple, several of whose novels were not only immensely popular Book Society Choices in this country in the nineteen-thirties and forties, and a great success in America, but also highly regarded by respectable critics, was unknown to me until I was sent a copy of *Someone at a Distance*. Although after its publication in 1953 she continued to write short stories and children's books, this was her last novel. It was also – surprisingly, since it is to my mind her best – the only one of her novels not to receive a major review in a national newspaper.

It is strange because she was, if not a great writer, a remarkably good one, setting her plain, forceful tales in the same geographical and emotional area as Mrs Gaskell. Her distinction had been widely and approvingly noted by – among others – Hugh Walpole, who foresaw that she would be a novelist of 'true importance', Orville Prescott (the notably stern reviewer of the *New York Times*), and Terence de Vere White, who wrote about her at length in the *Irish*

Times. For Frank Swinnerton she brought to her work 'a human talent, a seeing eye and the freshness and humour of one to whom the writing of novels is still a happy adventure.' And Anthony Burgess, reviewing her last collection of short stories, called them 'illuminating and startling'.

Of course there is nothing new in Dorothy Whipple's fate. Time is a notorious monster of ingratitude. And fashions change. The kind of gentle – well, apparently gentle – domestic tales she tells, no violence except of the spirit, sex only hinted at, may have had something to do with her disappearance from the paperback lists and the library shelves. As her publisher John Murray said, writing to her about the comparative failure of *Someone at a Distance*, 'Editors have gone mad about action and passion'.

But it does not explain her exclusion in more recent years from the general revival of interest in women writers. Perhaps this is because she is not a 'woman's novelist' in the way that the term is commonly used. Dorothy Whipple once said, 'The world of men is so different from the world of women, it is a wonder they speak the same language' and she herself possessed what Virginia Woolf insisted that all good writers should have, an androgynous mind. She writes about men as she writes about women, with understanding, from within. And her style is clear and precise, graceful without being showy, and never fancy or fey.

She is conscious of the disadvantages sometimes attendant on being a woman, but sees those disadvantages as mainly financial. Mrs Beard, the splendidly abrasive manager of an old people's residential hotel in *Someone at a Distance* puts it clearly to the heroine of this novel whose husband has left her. 'D'you know how hard money is to come by for women like us? . . . We're not the new sort of women with University degrees in Economics, like those women who speak on the Radio nowadays, girls who can do anything. We're ordinary women who married too young to get a training and we've spent the best years of our lives keeping house for our husbands. Not that we didn't enjoy it, but now you're out on your ear like me at over forty.' Mrs Beard is not a modern feminist. Nor is her creator. Dorothy Whipple is a storyteller in the straightforward tradition of J. B. Priestley and Arnold Bennett rather than Virginia Woolf or Elizabeth Bowen. And she is a very good storyteller indeed.

Someone at a Distance is, on the face of it, a fairly ordinary tale of a deceived wife and a foolish husband in rural suburbia not far from London and, perhaps because the author was nearing sixty when she wrote it, there is a slight pre-war flavour about the domestic expectations of the characters. Ellen, the wife of Avery North, a London publisher, finds it strange that her two 'day-women', her only household help, will only work for her in the mornings.

Ellen is a genuinely good woman, however, unselfish, loving and kind. It is always difficult to portray virtue, which has been out of fashion in fiction for a long time, but Ellen is virtuous: she is conscious of a moral dimension in the way people conduct their lives. She and Avery have two children, eighteen-year old Hugh, away on National Service, and fifteen-year old Anne, the apple of her father's eye.

The serpent that enters this happy family's Eden is a latter day Emma Bovary in the person of Louise Lanier, the spoilt, imperious daughter of a bookseller in provincial France. She is escaping to England after a humiliating rejection by her lover, the son of the local landowner, who has discarded Louise in order to marry a girl of superior social position. Louise has put an advertisement in *The Times*, offering French conversation and the performance of light domestic duties and Avery's mother, old Mrs North, who is both rich and lonely, has answered it.

The seduction of old Mrs North is swift and easy. She is a difficult, disputatious woman, the sort of woman who, greeting her grandson, home from the army for the weekend, can merely say, grudgingly, '. . . you get a good deal of leave, don't you?' Since Mrs North's husband died she has not 'come first with anybody' and Louise rapidly makes herself indispensable. When Mrs North dies, she leaves the young Frenchwoman a thousand pounds and her furs and Louise decides to stay with the Norths until the money is safely paid over.

It is, as I said, a fairly ordinary tale. But it is a great gift to be able to take an ordinary tale and make it compulsive reading. It is all in the telling and Dorothy Whipple is a storyteller – an art that cannot be taught, cannot be learned, an art only a few writers are lucky enough to be born with. At the end of the novel you can look back and see how it was done, how the author held your attention and persuaded you how one thing was bound to lead to the next, but while you are reading you are only aware of the suspense, the need to turn the page.

Thus the seduction of Avery is much slower, and surprisingly painful to read about. We know it is going to happen, the ground has been prepared from the beginning, but not how it will be brought about nor what will come after. A few lines at the very beginning of the book set his character clearly before us: when Avery and Ellen were first together, 'he sulked heavily when she offended him. To punish her, he wouldn't eat. He would either fling away from the table leaving his food untouched, or would refuse to come to the table at all. Ellen was astonished. Very young in those days, she didn't coax him as his mother had done, but kept going to look at him with wide grey eyes, rather like one child staring at another who is behaving unaccountably.'

This little scene is exactly the right one to bring Avery to life. Not that it is particularly remarkable on first reading. It is only later on in the story that we can see how cleverly it was planted, how economically it illuminates a great deal of what follows. Avery cannot bear to be in the wrong. It is why he cannot disentangle himself from Louise after his wife and daughter have caught him with her on the sofa in 'an embrace that should have had no witnesses'. It casts a light on his relationship with Ellen, as suitably discreet as when we learn that their single beds are 'three feet or so' apart. And when Ellen refuses to take money from him after the divorce and he writes, 'I beg you to take it, if only to make me feel better about all this', it echoes that earlier detail with, to me, devastating effect. The man who wrote that letter is recognisably the same as the man who flounced away from the dining table. It could be no other.

Writing about an earlier novel, *Greenbanks*, a Book Society Choice, Hugh Walpole says that 'this business of characters leaping strongly to individual life is one of the oddest and most unaccountable things. No novelist, however hard he try, can be sure whether this miracle will be granted to him or not.' To his mind, it had been granted to Dorothy Whipple who has 'performed splendidly the great job of the novelist, increased for us infinitely the population of the living world.'

High praise, but deserved, I think. All the characters in this novel have a strong, independent reality, both emotionally, in their actions, and in their physical appearance. Take Mrs Beard with her 'built up hair, large bust, curved hips and that thrown-forward look which may have been due to her stays or to the fact that she wore high-heeled court shoes which tired her and made her cross, but which she thought necessary to her appearance.'

Although she is a minor character, she is not stock or off the peg. Nor are Monsieur Lanier and Madame Lanier, Louise's unfortunate parents whose world is their shop, the 'Librairie-Papeterie Lanier, Spécialiste du Stylo', the cosy back room behind it, smelling of innumerable good dinners; their friendly shopkeeper neighbours, their daughter whom they both love and fear. Dorothy Whipple conjures up the Laniers with small delicious touches – for example, Monsieur Lanier wears his eyeglasses on a black ribbon and in moments of emotion he is liable to lasso himself with it. They are a couple who inspire affection, so much so that their distress when they finally see their daughter plain, as not only cold-hearted and ungrateful but depraved as well, you ache in sympathy.

In *Random Commentary*, an engaging fragment of auto-biography, Dorothy Whipple confessed, 'I don't like having to concoct plots, I like doing people', and perhaps there is a sense that the ending of *Someone at a Distance* is too neat; a modified happy ending to what is, essentially, a brilliant account of frailty and folly. On the other hand there is a moral satisfaction in the right people getting their come-uppance and an intellectual pleasure in the recognition of the part played in all human affairs by malicious chance.

But Dorothy Whipple has 'done' her people so well they each have their own fully realised world within the structure of the novel, from Ellen at Netherfold, to Mrs Beard at Somerton, the Laniers at Amigny, Avery at work in London. Things far apart in distance, actual or metaphorical, draw together as the novel comes to an end.

Nina Bawden

SOMEONE AT A DISTANCE

CHAPTER ONE

⟨∘⟨◇⟩∘⟩

I

Widowed, in the house her husband had built with day and night nurseries and a music-room, as if the children would stay there for ever, instead of marrying and going off at the earliest possible moment, old Mrs. North yielded one day to a long-felt desire to provide herself with company. She answered an advertisement in the personal column of *The Times*.

Old Mrs. North's husband had spoilt her, but now that he was dead and her three children married, no one spoilt her any more. She didn't come first with anybody and she didn't like that.

She considered that a woman who had brought three children into the world is entitled, in old age, to be the object of their care and attention. What was the good of having children if, half the time, you never saw them? Cicely, her daughter, who might have been a comfort, had chosen to marry an American and lived in Washington, sending lavish parcels, it is true, during the war and coming herself as soon as it was over, but going back, of course, and leaving her mother lonely as before.

The late George North had founded and brought to prosperity a hosiery factory, but though his sons still drew substantial incomes from it, neither had gone into the business. Howard, the elder, was in the Foreign Office. It had seemed a distinguished career when his father had arranged it for him, but as a consequence, Howard spent his life with his wife in the East, both Near and Far, and his mother rarely saw him. Only Avery, the youngest of the family, remained near her.

Avery had acquired a partnership in a firm of publishers with offices off the Strand, known for fifteen years now as Bennett and North. He had a house in the country three miles out of the little town of Newington, where his mother lived, and went up to London every day, which took him an hour.

Old Mrs. North incessantly complained that she saw next to nothing of Avery, his wife Ellen or his two children. Of the children, the boy Hugh had just started his compulsory army service and the girl Anne was away at school. Avery was always in London and Ellen was always busy, because she had no maids. Nobody had maids nowadays, certainly not those who lived in the country.

'Why don't you all come and live with me? This great empty house . . . !' said old Mrs. North from time to time.

But her invitation was not accepted and she really didn't want it to be. As it was she was able to nurse a perpetual grievance against her daughter-in-law for not coming to see her more often, and if she had her on the premises, she would have had to let that grievance go. Also the children would be too much for her. The young were so exhausting. So she was able to go on pressing them to come, well knowing they would not, and to complain that she never saw them and had nothing to do with herself.

Mrs. North had a housekeeper, a Miss Daley, who, reinforced by day-women, kept everything in apple-pie order, but who had an unfortunate passion for singing in the chapel choir. Unfortunate, that is, in Mrs. North's opinion, because for one thing she considered that Miss Daley's voice should never have been heard at all, it was far too powerful, and for another, it took Miss Daley out on Wednesdays for practice and on Sundays for performance. The chapel choir was Miss Daley's burning interest, and Mrs. North resented other people's interests. Her housekeeper's singing and her daughter-in-law's gardening took up time that should, she considered, have been spent with her. She felt entitled to their time; Miss Daley's because she paid for it, and Ellen's because, as Avery's wife, she had a duty to Avery's mother.

'But I'm an old woman,' said Mrs. North to her son. She said it bitterly because she didn't like being old. 'I suppose I can't expect Ellen to spend more time with me than she can help.'

'Ellen's always busy, Mother,' defended Avery. 'You know day-women have it all their own way these days. We simply can't get anyone to come so far out of the town in the afternoons. So Ellen always has to cook the dinner herself. And she does an immense amount of gardening. William Parkes is old. He has as much as he can do with the kitchen garden and with looking after the mare when Anne's at school.'

'You should turn Parkes out of that cottage and get someone more competent, then. And why you keep a horse when Anne can only ride it for about fourteen weeks out of the year, Avery, I simply cannot understand. It would be far better to hire. . . .'

She was off at a tangent, forgetting her complaint that Ellen didn't spend time with her because she was old.

It was not because she was old. At Somerton Manor, a country hotel where Ellen had taken the children for holidays during the war, was a Mrs. Brockington who was old too, but there was no one with whom Ellen would rather have spent more time.

Old Mrs. North didn't really want Ellen's kind of company. She wanted something Ellen could not supply and Ellen didn't even know what it was. She only felt they didn't get on very well, which was a pity, because they both loved Avery. She considered herself very much to blame because she forgot about her mother-in-law for reprehensibly long periods, sometimes as much as three days together, and then remembered her with a sense of shock.

'Oh, dear, I haven't been . . . I haven't rung up. . . . When did I go last?' she had to say to herself and would throw down her gardening tools, take off her gumboots, do her hands, her hair, change into a coat and skirt, get her car out and go and sit with her mother-in-law; and was able to go to bed that night with a sense of relief that she wouldn't have to go again for a day or two. All the same, she was ashamed.

This remembering of old Mrs. North occurred to her suddenly one evening in June as she was bringing Avery up from the station in her car, because his was under repair.

'Your mother!' she exclaimed.

'What about her?' said Avery.

'Do let's go and see her for five minutes. I've only been once this week and you haven't been at all.'

Avery grumbled. It had been hot in London and he wanted to get home, he said.

'I know, darling. And I'm anxious about my oven – but just for one minute,' she persuaded.

She drove in at the gates, behind which stood the late-Victorian house with its turrets and brick battlements, the windows of its mostly unused rooms glittering with the special plate-glass the late George North had insisted upon.

Old Mrs. North was sitting on the sofa in the drawing-room, some battered schoolbooks beside her, and behind her on the wall a collection of miniatures of her husband, herself and her children in infancy. The whole family looked chronically ill on ivory.

'Good afternoon, strangers,' said the old lady caustically.

'I know, Mother,' said Ellen, kissing her. 'But the days get past me so fast. My life seems to be one long scramble. . . .'

'Yes, my dear, I've heard you say so before. Are you going to sit down? No? I hadn't expected it. I suppose you want to get home. Well, it's only natural. Go along, both of you. I'm very well and everything's all right. Thank you for coming. Good-bye.'

Avery laughed. But it wouldn't have done for Ellen to. Besides, she didn't feel like laughing; she felt remorseful. Now they were there, she thought they ought to stay a little,

5

and made, while talking, for a chair. But Avery took her firmly by the arm and piloted her to the drawing-room door.

When they reached it, old Mrs. North brought them to a halt.

'I've answered an advertisement,' she said.

They turned.

'An advertisement?'

'In yesterday's *Times*.'

She held out the folded newspaper to her son. Round his shoulder Ellen read at the marked place.

'Young Frenchwoman desires to spend July, August, in English home. French conversation. Light domestic duties. . . . '

'But why do you want a Frenchwoman?' asked Avery.

'When you get to my age, Avery,' said his mother, 'you will find yourself in need of companionship occasionally.'

'But you could have an English companion at any time, Mother.'

'I'd like a Frenchwoman,' said Mrs. North firmly.

'So that's why the French grammars are out?' said Ellen, who had been puzzled by the school-books. 'I couldn't think. . . . '

'You could have asked, my dear,' said old Mrs. North. 'As a matter of fact, I'm rubbing up my French.'

Ellen found something so touching and forlorn in this announcement that she took up Mrs. North's hand and held it in her own. Avery laughed in affectionate amusement.

'You're a gallant old girl,' he said.

'I think it's a very good idea,' said Ellen. 'I think it will be fun.'

'At my age, I don't expect fun,' said Mrs. North. 'But I hope it will be interesting. I'm too old to go in search of change, so I'll try to bring change into the house. It's too quiet as it is.'

'Yes,' said Ellen, abashed.

Mrs. North removed her hand with some impatience from Ellen's.

'There's my old copy of French idioms,' said Avery, who had no idea of what was going on between the women. 'How I hated the thing! There are better books now, Mother. Shall I get you some from town?'

'No, thank you. If the young person is coming, I shan't have time to learn much. And if she isn't, I shan't learn anything at all. Now you can both go. I'm sure Ellen's got something in the oven that needs her attention.'

'Oh, I have, I have,' wailed Ellen, running out of the room, her coat flying. 'I'd forgotten. Avery, come . . . Good-bye, Mother . . . Good-bye. . . .'

II

The road from the town, on this fine summer evening, was thronged with bicycles. Ellen, driving home in a hurry, braked, sounded her horn, frowned and fretted.

'Why will they ride four abreast?' she asked, avoiding the bare legs of a girl-cyclist, who wobbled, then bit her lip with such smiling apology that Ellen's irritation vanished and, with perfect good humour, she smiled back.

'I ought to do more for your mother,' she said.

'She's all right,' said Avery, relaxed, letting himself be driven. 'In fact, she's lucky. Well looked after, enough money, quite fair health in spite of her complaints about her heart. Compared with other old people nowadays . . .'

'Oh, I agree,' said Ellen, willing not to feel uncomfortable too long. Avery was good at not letting her feel uncomfortable. He was good at putting things in a reasonable light.

'Fancy a French girl,' said Ellen, pursuing conversation in the desultory fashion of the married. 'I've forgotten any French I ever knew, haven't you?'

Avery lifted up his voice to show what he could do.

'Si par hasard tu vois ma tante,' he sang. ' Complimente-la de ma part.'

Ellen laughed delightedly.

'Go on,' she urged him.

'I can't.'

'I tell you a French phrase I'm always coming across nowadays and that I can't stand,' she said, skimming the ankles of another cyclist. '"L'homme moyen sensuel."'

'Mais c'est moi,' said Avery with a sudden flash of recognition. 'It fits me to a T.'

'Of course it doesn't,' said Ellen indignantly. 'You're not average.'

His family would never let him find anything wrong with himself.

'Am I fat?' he would say sometimes, spreading his hands over his ribs with some anxiety, and they all chorused no with such emphasis that he was almost able to believe them. Nevertheless, at forty-three, he was beginning to put on weight. So far it only added to his good looks. He was tall and it suited him to be slightly heavy in build.

'We're giving a party next week for Geddes Mayes. You know, the American,' he said now.

'Oh, are you?' said Ellen. 'Need I come?'

'No. Not if you don't want to,' said Avery.

'Hurray,' said Ellen. 'I'd rather be in the garden.'

Guiltily, pleasurably, she avoided the parties Bennett and North gave for authors, agents and the like. At first, she had youthfully tried to do what might be considered her duty as a publisher's wife. She moved from group to group, smiling. But everybody talked vociferously, and though here and there people moved aside, smiling, to let her pass, nobody interrupted conversation for her. Slight, fair, with no idea at all of trying to make an impression, she didn't look important and nobody wondered who she was. The rooms got very hot and the air so blue and fumey from the drinks that she felt if she put a match to it, it would light. Then little flames might stand above the authors' heads like the old picture of Pentecost. But it wouldn't necessarily mean they were inspired, though Bennett and North might benefit if they were.

There was a bachelor's flat off Avery's office where he spent the night when he had to stay in town and she kept escaping to it to get cool and pass some of the time. She went through the clothes he kept there, to see if moth had got into them. She straightened the contents of the drawers and collected a few forgotten handkerchiefs for the laundry. Not that she was incurably domestic, but it was something to do.

In the empty adjoining office, she sat at his desk, trying to imagine his life away from her. What did it feel like to be Avery here? He was important, powerful, waited upon by secretaries and typists, some of them very attractive young women. Probably some of them adored him, thought Ellen, unperturbed. She was so happily certain of him.

When she felt she had been away too long, she went back to the party, which was just as before, except that the air was even hotter and bluer. She smiled rather fixedly, standing at Avery's elbow, and was glad when it was over.

Nowadays, feeling that no one knew whether she was there or not, she stayed away.

The business of party going and giving fell mostly on Avery, because his partner, John Bennett, didn't like parties any better than Ellen did.

When old Thomas Bennett, John's father, was on the point of retirement, he considered the state of affairs within the firm with much misgiving. He knew that John, left to himself, would stick to the office like a snail to its shell. His interest was in books and their production. He would sit all day reading, discussing, turning over projects, but he wouldn't go out. He was shy, he wasn't a good mixer. He needed someone to make the contacts with the outside world, someone to keep the firm in the public eye, to keep it up to date and keep it moving. Avery presented himself at the right time. He knew nothing about books and seemed to have no natural interest in them, but he had possibilities on the social side. He was good-looking, he was likeable. They thought he would do; and his father was ready to put up a good deal of money.

George North had been one of those Victorian industrialists with a wistful admiration for culture. He encouraged literature and music. Hence the music room at The Cedars, mostly given over to his daughter's weak soprano, but where sometimes a celebrated artist appeared to give a recital to intimidated and impressed assemblies who never knew what to say when it was over. George North was pleased and proud to think his son would be a publisher and Avery himself thought anything better than going into stockings. He liked the idea of working in London and coming back to the country every night.

He set himself to learn his part. In the early days with Bennett and North, he was wise. He never gave himself away. He said little. He smiled, raised an eyebrow, murmured and was secretly amused to get away with it. He often laughed at himself, but he saw to it that no one else had occasion to laugh at him. He felt his way along and gained confidence. He hardened; and people, lunching with him and thinking him easy, would find his air of lazy well-being pierced on occasion by a look of purpose so acute, that they realised suddenly he was nothing of the sort, and that they had better look out.

His wife knew this tenacity. She smiled to remember how relentlessly he had pursued her. She hadn't wanted to marry him at first, but he kept on, and in the end, she gave in and had loved him whole-heartedly ever since.

Not that he had not bewildered her at first. In their early days together, he sulked heavily when she offended him. To punish her, he wouldn't eat. He would either fling away from the table leaving his food untouched, or would refuse to come to the table at all. Ellen was astonished. Very young in those days, she didn't coax him as his mother had done, but kept going to look at him with wide grey eyes, rather like one child staring at another who is behaving unaccountably. She herself continued to eat throughout his sulks, never dreaming of abstention.

By the time his children, inheriting their mother's candid, interested eyes, were old enough to look on at his sulks with the same surprise, Avery gave them up. He really had no need of them any longer, because he and Ellen rarely quarrelled and never seriously.

There was an Avery that only Ellen knew. The one who came to kneel beside her bed the night her first child was born. After Ellen's long terrible labour when he was allowed to see her at last, he knelt beside her bed, his face on a level with hers, his eyes full of tears.

'Darling, I thought you were going to die. . . .'

'Ssh. I'm all right now. Have you seen him?'

They smiled into each other's eyes. She was at one with him and he with her. It was the most precious moment of their life together. The second child's birth was easier and Ellen was never in such danger again. But she never forgot the time he knelt beside her bed, so absolutely himself, so much hers. That, shorn of minor vanities and petulances, was the real Avery and she loved him with all her heart.

'Nearly home,' said Ellen happily, leaving the main road and turning in under the elms.

'In spite of its rather suburban air, the lane looks nice

to-night,' said Avery, running his eyes over the lawn-like grass verges, the neat hedges, the ornamental trees.

'It's always nice,' murmured Ellen affectionately. 'I'm quite used to the houses now.'

Twenty years before when Avery's father had given Netherfold to them as a wedding present, theirs had been the only house in the lane, a charming little manor, three hundred years old. Now there were about twenty houses gathered around it, but though the Norths had been furiously resentful at first, they gradually became resigned to neighbours, if for no other reason than that they provided children for their own to play with.

As Ellen drove in at the gate, a little cat, black with white front and paws, hardly more than a kitten, galloped, giddy with welcome, to meet the car.

'Moppett darling,' said Ellen extravagantly, clambering out and gathering her up. 'Have I been a long time? Avery, take her, I must fly.'

Avery took the little cat, of which he was extremely fond, and Ellen flew.

Mornings and evenings were Ellen's busiest times and it was just when she most needed help that she had none. Maids had disappeared from the domestic scene long ago. Foreigners, housekeepers both 'lady' and 'working', mother's helps, helps under other names, having been tried and found wanting, Ellen now did as her neighbours did and employed day, or, more properly, half-day, women. Mrs. Pretty and Miss Beasley came separately on alternate mornings, and that was all Ellen could get of them. They were in great demand in the lane, because they were two of the few women who could be persuaded to come so far out of the town when there was plenty of work to be had in it.

Ellen might have had more help if she had been less 'weak', as old Mrs. North said. Adjoining the stable was a cottage where a capable gardener and cook might have been installed, but William Parkes and his wife Sarah had been there when the young Norths came to Netherfold. They were there still, Sarah, as she was the first to admit, 'past it' and William, as he often said, 'getting past it'. Ellen hadn't the heart to turn them out. They were so old, she said, and had been in the cottage such a long time.

She said she could manage. She always said that. Mrs. Pretty wasn't particular about her work, and when she had gone Ellen did most of it over again. But she was so nice, Ellen said, so warm-hearted and comfortable.

'All right,' said Avery, washing his hands of the matter. 'If you will do everything yourself.'

Ellen had an alarm clock, which she took into bed with her so that Avery shouldn't hear it ticking. She got herself up at seven, winter and summer. Breakfast was preceded on her part by a good deal of rushing about, waiting about and calling upstairs, because Avery wasn't good at getting up and in consequence made himself late. In the evenings she was occupied in cooking, serving up, washing up, clearing up and getting ready for morning. All of which she did as usual on this particular June evening, while Avery, the little cat on his arm, padded round the garden, calling out now and then to Ellen in the house. She wouldn't have him in the kitchen, because she said he needed fresh air after London, and though he protested, he agreed.

It was still light at half-past ten when the Norths locked the doors and windows and went upstairs. Ellen was glad, after rushing about, to get into her comfortable bed, three feet or so from Avery's. The curtains were drawn back and all the windows wide open to the gentle sky. The delicious scent of the night-scented stock came in from the garden. Ellen gave a happy sigh as she found the right place for her head on the pillow.

'Oh, dear,' she said after a moment. 'I forgot to say my prayers.'

'Can't you say them in bed?' murmured Avery.

But she was out, kneeling with her face buried in the eiderdown. Avery didn't believe in God. But illogically he liked Ellen to. It suited her somehow, and it was better for the children to be brought up by a mother who believed in something, especially in these days.

In bed once more, Ellen returned to a subject that had distracted her somewhat during her prayers

'Do you think that French girl will come?' she said.

'I shouldn't think so,' said Avery. 'She'll get lots of answers. "Light domestic duties" will fetch people all right. Why should she choose Mother?'

CHAPTER TWO

‹⊸◇⊸›

The postman, pursuing his early morning way along the Rue des Carmes, paused at the 'Librairie-Papeterie Lanier, Spécialiste du Stylo' and thrust several letters through the box in the door.

Madame Lanier, in peignoir and felt slippers, an apron tied round her ample middle, padded along the stone passage by the staircase, crossed the shop, where the counters were still sheeted, and picked the letters up.

Examining the envelopes, she went slowly through the shop again. Her daughter was just coming down the stairs.

'Are those letters for me?' she asked sharply.

Madame Lanier started, caught out in guilty interest.

'Yes, I think they are all for you. Yes, they are.'

'Then give them to me, please,' said Louise, holding out an imperative hand.

Madame Lanier surrendered them and Louise turned back upstairs. Her mother went to the kitchen and carried a jug of café-au-lait into the dining-room where Monsieur Lanier was already at table.

'What was the matter?' he said, as he poured the coffee into his bowl.

'It was the letters. They were all for her,' said Madame Lanier. She poured out her own coffee, and, unfolding the large, limp napkin, inserted one corner between the top buttons of her peignoir. Her husband had already tied his round his neck.

For a few moments they occupied themselves in tearing up crusts of bread and throwing them into their coffee, where they bobbed like ducks on a pond. Then they took up their large leaden spoons and began to eat with an appetite not even the unsatisfactory behaviour of their only child could impair.

'I don't know why she wants to go to England again,' said Madame Lanier. 'The three months she had at Foxton were surely enough. When Americans come into the shop they all say how well she speaks English.'

Monsieur Lanier shrugged that away. He was a big man with a head of thick dark hair, a beard, eye-glasses on a black ribbon and a strong resemblance to Zola.

'She is twenty-seven,' he said. 'It is time she married. She is leaving it too late.'

'But if she won't have anybody, what can we do? The days are gone when children were willing to marry those their parents chose for them. Which is a pity, because it saved a lot of trouble, and God knows it was usually more successful than allowing them to choose for themselves,' said Madame Lanier, pressing the loaf to her large bosom and cutting off two pieces towards her with a sharp knife.

'But you must also remember that our girl is very intelligent,' said the father in his precise way. 'She is a little above those who have suggested themselves.'

'She is, yes,' Madame Lanier was happy to concede. 'And though even I cannot call her beautiful, she has something. She has style, she is distinguished.'

'Psst,' warned her husband. 'She is coming. Good morning, Louise.'

'Good morning, Papa,' said Louise with reserve, but they saw all the same that she was in a better humour to-day, and their faces lightened.

'One little moment, my darling,' said Madame Lanier, getting up from the table. 'I will bring your coffee.'

Drumming her fingers on her letters and looking before her with a blank expression, Louise let her.

Her face was as smooth as ivory and the same colour. Her dark eyes slanted upwards a little at the outer corners. Her shining dark hair was parted in the middle and drawn into a knot on her slender neck. Her lips were made up, even for breakfast, in a magenta colour, which nevertheless became her and matched the varnish on the nails of her narrow hands.

As she sat in that back room where the smells of innumerable good dinners lurked in the dark corners, where the porcelain stove, the colour of milk chocolate, was cold for the summer, where the table was covered with a limp cloth of large red and white checks, where there was not, in fact, a vestige of taste or any aspiration to it, what was remarkable about her, the offspring of two large, baggy parents, was her clear-cut, almost exquisite finish.

She wore a dress of thin black stuff with a narrow white collar. On the wall behind her was an enlarged photograph of her at eight years of age, standing with a doll's perambulator in the garden of the town square. She wore a velvet dress, a lace collar, white stockings and a frilled hat from under which her dark eyes stared with unchildish melancholy.

It was this very dress that had provoked her first furious passion and marked her first victory over her mother.

'I hate it,' she had screamed coming in from school one day. She clutched the bodice with both hands as if she would tear it off. 'I won't wear it. You want everybody to laugh at me. You don't know what is right to wear. I want a blue serge dress. I want a blue serge. . . .'

'My darling, you shall have one. Don't cry, my angel. You will harm yourself. Mother only thought you would like . . .'

'You don't know anything. You are so stupid. . . .'

From that time onwards, Louise told her mother what to buy for her; until the day she bought clothes for herself. Now she was in plain black, with, nevertheless, a gold bracelet dangling with dozens of little charms. Her mother wondered where she had got it from, but dared not ask.

'There, my child,' said Madame Lanier, bustling in with the coffee.

'Merci, Maman.'

Madame Lanier was delighted. She wasn't often thanked, less than ever lately. She sat down to her cooling coffee, with an expréssion of happiness. No one could be sweeter than Louise when she chose, she reflected. She waited comfortably, feeling sure that Louise would say something about the letters before long.

19

All the same, she was careful to keep her glances from them as they lay on the table. She knew better than to display open interest.

It was not until her daughter's coffee-bowl was almost empty that her discretion was rewarded.

'I have five answers to my advertisement this morning,' said Louise. 'That makes seven in all.'

'Really?' exclaimed her parents simultaneously, falling like two famished fowls upon this crumb of information. It was gone in a flash and they waited eagerly for more.

'I think I have what I want here,' said Louise, with satisfaction, bringing a letter from its envelope and displaying the embossed address.

'Good paper,' murmured her father appreciatively. 'It is distinguished to have the address printed like that and it costs money.'

'Oh, the letters are all like that,' said Louise, bringing them out and scattering them over the table. 'All good places too, but this is the one I have chosen.'

Her father adjusted his eyeglasses, her mother bent forward and articulated slowly: 'The Cedars, Newington.'

'What is the name of this person?' asked her father.

'North.'

'Ça veut dire Nord, je crois?'

'Yes.'

'Tiens, Madame Nord. C'est assez curieux, ça,' marvelled Madame Lanier.

'And what does she say?' asked Monsieur Lanier, getting to know as much as he could while he could.

'She says she is a widow, elderly but of good health. And rich, I suppose, since this is the photograph of the house.'

She flicked a snapshot towards them and they pored, impressed, over the towers and battlements, the oriel windows and terracotta embellishments assembled with such pride by the late George North.

'C'est une maison solide,' pronounced Monsieur Lanier.

'What does this Madame North wish you to do?' asked Madame Lanier.

'Speak French with her,' said Louise.

She said nothing of her offer to undertake domestic duties. She was so anxious to go to England that she had presented herself as attractively as possible. But she avoided domestic duties so successfully at home that she didn't want them to know that she would undertake them abroad.

'Has this lady any children?' asked her father.

'Not at home. That is why I am going there. I am not interested in children. She has a son who lives fairly near. He has children. He is a publisher.'

'Really,' said her father with lively interest. 'Now that is extraordinary. You would go from books to books, so to speak. But there are publishers and publishers. Shall I make enquiries? It would be easy, and more prudent.'

'As you like,' said Louise with a shrug. 'But I shall go. I can look after myself. I know the English and I can tell that this person is respectable.'

The eyes of the parents dwelt on their child with pride. From no more than the sight of the peculiar and to them illegible English handwriting she could estimate the character of the writer. Yes, she could look after herself. She was far from ordinary.

Louise finished her coffee. Her mother finished hers, now quite cold.

'And when would you go?' asked Monsieur Lanier.

'At the beginning of July.'

'So you will not be coming with your father and me to Binic for the month of August?' said her mother wistfully.

'Ah, Binic,' said Louise with a laugh. 'Thank God, no. I shall not be at Binic in August this year.'

She folded her napkin, put it in its linen case and rose.

'I will give you an hour or two in the shop this morning, Papa,' she said.

'Ah, that is nice of you, my child. I might be able to straighten things up a little if you will do that.'

'In that case, my darling,' said Madame Lanier, 'I will do your room.'

'Very well,' said Louise.

Father and daughter went to prepare the shop for opening. They were already dressed for the public eye, but Madame was not. Nor would be, until she had made the beds with Cécile, the femme de ménage who came by the day, finished Louise's room herself, since Louise would not allow Cécile into it, prepared lunch and made a Biscuit de Savoie to tempt Louise's appetite at dinner. After that, she would brush, searchingly, her husband's clothes, Louise's clothes and her own. Like all French women, Madame Lanier believed in brushing, and spent a considerable time at it on the landing every day.

She would then make a careful toilet and be ready to appear in the shop in her prim shirt blouse and voluminous black skirt, her hair scraped up and firmly secured to the top of her head in the shape of a quoit.

Madame Lanier belonged to the class and generation of French women who considered that one's appearance should indicate immediately that one is respectable. One must never, she had been taught, give rise to wrong ideas by making oneself attractive. She was in constant anxiety as to what people must think of her daughter and had to keep reminding herself that all young girls were the same nowadays. You couldn't tell the serious from the light.

On this particular morning when she appeared, corseted and coifed, in the shop towards half-past eleven o'clock, Louise said: 'At last.'

'I'll go out now and get a little air,' she said.

'Do, my darling, it's a lovely morning. It will do you good,' said her mother, who rarely went out from one Sunday to another.

Louise went out into the sunlit street. Amigny was a small town, but there was plenty of noise and movement, more than ever to-day because in the Place de la Cathédrale a little market was going on. Bicycle bells jangled incessantly, lorries rumbled, cars hooted, people crossed and recrossed from pavement to pavement, hailing each other, hurrying to shake hands.

Louise passed among them; she was greeted and she greeted in return, showing an amiability she did not feel. The place was provincial, the people were dull. She had long had enough of provincial life. She had always laughed at and despised it; now she hated it. But she did not show it. She might need both the place and the people some time. In fact, she probably would. She saw no other prospect now but marriage with someone in the district, probably André Petit, the chemist. But she would put it off as long as possible. She would give every other alternative a chance to present itself.

She made some purchases, so as to have some ostensible reason for being out. It had been her habit for a long time to cover her every move. She made nearly half the round of the town, along the tree-lined and almost deserted boulevard, before she turned into a little street, completely empty in the sunshine. Wisteria toppled over a high garden wall in dusty mauve cascades. As Louise walked, catlike, under this wall, a door opened within it, as she knew it would, and a young man, propelling a bicycle before him, came out.

This was one of the three sons of the Devoisy family, owners of a good deal of Amigny, including the profitable chalk quarries outside the town. They were rich, with some claims to aristocracy. This young man, Paul, his mother's favourite, was supposed not to be strong. He cycled home in the middle of the morning for the benefit of the fresh air, exercise and a cup of whatever his mother considered good for him at the moment.

At the sight of Louise, he stood stock still, an expression of embarrassment on his face, which was pale, romantic, with a slight dark moustache. He even looked about for a way of escape, which she did not fail to notice. Her lip withered. She came on, fixing him with her dark eyes, and his embarrassment became acute.

'Don't be frightened,' she said. 'I'm not going to compromise you. In fact, I am removing myself very soon. I am going to England in a fortnight.'

His eyes flew wide; he had eyelashes like a girl.

'England!' he said. 'That's sudden, isn't it?'

'Did you think I would stay to assist at your wedding?' said Louise.

He frowned and looked away.

'That's all I wanted to tell you,' she said, making one of her smiles and showing her small, flawless teeth. 'Good morning and good-bye. You see, you have got out of this very easily, which is more than you expected, isn't it?'

She walked away, consumed with anger and pride. It was not that she loved him now, she told herself, but it was intolerable that she should be treated like this because her father was a bookseller. Put aside so that he could marry Germaine Brouet, the daughter of an advocate, a model girl, full of piety and good works and, in Louise's opinion, incredibly, incurably dull.

At the end of the street, she turned. He was pedalling away in the opposite direction. He didn't look round. She remembered how he used to stand to watch her out of sight. And how she herself, once he turned the corner, would come back to it again to see if he was still there. He always was, and they would run together, laughing, and have to part all over again.

God, what a thing life was when everything ended, when everything petered out and left you to look for something else.

England! What a bore to have to go. But she had to. She had to get away.

CHAPTER THREE

◦◦◇◇◦◦

At Netherfold, Anne North had spent the first day of the summer holidays lying blissfully in the garden under the cherry tree because it had been too hot to do anything else. But after supper it was cool enough to do as she always did on her first day at home, which was to go out on Roma, the mare, with her father wobbling along on the old bicycle, never used for any other purpose, beside her.

Ellen leaned from the landing window to watch them go, laughing together. When she had laughed with her father, now dead, it had always been politely and she imagined that this easy, loving companionship between Avery and Anne was something quite unusual.

She beamed down on their disappearing heads, Anne's silvery fair, Avery's dark, with hair thinning so slightly on the crown that you could only see it from an upstairs window or over the banisters.

When their voices and the leisurely clop-clop of Roma's hoofs had died away in the lane, Ellen drew in from the window, after a last look at the sky which was indigo over the elms, giving promise which it did not perform. It had been as black as that many times in these last few days and still no rain had fallen.

She went down to wash the supper things she was tempted to leave overnight for Mrs. Pretty, but couldn't because there was quite enough other work to be got through every morning. So she washed and dried, and from the sink under the wide-open window, she mourned over her garden. It was so dry. The lawns were like loofah, and roses, phlox, pansies, snapdragons sickened for rain.

The bird-bath was empty again. The thirsty birds, the thirsty stone, the sun, had drunk up all the water. She took a jug and went out to fill it. Immediately, the garden robin came to take a bath, as if he had been waiting for it. Back at the sink, Ellen watched him with satisfaction.

She liked looking after things. In the garden, she was always rescuing some plant or other, finding a better place for something, nursing something round.

She scoured the pans, looking out. The garden was absolutely still. She heard the thud of the tennis balls from the Wilsons' court in the distance. Near at hand, a blackbird suddenly clicked like scissors.

'Moppet,' called Ellen, leaning from the window.

Under the thick hedge, a little black-and-white cat-face appeared enquiringly.

'I thought so,' scolded Ellen. 'Leave the birds alone and come here. Come along. I'll give you some milk.'

Moppet had the endearing habit of coming when she was called. She galloped over the lawn, sprang through the kitchen window and crouched immediately to her saucer.

'Now I've finished,' said Ellen with satisfaction and hurried for the watering-can. The reservoirs were so low in the district that the use of the hose was forbidden.

With a heavy can in one hand and a heavy bucket in the other, she went backwards and forwards, backwards and forwards from the wash-house to the borders, spilling a good deal of water down the front of her linen dress, until she was too hot to do any more and sank into the hammock-seat for a rest. There she rocked gently, looking out over her kingdom, her garden.

In no time at all, or so it seemed, Anne came running up from the paddock, up the flagged path between the apple trees, across the lawn, and flung herself down on the hammock-seat, making the springs leap. She rubbed her cheek against her mother's bare arm and sighed happily.

Ellen looked fondly down on her fifteen-year-old daughter. All she could see was pale gold hair, pure brow and the upward curve of dark lashes.

'It was a heavenly ride. Roma is a lamb, isn't she? Oh, Mummy, I'm so glad to be home.'

She rolled round against her mother to gaze at the house.

'Nobody could have a better place to live in than this, could they? I always conjure it up before I go to sleep at school. I pore over it. But sometimes I have bad dreams about it. That I've come back and it all looks different. Deserted or somebody else living in it. And I'm so terribly unhappy, and then I wake up and find it's only a dream after all.'

She had been holding her mother's hand and became aware, all at once, of its seamed and polished palm.

'Mummy,' she said in amazement. 'Your hands are hard. Inside they are just like that stuff they put into bird-cages for the bird to sharpen its beak on. You know – cuttle-fish.'

She was very tickled with the idea that her mother's hands were like cuttle-fish, and holding them both, she laughed up into Ellen's face.

Ellen laughed too, though ruefully.

'It hadn't struck me, but it's just what they *are* like,' she said. 'I must do something to them. But gardening and washing-up . . .'

'Oh,' Anne groaned in contrition. 'I did mean to wash up to-night and then I forgot. I'm so sorry, Mummy,' she said, kissing her mother to make up. 'But isn't housework a nuisance? You don't like it, do you? You couldn't possibly like washing-up and cleaning pans and doing fires, Mummy?'

'Well,' said Ellen, considering it, 'I don't actually like doing those things, I suppose, but it's all part of looking after the house and all of you, and that I do most certainly enjoy.'

After the anxiety, the separations and dangers of the war, it was wonderful to have them safe and all together, except for mild interruptions in the form of school terms and military service.

'I'm very glad to have the house to look after,' she said. 'And the garden too.'

'Well, I hate housework,' said Anne. 'What I have to do at school is far too much for me. We're so short of maids we have to wait at table some days and take turns to do our classrooms and our bedrooms. Everybody simply hates it. When I leave, I'm going to do a job with no housework in it.'

'What are you going to do?' said her mother.

'I might go on the stage,' said Anne. 'Or I might write novels. What's the use of having a publisher for a father if one doesn't make use of him?' She smiled up under lashes to see how her mother took this piece of sophistication.

'No,' she said, rearranging herself with her head on her mother's lap and her knees up. 'I shall probably have a riding-school and then I don't need to leave home. I can run it from here, can't I? Because whatever I do and wherever I am, I'm always going to have Roma. Horses do live a very long time, don't they?' she asked anxiously.

'Yes, they do,' Ellen assured her. 'Was that a car in the lane? I hope nobody's coming.'

'It can't be,' said Anne, repulsing the idea. 'There's nobody to come.'

They swung gently. Avery had appeared in the borders, nipping off dead flowers here and there and throwing them, Ellen noted regretfully, on to the lawn.

Ellen closed her eyes. She was comfortable and rather sleepy. Anne's eyes were shut too.

Ellen opened her eyes to see two figures before her. One familiar and one strange.

'Oh, Granny,' she cried.

Anne swung her legs to the ground and came upright in astonishment.

'We've been in the house for some time,' said old Mrs. North with reproach. 'But there was no one about. Anybody could have taken anything.'

Ellen was looking at the stranger. This unsmiling, highly-finished person must be the French girl. Ellen was immensely surprised, she hadn't expected anyone in the least like this.

'Ellen, this is Mademoiselle Louise Lanier,' said Mrs. North. 'Mademoiselle, my daughter-in-law. Ma belle fille, n'est-ce-pas?'

'Oh, Mummy, what a compliment for you,' cried Anne.

'Not at all,' said old Mrs. North. 'It is French for daughter-in-law, as I should have thought you would know at your age, child. My grand-daughter, Mademoiselle. Ma petite fille.'

'How do you do,' said mother and daughter.

'I thought you would have come to see your grandmother before this, Anne,' said the old lady, lending her cheek to the girl's kiss.

'Oh, Granny, I was coming. But I'm always so glad to get home that I can't possibly leave it for even five minutes for the first two days, can I, Mummy? But I was coming very soon, Granny, really . . .'

'Well, I don't expect to compete with your horse, certainly,' said the old lady. 'And it hasn't mattered. I haven't been sitting alone waiting for some of you to call this time. We've been very busy, haven't we, Mademoiselle?'

'Yes, Madame, we have been very busy.'

'You speak English already?' said Ellen, smiling.

'I speak some English, yes,' said Louise, not smiling.

'Avery,' called Ellen to the borders. 'Your Mother's here. And Mademoiselle – er – Lanier.'

'Who?' called Avery in a family voice, turning from the waist.

'Oh,' he said, more politely, and stepped out of the border.

'Mother,' he said, coming to kiss her, and having kissed,

stood smiling at the stranger, waiting for some explanation. He couldn't think who she could be.

'Mademoiselle, this is my son, Avery,' said old Mrs. North. 'The youngest of my children. Avery, Mademoiselle Lanier.'

'I didn't know you'd arrived, Mademoiselle,' said Avery, achieving recollection, offering his hand.

Louise pressed it slightly with the tips of her narrow fingers, watched with interest by Anne.

'You don't listen to what I tell you, Avery,' said his mother. 'I told you all about it. Ellen even suggested she should come with me to meet Mademoiselle at the station. But no.'

'Oh, I'm so sorry,' said Ellen, looking very like Anne stricken with contrition about the washing-up. 'I forgot all about it. You should have rung me up. I was so excited about Anne's coming home. Mademoiselle, do excuse me, won't you?'

'Madame,' said Louise, shutting her eyes briefly, 'since I did not know of your existence, I did not miss you from the platform.'

The Norths were slightly taken aback. Avery's eyes met Ellen's with a suppressed twinkle.

'No, of course not,' said Ellen. 'Granny, do sit down. Sit here and let me get you something cool to drink. What will you have?'

'She'll have lime-juice and soda-water with a little gin in it,' said Avery. 'I'll get it. Mademoiselle, what may I get for you?'

Louise faintly raised eyebrows and shoulders as if it were a matter of indifference to her what she drank.

'A syrup of any kind then, thank you. Grenadine, Groseille, what you have . . .'

'Syrup?' murmured Anne in astonishment.

'I think it just means fruit juice,' said Ellen.

'Will you have a glass of wine?' said Avery. 'Madeira? Marsala? Sherry?'

'Thank you, no. I will have what Madame votre mère has, if you please.'

Old Mrs. North smiled with pleasure to be called Madame votre mère. How much better than "Old Mrs. North." In England she was called old Mrs. North simply to distinguish her from Ellen, who was "Young Mrs. North." A misnomer in both cases, Mrs. North considered, since she wasn't old and Ellen at forty-two certainly wasn't young.

'I'll get the drinks, Avery. You stay with your mother,' said Ellen. She pressed his arm surreptitiously, her sign that she wanted to get away.

Anne went with her.

'What a queer person,' said Anne. 'I thought the French were fearfully polite, but she isn't, is she?'

'There's as much difference between people in France as in England,' said Ellen, taking ice-cubes from the refrigerator. 'The French wouldn't think much of Mrs. Beard's manners for instance, would they?'

'Oh, no,' agreed Anne. 'Shall I get the painted tray?'

'No, the square silver one.'

'Is it clean?' asked Anne in surprise.

'Yes. I cleaned it for you to come home to.'

'Oh, Mummy, you are funny, as if I notice! I say, did you see the French person's nails? They're like pen-nibs. She need only dip one in the ink to write with it.'

'Get me another syphon, darling.'

'Mummy, I feel I shall get a fit of laughing if Granny practises her French again. Why does she want to learn French at her age, Mummy? I mean, it's not worth it, is it? Actually, I can't understand why anyone wants to learn French when they don't have to. I loathe it.'

When Louise accepted the glass with the pale green liquid cloudy with ice, she said: 'Is this Pernod?'

Ellen didn't know what Pernod was, but Avery said, 'I'm sorry, no. You don't often get absinthe in England.'

As she drank, the stranger's eyes were on Ellen's linen frock, creased, and damp down the front where the water had spilled from the watering-can.

'I know, I know,' Ellen protested mutely. 'I ought to have changed, and I wish I had.'

The girl was so beautifully finished: the cool suit, the white Juliet cap on the smooth dark hair, the white lawn blouse – all exactly right.

'And how do you like England?' asked Avery, making conversation.

'I have been before,' said Louise, as if there was nothing more to be said.

Again Avery's eyes twinkled with amusement.

'What a queer person,' said Anne when they had gone.

'She didn't seem to like us,' said Avery.

'Perhaps she's homesick,' said Ellen. 'That's probably it. She's homesick, poor girl.'

* * *

Old Mrs. North accompanied Louise to her room to see that she had everything for the night, although this was the second she would spend in it.

The old lady looked with interest on the signs of French occupation of her best room. At the calendar with saints' names besides the dates, and such French saints too. 'Ste Ursule . . . S. Isdore . . . Ste Geneviéve.' It struck Mrs. North with the force of a revelation that the French idea of God and his saints must be entirely different from the English. She regarded Louise for a moment with astonished speculation before continuing round the room.

A little gilt cupid took aim from the dressing-table.

'Pretty,' said old Mrs. North, admiring Paul Devoisy's gift.

'You haven't put any photographs of your parents out,' she said.

'I didn't bring any,' said Louise.

'I should have thought you'd have liked to look at your parents. . . .'

'Oh, pour trois mois,' shrugged Louise.

Left to herself she pored with passionate concern over a damaged cuticle on her forefinger. She removed a minute piece of skin with nail-scissors, she applied a soothing cream. She smoothed more cream into her hands, her face, her neck, spending a long time on her toilet for the night.

She got into bed, but before turning out the lamp she looked round at the room. It was different from her room at home, an old room in an old house there; a faded striped wallpaper, an iron shutter over the fireplace, Jeanne d'Arc on the mantelpiece, a parquet floor, a strip of carpet beside the bed that always slipped when you got out on to it and which, first thing every morning, was hung out of the window by her mother.

Her parents appeared in her mind's eye, bulky, humble, loving. But she thought of them with impatience, even with resentment. They knew nothing. Nothing of her sufferings, not only about Paul, but about all sorts of things from childhood upwards. They were no help to her. She thought they ought to be. Even without a word from her, they ought to be. She dismissed them and gave her attention to the English room.

It was pretty in a shining, unsubtle way. There was everything in it to make it comfortable, running water, a soft carpet, an armchair. The English were specialists in comfort. Le confort anglais was a byword in France. But their beds were not right. Why did they have such queer pillows? The wrong shape and not half big enough. The square French pillows were much superior, supporting the shoulders.

The English made their days more comfortable, the French their nights. According to the literature too of both countries, days were more important to the English, nights to the French.

She sighed sharply, remembering hers. What was he doing now? Playing the fiancé with much respect on his side, much virtue on Germaine's. Bah! She refused to think of him. Refused, she told herself, and turned out the light. She would dwell only on the present. It was not bad here. Not bad at all. Though devoid of interest. The family this evening, for instance, how dull in their mediocre happiness.

'Trop de simplicité' was her verdict on the North family, as she tried to accommodate her shoulders to the foreign pillows.

At Netherfold as Ellen was falling asleep, Avery gave a guffaw from his bed.

'What's the joke?' she murmured.

'I'm remembering our efforts to put the French girl at her ease, when all she did was to put us out of ours. She disposed of you beautifully and then of me.'

'When you don't mind how rude you are, you have every advantage,' said Ellen.

'But she amused me,' said Avery. 'I rather like a bit of salt now and again. There's so much sugar in people's talk.'

'Mmm. Perhaps,' mumbled Ellen, burrowing luxuriously into her pillows.

She wasn't to be allowed to burrow long. In the night the storm broke. Lightning crackled over the house. Thunder crashed and the sagging sky broke suddenly in torrents of rain. Ellen sprang out of bed and ran from room to room shutting the windows. Avery felt no responsibility in such matters.

Anne rose on her elbow as her mother ran into her room.

'Oh, Mummy, d'you think Roma will be all right?'

'Yes, yes,' said Ellen, enveloped in agitated curtains. 'Go to sleep, pet.'

She ran back to her own bed.

But Anne got up and went to the window. The next flash of lightning illuminated the scene and showed Roma standing at the paddock fence. A faint whinny made itself heard. It was enough. Anne put on her sandals and went as she was, in pyjamas, because it was no good getting her dressing-gown soaked. Fleeing noiselessly down the stairs, she went into the storm. Rain beat against her body, wet leaves drove against her face, she was drenched in an instant. Roma whinnied again, welcomingly. She was trembling when Anne reached her.

Child and horse went through the gate and into the stable. The field was illuminated in flashes, the poplars leaning this way and that. Anne rubbed Roma down in the dark, the mare blowing gently, nuzzling, talking in her own way.

'There you are, darling,' said Anne, kissing the velvet nose. 'Now you'll be all right. See you in the morning.'

She dashed back into the house. As she reached the top of the stairs the light went on, and mother and daughter confronted each other – Anne like a young Grecian goddess in her plastered pyjamas, her blue eyes brilliant.

'Anne! You're crazy! I suppose you've been putting Roma in?'

Anne nodded, showering rain.

'It was wonderful. But I'm wet.'

'Into the bathroom!' said her mother.

She brought dry pyjamas and rubbed Anne's hair.

'I rub Roma. You rub me,' said Anne.

'Have you a sweet handy?' she said, getting into bed.

'At this time of the night?'

'I'm frightfully hungry, Mummy.'

'I'll get you something,' said Ellen, remembering the fierce nocturnal hungers of her youth.

'Could I have a beef sandwich? Could you spare it? And some *beetroot*, please, darling . . .' she called after her mother.

CHAPTER FOUR

———◇◇◇———

I

On a warm Saturday evening, after supper Avery, Ellen and Anne sat together in the garden, variously absorbed. Avery, wearing horn-rimmed glasses, frowned over a thick typescript he had, for once, brought home. Anne, chewing a corner of her handkerchief in excitement, her legs doubled under her, raced through a book with the violent concentration of youth. Ellen read the morning paper, which she hadn't had time to look at until now.

The garden was peaceful, breathing scents of roses and stocks. The sky was glorious as if a flight of angels had just passed over, sweeping wings of gold from end to end.

Through the french windows of the sitting-room, a khaki figure appeared and waited, smiling his own particular smile, strangely kind for a boy of eighteen.

The effect of this appearance was all he could have wished. Cries of delight and astonishment flew up like birds.

'Oh, Corporal,' cried Anne, rushing over the grass and almost knocking the breath out of her brother by flinging her arms about his middle.

'Hugh,' cried Ellen, her face lit with loving welcome. 'Well . . .'

'I've got till Monday morning,' he said, and over Anne's head, kissed her and his father.

He kept coming home taller, broader and more of a man and still he kissed his father. Ellen was glad. She feared when Hugh no longer kissed his father it would mean that he had gone so far into the masculine world that she could no longer follow him.

'Hugh, you're so brown,' she said.

'And you all look marvellous,' he said, beaming round upon them. 'Anne's grown again. Oh, there's Moppet. Moppet, come on! Up!'

The little cat sprang and was gathered up. She settled herself on Hugh's arm, her back to the company, her paws on his collar, purring a rich rolling purr.

'You see?' said Hugh proudly. 'She remembers.'

It was he who had taught her the trick.

'Are you going to press your trousers?' said Anne. 'Because if you are, I'll come with you.'

'I don't bother much about them now,' said Hugh, smiling down at her.

When he first joined up, he fussed about the state of his uniform, not because he minded about it, but because he had orders to. Rules and regulations were on his nerves, but he was easier about things now, his mother was glad to see.

He hadn't said much about his life in the Army. He didn't complain except to say you never got any time to yourself, that he didn't like cookhouse fatigues, but who did? He said

42

the food was terrible, but you got used to it. He said you felt a bit out of depth with the chaps to begin with, but liked most of them before long.

His mother suspected he must have had a bad time at first. His quiet manner probably led army toughs to think they could be rude to him. If so, they must soon have found out their mistake. Avery had had his son specially instructed in boxing and Hugh had never any difficulty in looking after himself. All the same it must have taken a boy of his temperament some time to adapt himself to life in the Army.

He liked to read, for hours, he liked to play records over to himself in his room. He liked to go about with his friend Harding, who had been with him at Harrow. They might have been together still, if Harding had not elected to go to Cambridge before doing his military service, and Hugh afterwards. Hugh wanted to get it over, to clear it out of the way. And that was what his mother felt he was doing. He was getting through it.

* * *

When Ellen worried about Hugh, Avery always said it would do him good. It was all very well for Ellen to keep on escaping from people, but it wouldn't do for Hugh. He must learn to mix if he was going to be any good to the firm. He mustn't be a hermit-crab like John Bennett, said Avery.

But in spite of this stricture Hugh's admiration of and affection for his father did not blind him to the fact that John Bennett was the better man, as far as publishing was concerned, of the two. Not that he wished to be wholly like

John Bennett, who was, in Hugh's youthful opinion, too cautious altogether.

There had never been any doubt about what Hugh wanted to do. He wanted to be a publisher and his mother considered it almost providential that a place should be waiting that he was so exactly fitted for and so anxious to fill.

'I'll go and get something to eat for you, darling,' said Ellen now. 'You stay here. I'll bring a tray out.'

'Oh, nice,' said Hugh. 'This is marvellous after the train. Phew! – it was packed.'

At that moment, the telephone rang in the house.

'I'll go,' said Ellen. 'It's on my way.'

It was John Bennett on the telephone, asking if he could come for Sunday.

'Do,' said Ellen warmly. 'That will be nice. Hugh has just come.'

'Then you won't want me,' said John, ready to withdraw like the hermit-crab Avery said he was.

'But we do want you,' said Ellen, and persuaded him.

John Bennett's wife, Marianne, had left him during the war for an officer in the Army. She subsequently left the officer, but did not return to John. He had not divorced her.

'She hasn't asked me to,' he said. 'And until she does I can continue to support her. She never had any idea about money.'

Ellen was indignant for him.

'It's just because he's so kind and unselfish that Marianne treats him so badly,' she told Avery. 'She knows she can.'

'Poor old John,' said Avery and by his smile implied that

John was perhaps the sort of man women leave. A very good fellow, of course, but a bit tame perhaps for a fascinating creature like Marianne, who was, too, so much younger.

Avery liked his partner and respected his immense interest in and knowledge of publishing, but as a man, he rather smiled at him. Physically, Avery had much advantage. John was of middle height only, bald, pale, with a worried expression. He looked as if he was worried, not about himself, but you.

'Uncle John always seems so sorry about everything, doesn't he?' Anne remarked thoughtfully after a visit, and her father gave one of his shouts of laughter.

John lived alone, looked after by a housekeeper who had too much respect for him to do it properly. When he said he would dine on an egg on a tray, she brought it to him. Since Marianne's departure from the house in Kensington, a flood of books and manuscripts had crept unhindered from room to room, from floor to floor, until now you could hardly open the front door for books. In some of the great lofty rooms, John had scooped out places for himself, where he read, ate, smoked and slept.

Ellen had patiently encouraged him to look upon himself as one of the family, until now he was quite at home with them. He was fond and proud of the children, and for Ellen he had a deep affection which he disguised under extravagance of expression, so that, by seeming to play at it, he could show his gratitude for being rescued from the worst of his loneliness. Avery professed to be very tickled by these antics on the part of his partner, and teased Ellen about them to make Anne laugh. He would do almost anything to make Anne laugh.

On this Saturday evening, having at last overcome John's scruples about breaking in upon Hugh's short leave, Ellen put the telephone down and, still smiling, went into the pantry to get something to eat for Hugh. At the sight of the meat, a ration for three people which must now do for five, she became thoughtful.

'I've got an idea for to-morrow, if you approve, everybody,' she called, carrying the tray into the garden.

'Oh, what?' cried Anne, who loved her mother to have ideas.

'Well, that was John, Avery.'

'Ah, your devoted admirer.'

'Don't be silly,' said Ellen, and they laughed at her. 'He wants to come to-morrow,' she said. 'And the meat simply won't go round. So I thought we might go down to Somerton for lunch.'

'Oh, yes,' said Anne. 'You do have some lovely ideas, darling. And Daddy's actually never been to Somerton, have you, Daddy? You must see it.'

'The only thing is,' said Ellen. 'Will Hugh mind going there to-morrow instead of being at home?'

'Not I,' said Hugh. 'I'd like to see it again, and all the old ladies.'

'Some of them are sweet, Daddy. Mrs. Brockington especially. Oh, don't nice things happen?' said Anne. 'Hugh coming home to-night and all of us going to Somerton to-morrow. I'm so happy. But I wish I could ride over on Roma. Still, twenty-five miles is rather far, isn't it?'

'It is, unless you'd like to be arriving when we're coming back,' said her father.

'I'll just go and explain to her,' said Anne, dashing away, long-jumping a flower-bed in passing.

'Still crazy about the mare, I see,' said Hugh.

'Still crazy,' said Avery indulgently.

II

The former Manor House of Somerton, withdrawn into its little park, was now a private hotel, prospering quietly on its residents, mostly old ladies. During the war, while Avery was kept in London at the Ministry of Information, and Netherfold shared with evacuees, Ellen had stayed with the children so often at Somerton that they were looked upon there as ex-residents.

On Sunday morning, towards twelve o'clock, Avery North drove his family and his partner between the old stone gateposts and round the gravel sweep to the door.

'We're rather late,' said Ellen. 'I must go at once and ask Mrs. Beard very nicely to give us lunch, or perhaps she won't.'

'And I must come with you,' said Anne. 'Because I never like to miss any of Mrs. Beard.'

They all got out of the car. Avery looked with interest at the face of the old house that had sheltered his family without him so often and John immediately began to bemoan its fate.

'That such a gem of English manor house architecture should have to be turned into an hotel is iniquitous. It's sad . . .'

'Hugh,' said Ellen in an aside. 'Show them the garden when they're ready.'

She turned the old iron ring on the door and with a clank let herself and Anne into the cool hall.

The old ladies, sitting about among the flowers and the chintzes, peered for a moment to see who was coming in. Then those who knew Ellen and Anne exclaimed in greeting and those who did not observed them from behind their papers. It was pleasant to have this little stir made by an arrival on Sunday morning.

The old ladies tended to group themselves. Grandmothers sat together with knitting and family snapshots in their handbags without which they did not stir. Intellectuals, like Miss Welling, once headmistress of a famous girls' school, and Doctor Bell, who had been a medical missionary, sat together, but were engaged, separately, on the 'Ximines' crossword puzzle. Mrs. Vereson, who had been a beauty, kept state alone in a corner, but her mischievous and still lovely dark eyes invited the visitors to come and talk to her. Her hearing-aid, draped in black lace, was ready on a table beside her. She thought lace disguised it, but it whistled and whooed like a muffled owl and gave itself away.

Ellen waved a hand to Mrs. Brockington over by the far windows and Mrs. Brockington took off her glasses to be ready. She waited smilingly while Ellen and Anne spoke to Mrs. Vereson, then to one and then to another. The old ladies were like gentle briars in the path to Mrs. Brockington; you had to disentangle them very carefully, in case you hurt, not yourself, but them.

'Come here, dear,' said old Mrs. Fish, stretching out both hands to Ellen. 'Come and tell me how you are. We were talking of you only the other day. How Anne has grown! What lovely hair you have, child. Have you brought Hugh too? And your *husband*? Oh, that is nice for us. We've all wanted so to see him. Now, we shall see the whole family, Mrs. Ashburne. Mrs. Ashburne is new, dear. She's come to see if she would like to be resident here. She's rather hesitating, and between our-selves,' said Mrs. Fish, nodding her head significantly at Ellen, 'I'm not surprised. Our friend Mrs. B. has been distinctly rude to her once or twice. But I tell her not to take any notice. She mustn't be driven away, because the place is very pleasant, and whatever else she is, Mrs. B. is a good manager. Mrs. Ashburne,' she said, leaning backwards in belated introduc-tion, 'this is Mrs. North, who comes to liven us up sometimes.'

Standing to smile for a while at old Mrs. Fish and new Mrs. Ashburne, Ellen and Anne reached Mrs. Brockington at last. She was the only one they kissed.

'This is nice,' said Mrs. Brockington. 'It's been such a long time, Ellen dear. How well you both look. Anne, you're as tall as your mother.'

'How are you, how have you been, how are your hands?' said Ellen solicitously.

'I don't think they're any worse,' said Mrs. Brockington on looking down on them as they lay on her lap, swollen, reddened, crippled by rheumatism.

'Do they hurt terribly?' said Anne compassionately.

'No, darling, not terribly. But they're a nuisance. They won't let me write letters or knit or do my hair properly.'

49

'Oh . . .' mourned Anne.

'Now they're not bad at all, child. Not bad at all,' said Mrs. Brockington, hiding them from sight in her lace shawl. 'Tell me how you are, both of you. Have you brought Hugh?'

'Yes, and Avery's here and Avery's partner, John Bennett, is with us too. I haven't seen Mrs. Beard yet. I hope she can manage lunch for us.'

'Oh, you must go and see her,' said Mrs. Brockington at once. 'If she thinks you've been here for any time at all without paying your respects to her, you mightn't get anything to eat to-day.'

'I know, I know,' said Ellen. 'I'll go and find her and if I can't see you again before lunch, I'll come to your room this afternoon shall I?'

'Do, dear, I shall look forward to it.'

*   *   *

Somerton Manor was owned by a small Trust, composed of members of the Somers family who had lived in the house for generations, but found it impossible to keep up in these days. They were gentle, unpractical people with altruistic motives and when they turned the Manor into a private hotel, it made them feel better to stipulate that it should become a refuge, for the most part, of elderly gentle folk, because these were, the Trust considered, the people who had suffered badly, with themselves, during the last decade.

The Trust meant to do things properly and spent a good deal of money fitting up the old house with extra bathrooms, putting hot and cold water into every bedroom, modernising the kitchens and so on. They then became very frightened. Not only did the hotel not make money, it lost it very fast. The trouble was, as it mostly is in these days, staff. No resident staff would stay. The hotel was too far off the beaten track, they said. There was nothing to do, nowhere to go for time-off, it was too dark and lonely in the winter. They wouldn't stay, and because no staff would stay, no manageress would stay either. One after another, they came and went, and the Trust, established in small London flats, was extremely worried.

Then Mrs. Beard arrived on the scene. She was recently widowed and had never managed an hotel before.

'What of it?' she said, at the interview. 'You just use your common sense.'

She convinced the Trust that she had plenty of that and was engaged.

'Leave it to me,' said Mrs. Beard, outspoken from the first. 'And when I say leave it, I mean leave it.'

Though nervously at first, the Trust did. Mrs. Beard employed day-women from the surrounding villages and set them to work in shifts. She had one resident handyman, named Jim, who lived by himself over the stables. From the day of Mrs. Beard's arrival, the Trust had no more trouble.

Mrs. Beard was practically irreplaceable and knew it. It was not that she traded on the fact. She would have been the same in any situation in life. She had no inhibitions, no reserve. She was rude, even insulting, when she felt like it, she was impatient, she grumbled incessantly, she threatened, almost every day, to leave the place. She could do, and did, exactly as she pleased.

51

She bullied the old ladies, she often made the weak or sensitive ones feel quite ill, but nobody complained to the Trust. Mrs. Beard often told them that if she, the last of a long line of manageresses, took herself off, the hotel would close down and they would all have to find somewhere else to live. The old ladies feared this was only too true, so they kept quiet and Mrs. Beard continued to hang like a sword of Damocles over their white heads.

But there were many compensations. Under Mrs. Beard's rule, the whole place shone with cleanliness and good order, the fires were warm in winter, the food was excellent. Sometimes, too, Mrs. Beard was quite amiable and then everyone was grateful and felt there couldn't be a better place to live in anywhere.

On this Sunday morning, Ellen and Anne North penetrated the honeycomb of passages and pantries in search of the manageress. As they went, Anne squeezed her mother's arm and laughed in anticipation of Mrs. Beard's greeting. You never knew what it would be.

'Now be careful,' said Ellen. She meant 'Don't laugh too much'; a necessary warning.

They came upon Mrs. Beard in a cool little room with a sink and bars at the window, whether to keep burglars out or maids in, in the old days, has never been disclosed. Mrs. Beard was doing the salads. When Ellen and Anne appeared, she showed no surprise, though it was months since she had seen them.

'Oh, it's you, is it?' she said without expression. 'We've only got cold. I'm not roasting meat on a day like this for anybody.'

'We shall like cold lunch very much,' said Ellen. 'If you can do with us.'

'How many?'

'Five, I'm afraid,' said Ellen.

'Five?' said Mrs. Beard. ' How do you come to have five?'

'Us,' said Ellen. 'Hugh, my husband, and my husband's partner.'

'Oh, men,' said Mrs. Beard, suddenly gracious. 'It'll be a pleasure to see a man or two for a change. All right. I'll manage. Jim,' she called suddenly, out of the open window. 'Bring me three more lettuce. And some more radishes, about two dozen; little ones, mind.'

Mrs. Beard was a middle-aged Gibson girl, built-up hair, large bust, curved hips and that thrown-forward look which may have been due to her stays or to the fact that she wore high-heeled court shoes which tired her and made her cross, but which she thought necessary to her appearance. She had a high colour toned down by mauve powder, which gave her the look of a ripe nectarine; one that had been in the box rather a long time. She had green gooseberry eyes, often popping with temper. She wore a white linen coat this morning and looked, as usual, trim and capable.

Anne North, sitting at the table, her chin in her hands, watched her with absorbed interest.

'You're making those salads look very nice,' said Ellen appreciatively.

'I oughtn't to be doing them at all,' said Mrs. Beard. 'But they won't be fit to go on the tables if I don't. I do altogether too much. I do pretty near everything. I'm fed up. There are far too many old people here. All old people are tiresome, aren't they?'

'We shall be old ourselves,' said Ellen.

'You're telling me,' said Mrs. Beard. 'I'm old now. I've aged ten years in the five I've been here. Blast, where are those radishes? Jim – oh, there you are,' she said, subsiding as Jim appeared. 'And about time too.'

'We'll go now,' said Ellen, taking Anne by the hand.

'You don't need to,' said Mrs. Beard. 'You're not in my way.'

'But I must go and tell the others that it's all right about lunch,' said Ellen, extricating herself with the necessary care.

'May I go out the back way and look at the old laundry, Mrs. Beard?' asked Anne.

'Go where you like, medea,' said Mrs. Beard amiably. 'Your old play-house. You always liked the laundry, didn't you?'

'Mmm,' said Anne. 'Come with me, Mummy.'

'Good-bye, Mrs. Beard. We'll see you later, won't we?'

''Bye for now,' said Mrs. Beard. 'You lucky people. Nothing to do but enjoy yourselves.'

As mother and daughter went down the passage into the open air, Anne said: 'When Mrs. Beard calls me "medea," I always think of Jason and the Golden Fleece.'

'Ssh,' cautioned Ellen, smiling.

One of the nice things about the Manor House, Ellen always said, was that it was as attractive at the back as at the front. The little courtyard that faced you as you came out of the door in the passage was flanked on two sides by perfect period pieces; on the right a little brew-house and on the left a wash-house where Anne used to play on wet days at Somerton. This last was a two-storied building with good windows. In the great room on the ground floor were still the ancient appliances for washing: two fireplaces, a pump, coppers, tubs, dollies and a pair of huge wooden rollers, presumably for wringing, though it would have taken a giant to turn them. Anne did her doll's wash in this place, putting Gargantuan to Lilliputian uses. She ran up and down the wooden stair, through the three rooms above, and was busy and happy, while her mother, as often as not, sat at the old table, bleached and seamed with constant scrubbings and swillings, writing to her husband, her dear Avery, enduring the bombs in London.

Anne looked in at the door now and wished for her lost self.

'It was fun here,' she said. 'I always think it would make a nice little house.'

'We must go and find the others,' said Ellen. 'I must get Daddy and Uncle John introduced to everybody before the gong goes.'

Lunch was pleasant. The old ladies beamed from their tables at the Norths at theirs beside an open window, where Anne kept putting her hand out into the warm air as if from a boat into the water.

Hugh was getting all the publishing news he could from John Bennett. He had not asked his father for it; they had other interests in common. But John and he were two enthusiasts together. They leaned over the table towards each other and had to keep coming upright to allow plates to be put before them.

'I still haven't got over our not taking *Snow in Summer*,' said Hugh. 'They did well, you see. I was sure they would. Didn't I say so?'

'Mmm,' said John regretfully. 'It was a mistake. But too many short stories won't do, you know.'

'But they were so different,' said Hugh with vehemence. 'Have you come across her yet?'

'Yes,' said John Bennett. 'Yes, I have.'

'What's she like?' said Hugh, eagerly, leaning nearer.

'Hugh, the potatoes . . .'

'Oh, sorry,' said Hugh, turning to the waitress at his elbow.

Avery made no attempt to join in the book conversation. He was comfortably lazy, teasing Anne, chatting to Ellen.

'I daren't look about me,' he said. 'I catch a smile with every glance.'

'Never mind,' said Ellen. 'You're an event for them.'

Mrs. Beard walked majestically about in her white coat, surveying the scene. Some of the old ladies looked nervous when she approached their tables, but they needn't have worried. Mrs. Beard was propitiated by the presence of men in the dining-room, one of them so good-looking too. That Mrs. North, thought Mrs. Beard, had got damwell everything. As for her, buried in this hole, she'd forgotten there were men like that still in the world. To look at the North husband sitting there so easy and handsome filled her with vague sadness.

She went to stand beside him.

'Is everything to your liking?' she said, bending to look into his face solicitously.

'Very much so. All excellent, Mrs. – er,' said Avery warmly.

'Thank you,' said Mrs. Beard, turning away with emotion, Anne's eyes following her in surprise.

After lunch, Ellen was waylaid. Mrs. Fish waited beyond the dining-room door with her new friend.

'Mrs. Ashburne thinks you're a lovely family,' she said, putting a hand on Ellen's arm. 'And we think your husband suits you very well – such a good-looking fellow. Mrs. Ashburne thinks she is going to settle here. Won't that be nice?' said Mrs. Fish, who liked new blood. 'Mrs. Ashburne is in number fourteen, you know. Such a pleasant room. It has a powder-closet, hasn't it, Mrs. Ashburne?'

'Would you care to come up and see it?' invited Mrs. Ashburne.

So Ellen had to go. She stood with Mrs. Fish and Mrs. Ashburne and had all the family photographs explained.

On a table stood a silver pepper-castor, salt-cellar and mustard-pot, half-in, half-out of tissue-paper wrappings. 'I almost took them down to lunch,' confessed Mrs. Ashburne, laying a hand upon them. 'When I take my own table-silver down, it's practically irrevocable. It means I've settled. I think,' she said, turning to Mrs. Fish, 'that I shall certainly take them down to-night.'

'That will be splendid,' said Mrs. Fish. 'Do take them down, dear. You'll feel more like home when you get your own silver on your table. What a good idea it is. I wish I hadn't parted with mine.'

At last Ellen escaped. Although she liked people, she thought of getting away from them as 'escaping,' because there was always something she wanted eagerly to do, or somebody she wanted to be with; in this case Mrs. Brockington, to whose door she now hurried. She knocked and was told to come in.

'Here I am,' she said with a sigh of relief.

'Come along, dear,' said Mrs. Brockington, who had arranged two chairs before the open window. 'But not for long, because your son has only this one day with you. I mustn't take up too much of your time.'

'How are the plants?' said Ellen, bending over a stand with quite twenty pots on it.

'All thriving,' said Mrs. Brockington, who liked plants. 'You must grow something,' she always said. 'People who've had gardens can't cut themselves off from all growing things without feeling it. I must have something to watch and look after.'

Mrs. Beard grumbled about the plants and all the books too.

'The day-women simply can't get the room tidied up,' she said.

Books by Evelyn Underhill, Gerald Heard, Leslie Weatherhead, William Temple, St. Teresa, St. Francis, C. S. Lewis, Fosdick, Inge – showing catholic taste – spilled over the tables and chairs and often enough the bed.

'She's a very religious woman,' said Mrs. Beard, as if Mrs. Brockington suffered from some chronic illness.

Ellen could not remember her own mother. She and her brother Henry, now a surgeon in Manchester, had been brought up by her father and an aunt. She imagined that what she felt when she was with Mrs. Brockington was what one felt with one's own mother; a mother of the right sort, that is. She thought of it as a 'clear' feeling, compounded of relief and reassurance.

In spite of her happy, busy life, Ellen had need of both. Outside the warm, bright circle of home, there was darkness and fear. The war had appalled her. After the bombing, the gas-chambers, the concentration camps, how could life be the same again? Trust in mankind was undermined for ever. There was no limit to the cruelty and oppression wreaked by men upon men.

All sorts of things stabbed at and haunted her as she went about her daily life; the uncomprehending misery of a child's face in a photograph of Korean refugees in the morning papers; the sight of cattle, stupid with terror, being crammed into a truck when she fetched Avery from the station. A patient horse with sores under its saddle, standing between the shafts of a van in the streets. It was the suffering of the innocent and helpless that burdened her with what she considered useless pity, since she couldn't do anything about it.

When she was first married, she used to talk to Avery about what was in her mind. At twenty, she was full of questions she naïvely imagined he could answer. She used to lie in the crook of his arm, talking, seeking reassurance.

'But Jesus said, Avery, He said: "Not even a sparrow falls to the ground without my Father."'

'Yes,' said Avery. 'But they fall.'

Ellen was silent at that. She sat up in bed, looking at him with grave eyes.

He laughed and pulled her down again.

'Don't bother about it. What's the good? How can we ever know?'

But she continued to bother. She couldn't help it. She had to. But gradually she stopped talking to Avery about these things. Better not. He was too reasonable, and it needed more than reason.

In finding Mrs. Brockington, Ellen had found someone who had asked the same questions and who, towards the end of her life, now had found, if not the answers, some divine reassurance that answers would eventually be given. Mrs. Brockington had had bitterer questions than Ellen to ask. Her two sons had been killed in the first World War, her husband had died of a heart attack during a bombing raid in the second. But Mrs. Brockington, old, alone, almost crippled by rheumatism, had faith and courage. She had more. She had a warm serenity, and when Ellen was with her, she almost had it too. For goodness is catching. Mrs. Brockington was further on the road Ellen wanted to travel, and because Mrs. Brockington had got there, Ellen felt she might get there too.

Even quarter of an hour with Mrs. Brockington filled Ellen with mysterious peace, though she did nothing but talk and smile, looking into the sweet, worn face of her old friend.

'Now, dear, you must go and be with your family,' said Mrs. Brockington firmly. 'Come again as soon as you can. I'm so glad to have seen your husband. Now I can picture you all together at home, and a very happy picture it makes.'

Ellen kissed the old woman and drew her shawl more closely round her and reluctantly went.

She ran down through the quiet house, where behind closed doors the old ladies were resting, and out into the summer afternoon. She hurried about the garden looking for her family. Coming through the Maiden's Walk where the sunlight was quite shut out by the yews, seamed and twisted like a double row of witches, she saw them grouped in deckchairs on the lawn beyond, with an empty chair arranged for her. The empty chair touched her. She was happy to be waited for.

'What a time you've been,' said Avery as she appeared.

III

On their way home through the little town, drowsy in Sunday calm, they had to pass The Cedars.

'Shall we call in and see Granny?' said Ellen. 'John, can you spare five minutes or would you rather start for home?'

'Five minutes won't make any difference,' said John Bennett, who had parked his car in the town before setting off for Somerton in theirs.

'You'll see the French girl,' said Anne.

'French girl?'

'Granny's got a French girl for three months. You will be able to kiss her hand, Uncle John. She'll expect it.'

'Then she'll be disappointed,' he said.

'Oh, do kiss her hand,' said Anne.

'Indeed no. She might take it seriously.'

'What fun if she did,' said Anne.

'Sshh . . . ' warned her mother on the threshold of the

drawing-room, where old Mrs. North sat with Louise, having, presumably, French conversation.

'This is unexpected,' said the old lady, submitting her cheek to their kisses. 'And so many of you. Hugh, you get a good deal of leave, don't you? Good evening, Mr. Bennett.'

'Are we interrupting?' asked Ellen.

'We can continue later,' said old Mrs. North.

While her mother-in-law was making the introductions, Ellen went to speak to the housekeeper, whom she had seen to be engaged in setting the table for supper in the dining-room.

'Good evening, Mrs. Avery,' said Miss Daley, and from the heave of her shirt blouse, Ellen saw that something was wrong.

'I'm going to be late for chapel,' said Miss Daley. 'But do you think that French madam will give me a hand? Not she. And I'm singing a solo to-night, Mrs. Avery, though what my voice will be like with me in this state I can't imagine. I've never been late to chapel yet,' quavered Miss Daley.

'Let me help,' said Ellen, snatching the glasses from the tray.

'No, no, you've got your own supper to do when you get home,' protested Miss Daley. 'Now I wish I hadn't spoken. But why can't she do something? She's never lifted a finger all day, but it's no good to say anything. Mrs. North thinks Mademoiselle's the cat's whiskers. What's made me late is Mrs. North saying Mademoiselle didn't have much lunch because she doesn't like rice pudding and I'd better make some ice-cream for supper. And making ice-cream takes time, Mrs. Avery. I hadn't expected it. I'm all out of breath and I'll be worse by the time I've ran all the way to chapel. Mrs. North might consider my position. There's about two hundred people waiting to hear me sing to-night.'

'Get your hat on. I think we can run you there in the car,' said Ellen, hurrying to the drawing-room door. 'Granny, do excuse us if we fly. Miss Daley is worried about getting to chapel in time. If we go now, we could take her, couldn't we, Avery? So good-bye, Granny. Good-bye, Mademoiselle. Come along everybody. Miss Daley is coming downstairs.'

'It's always the same,' said old Mrs. North, as they went. 'They rush in and then they rush out again. Is it like that in France? Is everybody always in a hurry there too?'

'It is the same,' said Louise.

'I don't know what the world's coming to,' said old Mrs. North.

In the car, Miss Daley having been dropped at the chapel, where she would almost stun the congregation by her powerful rendering of 'Oh, Rest in the Lord', and John Bennett having been waved away down the London road, the Norths travelled homewards in a relaxed mood.

'Hugh, what did you think of the French girl?' asked Anne, leaning on him and digging her elbows into him with sisterly affection.

'Girl?' said Hugh. 'She must be thirty, surely. She's not flattering, is she? She wasn't at all interested in any of us.'

'She doesn't seem to be interested in anything,' said Ellen. 'But why do they come if they aren't? You'd think they come out of interest in the language, or the country, or the people. But goodness knows what this girl has come for. Still, Granny seems to be very pleased with her.'

CHAPTER FIVE

∽◇∾

Old Mrs. North was indeed pleased with Louise. She wished Louise had come years before. She regretted the time she had spent without her, and before a month was out she was dreading the day Louise would leave her. Old Mrs. North was happier now than at any time since the death of her husband.

As for Louise, she made herself pleasant, if only to her employer. The old lady was the means of absence from Amigny while Paul Devoisy was getting himself married. Louise passed the time with her; and she had the sense – no one had more sense than Louise – to know she was passing the time as comfortably at The Cedars as it was possible to pass it anywhere. Life at The Cedars was not exciting, but it was different; and it was difference that Louise was bent on procuring for herself at this time.

After the affair with Paul she needed rest and reparation. At The Cedars the air was fresh, the garden was large, there was plenty of milk. After this sojourn, her eyes would be clearer, her skin purer. She would go back with her looks renewed and when she passed Paul in the streets of Amigny he would see that his desertion had made no mark upon her. It was worth putting up with boredom at The Cedars. She was used to that. She felt that anywhere.

There was no need for her to exert herself much. To sit in the garden or the drawing-room, correcting old Mrs. North's French – not too much, because what could one do with it? – was not a strenuous form of work. And she turned the time she sat with the old lady to good account. She did quantities of her own fine sewing. Germaine Brouet might have her trousseau lingerie from the Rue de la Paix, but Louise thought with satisfaction that two or three of the things she was now making herself were no less exquisite.

The standards Louise set in the matter of dress and personal appearance filled old Mrs. North with admiration. When these standards were extended to her, she was astonished and delighted. She submitted like a pleased child to Louise's attentions. Louise arranged her hair, varnished her nails, applied a little colour to her lips, accompanied her to London to buy dresses, coats, hats. Louise picked over Mrs. North's jewels for exactly the right pieces to be worn. They spent hours at the dressing-table.

That anyone should think she was worth such care at her age delighted and touched the old lady. It was so different, she told Louise, from other people's attitude – Mrs. Avery's, for instance. 'They just think of me as Granny,' she said. She was sure Mrs. Avery never noticed what she wore. She should have said, in fairness, that Ellen rarely noticed what anybody had on, though she knew whether she liked the general effect and people remained in her mind looking pleasant or unpleasant without her being able to say whether they were wearing last year's hat or not.

'I thought it was too late to care how I look,' said the old lady.

'It is never too late,' said Louise firmly.

'I came to think it didn't matter,' said old Mrs. North.

'It always matters,' said Louise.

'You look like a duchess,' she said, standing back to look critically at Mrs. North posed on her dressing-stool in a corded lilac silk with lace at her neck and wrists. She even arranged a fold of the skirt as if the old lady would sit there for ever.

'You must never wear anything but real lace,' ordered Louise.

Mrs North touched it, and looked into the glass.

'You are very good to me, dear,' she said.

'But no,' said Louise. 'It interests me. Also, it is a pity not to use beautiful things. What good are they if no one sees them?'

'You are right,' said old Mrs. North, and turning over the jewels in her case, she brought out a ring, three diamonds embedded in a gold band.

'I'd like to give you this, dear,' she said, proffering it. 'Do have it, will you?'

Louise took it up and smiled.

'Tenez, Madame,' she said. 'It is very kind. But do not give it to me. Your family might not like it. Also, it is quite unsuitable for me. You see?' she said, putting it on. 'It is not for my hand, is it?'

Mrs. North blushed a little. The ring looked clumsy, even vulgar on that narrow hand.

'It is quite wrong,' she said, and hastened to take it back

and bury it under a little heap of gold chain in the jewel case. 'I beg your pardon,' she said, and shut the case up.

She did not offer anything in its stead, and Louise was annoyed with herself. She had given way to a moment of anger that anyone should think she would wear such an affair, and now she was not to get anything. The ring was ugly, but it had value. She could have sold it.

She had no need, however, to regret her refusal. Mrs. North, without saying anything, had the diamonds reset according to present fashion and gave the ring to Louise as a surprise a few weeks later.

Its reception was warm enough then. Louise was delighted with the ring and Mrs. North was delighted with Louise for being too honest to pretend to want the ring in the old setting and for being so pleased with it in the new. Old Mrs. North was indeed satisfied with Louise, but Miss Daley, the housekeeper, was not.

Before the French girl came, Mrs. North had depended upon Miss Daley for care and company. Now she did not. Moreover, she was becoming more and more critical. The French girl seemed to have initiated a lack of appreciation of Miss Daley and Miss Daley did not like it.

She didn't like the way the foreigner walked into her kitchen, either, asking questions and seeming to laugh at her ways of cooking.

As, for instance, one morning when she was making a jelly from a jelly-square. 'And what is this?' enquired Louise.

Miss Daley frowned. She detested the way Mademoiselle had of picking things up between finger and thumb, and when she did it now, Miss Daley felt it was an insult to the jelly-square.

'D'you mean to say you don't have jellies in France?' she said.

Louise smiled.

'Not like that,' she said. 'Coming in packets? We never have ready-made foods. Mon Dieu, no.'

Miss Daley asked Mrs. North what 'Mon Dieu' meant and when she was told, she said she would thank Mademoiselle not to use such words in her kitchen.

'Don't be foolish, Daley,' said old Mrs. North, who not only looked like a duchess on occasion nowadays, but behaved like one. 'The French always say Mon Dieu. It means nothing to them. Autres pays, autres moeurs, you know, Daley, which means in different parts of the world, one does differently. We don't want Mademoiselle to think the English provincial and narrow-minded.'

Miss Daley did not like to be spoken to in French words, or to be told not to be foolish. Also there were other incidents. She spoke to Mrs. Avery about them.

'I put a white collar on my best dress, Mrs. Avery – quite a nice bit of open-work. They're always so dressed up here nowadays, I thought perhaps something was expected of me. Nobody can say I don't try to please Mrs. North. Anyway, when I took the tea in on Sunday, Mrs. North said: "You've got a new collar on," she says. "It's pretty, isn't it, Mademoiselle?" And if that French girl doesn't get up and finger it. "It's not made by hand," she says. Not made by hand,' said the indignant Miss Daley. 'As if anybody ever makes anything by hand nowadays, or as if the likes of me could afford it if they did! But she took all the pleasure out of that collar for me, Mrs. Avery. And that's what she's always doing.'

'I served some tinned pea soup the other night. I do it up a bit, you know, with cream off the milk and dried mint sprinkled on at the last. Delicious, I call it. But that French woman put down her spoon and said "What is it?" and when Mrs. North asked me, I had to say it came out of a tin. Well, I went back to the kitchen and had a good cry. I have my pride, you know, Mrs. Avery.'

Though inwardly surprised that anyone should have pride in tinned soup, Ellen smoothed as best she could.

'You'll have to watch that French girl,' announced Miss Daley, in dark triumph one day. 'Mrs. North has given her a ring now. One of her old ones reset. I know, because I've seen the bill. You can see it on the girl's finger, unless she won't wear it when you're about. I know you're not the watching kind, but you've your children to think of.'

Ellen made non-committal murmurs. She did not mind what her mother-in-law did with her rings and did not think her children would mind either.

Whenever she called at The Cedars nowadays, Miss Daley waited to waylay her and get in a word or two about the French girl. But Ellen, though she recognised that Miss Daley had grounds for grievance, continued to be glad old Mrs. North took pleasure in Louise's company.

Louise soon found that a little implied criticism of Mrs. Avery, and even of the children, did not come amiss to the old lady, so she implied it. Not only to flatter, but because she had a natural asperity she liked to exercise. She was careful, however, to make it clear that the children would have been different if their mother had brought them up better.

Now and again Anne rode down on Roma to pay duty visits, tying Roma up in the drive and letting her graze the grass verges while she herself sat with her grandmother in the drawing-room or in the garden according to the weather. She was youthfully courteous, but stole a glance at the time now and again to see if she had been there long enough. She wore a shirt and jodhpurs and she laughed and blushed and shook her shining hair when they tried to make her speak French with them. In her youth and candour she was disarming enough, but Mademoiselle managed to find something to disapprove of when she had gone.

'Mais elle ne sait rien, cette petite,' she said in astonishment. 'Quelle education.'

'If you knew what it costs,' said old Mrs. North. 'But what a pretty child, isn't she?'

'She is very well. She is even exquisite,' allowed Louise. 'But she is always dressed the same, in those trousers and a chemise like a boy's. What idea will she have to dress herself later, if her mother does not teach her now?'

'But what idea has my daughter-in-law herself?' said old Mrs. North. 'She looks nice, I know, but in the summer she's always in a linen frock or something like it and in winter in a tweed skirt and a sweater.'

'Sweater! What a word!' shuddered Louise. 'It means something one sweats in, n'est-ce-pas?'

'In France,' she resumed, after clicking minute stitches

71

into some batiste, 'no young girl so beautiful would be content to spend all her time with a horse. She would expect more.'

'Je vous crois bien,' said old Mrs. North carefully.

'You said that very nicely,' said Louise. 'Vous devenez tout à fait française, Madame.'

They were very pleased with each other.

When Avery came with his wife, criticism could be indulged in afterwards. But not when he came alone. When he came alone, he was entirely his mother's son, and old Mrs. North was pleased to show Mademoiselle that he still belonged to her, though not so much as he would have done if he had no wife.

Avery called occasionally on his way up from the station. Sometimes he merely appeared, put the London papers in his mother's lap and went. Sometimes he sat down for a few moments. He was affectionately amused, even interested, in the change in his mother since the arrival of the French girl. He complimented her.

'Mother, you look wonderful. What have you been doing with her, Mademoiselle?'

'Is that a new diamond brooch, Mother?'

'This brooch,' said his mother, 'is no newer than you are. Your father gave it to me when you were born. It is precisely forty-three years old.'

'Hush,' said Avery. 'Don't frighten Mademoiselle by these astronomical figures. She will think me a very old man.'

Louise smiled.

'Oh, Monsieur, it is an age I should not like to claim for myself. But for a man, what is it?'

She bent her smooth dark head over a small square of lawn she was sewing.

'What are you making?' he asked, smiling at so much industry.

'A handkerchief.'

'I never heard of anyone making a handkerchief.'

'I make all mine,' she said.

'And very beautiful they are. Little works of art,' said old Mrs. North. 'Just look at the embroidery of that initial, Avery.'

Louise surrendered her sewing.

'And did you do that?' he asked, looking fully at her.

She gave a little grimace of self-deprecation.

'It's incredible,' he said, handing back the lawn.

'She has a passion for perfection,' said old Mrs. North.

'Really?' said Avery, looking at the girl again. 'Mmmm . . .

'Shall we have a glass of sherry?' he proposed.

'Certainly, dear. You know where it is.'

He went out of the room.

'Il est beau, Monsieur Aviary, n'est-ce-pas?'

'Not Aviary, dear. That is where the birds are kept. Avery. A-v-e-r-y. I had a brother of that name. Yes, he is handsome, isn't he? That's where the children get their looks from, of course.'

Avery came back with the sherry.

'You have very strong wine in England,' said Louise, taking hers.

'Come, you're the wine drinkers, surely?' he said.

'We send our strong wines to England. We drink much wine, yes. We drink it every day, but we put water into it.'

'That makes me shudder,' said Avery, laughing.

She laughed too. The wine cheered her. There had been so much water at all the meals. But now she laughed, showing her flawless teeth. She was animated. Her eyes shone. She made fun of the English. It was quite a pleasant half-hour.

CHAPTER SIX

—⋄⋄⋄—

Towards the end of the summer holidays, silences were apt to fall at Netherfold. Anne's return to school loomed over them all. As a rule the subject was shied away from by all parties, but one afternoon as she lay on the grass while, in the hammock-swing above, her mother sewed name-tapes on a few last things, Anne said sadly:

'Things make sort of graphs, don't they?'

Her mother knew what she was thinking, but said, 'What do you mean particularly, darling?'

'Well, the holidays,' said Anne, and was quiet again.

'For the first half,' she said, in a moment, 'it's absolutely perfect. I feel they're going on for ever. Then about the middle, I get a little weight in my chest. Only a little one, about an ounce. But as the time gets shorter, the weight gets heavier, and now it weighs about a ton,' she finished, turning her head away.

'But you like school, don't you?'

'It's all right,' said Anne, 'when I get there. I wouldn't like to go anywhere else. But I do hate leaving you and Daddy and Roma and everything. I sometimes wish I wasn't so fond of home, Mummy,' she burst out. 'It's so uncomfortable to have to keep leaving it and not being here.'

'But it works both ways. There's a school graph too. It might go down until half-term, but then it begins to rise, doesn't it?'

'Oh, it does! And then I get frightfully excited. What I nearly die to get to, is, first seeing you at the station, Mummy, and then to come home and stand just about here, before Roma knows. I watch her and I say "Roma", and she lifts her head and listens. Then I say "Roma" again, and she tosses her head and kicks up her heels and whinnies and gallops for the gate and so do I. Oh, the darling,' said Anne extravagantly, scrambling up from the grass. 'I must go and talk to her while I can.'

She was off and Ellen hastily dried her eyes.

'I'm silly,' she told herself. ' But Avery's nearly as bad, if not quite.'

He was. When, on the last day, as he was leaving after breakfast, Anne flung her arms round him, his eyes watered freely, though he said in a hearty way: 'Here – come on.'

'Daddy, you and Mummy will come for half-term, won't you?' she implored.

'Have we ever missed?'

'No, you're wonderful,' said Anne, hugging him. 'You're the best parents in the school. I'm terrifically proud of you. I love you both till I could burst.'

'I'm going to miss my train,' said Avery, tearing himself away. 'Good-bye, pet. See you soon.'

He could make a quick parting, but for Ellen it was more prolonged. She had to wave the train away. But first, on the way to the station, she and Anne must call at The Cedars to say good-bye there.

After a prolonged session at the dressing-table, old Mrs. North and Louise had just come down to the drawing-room where coffee was being brought in by a tight-lipped Miss Daley. Miss Daley resented this interruption of her work and disliked waiting on Mademoiselle in any shape or form.

'Shall I bring two more cups, Mrs. Avery?' asked Miss Daley, over the head of her employer, who looked at her like an affronted duchess. 'There's plenty of coffee here.'

'No, thank you, Miss Daley,' said Ellen. 'I'm afraid we haven't time.'

'Never time. Never time for anything,' said old Mrs. North. 'Why don't you come a little earlier then?'

'You'll hardly believe it, but it's taken me all my time to get here now,' said Ellen. 'Come along, Anne.'

'Good-bye, Granny,' said Anne, kissing her grandmother's presented cheek. 'Good-bye, Mademoiselle,' she said, offering her hand. 'I don't suppose I shall see you again, shall I?'

'Indeed you will,' said old Mrs. North. 'Mademoiselle has promised to come back. I can't possibly lose sight of her now. She has made such a difference to my life. Well, go along, child. Hurry off with your mother. Have a nice term. Good-bye.'

Anne dashed into the kitchen to kiss Miss Daley, who showed some emotion at the embrace.

'I bet she didn't kiss that French girl,' she said to the charwoman.

Ellen and Anne drove to the station.

'Well, are you off again?' said the cheerful ticket-collector they all liked. 'No sooner come than gone, it seems to me, though I expect the holidays seem shorter than what school-time does. Never mind, you'll soon be back. Your friends have gone through. Number four as usual.'

On the platform a group of girls was collected, the Mowbrays, who came by car from Benhampton, and the Westons, these last with their plump mother who always brought them in from the junction. At the sight of Anne, the girls rushed towards her.

'Oh, Anne, we thought you weren't coming. Good morning, Mrs. North. We thought you'd got measles or something.'

'No such luck,' said Anne.

'They're all the same,' said Mrs. Weston. 'Aren't they, Mrs. North? They might be going to gaol instead of to that lovely place.'

'It may be lovely, but it isn't home,' said Christine Weston, admonishing her mother. 'And you ought to be flattered that we mind leaving you so much. School's all right when we get there, but we hate going back. This term isn't so bad, as it happens, because it's the play. I do wonder what parts we'll get, Anne.'

'Oh, the train,' groaned one of the Mowbray girls.

There was a good deal of last-minute embracing before Anne, smiling, but looking quite sick, Ellen noticed, got into the carriage with the others. She hung out of the window, maintaining the smile, and as the train disappeared round the bend, a forlorn hand in a short childish glove was still waving.

'Children oughtn't to have to go away to school,' said Ellen resentfully, as she got into bed that night.

'There's no alternative,' said Avery. 'There are no schools here. You have to live in London for day-schools and we shouldn't like that. Anne wouldn't be able to have Roma, either, so that settles it.'

'Oh, I know,' said Ellen, drawing up the eiderdown because the nights were already chilly.

'Well,' said Avery sententiously. 'Either our children are fond of home and it hurts them to leave it, or they aren't fond of home and don't care when they leave it. You can't have it both ways.'

'No,' said Ellen, comforted, though it would be hard to say why.

'We called at The Cedars of course this morning,' she said in a moment. 'Your mother says the French girl has promised to come back before long.'

'Yes, I heard something about that before,' said Avery. 'I'm glad. It's been a good idea, having her.'

CHAPTER SEVEN

❖

I

When Madame Lanier heard the letters drop into the box behind the shop door, she left the coffee on the stove and hurried to get them. It was a fortnight since they had heard from Louise, and though she should have been used by this time to their daughter's irregularity of correspondence, her anxiety grew with every day that went by. But this morning she saw at once that there was an English envelope among the French.

'Papa,' she called in a voice made lively by relief. 'It's here. If you don't come at once, I shall have to open it.'

'I'm coming, I'm coming,' he called from above. He had been combing out his beard and enjoying the crackles of electricity, but he threw down the comb, lassoed himself with the flowing black ribbon of his pince-nez and reached for his jacket.

Madame Lanier, clasping Louise's letter to her immense bosom as if it were Louise herself, went back to the kitchen, which, though dark and inconvenient, was nevertheless the scene of excellent cooking. Over the old-fashioned range

80

gleamed a great battery of copper pans. There was a strong, warm, heartening smell of coffee.

'Oh, hurry,' Madame Lanier called out suddenly in an access of impatience. She burned to open the letter, but would wait, because to share things with her husband doubled her pleasure.

With muffled thumpings of felt boots, Monsieur Lanier came downstairs.

'Well, here am I, but where are you?' he called.

'Sit down. I'm coming.'

He tied his napkin round his neck, and since she did not at once appear, he rapped on the table with his spoon and shouted, 'Service!'

At the stove Madame Lanier giggled. They played like this when Louise was not there. Though they wouldn't have admitted it – they didn't even realise it – they were much more comfortable without her. In the shop, they enjoyed the pleasant interchanges with customers, belittled by Louise. In the house, they joked, chattered and permitted them-selves endearments as they never did when she was at home. Yet they were always longing for her to be there and when the letter was opened at last and they read that she was actually coming, they were exclamatory with happiness.

'She said she might stay another month and now she's coming next week. In seven days, she will be here.'

'I must air her bed,' said Madame Lanier. 'Marie must do her room to-day. The new curtains must come home at once. Oh, I hope she will like them. You know she never likes anything unless she chooses it herself. Henri, what have I done? I should have waited.'

She had ordered new curtains for Louise's room in a gush of love, and now she was full of misgiving.

'Of course she'll like them,' said her husband stoutly. 'What can she object to? They're very pretty and goodness knows they cost enough. Well, well, we shall see her next week! I can hardly believe it. More coffee, Maman, if you please.'

'This is cold now,' said Madame Lanier, rising. 'I must get some hot.'

'You know,' he called from the dining-room to the kitchen, 'they have made her promise to go back.'

'Yes, I saw that,' she answered. 'They have appreciated her.'

'That's all very well. But what sort of a life is she making for herself, weaving back and forth across the Channel? She ought to marry and establish herself.'

'Now don't begin about that,' begged his wife, coming back with the steaming jug. 'Don't say anything to her the moment she comes home.'

'You know very well,' said Monsieur Lanier, throwing bread into his bowl, 'that I never say anything to her. It is only to you I say what's in my mind. But it's getting serious.'

'Never mind. Not just now,' she said. 'I'm too happy to-day to concern myself with anything further away than next week.'

'Very well, very well,' he said indulgently. 'Be happy. I'm happy too. It's time I was taking the shutters down.'

He went out on to the pavement. Next door, Bonnet had come out to take the shutters from his shoe-shop.

'Louise is coming home next week,' called Monsieur Lanier.

'Ah – excellent. You will be glad to see her.'

Each shook the other's left hand, as they did every morning. Bonnet went inside, but for a moment, Monsieur Lanier stood looking about at the street, quiet as yet, with the water running clear and faintly audible in the stone gutter. At the end of the street, the sycamore tree, thinly leafed in gold, drooped over the old, wrought-iron gate of the Archevêché, the whole as delicate as a drawing in Indian ink. He wondered what England was like and if she saw anything more beautiful than she could see here in her native town. Yet she despised Amigny and all it offered. He knew it and sighed.

Across the road, Chaix, the jeweller, unbarred his door and appeared on the pavement.

'Bonjour,' they called to each other and met in the middle of the road to shake hands.

'Louise is coming home next week,' said Monsieur Lanier.

'Good,' said the jeweller. 'You must have missed her.'

Everybody who came into the shop that morning heard that Louise was coming home from England.

When young Madame Devoisy came in to order cards for her reception, she heard it too. A young matron so important had the services of both Monsieur and Madame Lanier; so they both told her, beaming across the counter.

Like Madame Lanier, although so young, Madame Devoisy could be summed up at sight as a good woman. A greenish blonde, or so Louise said, her hair was in a heavy chignon, which, although the mode of the moment, was nevertheless not modish. She was pale – the colour of celery, Louise had told Paul Devoisy in the first fury of hearing of the proposed marriage. Her lashes were pale too, but her eyes were amber and her lips wild-rose colour and very smooth. She did not use lipstick. She was, said Louise, too pious for that.

Everybody beamed with approval on young Madame Devoisy. She was rich and good and what they called 'simple,' by which they meant unspoilt. She was radiantly happy in her bridal state and enjoying to the full the important things she was now called upon to do, such as having a reception of her own and organising the Vente de Charité for the local pension, to which she had gone as a child before being sent to her Paris convent.

She listened amiably to the account Louise's parents gave of the size of the house and garden, the wealth and aristocracy of the family with whom Louise was staying. Madame Lanier felt that one who was rich and aristocratic herself must naturally be interested in people of the same kind. She felt she was meeting young Madame Devoisy on her own ground, and it gave her such satisfaction to tell the young woman how fond these rich people in England were of her daughter, that her eyes brimmed with tears and she had to wipe them away.

Also moved, though she did not know why, Madame Devoisy laid her hand on the mother's arm.

'Tenez, Madame,' she said with the faint lisp that maddened Louise, but which charmed everyone else. 'Mademoiselle Louise . . .' Her 'Mademoiselle' placed the shopkeeper's daughter exactly. One was amiable, but not familiar. 'Mademoiselle was also a pupil at Ste Colombe.'

'Oh, yes, Madame, she was at Ste Colombe for ten years.'

'I remember her. Although I was with the little ones when she was in the Cours Supérieur.'

'Ah, yes, you are younger by several years,' said Madame Lanier, with a pang that this one should be a matron and so well-placed, while Louise was still unmarried.

'You know I am arranging the Vente de Charité this year?'

'Indeed, yes, Madame. So young, but so capable you are.'

'Would your daughter, do you think, take charge of one of the stalls for me? Perhaps the embroideries? She had always so much taste.'

Madame Lanier flushed with astonished pleasure. This really was something. To be asked to take charge of a stall by the most important young matron in the town! It meant close association with her. It meant meetings at Madame Devoisy's house. It might lead to anything. Louise would be delighted. She had always complained of the sort of society the Laniers were forced to keep. But this would give her the entry to the best in the town.

'Madame!' she cried, clasping her hands. 'She will be enchanted. It will be something for her to come home to. Madame, she is clever. She has travelled. She has been to England before, you know. Yes, she spent three months at Foxton two years ago. Her father and I feel sometimes that it is a little dull for her with us. But she will so much enjoy taking charge of a stall under your direction, Madame, and meeting her old school friends again! It is charming of you, Madame, to have thought of her.'

'Not at all,' said young Madame Devoisy complacently. 'I take it that she will do it then?'

'Certainly, certainly. Put her name down at once,' said Madame Lanier. 'And, Papa, you will give a donation, won't you?'

'With pleasure,' said Monsieur Lanier, and taking a bundle of notes from Mademoiselle Léonie at the caisse, he presented them to Madame Devoisy with a bow.

'Oh, it's too much,' protested the young woman. 'Monsieur! Really!'

'I am delighted to give to the Charities of Ste Colombe. Take it, I pray, Madame. And in the subscription list, please put it down in my daughter's name.'

'You are too good, Monsieur. Thank you a thousand times. Madame, I'll send notices of the meetings and everything to Mademoiselle Louise. Now I must go. I promised to meet my husband at twelve o'clock and it's striking now. Au revoir, Madame. Au revoir, Monsieur, et merci. Merci beaucoup.'

Forgetting her matronly dignity, she ran out of the shop like a child.

'There, Papa!' said Madame Lanier in a state bordering on ecstasy. 'Isn't that nice? Won't Louise be pleased? I have always wished those people to see our daughter to better advantage than behind the counter or in church. She will astonish them, Papa. They can but admire her, can they? Mademoiselle Léonie,' she called towards the glass box where that middle-aged woman sat all day receiving moneys and making out accounts. 'We are going now. Call out if there is anything important. Come to lunch, Henri.'

'What is there?' he asked, shutting the glass doors on the tooled leather copies of Racine, Molière, Corneille and other classics that nobody bought.

'There is what you like,' said his wife. 'Cold ham and cornichons and a salad and some Camembert in an excellent state of putrefaction.'

'Good,' said Monsieur Lanier. 'Let us go.'

'I'm so very glad,' Madame Lanier's voice could be heard diminishing into the house, 'about the Vente de Charité.'

II

The Paris train was due at half-past six in the evening, so, as the shop was closed, both her parents were able to go to meet Louise. They waited, two bulky figures, Madame Lanier swathed in veils and a vast coat, Monsieur in his best suit with something elephantine about his trousers, an ancient cape, a woollen scarf and a large black hat. Being so much in the shop, they felt and feared the fresh air; and the air blowing unimpeded over the flat land round Amigny was very fresh to-night.

'It's winter, Henri,' said Madame Lanier, shuddering. 'It's absolutely winter.'

'I always think,' said her husband, 'that there is nothing more melancholy than a railway station at night.'

The cement platform stretched palely to right and left. The few lamps merely revealed the desolate scene without illuminating it. The parents kept their faces turned up the line, although the wind, blowing from that direction, made their eyes water.

'Ah, at last,' cried Monsieur Lanier. Far away in the night sky appeared something like a large loose caterpillar with a fiery stomach, gambolling and rolling madly and coming on at great speed – the smoke of the Paris train, which soon thundered up and clanked to a standstill, belching smoke above and steam below. This leviathan brought forth one slight and solitary figure.

'There she is!' cried the parents, running in spite of their bulk. 'Louise! Louise chérie! Louise!'

She was engulfed in their loving embraces. They took her hand-baggage and followed her, colliding with each other and with her, to the booking-hall. They stood respectfully while she claimed her travelling trunk. Under the lights, among blue-bloused porters, she looked so cosmopolitan, she had such an air.

'Is there a taxi?' asked Louise.

'I ordered Pouillot,' said her father.

'You look so well, my treasure,' said her mother as they rattled over the cobbled streets, over the bridge where the lights of the little town were doubled in the dark river. 'The air of England must have done you good.'

'England is a small country entirely surrounded by the sea,' said Monsieur Lanier. 'That's what it is.'

'I was nowhere near the sea, Papa.'

'No, no, but the sea air would reach you in England, wherever you were. It is so small.'

In the darkness of her corner, Louise shrugged her shoulders. Let him have it his own way.

'You were so thin when you went,' said her mother. 'But now you are even a little plump.'

'Oh, horror, I hope not,' cried Louise, roused. 'Is it true? Do you see any difference?'

'No,' said Monsieur firmly. 'Except that you look well where before you looked ill. That is the only difference.'

'Thank heaven,' said Louise, relaxing. 'To be fat is disgusting!'

And they who were fat humbly agreed.

They reached home. Louise felt the usual distaste at having to go through the shop into the house.

While her trunk was being brought in, she went upstairs with her mother.

'What a poor light,' she said when Madame Lanier switched it on. 'I'm used to good lights now.'

'Papa shall put a stronger bulb in, my love.'

Louise looked round her room. It was good after all to be back in it.

'What are these?' she said, walking to the window and taking the curtains into her hand.

Madame Lanier held her breath.

'They're new,' said Louise. 'Toile de Jouy, and not bad at all.'

'Oh, Louise,' said her mother, hurrying to embrace her. 'Do you like them? I was so afraid.'

'It is quite a coincidence,' said Louise, pressed to the billowy bosom. 'They are rather like the curtains in my room in England.'

'I am so happy,' said her mother, laying her cheek to her child's smooth head. 'I ordered them and then I was afraid they would not be to your taste. My treasure has so much better taste than her poor mother. Now I must run down to my stove. I have another surprise for you later. You will come down quickly, won't you, darling? I don't want the dinner to spoil.'

'I'll come at once. I'm very hungry and it smells so good, it makes me hungrier than ever.'

'One minute then. Only one minute.'

Madame Lanier hurried downstairs, full of love and happiness.

She was increasingly happy. Not only had she a success with the curtains, but with the dinner too. The consommé was crystal clear, but strong. The chicken was done to perfection. The crème was so smooth, so delicious, that no one could make it last long enough, but went on scraping out the little brown pots after there was nothing left.

'Well,' said Louise. 'I haven't had a dinner like that since I left home.'

'Is it possible?' said Madame Lanier, unable to believe this high praise. 'Is it really possible?'

'Well, Maman, the English are not noted for their cooking,' said Monsieur Lanier, 'and since I doubt if you have your equal in France – among the housewives, that is – I don't think Louise would find it in England.'

'But this is ridiculous,' said Madame Lanier delightedly. 'You flatter me, both of you. I never heard of such a thing.'

'It isn't flattery,' said her husband.

'So your old mother cooks to please you, does she?' said Madame Lanier, who could not resist the temptation to fish for another compliment or two while there was the chance of any.

'Of course,' said Louise, with one of her rare smiles.

These smiles enchanted her parents. She smiled as if she didn't want to, which somehow had always given a peculiar charm to her face. When one of those smiles began to dawn, her parents leaned forward beaming, as if the sun was coming out and they wanted to catch every ray.

'My treasure,' said Madame Lanier with emotion. 'It is so good to have you at home again. You will stay with us now, won't you? You won't go to England again?'

'Madame North wants me to go for Christmas, but I don't think I shall. I don't think I shall go before Easter at the earliest. I may never go again. I don't know yet. But don't bother about that now. I've only just come home.'

'Yes, leave the child alone, Maman,' said her father.

'Tiens!' said Louise, reaching for an envelope she had put on the sideboard behind her. 'I have brought one or two photographs for you.'

'Oh, that will be interesting,' said Monsieur Lanier.

'Wait for me, Louise,' said her mother. 'I must just get my glasses.'

'This is the house where I lived,' said Louise. 'The old lady's house. Those are the windows of my bedroom.'

Their heads together, her parents pored with deep interest over the snapshot.

'It is a very big house,' said her father. 'I don't think there is one of that size in Amigny – except perhaps the Devoisys'.'

'This is the son's house – Netherfold, it is called. Here he is. His name is Avery. You see he is not bad at all.'

'That is the publisher?' asked her father. 'You are right. He is tall and handsome.'

'There we are, all together,' said Louise, bringing out a

photograph taken by John Bennett one Sunday afternoon at Netherfold.

'My darling, it is excellent of you,' said Madame Lanier. 'How well your broderie anglaise has come out! And that is the old lady! Most distinguished. What a beautiful young girl!'

'That is Monsieur Avery's daughter. He adores her. She is pretty,' conceded Louise. 'There is Monsieur Avery again, you see, and that is his wife.'

'She has a sweet face,' said Madame Lanier. 'What a very nice family. They all look so happy.'

'That is Monsieur Avery's son. He is about eighteen. He is doing his service. They make such a fuss about that in England, Papa, while we, who have always had it . . .' She shrugged her shoulders and put the photographs back into the envelope. 'Those are for you,' she said. 'I have others.'

They thanked her profusely. It was all she had brought them from England, but it occurred neither to them nor to her that she might have brought any other gift.

Madame Lanier hurried out for the coffee. Her elbows on the table, Louise held her cup between the fingers of both hands, sipping now and again. The light of the red silk-shaded lamp, hopelessly old-fashioned, she thought almost affectionately, shone down on her head. The red light, her pallor, her dark eyes became her wonderfully.

'Well, tell me some news,' she said. 'What's been happening?'

'Ah,' cried Madame Lanier, putting down her cup. 'You want some news?'

This was the moment.

'Wait,' she said, smiling. 'We have one wonderful piece of news for you, haven't we, Papa? Something you will really like.'

'Oh?' said Louise, sipping. 'What is it?'

'It is this,' said her mother, clearing a place on the table and leaning her forearms on it. 'Last week – was it Wednesday, Papa? – well, the day doesn't matter,' she said, hurriedly in case Louise should say it for her. 'But it was Wednesday, because it was the day your letter came to say you were coming home and we were so happy about it, we told her, didn't we, Papa?'

'Told whom?' said Louise.

'Young Madame Devoisy,' said her mother.

The cup was poised in Louise's fingers. Her eyes were intent on her mother's face.

'She is organising the Vente de Charité at Ste Colombe this year. She is organising everything in the town now, it seems to me. When we told her you were coming home, she suddenly asked if you would take charge of a stall for her. Think of that! I accepted at once. I knew you would like it above everything. What is it, Louise?' faltered Madame Lanier. 'You do like it, don't you? I haven't done wrong, have I?'

Louise put her cup down. Under the lamp, her nostrils showed white.

'You had no right,' she said, speaking with difficulty. 'Why don't you wait? Why do you think you can decide for me? I shall not take a stall at the Vente de Charité. You can get out of it as best you can.'

She got up from the table. They raised distressed eyes to her face, which was now in darkness above the lamp.

'Louise,' said her mother humbly, ' I'm so sorry. You must forgive me. I thought you would like it, darling.'

'You were wrong,' said Louise. 'A stupid provincial sale of work . . . all those stupid people. Oh, it is always the same,' she said in disgust. 'I wish I'd never come home.'

They were silent, their heads bowed over the empty cream pots. They did not look at each other.

'I shall go to bed,' said Louise harshly. 'I am very tired.'

She went round the table and laid her lips without warmth to her father's brow. 'Good night, Papa. . . .'

'Good night, Maman,' she said, doing the same for her mother.

'Oh, Louise. I am so sorry . . .'

Louise flapped a hand.

'No more,' she said. 'I've had enough.'

She went up the echoing wooden stairs, but she did not seem to go to bed. Overhead, she walked backwards and forwards; unpacking, they supposed.

Madame Lanier washed up and put away the best dinner service, very handsome with its dark red decorations. It was not until she had finished that she realised the embarrassment of her own position. But when she had set the table for breakfast, she stood before her husband, with her hands rolled in her apron and a troubled look on her face.

'What shall I say to young Madame Devoisy, Henri?'

'Ah, that,' he said with a sigh. 'That is difficult.'

'And my donation?' he thought.

'I think perhaps, Maman, we were a little too much in a hurry,' he said.

CHAPTER EIGHT

—◦◇◦—

I

Madame Lanier usually enjoyed being in the shop. She liked serving people, exchanging news, taking the money. But now she kept out of it as much as she could. When she was obliged to take her place behind the counter, she stayed as near to the house door as possible, so that she could vanish through it if Madame Devoisy appeared.

She racked her brains incessantly to find something to say to that young person. She knew she would have to face her in the end, but how could she find the right way to tell her that Louise had refused her gracious invitation? Madame Lanier kept sighing, her plump forehead was corrugated with anxiety.

Monsieur Lanier worried too. One couldn't treat important customers in this way. It was bad for business.

And then after all, there was no need to make excuses to Madame Devoisy. Louise changed her mind.

'I have changed my mind, Mamma,' she said, after keeping them on tenterhooks for more than a week. 'I will take the stall.'

'Oh, Louise,' cried Madame Lanier, radiant with relief. 'I am so happy, darling. You think you will like it after all?'

'No,' said Louise. 'But since you have said I will take it, I will take it.'

Her mother was deeply grateful.

'How good she is, Henri. She really doesn't want to take the stall. It is only for my sake that she is doing it. To save me from the embarrassment of telling Madame Devoisy.'

The parents were much moved by this evidence of Louise's goodness of heart. Louise let them think what they chose. She was taking the stall for reasons of her own.

When she recovered from the first shock of hearing what her mother had arranged for her, she decided that she could not miss this unique opportunity of satisfying her curiosity and of embarrassing Paul. And how she would embarrass him by appearing in his house. How uneasy he must be already at the prospect! She was filled with savage pleasure at the thought of it and waited with impatience for the summons to the first meeting of the stall-holders.

It arrived. Young Madame Devoisy liked giving fashionable teas. To invite her helpers to a "Fiv o'clock" would flatter them and put them in the humour, from the start, to do their best for Ste Colombe. It would also give the young matron a chance to show off her house.

She prided herself on being a good hostess, and before the arrival of the helpers, she decided to be very kind to those who might feel a little overawed by the fact that they were visiting the house of a Devoisy; Louise Lanier, for instance, and people like that.

So when Mademoiselle Lanier was announced at the door of the white and gold salon, young Madame Devoisy hurried across the room to receive her.

'You probably remember most of your colleagues?' she said. 'Mademoiselle Ranaud, for instance? Yvette Courtan? Madame Vionne?'

'Naturally,' said Louise, giving her hand all round. 'Since we have seen one another constantly ever since we left Ste Colombe – except for my absence in England, of course.'

'Ah, yes, you have been in England,' fluted the hostess, bringing tea to Louise. 'You are quite used to fiv o'clocks, then, aren't you?'

'Well, to tell the truth,' said Louise with one of her smiles, 'the English don't have tea at fiv o'clock.'

They stared at her. They didn't believe her.

'Why is it called fiv o'clock then?' asked Madame Devoisy.

Louise shrugged her shoulders.

'A misapprehension on our part. Just a piece of ignorance. Or perhaps a hundred years ago the English did have tea at five o'clock. Now they have it at four or half-past. They have little sandwiches, scones, cakes,' she said, taking petits fours from Madame Devoisy's plate. 'And very good tea,' she said, stirring with a critical spoon the pale straw-coloured liquid in which twig-like leaves floated. The water had not been boiled and the milk was blue. She let the so-called tea run off her spoon while they watched her. 'The English make good tea,' she said. 'There is no tea like English tea.'

'But they can't make coffee,' said someone triumphantly.

She raised her eyebrows. 'I always had good coffee,' she

said, and Miss Daley would have been astonished to hear her. 'It depends on the household, of course. They don't like chicory in their coffee and I must confess neither do I now.'

The young hostess's pleasure in her fiv o'clock was ruined. She had thought she was doing the right thing and here, according to Louise Lanier, it was not the right thing at all. She smarted with humiliation and dared not ask anybody to have any more of the tea.

But, passing cigarettes, she recovered herself sufficiently to say she thought they ought to be getting down to business.

Louise, sitting in a pale gilt bergère before the fire, prepared to listen to suggestions and decisions. She was good at this sort of thing when she chose and it would have been easy to outshine and over-rule the others. But the associations of the room, of the house, of Germaine herself were becoming too much for her. He sat in these chairs, this was the woman he slept with. Worst of all there was his photograph on the writing table, the latest, the best of all, the only one she hadn't seen. She couldn't bear it, she was suddenly afraid that if he came home, she wouldn't be able to trust herself.

As soon as she decently could she said she must go. Madame Devoisy, somewhat restored by the brisk way the plans were going, said she would let her know the date of the next meeting and summoned the man-servant to show her out.

Louise crossed the courtyard alone. In a little wing to the left, through a window opened to mitigate the heat of the kitchen, she saw the cook slicing vegetables with a long knife for his dinner. She went through the great door, opened for her from inside the house. She hurried away. The dark mass of the cathedral loomed ahead. The night wind was cold and blew the bare branches of the trees across the stars.

What torment! She had to walk about a long time before she felt composed enough to go home. When she reached it, she gave no account of the meeting to her eager parents, except to say it was very dull.

In the house she had left, when the helpers had gone at last, the bride sat on the bridegroom's knee in the interval before dinner.

'She was so impolite, Paul. I don't know how she dared. In our house?' She looked round the salon as if it were the holy of holies. 'After all, her father is a tradesman, isn't he? Even if she does go to England.'

Her husband was as angry as she could wish, even more so. He wanted her to break up the meetings and tell Louise Lanier that she wasn't needed again. But Germaine would not agree to that. For a charitable cause one must put up with annoyances. All the same, it was nice to have him taking up the cudgels for her so vehemently and she kissed him for it.

Paul detached her arms from his neck. He was alarmed. What did Louise mean to do? She had removed herself to England and he had thought it magnanimous of her and was grateful. But here she was, back again, actually making her way into his house and being rude to his wife. How much further would she go?

Why couldn't she accept the fact that it was all over between them? It had been good while it lasted. He didn't expect the same intense excitements in his married life. But you can't have everything. He expected more solid joys: a home and a family. He had married not so much a wife as the mother of his children, and Germaine would make an excellent mother. The time had come for him to settle and he was doing it very well. He didn't want Louise to break in now and ruin everything.

'Write and tell her not to come again,' he urged his bride.

'Oh, darling, I can't do that,' said Germaine virtuously.

'Madame est servie,' announced the man-servant and Paul followed his wife in to dinner.

'Oh, women,' he thought with a sigh. 'Women.' Yet no one had obliged him to live with Louise at Folkestone and elsewhere, or even to marry Germaine.

II

Although Louise had found the first visit to his house almost unbearable, she was ready, when the second summons came, to go again. She resented having been made to suffer such a sense of loss and sadness that first time. She was used to feeling bitter; there was something stimulating about bitterness, but sadness was insupportable. No one should suspect her of being sad. She felt the need now of presenting herself as an attractive young woman leading an enviable, a cosmopolitan life, the sort of life none of the others knew anything about. So before she left home for the meeting, she put old Mrs. North's ring on her engagement finger. She mocked at herself for this childish subterfuge, but she gave in to it all the same. It could do its work. Someone would be sure to notice.

'Oh, Louise, you're engaged!' cried Yvette Courtan. 'And you didn't tell us! What a lovely ring! Who is your fiancé?'

Louise, with a show of embarrassment, changed the ring to another finger. She smiled and shook her head at the girls.

'I should have taken it off before I came here. Don't betray me, please.'

They were delighted with the mystery. Someone in England, they supposed. She didn't contradict them, but would say no more.

After that, she gained some subtle ascendancy over the company and all her suggestions for the sale of work were agreed to.

But as she was crossing the courtyard alone, Paul came in from the street.

In the light streaming from the house door, held open by the man-servant, she bowed and he raised his hat.

'Why do you come to my house?' he said in a low voice as he passed her. 'I thought you would have better taste.'

'My mother accepted for me before I came back from England,' she said furiously through her teeth. 'As if I want to look on at your ridiculous ménage.'

They continued, she to the great wooden door, he to the house.

'Oh, Paul,' cried his wife ecstatically, leaving the others to run to meet him.

Louise rushed away without knowing where she was going, her lips pressed tight together to keep her sobs back. She came to a deserted alley and there, her forehead pressed against the wall, she burst into tears.

'Oh, Paul. Oh, Paul, Paul . . .'

When she had cried herself out, she still stayed there, her forehead against the stone.

'I thought I could bear it,' she said. 'But I can't.'

She was weaker than she had bargained for.

After a while she dried her eyes and, in the dark, applied lipstick and powder to her face. She had to walk about now to get her eyes right before she could go home to be looked at by her parents. Hat in hand, she walked up one street, down another, down the boulevard by the river, round the cathedral and back again. What a place! There were eyes everywhere.

'I can't stay here,' she said. 'I shall have to go back to England.'

CHAPTER NINE

∞◇∞

I

It was made easy for her. Just before Christmas, a letter arrived from Ellen. Old Mrs. North had written several times to ask Louise to go back, but now Ellen added her persuasions.

Her mother-in-law, she said, was not well. If Louise would come back even for a few weeks, they felt it would help Mrs. North to recover her health. She missed Louise and seemed to have no wish to go out or to interest herself in any way without her.

'She is very attached to you,' wrote Ellen. 'I'm afraid you have made yourself indispensable to her happiness. We shall be very grateful if you will come; especially for Christmas. My mother-in-law wishes me to say that first-class expenses are to be paid and that your salary is to be doubled.'

Louise translated the letter at the breakfast table. Her parents, spoons suspended, looked at her in silence. They were impressed. First-class expenses. Salary doubled. They were also uneasy. Were these people trying to lure their daughter away permanently?

'I wish the letter hadn't come just now,' said Madame

Lanier. 'I was so looking forward to going to midnight mass all together on Christmas Eve. It's meant to be a family affair and you are all the family we have. And what is New Year's Day without you?'

Tears swam glassily in her eyes.

'I must go, Maman,' said Louise, compressing her lips as if it were a matter of duty. 'Madame needs me. Besides,' she said, 'the money is a consideration.'

'They must be very rich,' said her father.

'They are well off,' agreed Louise. 'But not fabulously so. They are, however, willing to pay almost anything to get me back, you see.'

Monsieur Lanier cleared his throat, adjusted his pince-nez and prepared to make a pronouncement.

'In my opinion,' he said, 'you shouldn't go. There is nothing for you in England. What can it lead to? I think it is time you took up your life here.'

'Look, Papa,' said Louise, leaning across the table and fixing him with her dark eyes. 'What is there in Amigny for me? Except marriage with André Petit? I haven't come to that yet, thank you.'

She got up abruptly and left the room.

'Now she won't eat her breakfast,' sighed her mother.

'I suppose we shall have to let her go, Henri,' she said in a moment.

'Have to let her go?' repeated Monsieur Lanier with irony. 'When have we been able to stop her doing anything she intends to do?'

They finished breakfast in heavy silence. Madame Lanier

wondered, as often before, why André Petit should be the only one to propose himself. It was humiliating that there was no alternative.

The truth was that the mothers didn't like Louise, and in Amigny the mothers were still the prime movers in the matter of marriage contracts. André Petit's mother had died years ago, so he was free to choose for himself.

During the morning, as Louise was coming downstairs, she heard the unmistakable lisp of young Madame Devoisy. She turned back to her room, threw on her coat, took up the letter she had just written and appeared in the shop.

'Ah, Madame,' she cried. 'This meeting will save me a walk.'

'Indeed,' said Madame Devoisy, who considered Louise's airy manner altogether unsuitable. 'Have you something to say to me?'

'Yes,' said Louise. 'It is that I regret I shall be unable to take the stall at Ste Colombe after all. My friends in England invite me most pressingly for Christmas. I'm sorry, Madame, but you understand, I am sure. Maman, I'm just going to the post.'

She waved her letter at her mother and bowed to the young matron, who told her husband all about it at luncheon.

She connected Louise's departure with the ring.

'I think she's engaged to someone in England,' she said.

Paul, forgetting himself, laughed shortly.

'I don't think she is.'

Germaine looked at him in surprise.

'Why shouldn't she be?'

'People don't get engaged to foreigners as easily as all that.

Besides, I should say she's very French. I don't think she'd like an Englishman.'

'Do you know her?'

'No, I don't know her,' he said. 'I've seen her in the shop, of course.'

The lie was unavoidable and he told it unflinchingly. He only wished Louise would get engaged to someone in England and take herself out of his life for ever. But things rarely turned out as conveniently as that.

Still it was an unexpected piece of luck that she should not be coming to his house any more and he smiled on his wife as if he had suddenly been given permission to enjoy his married life.

II

Three days before Christmas, Louise boarded the early morning train for Paris. It was still pitch dark and once inside the well-lit, well-warmed first-class compartment she could hardly see the faces of her parents outside the window. Clouds of steam rolled up from under the train, through which they made ghostly appearances, her father's white face and black beard, her mother's unwieldy black hat, under which nothing could be seen but her chin quivering with emotion. The guard blew his trumpet. Their voices came faintly through the glass. 'Good-bye, Louise. Good-bye, little one.'

She waved and smiled and they slid out of view. With a sigh of relief she settled herself against the dove-grey cushions of the corner seat.

It was pleasant to be travelling first-class and pleasant to think other people were paying for it. Money makes all the difference, she thought, watching the dawn break over the wintry scene. There was no money that could be called money in her family. The shop did well and they were comfortable. But that was all. Yet for a long time she herself had been associated with people with money. With Paul and now with the English family. For a long time, she had been looking on at money without having any herself. It was too bad. The lack of it had ruined her life. If she had had money, Paul wouldn't have left her for Germaine Brouet.

Paul had never given her money; she hadn't wanted it. She hadn't even thought of it. It's only when you haven't love that you begin to look for money, she said to herself. I threw away everything I had for nothing, she thought, but no one shall find me doing that again.

Her reflections, which had started in a detached, interested way, were turning to bitterness as they usually did.

By the time she reached the Channel steamer, she was deep in depression, which the prospect of the crossing did nothing to dispel. The grey sky leaned upon the grey sea, chopped with white foam. It was bitterly cold and as she went up the gangway, sleet began to fall. She went below at once and smoked and drank black coffee all the way over. She had been glad to leave France, but she didn't want to arrive in England.

There seemed no place for her. There was nowhere she wanted to be. Paul had made her homeless.

Cold, tired, irritated by the nuisance of passing through the Customs, she was walking through the barrier at Victoria when she caught sight of a noticeably tall man waiting beyond it. Light and warmth rushed into her face.

'Oh, Monsieur Avery! Have you come to meet me? Or there perhaps is someone else?' she cried, looking behind her.

'No, no – it's you,' he said, taking her travelling case. 'Is this your porter?'

'But this is charming on your part,' said Louise, hurrying along with him.

'I thought if I came to get you across, we should just catch the train at St. Pancras. And that will make all the difference to the length of your journey.'

'You are so nice,' said Louise, getting into the taxi, gratefully giving up effort, leaving all to him. How useful men were, how necessary!

'Well,' asked Avery, turning his handsome head towards her. 'How are you? Nice to see you again.'

She always had to listen carefully to what he said because, in common with many Englishmen, he barely moved his lips when he spoke. It gave her the air of hanging on his words, which he thought very attractive in her.

'I am well, thank you,' she said. 'And you, Monsieur? And how is dear Madame your mother?'

'She hasn't been well,' he said. 'Her heart isn't too good, though I don't think it's anything to worry about. I'm sure she'll be better now you've come.'

'I hope so,' said Louise.

'When I asked her what she wanted for Christmas,' he said, turning to smile down on her again, 'she said the best present I could give her would be to get you back.'

Louise smiled up at him, flattered. She knew her parents felt that too, but from them it didn't count. A compliment, to matter, had to come from outside.

'It is charming of you to come in search of me,' she said again.

'It's so good of you to come back,' he said, 'that we must do all we can to make it easy for you.'

It hadn't been his idea that he should meet her. He didn't put himself out much as a rule, except for his wife and children. But when his mother asked him to be at Victoria, he agreed. He was impatient to hand her over to the care of the French girl. Ailing, exacting, she had made great demands on Ellen's time lately, and even on his, which really was coming to something, he privately considered. The Christmas holidays were here and Ellen had her hands full at home. She couldn't go down for hours at a time to The Cedars and his mother had refused to come to stay at Netherfold. The only solution had been to get the companion back and that he was doing as quickly as possible.

At St. Pancras, he waved a hand to his usual travelling companions, Weston and Holmes, and got into a compartment with Louise. He thought he might find the journey a bit long and hoped she wouldn't expect him to talk the whole time.

But Louise considered conversation in a railway carriage a nuisance. You had to be very intimate to want to talk in a train; in love, or intensely interested in something in common. Journeys with Paul had been all happiness, but this Englishman was not Paul, so she arranged herself in her corner and after a few more pleasantries closed her eyes. There were two other people in the carriage, which made it unnecessary for her to exert herself further.

After waiting for a time to see if she wished for conversation, Avery took up his *Times* to finish what was left over from the morning's journey.

Now and again, he glanced round it. Astonishing girl, he reflected. When she was absent, he was able to think of her as the companion, but now that he saw her again, it struck him that he had never seen a more unlikely companion to an old woman. Lying there in the opposite corner with her eyes closed, she looked like a tired ballet-dancer. She had the typical smooth hair, the pallor, the slenderness. Her narrow hands with their crimson nails were folded on the cover of a magazine bearing the words 'Chic et Simplicité'. He didn't know what they referred to, but they summed her up – her appearance, at any rate. Certainly nothing else. The expression on her face at the moment was one of disillusion and bitterness.

She opened her eyes and he moved his own to the paper and was absorbed again. He wasn't much given to speculation about people. Unlike his wife, who jumped to conclusions or pursued eager enquiry, Avery didn't bother. People usually revealed themselves in time for what they were, and he left them to it.

By and by he exhausted *The Times*. He stuffed it down the side of the seat for the porters and, folding his arms, gazed at the dark window, smiling to himself.

Louise, who thought they must be approaching Newington,

put on her gloves, collected her magazines and then found she was ready too soon. She turned her attention to Avery, and found him still smiling as he gazed at the window, which was sightless in the winter night.

She leaned towards him.

'Something amuses you?' she said.

He leaned towards her, as if he were only too glad to be asked.

'Anne comes home from school to-day,' he said.

'Ah?'

'She'll be there when I get home,' he said.

'Vraiment?' said Louise and sank back into her corner.

She was irritated. He had been looking handsome and interesting, and all he had been thinking about was his schoolgirl daughter. These Englishmen, she thought. No Frenchman, if asked by an attractive woman what he was thinking of, would have answered so naïvely.

And now, thank God, they were really arriving.

*　*　*

On winter nights, Avery's car was brought to the station from a nearby garage. Within ten minutes of arrival, he was driving in at the gates of The Cedars. The door was flung open and old Mrs. North appeared in a beam of light, with the un-welcoming face of Miss Daley peering from the back of the hall behind her.

Louise ran up the steps and embraced the old lady on both cheeks with a warmth that would have surprised her parents.

'Dear child, I am so glad to have you with me again,' said old Mrs. North, almost in tears.

'And I am glad to be here, Madame.'

'Did you have a good journey, dear? Was everything all right?'

'Oh, yes, Madame, thanks to you it was all very comfortable.'

'Daley, take Mademoiselle's things. There's a good fire in your room, dear, but I won't come up with you. I am only allowed to climb the stairs three times a day and I have to go up to bed yet.'

'I am here to run up and down for you now, Madame,' said Louise. 'I will go up now and in a moment I will be down again. Good-bye, Monsieur, and thank you.'

Half-way up the stairs behind Miss Daley, she turned and thanked him again. Quite the daughter of the house, thought Miss Daley.

'Thank you, Avery,' said his mother too. 'Will you have some sherry before you go?'

'No thanks, Mother. I'll go straight on now. Anne's home, you know.'

'I know,' said old Mrs. North. 'They called.'

'Did they? How does she look?'

'She's grown again. Don't let her grow *too* tall, Avery,' advised his mother.

'Very well. Good-bye, Mother.'

'Good-bye, dear.'

When he drove in at his own gates, this front door was flung open in its turn and a figure with flying hair leaped from the house.

'Daddy!'

'Well, pet . . .'

They hugged each other.

'Glad to be home?' he said.

'Oh, aren't I just! I'll shut the garage doors for you.'

'No, go in. You'll get cold.'

'No, I must wait for you.'

'Hello, Avery,' said Ellen, appearing in the hall, basting spoon in one hand, oven-cloth in the other. 'Hasn't she grown?'

'Exactly three-quarters of an inch,' said Anne, hanging on her father's arm and turning up her face under the lights to beam at him.

'We must put a weight on your head,' said her father fondly.

'Come and get warm,' said Ellen. 'Did you meet the French girl?'

'Yes, I met her all right.'

'What was she like?' asked Ellen. 'Rude as ever?'

'Well, no,' said Avery. 'She was quite agreeable, really. Anyway, I'm glad she's got here.'

'Oh, so am I,' said Ellen fervently, and hurried back to the kitchen.

CHAPTER TEN

⊷◇⊷

When Ellen rang up to give the usual invitation to dinner at Netherfold on Christmas night, old Mrs. North said she would bring Louise, but not Miss Daley.

'Miss Daley won't come this year,' she said. 'Pure jealousy, of course. She says she's going round singing carols with the choir, silly woman.'

Ellen would rather have had Miss Daley than Louise. The French girl might be more decorative, but Miss Daley was more comfortable and certainly more helpful. For several years, she and Ellen had cooked the Christmas dinner together and shared the compliments at the table afterwards. This year Ellen must do it alone, since both Miss Beasley and Mrs. Pretty had announced that they weren't going 'out' at all in Christmas week.

Ellen would miss Miss Daley's help and got her privately on the telephone to tell her so.

'Hugh's coming home and Mr. Bennett's coming from London, of course. I shall never manage without you.'

'That's very nice of you, Mrs. Avery,' said Miss Daley, though Ellen had not meant to be nice, only truthful. 'But I've made my arrangements. I shall miss our fun in the kitchen and the dinner, of course, but I shall enjoy singing carols with the choir. I've never been able to go with them before. Mrs. North has always wanted me. Now she doesn't. But the choir do. So you see it's an ill wind, as they say. Don't worry, Mrs. Avery, you'll get through all right.'

Ellen put down the telephone and laughed with rueful amusement. She laughed at herself for being surprised, still, after all the social changes, that people like Miss Beasley and Mrs. Pretty, and now Miss Daley, should prefer to amuse themselves rather than help her.

'Now you can fend for yourself,' she told herself, and began her preparations.

Anne was busy decorating the house. Holly caught at every sleeve. Tinsel dripped. Lights were so draped with coloured paper that one could hardly read.

'Isn't this rather excessive?' asked Avery, peering at his book.

'Now let her,' said Ellen. 'Soon she'll grow out of this and then we'll be sorry.'

Decorations completed, Anne made toffee that wouldn't set and had to be eaten with a spoon, but which was good all the same, said the confectioner. She also undertook the cream, both ice and mock.

'If only we had real cream,' sighed Ellen,

'I'd rather have mock,' said Anne, beating sugar, cornflour and margarine together with enthusiasm.

'Anne, you couldn't . . .'

'I do,' said Anne stoutly. 'Sweeter.'

Ellen sighed again for a generation that preferred its substitutes.

On Christmas Eve Hugh arrived and was fussed over.

'We're complete now,' said Ellen. 'All gathered in.'

'Christmas Harvest,' said Anne.

Christmas morning and church bells in the dark. Squeals of delight from Anne, who rushed in before her parents were properly awake in their beds. Her silken hair fell over their faces as she kissed them.

'Oh, thank you, thank you, darlings. My lovely dress, Mummy! White tulle. What I've always wanted. Can I wear it to-night? And my saddle, Daddy! Oh, they're marvellous presents. Bless you both and Happy Christmas. Did you like what I've given you? I must fly. I've lots to open yet.'

Ellen dragged herself from her warm bed.

'Happy Christmas, love,' she said, stooping to kiss Avery.

'Same to you, darling,' he murmured. 'Is it really time to get up?'

'Not for you. Oh, this magnificent box! Oh, all the pots and bottles. What fun I shall have doing my face when I've time. Thank you so much, darling. I do hope you'll like your driving gloves?' She held them up before his sleepy face.

'Oh, wonderful,' he murmured. 'Yes, rather.'

Satisfied, she rewrapped them in the Christmas paper, so that he could undo them again when he was properly awake and went downstairs.

Breakfast was a cheerful confusion. The rooms were chaotic with bright wrappings and ribbons, but Ellen rushed about, tidying, washing-up with help from the children, making the beds, and got off to church with Anne, who said she couldn't possibly miss 'Oh, Come let us adore Him.'

They walked down the snowy fields to the village where the church stood among the thatched cottages. It was a scene of peace and simplicity, and for seven hundred years people had been making their way to this church on Christmas morning.

In the churchyard, graves were mobled in snow, ancient headstones leaning this way and that, a great many carved with cherubs' heads. A cherub's head with wings was a feature of eighteenth-century gravestones in these parts and no one noticed them much in the ordinary way. But this Christmas morning, by some freak of the wind, snow had stuck to the wings and the cheeks of the cherubs, claiming attention for them, showing how many there were, in ranks one behind the other, some low, some high.

'Oh,' said Anne, stopping in delight on the path. 'It's like a choir of little angels out here, isn't it?'

The bell warned and they hurried on to the porch, where people were whispering 'Happy Christmas' to one another before they went in.

The interior of the little church was illuminated by the snowlight from the fields, by white flowers and lighted candles. Against the whiteness, the faces of the few choirboys showed red and healthy.

'I didn't know Tom Mayes was in the choir,' whispered Anne.

'Oh, yes,' her mother whispered back.

'Do look at Mrs. Prestwich,' whispered Anne.

Her mother shook her head. Anne's sense of the ridiculous easily got the better of her and often had to be discouraged.

The Vicar was old and frail and his congregation watched with anxiety when he lifted his feet to go up or down the altar steps. Every one was relieved when, having started to climb the pulpit steps, he finally appeared above them. But he went unfalteringly through the service, bending his face upon his flock with stern affection.

The lessons were superbly read by a young bank-clerk, who walked to and from the lectern with fast-beating heart. His Sunday performances saved his whole week from drabness. They filled up a good deal of his time too, because they needed rehearsal. He was not taken up entirely with his own delivery; the significance of the words remained with him. The lesson from Isaiah, for instance, the one that ended: 'And righteousness is immortal.' How he enjoyed that!

'Young Sims excelled himself to-day,' said Ellen, as they hurried up the fields again. 'The B.B.C. really ought to know about him.'

'His head shakes when he's reading,' said Anne, taking a slide over the path. 'And when he gets to his place, he mops his brow. I think he gets into a bit of a lather.'

'Now, Mummy,' she said, laying a hand on her mother's arm as they reached the gates of Netherfold. 'Remember. I'll set the table for lunch when I come in. But at the moment, I'm just going to say hello to Roma.'

Cooking began in earnest at three o'clock and at four, when Ellen was getting tea, John Bennett arrived. He came into the kitchen with Anne behind him, clapping fur gloves together. 'Look what Uncle John's given me. They will be green with envy at school. Look!'

'Happy Christmas, my Christmas Rose,' said John Bennett, presenting flowers and boxes to Ellen as she turned from the oven. 'You look a bit hot, my love. What are you doing to yourself?'

'I've just basted the turkey and I'm toasting scones at the same time and I *am* hot,' said Ellen, putting her hair back. 'John, you shouldn't. All these things again. You're such an extravagant man. . . .'

He would kiss her hand, although it was floury. When she told him so, he said it made her hand more precious to him. At which laboured gallantry Anne laughed, waiting to see what he would say next.

'I must wash my hands before I open these innumerable boxes, anyway,' said Ellen.

'I'll open them for you, Mummy. I adore opening parcels,' said Anne, whipping off lid after lid. 'See – a lovely silk square! I say, will you lend it to me sometimes! Oh, see – hankershiffs!' (Anne always said 'hankershiff.') 'Look! – scent. Oh, what are these?'

'Oh, marrons glacés! My greatest weakness. It's years since I had one. I didn't even know they were back.'

'Back?' said Anne. 'Where from?'

'The war,' said her mother. 'Have one.'

'Oooh, I say. Oooh, how marvellous. Are they *chestnuts*?'

'Of course they're chestnuts, you chump,' said Hugh, coming behind her and taking several.

'That's what I call greedy,' said Anne, following suit.

'You're both going to spoil your tea,' said Ellen. 'And I'm just taking it in. Go along, all of you. John, thank you so much for all the lovely things. I'll take them upstairs and pore over them in peace by and by. In the meantime, could you carry the tray in?'

'Heavens,' said John, staggering with the massive silver tray. 'This needs a butler. Avery, I hope you never let Ellen carry this.'

Avery, who had spent a lazy afternoon and was feeling torpid, roused himself sufficiently to give his partner what Anne called his rather grand look, implying that he didn't need to be told how to look after his own wife.

'That tray,' he said, 'only comes out about twice a year.'

'Pity,' said John, putting it on the low table. 'Because it's a handsome thing.'

'Most handsome things are put away now,' said Avery. 'As you say, it needs a butler not only to carry it, but to clean it. And where are the butlers nowadays? Où sont les neiges d'antan?'

'What's that – French or German?' asked Anne, carrying tea to him.

Avery put a hand over his eyes. 'Is that your ignorance or my pronunciation?'

'I don't know. We must ask Mademoiselle when she comes to-night. I do wish she wasn't coming,' said Anne. 'She'll only spoil everything.'

'I don't think so,' said Avery. 'She's quite a cheerful soul, really, when you get to know her.'

He smiled into his cup as he said it because it struck him

that it was a singularly inept description of Louise. How she would hate it, too.

After tea, Ellen went back to the kitchen. Anne flitted about setting the table for dinner. Avery was busy with wine and glasses. Hugh was deep in talk with John Bennett about a manuscript he had brought with him.

'I'd like your opinion, Hugh,' he said, delighting the boy. 'As a young man on a young man. I don't think you'll put it down once you've begun it. So you'd better not start it now.'

'I'll take it up to bed with me,' said Hugh.

'Mummy gave me a dress, Uncle John,' said Anne, placing the crackers. 'White tulle. Yards and yards of it. I'm not putting it on until the last minute. Then I shall come down and make an impression.'

At half-past six, car wheels crushed the gravel of the drive. Old Mrs. North and Louise came in muffled in furs. Mrs. North had more than enough for the two of them.

'Happy Christmas, Granny. Happy Christmas, Mademoiselle,' cried Anne, kissing her grandmother. She didn't know if she was expected to kiss Mademoiselle too, since it was Christmas. But looking at her, she decided not to.

'Thank you awfully for the white bag, Granny,' she said. 'It's made of such nice shiny stuff. It'll go beautifully with my tennis things in summer.'

Old Mrs. North halted Hugh, who was helping her out of her fur coat.

'Your tennis things?' she said. 'It's a sponge-bag, child.'

'Oh, is it?' Anne's eyes flew wide in astonishment. 'Of

course,' she hurried to say, 'it's just as nice its being a sponge-bag.'

'I'm sorry you didn't know what it was,' said the old lady, and to John Bennett in the sitting-room, her voice was strangely reminiscent of Avery's telling him the tray only came out twice a year. 'I should have thought,' said old Mrs. North, 'that it was sufficiently obvious what it was from the lining.'

'I thought it was plastic,' said Anne.

'It is plastic.'

'Hop it,' said Hugh, passing with his grandmother's furs. 'You're only getting more involved.'

Anne fled to the kitchen.

Avery took his mother and Louise to have sherry. After a moment with them, Ellen went back to the kitchen, where Anne was stifling her laughter in the roller-towel behind the door. She was laughing too hard to explain why and Ellen smilingly waited, drinking her sherry and looking through the open doors at the scene in the sitting-room.

Old Mrs. North was regal in a winged chair, her dark blue draperies disposed with an expert hand by Louise, who stood beside her in a dress of pale grey chiffon, Grecian in simplicity, Parisian in subtlety.

'She's an artist about dress,' thought Ellen with respect. 'Not only for herself, but for Avery's mother too.'

At that moment, the old lady, receiving her glass from Louise, smiled up at her with affection.

'Never once,' thought Ellen, 'has she smiled at me like that. I haven't pleased her. But I didn't dream that she wanted me to take an interest in her clothes. There's something suppressed about this French girl,' she mused. 'Or concentrated. Something very uncareless. Not a bit like us. We're all careless; except Avery's mother. Now perhaps that's what they have in common.'

Anne emerged from the towel.

'Oh, dear,' she sighed, weakly and pleasurably. 'That was funny. I'll tell you later, Mummy. Granny might hear me now. I'll go and change, shall I?'

'Yes, off you go. A nice sight you've made of yourself, laughing like that.'

'Oh, it'll wear off,' said Anne, rushing away.

Ellen closed the kitchen door. The climax was upon her. Now she must get to it in earnest. She longed for Miss Daley, that capable hand at dishing-up. Without her, what plates, dishes, sauce-boats, to change round in the heat. What gravy-making, sauce-making, tossing, seasoning, testing, arranging. What returning to ovens to keep hot while she got everything to table. She hurried into the sitting-room to announce dinner just as Anne called from above: 'Are you ready, everybody. I'm coming.'

They all turned. After a pause due to a sudden fit of shyness on the stairs, she appeared in the doorway in the white tulle dress.

There was a brief silence. It might have been the dress, but her youth was so dazzling and lovely that no one spoke. Avery's eyes met Ellen's in a moment of emotion. Their little girl was growing up. Anne had divested herself of her childhood and uncertain, but trusting, was going forward into the world. Then everybody spoke at once.

'Come in and let's have a look at you,' said Hugh.

'You've got a pretty dress at last,' said her grandmother. 'And quite time too. Where did you get it, Ellen? Don't you like it, Louise? Almost worthy of France, isn't it?'

'You're growing up too fast,' said John Bennett. 'It's a pity. You've been such a nice little girl.'

'Can't I be a nice big girl?' said Anne, recovering herself sufficiently to pirouette in the tulle.

'Will you all please go into the dining-room?' said Ellen firmly.

The table looked wonderful and everybody said so. Avery put his mother on his right and Louise on his left. Ellen couldn't help coming in looking hot. She laid the backs of her hands briefly to her cheeks and sat down.

Topping the pile of plates was a saucer for Moppet, who rubbed ecstatically round Avery's ankles.

'I suppose she comes first,' he said, slicing a piece of turkey awkwardly with the carving knife and fork.

'Let me,' said Anne, removing the saucer.

'You probably think the English are crazy about animals, Mademoiselle,' said Avery, carving now in earnest.

'It is certainly something I have not seen before,' said Louise. 'But I suppose it is the fashion here.'

'Fashion?' said Anne indignantly. But her brother kicked her under the table and she subsided.

Hugh poured the wine, and when everyone was served John Bennett raised his glass.

'To the cook,' he said.

They drank to her and she smiled lovingly on them.

'I hope it's all right,' she murmured.

'The turkey's marvellous,' said Anne, trying it. 'And aren't the crackers gorgeous this year. I shall have to pull mine soon, because I'm dying to know what's in it.'

'You'll not pull it,' said Hugh. 'You'll wait till dinner's over. No good wearing a dress like that and behaving like a kid of two. You'll have to start living up to your looks, you know.'

'Oh,' said Anne in a cooing voice. 'Have I got any?'

'Well, to-night you have,' he admitted.

'That's the first compliment you've ever paid me,' she said, beaming at him across the table.

'You mustn't be too fond of compliments,' he said.

'But you'd be fond of compliments if you ever got any.'

'Anne,' said her mother reproachfully.

'I'm only teasing him,' said Anne, taking another large mouthful of turkey.

'Their conversation,' thought Louise, 'is for children and animals. I am here and there are three males. But they look at me with less animation than they look at the cat and don't speak to me so much.'

The sight of other people's happiness irritated her. Happy people were so boring. It was unintelligent to be happy, Louise considered. Her face took on an expression of cold reserve. Ellen saw it and felt she wasn't doing enough to make this stranger at home.

'Is our Christmas Day anything like yours in France?' she said in a friendly way.

Louise closed her eyes briefly.

'Oh, no. In France, Christmas is a feast of the Church. I think your Christmas is more German.'

She said it with a peculiar inflexion. They could take it as they wished, but they didn't take it at all. They had become aware of a scuffling at the front door, and as they listened, a contralto bellow assailed the night.

'I saw three ships go sailing by . . .'

Anne's look of incredulity changed to one of extreme delight.

'It's the Bull of Bashan,' she cried.

'It's actually Daley,' said old Mrs. North in deep displeasure.

'Sailing . . . Sailing . . . ' swooped the voice at the door, supported by a low groundswell from the rest of the choir.

'Avery, go and tell her to go away at once,' commanded old Mrs. North.

'Oh, Granny, let her,' begged Anne.

'Had got in . . . had got in . . .' swooped Miss Daley.

'Good heavens,' said John Bennett.

'Mais c'est formidable,' said Louise. 'Quelle voix!'

Miss Daley's voice was like a ball among the skittles. Everybody was bowled over in the end. Even old Mrs. North, even Louise, who, having begun to laugh, found herself crying. The others were laughing so hard they didn't notice that hers were not tears of mirth like theirs. She pressed her handkerchief over her eyes. She was full of tears, she must be careful still to give them no chance to flow. That old grief – would it never die?

Ellen got up from the table, mopping her own eyes.

'I must go and speak to her,' she said.

'Give her this,' said Avery, taking a note from his case. 'And tell her she'll be the death of us.'

The singing ceased, and suddenly the company at the table was startled by the sight of a Robin Hood hat, complete with pheasant's feather, popped round the dining-room door by Miss Daley herself.

'Merry Christmas everybody,' she said, rosy and happy. 'I just wanted to take a peep, seeing I can't be with you this year. Hello, Mademoiselle.'

Intoxicated by the exercise of her voice and the company of her choir-friends, Miss Daley had thrown off, together with restraint, all animosity towards Louise. Full of goodwill, she singled Louise out for a special word, a special beam. But Louise continued, without expression, to pat her eyes with her fine handkerchief.

'Thanks ever so much, Mr. Avery, for that lovely gift. I'm sure we shan't equal that again to-night,' said Miss Daley.

'Have a glass of wine,' said Avery, pouring one. 'Warm you up.'

'Oh, I couldn't,' protested Miss Daley. 'I've got ever such a weak head. Well, just to drink your healths then.'

She raised her glass to them and they theirs to her.

'Better luck and less need of it,' said Miss Daley, surprisingly. 'Lovely,' she said, draining the glass. 'Thanks ever so much. Now bye-bye.'

Another beaming smile and the green hat withdrew.

Anne raised a hand, listening in delighted anticipation, and as Miss Daley's voice began to boom again, she was off on another gale of laughter.

'Well, I shall just have to wait to bring the pudding in until all this is over,' said Ellen.

After dinner, Ellen closed the others in with their coffee and, as she always did on Christmas day, rang up her brother in Manchester. They talked together across the distance. They remembered their childhood for a few moments. They said, as usual, that they wished they weren't so far apart.

'But everything's all right for you, isn't it, love?' said Henry.

'Yes, everything's all right,' said Ellen happily. 'Good-bye, old chap.'

Then she rang up Somerton Manor to speak to Mrs. Brockington, whose hands were so crippled now she could hardly write letters at all.

'Have you all had a nice day?' asked Ellen.

'Yes, dear, thank you,' said Mrs. Brockington in a guarded way.

'How's Mrs. Beard?' said Ellen, getting to the heart of the matter.

'Well – er – I think she's rather tired,' said Mrs. Brockington.

'Rather cross too?' said Ellen.

'Well, she has a great deal to do,' excused Mrs. Brockington. 'But she's just cooked an excellent dinner for us.'

She forbore to mention that Mrs. Beard, in a loud voice and before the others, had told Mrs. Fish she was senile and ought to be put into a Home, and that poor Mrs. Fish had spent the day in tears in consequence.

When Ellen left the telephone, she went to see what was happening in the dining-room. John Bennett and Hugh had taken old Mrs. North into the other room, but Avery, with a glass of old brandy, and Louise with a cigarette stood by the dining-room fire watching Anne, who was clearing the table to the dance-music pouring from the radio.

When Anne waltzed away to the kitchen, letting the white tulle fly out, Louise, mellowed with wine and laughter, said surprisingly: 'Yes, she is very pretty. To-night she is made up of flowers and stars and pearls, as someone once said of the Duchesse de Longueville.'

Avery turned warmly towards her and Ellen smiled up from the glasses she was assembling on a tray.

'That's a very graceful compliment to pay to our little girl,' said Avery.

'Oh, she is very pretty,' repeated Louise. 'She will go a long way.' She drew on her cigarette and threw the end of it into the fire. 'If she is careful,' she said, exhaling smoke through her nostrils.

Ellen stared in frowning displeasure, but Avery laughed, and loudly. Louise asked in surprise if she had made some mistake.

'No, no,' he assured her, picking up his brandy. 'Come into the sitting-room to the others.'

He steered her past Ellen, from whom he feared an explosion, she looked so angry.

She was still seething when he went into the kitchen a few moments later.

'What a hideous point of view!' she said.

'My dear girl,' said Avery, raising his eyebrows. 'It was funny. You should be able to laugh.'

'Well, I shan't laugh,' said Ellen, snatching forks and spoons from plates to put them into water until the morning. 'What have her commercial calculations to do with Anne? It just makes an ugly smear on something young and touching.'

'My, you are cross,' said Avery amiably. 'I came out for matches. My lighter won't work.'

'Again?' said Ellen, finding the matches to show it wasn't he whom she was cross with. Although she was, a little, secretly.

'Aren't you ever going to sit down, Ellen?' said John Bennett, appearing later.

'I am, John dear, in five minutes. I'm just filling the hot-water bottles.'

'Can't I do it?'

'I'm sure you've never filled a hot-water bottle in your life. Go back to the fire. I won't be a minute now.'

Five bottles in five beds, beds turned down, curtains drawn and, after subduing her ruffled hair and doing her face again, she joined the others in the sitting-room.

'Haven't we had a marvellous Christmas, Mummy?' said Anne, when at last they were on their way to bed. 'The best we've ever had.'

'You always say that, pet.'

'But it really has been the best this time,' Anne insisted.

Before she got into bed, Ellen looked through the curtains and caught her breath at the sight of the snow in the moonlight. All was radiant, white and absolutely still. Christmas night, silent and holy. The most significant night in the history of the world.

'How much longer are you going to stand in the cold?' asked Avery from his bed. 'I should have thought you were tired enough after all you've done to-day.'

'Oh, I am, I am,' said Ellen, and making a rush for the warmth of her bed, she turned out the light.

The house was settling down. In the spare room, John Bennett brooded a little on his companionless, comfortless life in Kensington and wondered if Avery knew his luck. Anne was already asleep, the white dress glimmering over a chair. By and by at Hugh's door there was a small scratching, and Hugh, laughing, sprang out of bed and caught up the little cat. He put her under his eiderdown and, still smiling at her happy purring, went to sleep, feeling he was home indeed.

CHAPTER ELEVEN

———◦◇◦———

Old Mrs. North could not take quite the same pleasure as before in dressing-up. She put herself passively into Louise's hands, but she often flagged, sitting at the dressing-table, and said she thought that would do for to-day.

She gave up trying to speak French too.

'I can't think of the words, dear,' she said apologetically to Louise. 'But read to me. I love to hear you read in your own language. There's a copy of *Madame Bovary* in the book-case. Shall we read that?'

Louise smiled wryly. It was a book she knew by heart. The only character in literature for whom she felt profound sympathy, with whom she felt affinity even, was Emma Bovary. No one, she often said to herself, understands better than I do why she did as she did. It was the excruciating boredom of provincial life.

It came at a bad moment for her that she had to go over *Madame Bovary* again, because she was finding the English winter depressing. The drawing-room, where she sat with old Mrs. North in the afternoons, was high, built on a terrace. The arched windows looked over a wide stretch of fields and woods rising gently to the sky-line. The late George North had been proud of this view, but it afflicted Louise. Snow or sleet or fog so often drifted across it, and it was so empty, empty of interest, empty of anything for her.

A page or two of *Madame Bovary* sufficed to send old Mrs. North to sleep and Louise was left to stare at the winter view and brood over her past and her future.

Paul had poisoned both, she told herself. She seemed to have been fated from the beginning. Their paths had crossed so early. As a child, on her way to and from Ste Colombe, she had gazed in admiration at the three Devoisy brothers, distinguished, aloof, always together, coming from or going to the Lycée in their dark blue capes and peaked caps, like naval cadets.

She had chosen Paul as the one she liked best and soon he became the only one for her. At Mass in the cathedral on Sundays, she never took her eyes off him, and sometimes in the press of people going out, she managed to walk so close that she was able to take the edge of his cape in her fingers.

He didn't notice her in those days. He was as remote as a young god. But, later, when she had left school and used to pass the gates of the Lycée during recreation, some of the students used to hiss surreptitiously at her, if their masters were far enough away. Louise took no notice. But once she turned her head and saw Paul standing far back and their eyes met.

His attention was caught and he began to look for her in the streets of the town. He went to the shop for his books, and after that it was only a matter of time before they were meeting behind the church of St. Eustache, falling into ruin since disestablishment, in the fields by the river.

In the little town where the code of behaviour was so strict and both were well known, though on different levels, they had to be very careful. To live dangerously became the most exciting of games to Louise. The double life she led, the lies she told, the necessity of deceiving, became almost second nature to her. So that, when it was all over, everything seemed terribly dull; not only because she had lost her lover, but because she was like a skilled actress without a part. Also, her inclination to despise people had been fostered by finding them so easy to deceive. They were stupid to be so gullible. If you were clever enough – and she was – you could get away with anything.

When the time came for Paul to marry, there was nothing for him but to break with Louise. A bookseller's daughter could never be considered a suitable match for a Devoisy. Besides, her dowry wasn't half big enough. So, to please his parents, to found a family, to return to the Church and the respectabilities in general, he married Germaine Brouet and there he was, waiting for his children to arrive.

And here was Louise, sitting through the winter afternoons in an English drawing-room.

'What am I doing, spending my time with an old woman?' she asked herself. 'What is there here for me?'

It was all very comfortable, but there was no future in it.

She must go home, she told herself. She must accept her fate. She must marry André Petit, since he was the only one that offered, and wring some kind of life for herself out of the marriage. He was well-off, nothing like the Norths, of course, but much better off than her own parents, and he was so infatuated with her that he would let her do as she liked. She would do as she liked, anyway.

When she had made up her mind, she wanted to go at once. On the afternoon she came to her decision, she switched on the lamps long before the usual time so that she could wake old Mrs. North and tell her she must go home.

The old lady blinked her eyes and sat up.

'That was a very interesting chapter, wasn't it?' she said, as she usually did. 'Will you ring for tea, dear.'

'It isn't yet tea-time,' said Louise. 'But I want to speak to you first, Madame.'

'Do you, dear? What about? Is it Daley again? I do wish she wouldn't annoy you so.'

'No, it isn't Daley, Madame. It is that I must go home. And as soon as possible.'

'Louise!'

'Now, Madame, don't distress yourself. I can't stay here for ever, you know.'

'Don't leave me, Louise,' begged old Mrs. North. 'Stay a little longer, if only for a few weeks, Louise.'

'Mais, voyons, I have my parents.'

She enlarged on having her parents.

'Stay with me until I am better,' pleaded the old lady. 'I'm not well, Louise.'

'But of course you are well. You are all right,' said Louise, rallyingly. 'You are just a little tired, that's all. You must rest and then in the spring I will come back.'

She had no intention of coming back. What was the good?
'Oh, Louise . . .'

'Now, Madame, Madame . . . See, I have rung for tea. A cup of tea will do you good. You always say that in England, don't you?'

'Louise, can't I persuade you?'

Louise shook her head.

'No, Madame. I have my duty to my parents. They didn't want me to come to you, but I persuaded them. It has been long enough for them to have been without me.'

'But why have you made up your mind so suddenly to go?'

'Well, Madame.' Louise shrugged her shoulders. 'You wouldn't have liked me to tell you as soon as I came, would you? Now here is tea. On this table by me, Miss Daley, please. Madame is a little tired. I will pour out the tea.'

Miss Daley cast a look of dislike at her and went to draw the curtains.

'Oh, Daley,' said old Mrs. North in distress. 'Mademoiselle says she must go back to France.'

Miss Daley turned from the windows.

'Oh,' she said with animation. 'When?'

'Very soon,' said Louise, pouring tea. 'Next week.'

'Next week, Louise?' said old Mrs. North, shocked again.

Miss Daley tugged the curtains together, stroked them appreciatively and left the room. Back in the kitchen, she burst into song. 'Praise God from whom all blessings flow,' sang Miss Daley.

Mrs. North sent for Avery to plead with Louise. When he came up from the train one wild wet night, she sent him into the drawing-room where she had left the girl alone. She herself hovered about in the hall to wait for the outcome of his persuasions.

Louise looked up from the letter she was writing home to announce her arrival for the following week.

'Ah, Monsieur Avery,' she said, with a flattering note of welcome, and put the letter aside.

He came to stand by the fire and she got up to give him her hand. He was always a little uncertain about these French hand-shakings and was again not ready for this one. But when he took her hand, he kept it for a moment.

'I hear you want to leave us,' he said gravely.

Louise raised her eyebrows.

'I must.'

'It is a great shock to my mother.'

'Yes, I am sorry.'

'I think she hoped to keep you for a long time. Perhaps for the rest of her life.'

'But that is impossible.'

'I know, but couldn't you let her down gently?'

'Let her down?'

'Couldn't you give her more time to get used to the idea of your going?'

'What would be the good of that? I should have to go in the end, and she would only worry, worry, worry all the time trying to keep me.'

The charming growl of three worries running made him smile.

She tilted her chin.

'Why do you laugh at me?'

'I like the way you say "worry," that's all.'

'You speak French and then I can laugh at you,' she said.

She was standing beside him at the fire, so close that he was aware of the faint, delicious scent she used. They considered each other, smiling.

'Don't go,' he said suddenly.

In one instant, from the mere tone of his voice, the situation changed. Both knew it and both were amused. Incredibly, Avery felt his heart beat faster. He folded his arms and his smile deepened. Louise felt a sudden gaiety and freedom.

'I shouldn't go,' he said, more lightly this time.

'Mais, voyons,' she mocked him. 'I must.'

'Why?'

'But be reasonable. I can't stay here for ever. I must think of my parents. I must think of myself. It is time I got married.'

She began to walk up and down the room, her hands spread at the back of her waist.

'Married?' he said. 'Are you engaged?'

'No, but I ought to be.'

Her matter-of-factness tickled him. She said the sort of thing other people didn't say. It seemed not only amusing, but honest. He watched her as she paraded before him.

Then she came to stand in front of him, her head almost under his chin.

'Well?' she said challengingly.

The door opened. Old Mrs. North couldn't wait any longer. She came in, her face puckered with anxiety, her eyes going from one to another. Avery was glad to see her. He had no intention of playing games with the French girl, attractive though she was.

'Have you been able to persuade her, Avery?' said old Mrs. North.

'I don't know,' said Avery. 'I was just trying to find out. Have I, Mademoiselle?'

Louise was used to assessing tones of voice and shades of expression. For years she had watched people's faces to see if they suspected what was going on between her and Paul. She knew at once that Avery had withdrawn. It was the flick of a whip to her pride, still raw from Paul's desertion.

She turned away to pick up her writing things and obliged Avery to repeat his question.

'Have I been able to persuade you to stay, Mademoiselle?'

'No,' she said, tilting her chin as she faced him. 'No. I have to go. I regret, Madame, but I must go. And now if you will excuse me, I will go to my room and finish my letter. Bonsoir, Monsieur. I shall see you again to say good-bye, perhaps.'

She threw him one of her mocking glances and went out.

* * *

Reaching her room, Louise turned on the lights and walked over to look at herself in the glass.

'So I am alive after all?'

Her own face looked back at her, her dark eyes shining, her lips parted, her ivory skin glowing with mysterious vitality. A moment like that was better for the looks than any beauty-treatment in the world.

For one moment, she had been strongly attracted to him and he to her, she knew. Then he was frightened and retreated. Stupid man, he need not concern himself. Never again a secret love-affair for her, she thought, collecting her belongings as if she would be leaving within the hour. What was there in such an affair for her but to be left planted in the end? Never, she said to herself. Never again.

But it was something to know that the blow dealt by Paul had not been as mortal as she thought. She must be recovering, if she could feel attraction even for a moment. Hard, she thought, sweeping the calendar from the mantelpiece and the gilt cupid from the dressing-table, hard to know oneself recovering, and to have to go home and marry André Petit. But it must be done. There was nothing else for it, she told herself.

CHAPTER TWELVE

———◦◇◦———

She went home, Her parents received the disturber of their peace with the same gratitude as before. But though there was no scene so distressing as on the first night of her previous homecoming, they were not allowed to rejoice for long. Louise, they soon found, had come back in a harsh mood. Demonstrations of affection were discouraged. Conversation was nipped in the bud. Nothing was right.

Yet when she told them she would not be going back to England, their faces brightened.

'That is the best news,' said her mother, 'that I've heard for a long, long time.'

'It is indeed,' said her father. 'Now perhaps we can settle and make plans for the future.'

'And perhaps you will be coming to Binic with us for August this year?' said Madame Lanier.

'I suppose so,' said Louise.

But she made it so plain that she took no pleasure in the prospect of going with them to Binic or being with them at all, that her parents were saddened. They wondered where they had failed. They had meant to do their best. They had tried to be good parents. But they had not satisfied her, it seemed.

They hadn't even understood her. Monsieur Lanier no longer made his jokes, and Madame Lanier's forehead soon showed her anxiety again. Like the rest of her person, her brow was plump, and when it was furrowed it was more deeply furrowed than other people's. The furrows were flushed too, so that her anxiety was very noticeable, in the shop and everywhere else.

Louise let the weeks go by without broaching the subject of André Petit. She had seen him several times, walking on the boulevard on Sundays, so horribly provincial, so much another Charles Bovary that she couldn't face the prospect of marrying him. She told herself she must wait until her situation became intolerable, as she knew it would, before she said anything to her parents.

She seemed to take no interest in anything that went on around her, but one morning she came into the shop as young Madame Devoisy left it.

'Well?' she said to her mother in the almost brutal manner she had come home with. 'Any signs of a family there yet?'

Her mother's face brightened. She welcomed any indication of interest in Louise. 'No, my darling. Not a sign. Their first child should be on the way by now. It is disappointing, isn't it? Everybody wonders. No, no sign yet.'

'He won't like that,' said Louise.

'No, he won't. Every man likes to have a family. Perhaps if this goes on, she ought to take a cure. They say Madame Pouillet owes her son to Vittel.'

Louise was temporarily cheered by the lack of family for Paul. She was glad he wasn't getting what he wanted. But the lighter interval was soon over and she fell back into what seemed a darker mood than before.

One evening, after hardly uttering a word all day, she said, as she finished her coffee at the dinner-table: 'Perhaps you had better speak to André Petit.'

Their hands fell from their cups to the table.

'Louise!'

'My child, my dear child.'

They got up from their places and went round the table to kiss her. She let them, turning one cheek and then the other.

'I am sure you are wise, my child . . .'

'You will make him so happy, darling, and I'm sure you will be happy yourself in time.'

'Perhaps,' said Louise.

They wanted to exclaim, they wanted to discuss it, but she left them and went up to her room.

Madame wiped her eyes.

'Oh, Henri, I am so thankful she has come to it at last. He's such a good fellow.'

'He is indeed and his business is so sound. A pharmacien is not to be sniffed at, you know. I always wish I had been one myself.'

'My dear, you know you have been very happy with the books.'

'I am happy. But a pharmacien is almost a doctor, you know. He has a great many human contacts. He helps a lot of people. I should have been interested.'

'You're very well as you are,' said his wife, kissing him. 'And perhaps your grandson can be the pharmacien you wanted to be yourself. Life often works out like that. Won't it be wonderful to have grandchildren, Henri? Madame Piquet was telling me only the other day that grandchildren are a woman's greatest happiness. Just pure pleasure without any anxiety. I am so looking forward to mine.'

'I think we must have a glass of Bénèdictine to celebrate,' said Monsieur Lanier, getting a bottle and glasses from the cupboard. 'Will you call Louise or will you take a glass up to her?'

Madame Lanier hesitated.

'I don't think I shall do either, dear,' she said. 'Because I don't think for her this decision is something to be celebrated. Not yet. I hope in years to come she will look back and see it was. I feel sure she will.'

'I'm sure too,' said Monsieur Lanier. 'I'm perfectly sure. She couldn't go wrong with André Petit.'

'But at the moment,' said his wife, 'I think we'd better leave her alone.'

They took up their glasses.

'To her happiness,' said Monsieur Lanier.

Madame Lanier repeated it, her lips trembling against the rim. Poor Louise. She expected too much of life. That was it. She expected far too much.

'I suppose it's too late to go round and see André Petit to-night,' said Monsieur Lanier, sipping the last rich drop of the liqueur. 'I should like to, really. But perhaps it's rather late.'

'Yes, it's too late now,' said his wife. 'Never mind, you can go round first thing in the morning.'

But in the morning there was a letter from England.

The letter was from Avery.

'Don't worry,' said Louise, slitting the envelope at the breakfast table. 'I shan't go back, no matter how they press me to.'

'Oh,' said Louise, reading it. 'Oh, Mon Dieu!'

'What is it? What is it?' asked her parents. 'What is it?'

'She's dead. Old Mrs. North is dead. Alas, I never expected that . . .'

'But was she ill?' they cried. 'You didn't say so. Was she ill then?'

'Wait a minute,' said Louise, frowning. 'Wait till I read. Oh!' She gave a loud cry and clapped her hand to her cheek.

'For the love of heaven what is it?' they besought her.

'Papa! Mamma! Can you believe it? Can you believe it?'

'No, we can't if you don't tell us what it is.'

'She has left me some money in her will. She has left me a thousand pounds.' They all stared at one another in silence.

'Are you sure, Louise? A thousand *pounds*?' said her father.

'What is that? Is it a thousand francs, Henri?' asked Madame Lanier.

'A thousand pounds, Mamma!' said Louise indignantly. 'Look – it says a thousand pounds. Mon Dieu, how much is that, Papa, with the exchange?'

'A thousand pounds is roughly nine hundred thousand francs!' he said.

'No!' cried Madame Lanier, as if on the verge of collapse. 'Nine hundred thousand francs!'

'I can't believe it,' said Louise, picking up the letter again.

Madame Lanier's face puckered slowly up. Tears spilled from her eyes.

'Oh, Maman,' said Louise impatiently, looking up from the letter, 'you never knew her. It's pure sentimentality on your part to cry for her.'

'It's because she must have loved you,' said her mother.

'Ah, yes,' admitted Louise. 'She did. I did a great deal for her. But I certainly never expected anything like this. She has not only left me money,' she said. 'She has left me furs and jewels too. Her son suggests that I should go and collect them. He says it would be much easier to get them out of the country, if I took them myself.'

'Furs and jewels,' breathed Madame Lanier.

'Oh, there won't be anything much there,' said Louise dismissingly. 'All rather old-fashioned stuff, I'm afraid. Still, they have value, I dare say. And probably there will be a fur coat that will do for you, Maman.'

'Oh, Louise,' said Madame Lanier, wiping away the tears she had shed for old Mrs North. 'A fur coat for me! I've always wanted a fur coat, haven't I, Papa?'

'I believe so,' he said, making calculations in the margin of the newspaper. 'Louise, this is a very large sum of money. The Bourse is favourable to you at present.'

'Free of tax, Monsieur Avery says. She seems to have thought of everything, the poor woman. I shall have to go back to England, you know, Papa,' she said in a business-like way. 'To see to things.'

'Of course,' he agreed gravely. 'You must certainly go. Emilie, if you will take charge of the shop this morning, I'll go and see Vignet at the bank and make a few enquiries.'

'Then I must go and get dressed,' said Madame Lanier briskly. 'Oh, Louise, I am so happy for you. Come and let me kiss you. We haven't embraced her yet, Papa. We've been so busy being astonished by her good fortune that we haven't felicitated our child. Oh, Louise!'

Louise, smiling, was engulfed. She leaned against them as she hadn't done for years.

'Oh, Papa,' she said, rubbing her face against his beard. 'A thousand pounds! You do think I'll get it, don't you?'

'You'll get it,' he assured her. 'The English are still an honest nation. Now I must get into the shop, and as soon as you can relieve me, Emilie, I'll be off to the bank.'

'Wait,' said Louise, halting them. 'One moment. You won't speak to André Petit now, of course. This makes all the difference.'

'Ah,' they said and were thoughtful. It made a difference. A thousand pounds had been added to her dowry. The matrimonial net could be cast in a wider circle. Louise herself did not want André Petit as a husband; she now had more choice. André Petit, good fellow though he was, could be discarded for the moment. If necessary he could be considered again later. But not just now. Let the child, who had, after all, acquired a thousand pounds, please herself for the present.

The Lanier family spent a wholly delightful morning.

Stepping to the Bank, Monsieur Lanier told two or three people in the strictest confidence and received congratulations.

In the shop, Madame Lanier told her favourite customers, whispering some of the news across the counter, coming round to add more, conducting to the door to add still more.

Her bulky figure tipped towards her hearers, her hands clasped under her chin, she was very happy.

It was not so much the money they were elated about, though they had saved too long and too painfully for Louise's dowry to underestimate that. It was that the handsome legacy was both a triumph and a vindication for Louise. Their daughter, in spite of looks and intelligence so far above the average, had not had much success in her native town. And only one 'parti' had been proposed in marriage. But now it was clear that, whatever the neighbours thought of her, *other people* valued Louise.

'Now see what you've missed by not appreciating her,' implied the drawing back of Madame Lanier's head after imparting the news. 'Our child has only to set foot in the world to be estimated at her true worth.'

Madame Lanier enjoyed to the full her morning in the shop. The news of the legacy, she reflected, made a better impression and gave Louise more credit in the eyes of her fellow townsfolk than the betrothal to André Petit would have done. It was more unusual, thought Madame Lanier complacently. Also it was a tribute from outside.

In her room above, Louise had thrown back her windows because the sun was quite warm. It seemed like the first morning of spring. She leaned out over the street to look at the people passing up and down, calling out to each other, stopping to talk. She looked on them with something approaching benevolence. She had never felt more amiable in her life. The legacy had, on her, almost the effect of religious conversion on other people. She almost loved everybody.

She sat down to her desk, which was scrupulously neat. Dust could lie thick elsewhere in the house and often did, because the house was old and exuded powdered plaster, wood, paint from its ancient seams and cracks, but Louise saw to it that her own room was always fresh and polished. She was possessive and no one dared to lay a finger on her belongings.

She sat down to her desk now, pushed up her cuffs and the gold bracelet with all the charms and read Avery's letter again. She felt nothing in particular for old Mrs. North, except that it was very nice of her to have left her the money. After all, Mrs. North was old. She had to die some time. And it was not as if she had known her long or had had time to become attached to her.

She did regret, briefly, that she hadn't done more for the old lady, but chiefly because she might have got more if she had. If she had a thousand pounds without trying at all, what would she have got if she had really exerted herself? Probably the whole fortune. Still, it was no good thinking about that now; and what she had got was very gratifying indeed.

She drew some rough paper towards her and gazing unseeingly at the cupid Paul had given her, she considered how to word the letter to Avery.

It was difficult. She must express both grief and gratitude. She must also ask how to get hold of the money. They didn't look well together, and after several attempts at combination, she hit upon the idea of writing two letters, the first of condolence and gratitude, the second about business and her journey. The first letter should arrive as if she had been too grief-stricken to think of the money; the second should come as an after-thought. After this, composition was easier. She completed her letters to her satisfaction and ran down to the shop for special writing paper.

There were several people with Madame Lanier and Louise knew from their smiles that her mother had told them. She had told them as a secret, so they dared do no more than smile significantly at the heiress. Louise smiled back. She didn't mind who knew. The more the better. Then it would get to Paul.

'Mamma, I'm taking a box of the grey,' she said, waving a box of the best paper in the shop. 'For my letter, you know.'

'Certainly, my darling,' beamed her mother.

'So she has done very well for herself?' resumed one of the ladies as Louise went out.

At noon, his wife gave Paul Devoisy the news at table.

'I don't believe it,' he said. He knew Louise was capable of putting about a rumour like this for no other reason than to let him see she could do perfectly well without him, that other people appreciated her if he did not.

'But, Paul, it's true. Her mother told me herself.'

'And who told her mother?' he said.

His wife looked up from the salad she was turning over in the bowl with two forks. 'How strange you are about Louise Lanier,' she said. 'Do you know something about her?'

'Not I,' he laughed. 'Nothing. But first there was a rumour that she was going to marry someone in England, and now

there's one that she has been left a lot of money. It strikes me as unlikely, to say the least of it.'

'All the same, Paul,' said Germaine, 'she has been left a lot of money, whether you like it or not.'

CHAPTER THIRTEEN

⟨⟩

Avery asked Louise to come for the things his mother had left her, because it seemed the easiest way of getting them off his hands.

He was appalled by the clearing-up there was to be done at The Cedars. For years and years, old Mrs. North had hoarded, filling drawers, shelves, cupboards, boxes, pigeon-holes, with papers, photographs, stuffs, relics of all sorts. Now they had to be brought out, gone through and disposed of.

Ellen and Miss Daley toiled day in, day out, but Avery still felt he was doing it all. He thought his brother and sister ought to be on hand to do their share. But Cicely was in a Washington Hospital after an operation and Howard wrote that he couldn't get away. To have to make decisions about his mother's many possessions made Avery tired.

It also saddened him. He hadn't been particularly disturbed by the thought that his mother must die some time, but now she was dead, he found a blank he hadn't expected. It was as if he had lost, not her, but part of himself. He felt as if his childhood had suddenly dropped off. There was no one left to tell him about it. Now that his mother was dead, he remembered all sorts of things he wanted to ask her. The answers were with her in the grave; he would never know them now.

It seemed strange to him that, after looking upon his mother as an old lady who had become rather a trial, he had to keep remembering her now as she was when he was a little boy. He had only to call out in the night then, and she came. She held his head when he was sick, she calmed his fears and comforted him. He kept remembering a certain yellow silk dress she used to wear, all flounces, in which his short white-socked legs were engulfed when he leaned against her to be read to on the drawing-room sofa after tea. The tenderness he felt for her, too late, was painful.

Her death had shocked him. Like him, she had complained easily and he had attached no more significance to her last complaints than those she had made before. He jollied her about her heart as he had done for years. Then one morning while he was at the office, she died.

The trappings of death appalled him and he left them to Ellen, pointing out that since it wasn't her mother she had to make the ghastly arrangements for, it couldn't matter so much to her.

'Excuse me, sir, but there is one question I must put to you personally,' said the undertaker, who found Avery elusive.

'Can't my wife answer it?' said Avery, caught on the hearth-rug with the man between him and the door.

'No, sir,' said the undertaker firmly. 'I won't keep you a minute.'

He advanced on tiptoe, Avery watching him with horror.

'It is this, sir,' said the undertaker, peering up at Avery

through powerful glasses. 'I think I ought to inform you that there won't be room for you in this grave. Your late mother will take up all the remaining accommodation. . . .'

Avery put out a hand and moved the man aside.

'I'll see about that when the time comes,' he said, and strode out of the room.

The undertaker looked hurt and turned his strong lenses upon Ellen, who choked back sudden unsuitable laughter and soothed him as best she could. She talked him out of the front door and came back to the fire to laugh again at the outrage on Avery's face when the undertaker reminded him that he too must die and be buried. Then she sobered. Avery couldn't bear the thought of his own death, but who could? Death! Don't let's think about it. Let's go to the pictures. Let's have a cup of tea. Let's have a drink.

'Mr. Porter's gone, Avery,' she called from the foot of the stairs.

About Louise's legacy, Avery was short-tempered. Not about the legacy itself, he said, but about the trouble it entailed.

'Let her come and get her own things,' he said. 'They're hers, aren't they? She should do something for her thousand pounds. She's been very lucky.'

As for the moment of attraction in the drawing-room at The Cedars that night, it wasn't worth a thought. Such moments are common in every man's life. Let her come. She could help Ellen and Miss Daley to clear up. Ellen agreed that it was best for her to come and herself pick out what she wanted from the furs and jewellery.

154

Both of them took it for granted that she would stay at The Cedars as before. But when Ellen asked Miss Daley to get the room ready, Miss Daley went red in the face and refused.

'I'm not going to be here on my own with that French girl, Mrs. Avery. I'm only staying on here to oblige until everything's tidied up and I'm not waiting on that young woman any more. I've had enough of her.'

Ellen was taken aback and didn't know what to say. When she told Avery, he was cross.

'Damn it all, there's no end to the bother,' he said. 'I suppose we shall have to put her up now.'

'Oh, I don't want to,' said Ellen.

'I can't help that,' said Avery. 'We'll have to. We'll have to accept it as part of the general upset.'

'Then I hope she won't stay long,' said Ellen.

'Why should she? She ought to get through in three or four days.'

'It's a long way to come for three or four days.'

'She's coming for a thousand pounds, isn't she?' said Avery, in whom affliction took the form of irritation. 'People are usually willing to put themselves out a bit for that.'

'But I have to put myself out too,' said Ellen.

'What?' said Avery as if he really didn't know what she was talking about. 'Put yourself out?'

'Oh, never mind,' said Ellen, cross too by this time.

She was unwilling to have the French girl in the house, but she made the spare room ready as if for a welcome guest. This room, though next to her own, looked out on a different part of the garden, a little lawn backed by a shrubbery and edged now by primulas and hyacinths and violets. When you came into the room, fresh with Chinese yellow chintzes, you were almost startled by the blaze of yellow light flung up by the forsythia bush in bloom below. Looking in at the last moment to see that nothing was missing, Ellen wished she could be a guest in her own spare room. Then she went to the station to meet Louise.

She was astonished at the difference the thousand pounds seemed to have made in the girl. She kissed Ellen on both cheeks and was voluble in sympathy.

'Ah, Madame North was so good,' she said, as they drove up the hill from the station. 'So good and kind to me. But never did I think she would die, and never did I think she would leave me so much money, or any money at all. You and your husband don't think I tried to persuade her to that, do you?'

'Goodness, no,' said Ellen. 'We know how fond she was of you. By the way, I hadn't time to let you know, but you are staying with us. Not at The Cedars. You won't mind, will you?'

'On the contrary,' said Louise. 'It would be so sad there for me. You are too kind, Madame.'

She was glad to be staying at Netherfold. It was more attractive and altogether better. Also it was not all women there; it would be more interesting.

When she walked into the spare room and received the golden welcome, she was warmer in her pleasure than Ellen thought she could be and Ellen herself warmed in response.

'I'll run down and make tea,' she said.

'Ah, tea,' said Louise, taking off her hat. 'That I have certainly missed – your tea.'

When Ellen left the room, Louise closed the door.

'I shall do very well here,' she said to herself, walking about with satisfaction. 'It is a good thing I brought all I wanted, because I think I shall stay some time. No point in going before I have the money. I can do nothing until I get it and it's best to make sure of it.'

She opened drawers and cupboards, surveying the places she would fill with her things, taking possession.

Gradually, the French scent stole under her door, faintly permeating the atmosphere, changing it, establishing her presence.

'No need to ask if she's arrived,' said Avery gloomily, arriving himself in the evening.

'Why?' asked Ellen, flying round the table with the silver, rather late.

'Scent.'

'Goodness, from here? Is it so strong?'

'No, but it's unmistakable.'

He was still in his heavy mood and made no attempt to hide it. He gave Louise an indifferent hand and after one look at him, she knew what the situation was or what he wished it to be. With an invisible shrug she left him to his distance and attached herself to Ellen.

Ellen hadn't wanted Louise, but she soon had to admit that she made a great difference to the pace of clearing-up at The Cedars. Ellen herself hadn't liked the task at all. She found it both wearisome and saddening. Homes, like people, died. This had been a cheerful, comfortable, beloved house but now it was dead, and they were trying to dismember it as quickly as possible and finish with it.

There was something that induced melancholy in bringing old Mr. North's pepper-and-salt suits out of moth balls, in handling rusty sealskin jackets, cracked silks, and innumerable old kid gloves laid together like pairs of kippers. There was so much of everything. Ellen and Miss Daley had groaned and made up indiscriminate parcels. They sent for the Salvation Army and the Youth Clubs. They piled up the handcarts of all sorts of Associations and still seemed to have made no impression on the accumulations.

But now Louise came. Giving her attention first to what would be hers, she turned over Mrs. North's furs with the knowledgeable hands of a business woman and soon made her selections.

'You don't mind that these things should be left to me?' she asked Ellen.

'Not at all. Not in the least. What do I want with them?'

The jewellery was gone through in the same brisk way. Wishing to appear fair, she gave Ellen a chance of the worst things.

'You're sure you don't want this?' she said, holding up a garnet necklace.

'Goodness, no. It's like a string of jujubes,' said Ellen.

Louise smiled. It wouldn't look like a string of jujubes when Monsieur Chaix had finished with it, but if Madame Avery didn't think of that, so much the worse for her.

Far from finding it tiring, Louise was interested in pulling the house to pieces and seeing what it had been made of. She quickly cleared the rooms, assessing at once what was of value and what was not. She acquired a good deal in the process. She fitted her mother up for years, and her father too, sending off great parcels expertly packed and marked 'Worn Clothing', so that they should not have to pay duty. Miss Daley watched with compressed lips.

'I'm glad to say I'm not like that myself,' she said, and it was true. She would only accept Mrs. North's work-box and some felt hats.

She didn't know, and there was no point in telling her, that the old lady, in the codicil to her will in which she had left a thousand pounds to Mademoiselle Louise Lanier, had cancelled a previous legacy of two hundred and fifty pounds to Miss Alice Eva Daley; presumably because Miss Alice Eva had not behaved as Mrs. North wished to Mademoiselle Louise.

Louise sighed because she couldn't take more from the house. The Norths, she saw, would have given her practically everything. As it was, she took possession of the drawing-room curtains at the last minute. It was unthinkable that such brocade should go to a sale. She made up five enormous parcels and got them off home. At the receiving end, her parents were dumbfounded.

At last the house was cleared. Not a trace of old Mrs. North remained. Ellen went upstairs to say good-bye to Miss Daley and found her taking her corn cure, chilblain lotion, health salts, glycerine and cucumber and the photograph of her father from the mantelpiece of the room she had slept in for six years. Miss Daley was going as 'mother's help' to the house

159

of the minister of her chapel and was awaited with anxiety because another baby was due to arrive at any moment.

'I shall see you about the town, I hope,' said Ellen, who liked Miss Daley.

'Oh, yes,' said Miss Daley cheerfully. 'That is, if I ever have time to go out. It'll be much harder at Mr. Salter's and I'm not getting half the money. This was a very good place for me until that French girl came and spoiled it. And if you don't mind me saying so, Mrs. Avery, I'd see I didn't get too tied up with her if I was you.'

'She'll be going back soon,' said Ellen. 'And then I don't suppose we shall ever see her again.'

'And good riddance,' said Miss Daley.

The doors of The Cedars were locked and the key given up. The house was to be turned into Government Offices.

'I think you've been wonderful,' said Ellen to Louise as they drove away for the last time.

'I wouldn't say that,' said Louise, laughing. 'But I feel very dusty and rather tired.'

'You must have a good rest now,' said Ellen. 'Before you go home.'

CHAPTER FOURTEEN

—✦◇✦—

I

Ellen set herself to see that Louise had the promised rest. She took her breakfast upstairs, putting the tray outside her door as requested by Louise. She gave up her own corner of the sofa in the sitting-room. She invited her to pick flowers for her room and still smiled when she took all the best roses. She put herself quite aside. She didn't read when she wanted to, she cooked elaborately when she might have been sitting down. She ran about incessantly as women do when they have a visitor in the house.

She had said vaguely and warmly 'a good rest.' She thought Louise would stay on for about a fortnight.

But the fortnight ended and Louise showed no sign of going. Ellen was almost apologetic to Avery. After objecting so strongly to her coming in the first place, Ellen didn't like to say she had asked Louise to stay on. Life is full of these inadmissions, even between husband and wife.

'I think she'll be going soon,' she said in a reassuring way to Avery.

She was beginning to hope so. She thought of the Spanish

proverb: 'After three days, fish and a guest begin to stink.' It wasn't as bad as that yet, but she looked forward to having the house to herself once more.

Avery had begun by avoiding Louise. He still felt he couldn't make the effort to be agreeable. He had to make himself agreeable to too many people during the day, he wasn't going to start again when he came home.

It was some time before it dawned on him that Louise was also avoiding him. In the mornings, she didn't come down until he had left the house; in the evenings, she went upstairs as soon as possible after supper. If he came into the room where she was, she soon left it. At times he looked after her in some surprise.

One evening, he stopped her.

'I saw the lawyers to-day,' he said. 'It will be about three months before the money my mother left you will become yours. But you don't need to concern yourself about it any further. It's quite simple. When the Bank of England has approved, it will be transferred to your bank in Amigny.'

'I understand,' she said, turning towards the door. 'Thank you.'

'So that – er – ' he said, taking his sherry from the mantelpiece. 'I mean, there's nothing for you to stay for, if you feel you ought to be getting home.'

He stood there, glass in hand, in his well-cut English clothes. It was because he was handsome and in such a position of strength in his wealth and maleness that she was infuriated. From such an advantage, he was telling her to go home. He was dismissing her. And at one time she had him dangling on a string, or could have had if she had remained with his mother.

'Mrs. North has asked me to stay,' she said, and left the room.

'She says you asked her to stay,' said Avery challengingly to Ellen, who came in a few moments later.

'Oh, I did. A long time ago,' said Ellen guiltily. 'I did. When we'd finished at The Cedars. I said she must have a good rest. But I didn't mean any longer than about a fortnight.'

'Well, there you are,' said Avery, finishing his sherry and picking up the paper. 'If you didn't fix a date, you've asked for it.'

In the room above, Louise was writing to her parents.

'I have news for you,' she wrote. 'I hear to-day that it will take about three months for the money to be handed over to me. I think I ought to stay, if for no other reason than I might be required to sign something.'

Her parents wrote back that, though they longed for her to come home, it was better to stay. After all, no country at the present time wanted to part with money. One never knew. Much better to be on the spot and supervise in person, they wrote, with other cryptic phrases.

And now they on their part, they wrote, had news for her. Young Madame Devoisy was expecting a baby. It would be born in November. Madame Devoisy was so delighted she was telling everybody. Wasn't it nice, they wrote? It would have been sad if there had been no children for such an inheritance. They were sure Louise would agree.

Louise did not agree. The news was hateful. Why should he be happy? She suffered from their association, why shouldn't he? Men had everything. She was still smouldering from Avery's attempt to dismiss her. She hated men, she told herself. But unfortunately it was through them that women had to get what they wanted, at any rate, women like herself. She was no career woman. No slaving in any office or profession for her. For a woman gifted in her own particular way as she was, there would be no need for that, she remarked to herself, as if discussing the situation with a friend such as she had never had.

Her fellow creatures were largely objects of indifference to Louise and she had never made a friend of girl or woman. But now, principally from motives of her own, she conceived the idea of making a friend of Ellen.

She liked Ellen, she told herself, although she was exasperated by her. Surely Ellen was a little too good to be true? A little too kind, trusting and happy? An example of the well-known English hypocrisy, she supposed. Either that, or Ellen was what she was because she had never had reason to be otherwise. She had everything: a handsome husband, money, children, a charming house. All the same, Louise quite liked her.

But she thought Ellen managed her husband badly. Ellen was unselfish, so in consequence, he was not. Ellen took responsibility for everything in the house and evidently for the children too; so he did not. He took Ellen for granted and that was, Louise considered, Ellen's own fault. She was altogether too open and simple. A woman needed art and subtlety and Ellen had neither.

So from complicated motives, from a wish to ingratiate herself with Ellen and prolong her hospitality as long as she should need it, to get her own back on Avery by isolating him and forming a feminine partnership against him, Louise tried to strengthen Ellen's hand by putting into it some of the cards she herself considered essential to the feminine game.

She began one afternoon. Ellen, in a cotton frock and gumboots, was digging in the borders, her hair falling over her face. Louise, in sun-glasses, a cigarette in her fingers, was walking round and round for the good of her figure and to the detriment of the lawn, which was now so spiked by French heels that Ellen could hardly keep her mind off it.

'I shall have to say something,' she kept resolving, but didn't know how to put it so that it wouldn't wound the guest.

'Shall I make tea and bring it out into the garden?' called Louise, who liked making tea because it was something Germaine Brouet could neither do herself nor get her servants to do.

'Er – thank you,' said Ellen, groaning inwardly.

Although Louise talked as if she were the only one in France to be able to make tea, she still couldn't make it. She warmed the tea-pot, she boiled the water, or so she said, but the leaves still floated.

But Ellen decided she must put up with it – she was always putting up with something nowadays – because her gumboots were so thick with damp earth she couldn't go into the house to make it herself. She felt like a cart-horse coming out of the plough as she made for the bench when Louise brought the tray out.

'We must get the garden chairs out to-morrow,' she said. 'I love the day we bring the chairs out for the first time. It means summer's begun. Oh,' she said as she sat down. 'I'm stiff from digging.'

'Ah, but you will do it,' said Louise, taking the opportunity. 'All this gardening. It's not for a woman. You have William. Why do you not leave it to him?'

'He has other work. Besides, I like it,' said Ellen, drinking the poor tea.

'But it ruins your hands. It disarranges your hair. It makes you wear such ugly boots.'

Ellen laughed.

'You don't take yourself seriously enough,' said Louise. 'You don't appear to advantage.'

'What – just now? Of course I don't. I don't expect to. I don't even want to.'

'I don't mean only at this moment,' said Louise coolly. She didn't like to be laughed at. 'I mean all the time. You don't make the best of yourself.'

Ellen laughed again. People were rarely so frank.

'I haven't time,' she said.

'There is always time for what one wants to do,' said Louise. 'You don't really want to make the best of yourself. You think it isn't necessary.'

'Oh, no,' said Ellen amiably. 'I should like to look my best.'

'But you would rather read in bed at night, and cook, and rush about the house, and most of all, you would rather garden, scratch the ground,' said Louise, with disgusted

166

rolling of the r's. 'You can't be soignée and dig in the earth as well. It is impossible.'

'But what about the garden?' said Ellen, still laughing. 'It would be in a dreadful state if I didn't look after it.'

'It is more important to cultivate oneself, Madame,' said Louise gravely.

Ellen was amused. But when she went up to change, she considered herself in the glass.

'Am I such a sight as all that?' she wondered.

She tried to look at herself with other people's eyes. What she saw was a woman who still, she thought, looked young, with ruffled light brown hair, no grey in it yet, a figure as slender as ever, long slender legs. She didn't know what to think of her own face, but she remembered her most cherished compliment. 'Now *that*,' said one of two strange women once in her hearing, 'is the sort of face I like.' They smiled at her as if they liked her too.

'I don't think I'm so bad,' said Ellen rather uncertainly to herself, and went to have a shower.

When she was back at her dressing-table, Louise knocked at the door. That was the worst of having someone in the house with you, you had to close the door.

'Come in,' said Ellen, and Louise appeared with a hat.

'I should like you to try this,' she said.

This was getting tiresome, thought Ellen, who wanted to go down and start the evening soup.

'Let me finish your hair,' said Louise.

Ellen unwillingly sat, suppressing a sigh.

'You are lucky to have this hair, curling of itself, but you do nothing with it,' lectured Louise. 'See, I do it like this. Now I put on the hat – so. You see? You have a charming face.'

'You think the hat makes the face then?'

'The hat makes more of the face.'

'It is certainly a pretty hat,' said Ellen. 'But I can't very well walk through the fields among the cows in a hat with a veil on.'

Louise turned out a hand in despair.

'But who wants to walk among the cows,' she said. 'Among cows, Mon Dieu! Ah, Englishwomen. What can one do with them? As you say in your language – they ask for it.'

'Ask for what?' said Ellen, laughing and taking off the hat.

'Ah, Madame, may you never know,' said Louise darkly, turning to leave the room.

Ellen went after her.

'I know you know all about dress,' she said in a conciliatory way. 'Not only for yourself. You used to make old Mrs. North look marvellous. And it's very kind of you to try with me. But it would be waste of time both for you and for me. My interests don't lie that way. I like clothes, I'm glad when I look nice, but I can't spend my days and nights thinking about them. I *like* gardening,' she said. 'And if I have to choose between smooth white hands and gardening, I choose gardening every time.'

'Hélas,' said Louise and went into her own room with the hat.

From her bed that night, Ellen repeated the conversation to Avery with amusement. She expected him to be amused too, but he only said: 'Well, she certainly does a good job on herself. What *is* the scent she uses?'

'I don't know. I asked her once, but she seemed to think I was trying to find out for my own advantage and she didn't tell me. There are women who won't part with a good cake recipe, you know, in case anyone else should be praised for it,' said Ellen, as if Avery could know what she meant.

'You don't think I look a sight, do you?' she said, suddenly rising on her elbow and looking through the dark towards Avery's bed.

'Of course not.'

'Do you think I ought to do myself up more?' she persisted.

'No,' said Avery, turning over and pulling up the blankets. 'It wouldn't suit you.'

'Oh,' said Ellen, lying down again. 'That's all right then.'

But somehow she felt rather flat. Until Avery, after a silence, said suddenly: 'When's she going home?'

'I don't know,' said Ellen. 'It looks as if we shall have to give a hint soon.'

'It looks like it,' said Avery.

After that, Ellen fell comfortably asleep.

II

'What shall we do when we go for Anne's half-term next week? We can't very well take Mademoiselle with us,' said Ellen, looking apprehensively at Avery. He had been slightly more agreeable to Louise lately and might think they ought to take her.

But he said at once: 'Good heavens, she can't come,' and Ellen's face cleared.

'It would spoil everything,' she said.

'Of course it would. Anne would hate it,' said Avery. 'And it's her day.'

Anne's name had only to come up for them to chime together like a pair of perfectly synchronised clocks.

'I suppose we take masses of food as usual?' said Avery.

The School didn't provide tea at half-term. Parents and children had what was called a picnic-tea in the Library.

'She wants tinned pears, mock cream, ham-sandwiches, meringues, my rock-buns and biscuits, and all the sweets we can collect without using our own points for her.'

'The stuff the child can eat,' said Avery. 'She can have my sweet-points, of course, but I'll look for something else in London to-morrow.'

The something else proved to be a box of marrons glacés, which he exhibited the next evening when he came home.

'She loves those,' said Ellen.

'Now those – they really are something,' said Louise with animation. 'Your English sweets seem so synthetic to me, but marrons glacés, the product of France – what perfection!' She put the tips of finger and thumb together and blew them a kiss.

She waited to be offered some. But it appeared no one was to have any. They were for his daughter. Louise withdrew herself. Never had she been *shown* sweets before. Shown, and then told they were for someone else? It was unheard of. He was crazy about his daughter. He was like a lover. Somebody should say something to him. It was unnatural.

She was cool at supper, and afterwards, although she had been staying down longer of late, she went early to her room.

It was not until he was supposed, by Ellen, to be asleep that Avery said. 'I think Louise thought I ought to have offered some marrons glacés to her, you know.'

Ellen had raised her head with an effort from the pillow to listen and now it didn't seem worth it.

'But they're for Anne. To take any out would have spoiled the look of the box.'

'It would. But she seemed a bit annoyed not to be offered any.'

'She shouldn't have expected it,' said Ellen, sinking back into her pillow and oblivion.

Although she thought Avery concerned himself unduly with Louise's feelings in this case, Ellen herself apologised a good deal for not taking her to Mershott.

'It's really just a day for parents and children. You do understand, don't you?' she said several times.

'Perfectly, Madame,' said Louise.

On the Saturday morning as they drove away in the car, she stood at the gate waving so amiably that they were smitten with compunction at leaving her behind.

'I don't know what she'll do with herself all day,' said Avery.

'Neither do I,' said Ellen. 'I hope she'll be all right.'

When they were out of sight, Louise walked back, with a lively sense of anticipation, to the house. This was the first time she had been alone in it. Neither of the day-women would come to-day. She had the chance she might never have again of going through everything.

The house was defenceless. The morning sunlight came innocently through the landing window and lay upon the stairs. The lives, the very beings of the Norths were exposed to the stranger's inspection.

She began with Avery's dressing-room, because that interested her the most. There was a photograph of Anne on the table. There would be, she thought. He made a parade of his fondness of his daughter. She picked up his hairbrushes and smelled them with a sensation of pleasure. There was amber in his brilliantine. Paul had used it, probably used it still. What memories that smell brought back.

She fingered Avery's dressing-gown hanging behind the door. It pleased her to be among a man's things again. She walked about, her hands lingering on them.

There were rows of shoes on trees. Unlike his wife, he provided himself with the best of everything. She admired him for that. She looked into his drawers, carefully replacing the contents as before. He had a packet of letters in one. She drew them out with excitement. Now she would come upon the core of the man. But they were in a child's hand – Anne again. She tried to make out one or two. She was puzzled by: 'Send me some sweats, please. It is ergent.' Also by: 'There is a box for seggestions at this school,' and on the back of the envelope, triumphantly: 'I put a seggestion in the box.' She didn't know that this missive, after half a dozen years, had power still to move Avery to laughter, almost to tears.

She left the drawers with disappointment. There was no key to the man here. His life must be lived elsewhere, she decided. He might have a mistress. Even in England, men had.

She went into the wide bedroom where the curtains stirred gently at the many windows. Here they slept. Sunlight lay over their beds. All was serene, charming. She felt a sudden violent wish to upset it all. Why should these people, other people, Paul and his wife too, have so much while she had nothing? Why must she always be the one to be outside?

Not that she would be contented with what these women had. She despised them for wasting their chances. If she had this husband, she would see to it that he took her about the world. To Rome in winter, to the mountains, the plages, the casinos in the summer. America, Spain, where would she not go? This man could afford it and yet his wife lived like a peasant, doing her own cooking and working the soil.

'What a fool she is,' said Louise, snapping the cupboard doors on Ellen's coats and skirts and linen dresses.

'So she reads books of devotion in her bed at night?' she said, turning them over on Ellen's table. 'Surprising, since she is not Catholic.'

She went down to make coffee. There was plenty of time, she had all the day before her. She took it into the sitting-room and going through the desk there she found an album of snapshots. There were dozens of photographs of Avery and Ellen together. Florence, was written below; Fiesole, Corsica, Malta, Rome, Venice. She was annoyed. They had been about the world after all.

Towards two o'clock, as she started her investigations again, Avery and Ellen were driving in at the gates of the School, once a great country house. Cars were arriving from all sides and were parked in the drive. Parents, brothers, sisters, aunts, even dogs, got out, and after much banging of doors, converged with one accord towards the wide gravel sweep in front of the house, where they waited.

At upper windows, faces were pressed against the glass. These were the girls, Anne had told them once, whose parents were not coming. Ellen, looking up at them, felt a sharp pang for the children of the world with no parents, or indifferent ones.

The stable clock struck two. A bell rang. The doors under the Palladian portico seemed to burst under pressure, and hundreds of girls poured out in a tidal wave of tossing hair, laughing faces, flying legs. The air was full of young voices uttering cries of joy and excitement. On the drive the parents braced themselves and were engulfed. Each girl made unerringly for her own family. Anne reached hers.

'Oh, Mummy. Oh, Daddy . . . oh . . .'

The great knot of ecstatic greetings began to dissolve. Children were soon hauling parents away in all directions.

'You must come and see my room, darlings. Because I've changed, you know. Let's go up straight off before Pug gets her people up. It would be such a squash with all of us. Oh, Mummy, Pug can come and stay with us in the summer – her mother says so. Oh, the Head wants to see you. Isn't it a bore? Taking up our precious time. I bet anything it's about my not being ready to take the exam next year. You know, the one instead of the School Cert. whatever it is. Oh, Mummy,' she squeezed her mother's arm in an access of happiness. 'Oh, Daddy, you're sweet to come. Lots of fathers don't, you know. I'm so glad you do.'

Rattling away, she took them up flight after flight of stairs. Ellen was breathless, but wouldn't say so. The room, when they finally reached it, was like a room in a good country hotel; two beds, white paint, chintz armchairs, flowers on the wide window-sills.

'This is the bathroom. Pug and I share with two others,' said Anne.

'So this is what we pay for,' said Avery.

'How times have changed,' said Ellen. 'I was in a cubicle with white curtains. We used to be fined for looking over. My bath nights were Tuesday and Friday. Hair washed once a month.'

'I wash mine whenever I feel like it,' said Anne. 'Let's go down and see when you have to see the Head. I hope we can get it over soon, so it doesn't hang over us. Did you bring plenty of mock cream, Mummy?'

'I brought plenty of everything,' said Ellen, and Anne hugged her for it, and Avery too, so as not to leave him out.

'If only you could have brought Roma. Is that French person still with us?' said Anne, clattering down the stairs again. 'I hope she'll be gone by the time I come home.'

'Oh, yes, six weeks. Oh, yes, surely,' said Ellen. 'She's got time to go before you come home. We don't know why she stays, but she does.'

'Now here's the board for the interview. The Headmistress will be glad to see Mr. and Mrs. Weeks at 2.30 . . . Mr. and Mrs. . . . . Here you are. "Mr. and Mrs. North 3.10." Oh, not so bad. I should have been mad if it had interfered with tea. Come on, darlings, please come and look at our classroom because I did it. It was my turn. I'm very particular. I make them pick their papers up.'

'Don't be long,' she implored, leaving them outside the Headmistress's door. 'Remember, time's going and I'm waiting outside. Cut the Head off if you can. Don't let her get long-winded about me, will you? Good-bye; sooner you than me, though she's not bad really.'

If schools had changed since Ellen's time, Headmistresses had changed with them. Miss Beldon was calm, smiling and natural. The room was full of flowers and a tabby-cat dozed comfortably on her desk, blinking lazily at successive parents.

'Anne's a clever child,' said Miss Beldon. 'But I don't think she feels she need work very hard.'

Anne's parents smiled and murmured.

'She's a very happy person,' said Miss Beldon.

'That's the main thing,' said her father.

'But we do want her to pass the school-leaving examination at the highest standard. Scholarship standard it is called, though she may not wish to take up a scholarship to the university. She's quite capable of passing at that standard if she will exert herself. But her French is so bad,' said Miss Beldon.

'She doesn't seem to like French,' said Ellen.

'I was wondering if she could spend a holiday in France this summer,' said Miss Beldon.

'She hates to go away during the holidays,' said Ellen. 'She won't leave her horse, you know.'

'I've heard about Roma.'

'But we have a French girl with us at the moment,' said Ellen. 'Perhaps she would stay on and coach Anne during the holidays, Avery. Would that be enough, Miss Beldon?'

'It would help a good deal, I think,' said the Headmistress. They both looked to Avery.

'Mademoiselle will probably stay whether we ask her to or not,' he said. 'So she may as well coach Anne. If she will.'

'Oh, I think she will,' said Ellen hastily. No good running off into a sideline about Louise with Anne waiting outside.

Miss Beldon soon said she knew they wanted to spend as much time with their daughter as possible and smiled them out.

'It's your French, darling,' said Ellen, after being hugged as if the quarter of an hour away had been another half-term.

'Oh, it would be. I loathe French,' said Anne.

'Which do you choose – to go to France for the summer holidays or be coached by Mademoiselle at home?'

'Oh, Mummy, I couldn't possibly leave Roma. I shall have to put up with Mademoiselle. But you know Pug's coming to stay with me. I'm not going to have to do lessons all the holidays, am I?'

'No, no,' Ellen assured her. 'Just conversation now and again.'

'All these girls,' marvelled Avery, as a torrent passed him on the way to secure tables for tea. 'Some of them are very hefty. Look at those legs. They're like young trees.'

'Oh, nobody bothers about legs here,' said Anne. 'Let's hurry. I've laid our food out on a grand table in the window, but if we don't be quick, somebody might remove it.'

'I'd be ashamed of this immense amount of food,' said Avery, sitting down, 'if other tables weren't just as bad.'

'As good, you mean,' said Anne. 'We look to to-day to keep us going till the end of the term. Now, I'm going for the tea to the hatch, darlings. Don't let anybody join us while I'm away.'

Ellen knew the visit was making one of Anne's graphs for her. Until tea-time it rose steadily in happiness; after tea it began to fall away towards the parting. When tea was cleared away and empty boxes and baskets packed into the cars, parents and children walked soberly about the gardens or sat in groups in the Library and playrooms. When the Norths had walked about as much as they could, they came to sit down too. Conversation was difficult; it was like waiting for a train to go out. Anne maintained a small, aching smile which wrung her parents' hearts.

It was always like this after tea at half-term.

'We might be at a funeral,' said Avery, and Anne laughed and took the opportunity to blow her nose.

At half-term times, Ellen loved Avery with an intensification of her constant everyday love for him. He was endearing in the way he put off masculine grandeur and worldly business ways for this day. He gave himself up to being Anne's father, putting himself entirely aside to make her happy, and because she was happy, he was happy himself in a deep humble way.

Although perhaps absurdly painful, the time after tea at half-term drew father, mother and child very close, knitted them up. Indissolubly, Ellen felt.

Seven o'clock struck.

'I won't watch you go,' said Anne. 'I'll rush upstairs with Pug. We've arranged. I won't even say good-bye.'

'No,' said Avery, turning his back. 'Rush off . . .'

CHAPTER FIFTEEN

⊸◇◦⊷

I

'Well,' said Ellen, in the car on the way home. 'Louise has hung on and on with us and we've kept wishing she'd go and feeling we'd have to give her a hint. And now you see we have to ask her to stay.'

'And perhaps she'll say no,' said Avery.

'I don't think so,' said Ellen. ' I think she wants to make sure of her money.'

'You think she's mercenary, do you?' said Avery.

'I don't say that. I think she's highly practical and has everything weighed up. No loose ends about Louise.'

Avery drove on, smiling lazily.

'But if she stays,' Ellen began again after a time, 'you will be nicer to her, won't you? You've been rather distant so far. I don't suppose she's noticed, because she doesn't know what you're usually like. But I could see that you didn't like her being always with us. Still, if she's going to help Anne with her French, you'll be a bit more friendly, won't you?'

Avery made murmurs, which she took for agreement. She had had a happy day and was full of warmth and good will towards everybody, Louise included. Louise should be gathered into the family now. Anne's French would improve, Hugh would get leave before long and altogether it would be a good summer for everybody. She was at her usual game of making everything cosy.

The car turned the corner of the lane and the house waited, evening falling softly about it. The lilac smelled sweet and a blackbird was singing. 'I'm a lucky woman,' thought Ellen, running into the house. Though over forty, she still ran.

'Here we are,' she called out. 'We're back.'

But Louise was far away in the garden, smoking a contemplative cigarette. She was as full of information as a cat of stolen cream and showed as little trace of it.

'Tiens, is it time for you?' she said, looking at her watch when Ellen came upon her. She spoke as she felt, without welcome, unwilling to see Ellen turning up again.

On the way home, Ellen had been busy building up Louise into a friend of the family. But face to face with her now, she saw that she was as before – cold and self-centred.

Besides, she hadn't even set the table for supper. Only a woman and a housewife, perhaps, would have judged Louise on this point. But she was right; it was an indication of character.

If we could be seen thinking, we would show blown bright one moment, dark the next, like embers; subject to every passing word and thought of our own or other people's, mostly other people's.

'I don't think I shall ask her to stay,' thought Ellen, preceding Louise to the house.

But Avery did it. No sooner had they sat down to supper than he said: 'We had a talk with Anne's Headmistress to-day and she tells us Anne's French is very bad.'

'I could have told you that myself,' said Louise with one of her rare smiles.

'The Headmistress suggests she should go to France for the summer holidays,' said Avery.

'Ah?'

Reserve closed Louise's face. She thought they were going to ask her to take the girl to Amigny and that she would not do.

Ellen was looking deeply at Avery, trying to convey to him that she didn't want him to go on. But he noticed nothing.

'Anne doesn't want to leave home during the holidays,' said Avery. 'And we don't want her to either, so we wondered if you would care to stay on with us and coach her.'

'Coach?' said Louise.

'Coach means teach,' said Avery.

'Ah – teach,' said Louise on a note of distaste. Now she had a thousand pounds, she didn't think she should be asked to teach.

'We mean, will you talk to her in French for a little while each day . . .?'

The more persuasively Avery put it, the more difficulties Louise made.

'I don't know that I can stay so long,' she said.

'How long did you think of staying?' said Ellen.

Avery looked across at her in surprise.

Louise could not say she had intended to stay until she got the money. So she closed the subject by a show of filial piety.

'I must ask my parents what they wish me to do,' she said
primly.

'Of course,' said Avery. He smiled at her as if he saw
through her and Louise, lowering her eyes to her soup,
smiled too.

But Ellen was restive.

'I'd changed my mind,' she told Avery as soon as they were
alone in their room.

'Changed your mind?' said Avery in amazement.

'Yes,' said Ellen rather testily, as if he ought to have known.

'How on earth was I to know that? Why did you change
your mind?'

'Well . . . she hadn't even set the supper table. . . .'

Avery shouted with laughter.

'Sshh,' said Ellen. 'She'll hear.'

'How will she know what I'm laughing about?' said Avery
impatiently. 'Really, Ellen, you're absurd.'

'I may be,' said Ellen. 'But I suddenly felt it was a mistake
to ask her to stay.'

'You're too changeable,' said Avery, going into his dressing-
room. 'I can't keep up with you. But you don't need to concern
yourself. She's evidently not going to stay.'

When the light was out, Ellen felt she must dispel the
slight coolness there was between them.

'Perhaps I was absurd,' she said. 'Besides it doesn't matter
if she doesn't stay, does it? We can always get someone else for
Anne.'

'I suppose so,' said Avery, willing to be mollified. 'Except
that we're used to this girl. I don't like strangers in the house.'

'Neither do I,' said Ellen. 'Well, we'll wait and see what she decides. Good night, darling,' she said, quite restored.

'Good night, darling,' said Avery.

'Anne will be asleep in that nice room,' said Ellen contentedly. 'She has a happy life, bless her. I suppose Hugh's in a tent to-night. You know, count no man happy until he's dead and all that, Avery,' she said, rising on her elbow. 'And I really shouldn't say it until they are grown up, but I do feel, as far as happiness is concerned, that we've made a success of our children.'

'I hope so,' said Avery. 'But go to sleep.'

'Yes,' said Ellen, lying down again.

The following morning, having decided that even if she had the money by that time, it would be better to stay at Netherfold than go to Binic with her parents, Louise said she might manage to remain until the end of August. There was nothing for it but to thank her, which Ellen did with some reserve at first.

But after taking a quarter of an hour off to look round the garden, carrying apples down to Roma and coming back to drink coffee with Louise in the sunny corner outside the sitting-room windows, Ellen was full of plans and goodwill once more.

'I think you should go to London for the day now and again,' she said. 'It's so easy from here. You could go up with my husband. He wouldn't have time to take you about, I'm afraid, but you would get a lift to the station and back again.'

'I will go,' said Louise. 'I should like it.'

'The summer's lovely here,' said Ellen, stretching luxuriously to the sun. 'We must take you to Somerton Manor some time soon.'

Louise allowed her to exercise her expansive feelings in this way.

II

There are times in our lives when the slightest move is dangerous. From some notion of making up for not giving her any from Anne's box, and from a wish to thank her for agreeing to stay, Avery brought home a box of marrons glacés for Louise.

It happened that Ellen had gone to William's cottage and Louise, alone in the house, was crossing the hall as he came in from the car.

'For you,' he said, presenting the round beribboned box with a mock-ceremonial bow.

Louise's eyes flew wide. Turning from the stairs, she looked as if she had suddenly come to vivid life.

'Mais c'est charmant,' she said. 'For me? Tiens!'

She clasped the box and smiled radiantly.

'I'm sorry I couldn't give you any the other night,' he said, lamely for him.

'Oh, but I knew that,' she said. 'I knew. This is a marvellous surprise. . . .'

As they stood there, smiling, Ellen called to the little cat as she came through the French windows of the sitting-room.

'Moppet. . . . Moppet. . . .'

Louise turned swiftly and ran lightly and noiselessly upstairs to her room with the box.

Avery was taken aback. He hadn't meant to make a secret of it. What had he meant? He should have brought a box for Ellen too. But he hadn't thought of it. Now Ellen was here and the thing was done. He stood, hesitating.

'Oh, you're here,' said Ellen happily. She was always glad when he came home.

As he kissed her, he glanced over her head at the stairs. Louise was coming down again, without the box. What could he say now without giving her away and turning Ellen against her? He couldn't say anything now. He must do something about it later. He couldn't let the situation develop as Louise evidently meant it to. And yet he was amused. He was distinctly amused.

'I think we'll all have a glass of sherry,' he said.

He almost worked on that axiom. When in doubt, have a glass of sherry. It tided him over. It put things off, and after a glass of sherry, problems mostly solved themselves. At any rate, sherry to-night rid him of the feeling of slight disloyalty to Ellen. Though it was ridiculous to think of it as disloyalty, really, he told himself. It wasn't his fault the girl had made a secret of the box, giving it a significance he hadn't meant.

'I went to ask William to take Roma to the forge to-morrow. She has one shoe loose,' said Ellen. 'Do you ride, Mademoiselle?'

'No,' said Louise.

'Wouldn't you like to try?' said Ellen, still bent on helping Louise to pleasure.

'I don't think so,' said Louise. 'I haven't the trousers.'

When Avery laughed, she did not withdraw into dignity as she usually did. She laughed too.

'What is wrong now?' she said gaily.

'I don't know why trousers should sound funnier than breeches,' said Avery. 'But it does.'

'Britches. It is an ugly word.'

'You're right,' said Ellen. 'It is. But you could have Anne's jodhpurs. They'd fit you.'

'Jodhpurs? Oh, this is too much,' protested Louise. 'I cannot follow.'

They tried to explain and they laughed a great deal. Ellen thought how nice it was that they should be all getting on so well together and smiled at Avery for lending himself to it.

In her room that night, Louise took the box of marrons glacés from her trunk. Not to eat from it, but to smile over it while she smoked a last cigarette.

Smoking was an art with her. It enabled her to show off her hands, to make inscrutable faces, narrowing her eyes against the smoke, tilting her chin to blow it away. She never allowed her companion to forget that she was smoking a cigarette, and even when she was alone, she kept up the tricks.

As she smoked now, she smiled, and her smile was compounded of triumph, scorn and excitement. Triumph because she had won, and excitement because the game had started in earnest now. She had dangled the bait. No need to take any more notice of it now. She herself was the bait.

It was not that she had any particular design at this time. She was attracted by Avery and she meant to pay him out for ignoring, or pretending to ignore, her so long. Also, at the back of her mind, was an idea of being ready to follow any advantage to herself that offered. In spite of her thousand pounds, her future was a blank before her. She was casting about, almost instinctively, like a caterpillar at the end of a stalk, for something to get hold of and climb on to.

She leaned into the glass, blowing smoke and looking at herself provocatively from under her lids. She had no intention of losing her head again, she told herself. If he lost his, so much the worse for him.

Her gaze sharpened. Was that a freckle? She leaned into the glass again in passionate concern. No, thank heaven, it was not. Freckles were all very well for his wife, but she would never permit them.

It might not be a freckle, she decided, but it was a faint blemish of some kind. Reaching for a little jar of unguent, she carefully, tenderly, smoothed it on.

She went through a long ritual of cleansing and creaming her face, neck, hands and arms; she avoided water. She brushed her hair, did her nails, laid out fresh underclothes for the next day, washed out her silk stockings. She maided herself very thoroughly, and Ellen, seeing the beam from her window shining out into the trees long after their adjoining room was in darkness, wondered what on earth the girl did every night to be so long in getting to bed.

It was not until she had finished her elaborate toilet that Louise noticed again the box of marrons glacés. She returned it to her trunk and, smiling, got into bed at last, as plain as a nun with her hair screwed back and her lips pale.

CHAPTER SIXTEEN

⊸◦◇◦⊸

A grain or two of sand can start a downward trickle on the sand-hills which eventually alters the shape of the immediate scene. After the invitation to stay for the summer and the box of marrons glacés, invisible displacements and shiftings began at Netherfold.

Louise did less and less in the house. Her attitude was that, if she was going to work with the girl in the holidays, she wasn't going to work now. She suspected Ellen, unjustifiably, of trying to put her on an 'au pair' basis and she wasn't going to have that. She was a guest. She had been invited to come and persuaded to stay. As a favour, she would speak French with the child in the holidays, but nothing must be exacted or expected of her. Also, although she might conceal the fact, she had Avery behind her now.

So she came down later in the mornings, causing asperities to fall from the lips of both Mrs. Pretty and Miss Beasley, who, when they met in the lane, said they didn't know why Mrs. North put up with her.

'Takes good care of number one, doesn't she?' said Mrs. Pretty. 'She never so much as passes the time of the day with me. Does she with you?'

'Not she,' said Miss Beasley. 'Not that I give her the chance. I don't hold with these foreigners coming over and doing our work.'

Which was hardly to the point, since Louise did no work, except to keep her own room in order. She was possessive and secretive about that, keeping the door firmly closed. It was weeks since Ellen had had a glimpse of her own spare room. Not that it mattered, she told herself.

That was how Ellen felt about the situation. Louise was not the companion she would have chosen. They had little in common. They would never really get on, but what did it matter? Ellen's busy, happy life went on as usual. There was the house to see to, and the garden. Hugh would be coming home on leave before long. Anne would come for the holidays. So that if Louise took possession of Ellen's own corner of the sofa, if she spent an unconscionable time in the bath when other people wanted it, if she made extra work, if she joined Avery for sherry in the sitting-room as soon as he came home, while Ellen got supper to table unaided – well, irritating though it was, did it really matter? That was what Ellen asked herself, being reasonable about it. And Avery asked her the same thing when she told him sometimes about things that had annoyed her.

So, for a time, Ellen went blindly and happily on. There was until now a sort of naïveté about Ellen. If she wasn't quite as gentle as a dove, she certainly wasn't as wise as a serpent. She had no experience of serpents. She had really never come across one before.

'You're going to have your first riding lesson this afternoon,' said Avery to Louise at lunch one Saturday.

'Aren't you going to golf?' said Ellen in surprise.

'No. I played badly last week. I don't want to depress myself again yet. So I'll give Louise her first riding lesson.'

Louise?

'Yes, it will be better if we call you Louise,' said Ellen. 'Will you call me Ellen?'

'Ah, Madame,' said Louise, turning out a hand. 'You are much older than I am. I think it would not be polite.'

Ellen and Avery laughed aloud.

'I forget my advanced age,' said Ellen. 'Stick to Madame then, if you feel you would be irreverent.'

'I am used to calling you Madame,' said Louise. 'I am afraid I could not remember to call you anything else.'

'Where are Anne's riding things, Ellen?' said Avery when lunch was over. 'Can you get them?'

'Why can't he wait?' thought Ellen. 'Why must he clamour for riding things for her before even the table is cleared?'

Neither he nor Louise offered to clear it. They lit cigarettes and sauntered to the windows, while she went up to get jodhpurs and a shirt.

She intended to take them to Louise's room, but to her astonishment the door was locked.

'I was going to put them on your bed,' she said, appearing in the sitting-room and speaking in such a brisk way that Louise turned in surprise from the window. 'But your door was locked.'

Her eyes were very direct.

'Yes,' said Louise, blowing smoke and waving it away with a narrow hand. 'Mrs. Pretty was here this morning.'

'Mrs. Pretty is entirely honest,' said Ellen. 'I never lock any room or even any drawer or cupboard against her, and I don't like it to be done by anybody else.'

Louise's nostrils fluttered. Without a word, she took the riding things from Ellen's arm and went upstairs.

'You shouldn't speak to her as if she were a servant,' said Avery.

'She shouldn't treat us as if we were servants,' said Ellen, clearing the table. 'And ones she couldn't trust too.'

'Oh, come,' said Avery in a conciliatory tone. 'Perhaps they do lock their bedroom doors in France.'

'Perhaps they do,' said Ellen, unmollified, taking the tray out.

She shut herself into the kitchen and began to wash up at a great rate.

'Louise,' called Avery from the foot of the stairs. 'I'm going to saddle Roma. Come down to the paddock when you're ready.'

In a few moments, Louise passed the kitchen window looking distinctly odd. Some women do not wear jodhpurs to advantage and Louise was one of them. Ellen stared, forgot her anger in amusement, the cause of which she did not go into, threw down the towel and went out to see the fun.

In the paddock Avery was holding Roma, saddled and as quiet as a lamb. Louise reached him, but when Ellen appeared at the railings, she looked over her shoulder and waited pointedly, implying that she didn't want an onlooker. But Ellen stayed where she was, and Louise had to put her foot into Avery's hand and be hoisted up. She sat on the mare with apprehension and distaste. Avery instructed her about her hands and began to lead Roma round the paddock. All went so quietly that Ellen went back to the washing-up.

But in another moment, she heard a shout of laughter from Avery and Louise came stalking past the kitchen window, looking furious.

'Oh, come and try again,' called Avery. 'Louise! Don't be silly! Don't give up.'

'I don't like it,' she called back coldly. 'The horse is too wide.'

He shouted with laughter again and Ellen smiled. The first riding lesson was soon over.

'Now I will do something I like much better,' called Louise petulantly and went through the french windows into the house.

Avery rode Roma down the lane, but not for long. The sun was hot. He turned back, unsaddled the mare and turned her loose. She made for the shade of the great chestnut and stood there, flicking at the flies with her tail.

Avery walked slowly towards the house. He wished he had gone to golf. Hanging about like this . . . he said furiously to himself.

He, coming into the garden, and Ellen, still at the kitchen window, were simultaneously startled. On the lawn, a moment before green and empty, appeared a slender shaft of dazzling whiteness – Louise, naked but for sun-glasses and what looked like two striped handkerchiefs. As Avery stared from the trellis and Ellen from the window, she spread a rug on the grass and lay down to take a sun-bath. She had appeared to disadvantage; now she would appear to advantage. The horse and the jodhpurs had made her look funny; but she didn't look funny now.

Ellen stared in amazement. Sun-bathing was a commonplace, everybody sun-bathed. But she had never seen anyone expose so much body before. The body was beautiful, Ellen told herself, and that should excuse everything. But what an apparition – in the middle of the lawn on Saturday afternoon!

Avery's first reaction was that if he crossed the lawn as he had intended, he would be intruding on Louise's privacy. So he went into the house by way of the kitchen.

'Good heavens,' said Ellen, still looking through the window.

'As you say, good heavens,' said Avery, with an attempt at a laugh.

The girl was dangerous.

'Just look at her,' said Ellen.

Avery felt a stab of anger. Really Ellen shouldn't . . . she should realise . . . She shouldn't take it for granted that he was as safe as all that. Damn it all, he was a man like any other, and whether she knew it or not, this girl was more provocative than any he had come across.

He was afraid to betray the fact, but he looked.

On the rug, Louise was curled round, her knees under her chin. She seemed to have no bones, her ivory body was narrowly banded with bright stripes.

'She looks like a Catherine wheel,' said Ellen. 'Or a wasp. Or even a snake.'

'Huh,' said Avery briefly, with what Ellen took for disgust, and went out of the kitchen. Late though it was, he decided to go to golf after all.

When Louise heard him go away in his car, she went into the house for her sun-oil and spent the rest of the afternoon on the rug assiduously oiling her body. If one did not amuse oneself in one way, one amused oneself in another. She furthered her own ends whichever she did.

Ellen left her in possession of the garden. She was unaccountably tired and went to lie down on her bed with a book. But she could not forget the naked figure on the lawn and kept getting up to look through the curtains at it. Whenever she looked, Louise was still engrossed, using the sun, thought Ellen with disgust. Like everything else, the sun had to be pressed into the service of Louise.

*   *   *

Ellen had asked Avery to be nicer to Louise, but soon she thought he was overdoing it and said so.

'I don't think you should play up to her,' she said, when Avery had let Louise get away with some cutting remark or other. All he did in defence was to smile at the girl and she, in the end, smiled too in spite of herself. It gave the impression that Avery alone knew how to manage her.

'I don't think you need follow her about,' said Ellen, who was getting tired of fetching them in to meals from the garden or the paddock or the stables or sometimes from upstairs, where they would sit smoking and talking on the landing window-sill.

One evening she appeared heatedly in the sitting-room.

'I've been making jam all afternoon,' she said. 'I cooked supper, I set the table and cleared the table and now I think you might help to wash-up for a change.'

'But certainly, Madame,' said Louise in cool surprise, stubbing out her cigarette and going straight to the kitchen.

'We'll do it between us,' said Avery, getting up from his chair. 'I'll wash-up. Louise shall dry. You sit down.'

'No,' said Ellen. 'I'll wash, but you can both dry.'

'Nothing of the kind,' said Avery, taking her by the elbows and putting her into her chair. 'Sit there. Here are the papers. You have a rest.'

'Avery,' she whispered fiercely as he made for the door. 'Let her do it. Why shouldn't she for once? Avery . . .'

But he continued to the kitchen and she had an angry, hurt feeling that he was paying her out. Both had implied that she had been peevish. But who wouldn't be, she asked herself.

In a moment, she went out into the garden. She could always garden herself into some sort of calm and she did it now. But when she was in bed that night, she said nothing to him of what was in her mind. The first silence fell between them.

Although, like an early snowflake, it didn't lie. It melted away in the morning, and everything seemed as before.

* * *

'I will go to London,' said Louise a few days later. 'Like you suggested.'

'As you suggested,' corrected Avery, who was there. She had waited to announce her intention until he was.

'As you suggested,' said Louise with docility. 'I will go to London for the day to-morrow, as you suggested.'

'Yes, do,' said Ellen, whose first thought was that it would be nice to be without her.

'I will go with Avery in his car and on his train, as you suggested,' said Louise.

It was true. Ellen had suggested it in the days when she had no suspicion of Louise. She wouldn't have suggested it now. In fact, if she had not had an appointment with the dentist, she felt, for a moment, that she would have gone to London too.

Then she told herself she ought to be ashamed. She might have doubts of Louise, but never of Avery. Never, never of the Avery who had knelt beside her bed the night Hugh was born. He might flatter and spoil this girl in a way any wife would consider unnecessary, but of course there was nothing in it. It was just because Ellen had never so far seen him pay the slightest attention to any other woman but herself.

'I'm jealous,' she thought next morning as they went away together in the car. 'That's what it is. I'm jealous and I didn't know I had it in me.'

All those years, jealousy had been lurking unsuspected in her character, like a toad under a stone that had never been turned up before. And somehow as soon as she could put down all her misgivings to jealousy, she was immensely relieved and spent an energetic morning with Mrs. Pretty. Louise's name cropped up once.

'On my way here,' began Mrs. Pretty in a guileless way,

'I thought I caught sight of Mademoiselle with Mr. North in his car. Going somewhere, was she?'

'Yes. To London for the day,' said Ellen.

'Oh,' said Mrs. Pretty. 'Fancy,' she said, and fell to polishing the legs of the table.

'Mr. North was taking her to the station,' Ellen felt obliged to add.

'I see,' said Mrs. Pretty, as if a child had offered her something it took for a sweet and she was obliged to pretend to swallow it.

'All I know is I wouldn't let my husband go off to London by himself with that girl,' she said to Miss Beasley when they were on the bus.

'Oh, husbands,' said Miss Beasley, darkly.

'She's asking for trouble, letting him,' said Mrs. Pretty.

They wrung every drop of interest out of the topic, as if it had been one of the floor-cloths they also shared at Netherfold. They wrung it out and left it. Later they would pick it up again, soak it in their mutual interest and pass it from one to the other as before.

Avery spent the day with Louise. He made some show of telling himself that it was all very awkward, that Ellen had let him in for it by suggesting in the first place that Louise should go to London for the day. The girl couldn't go about London by herself, so what else could he do? But it must never happen again, he told himself. He was far too busy. Also, though it was her fault, Ellen wouldn't like it and she was far too dear to him. . . . Not that he wasn't always with women, some of them very attractive too, taking them out to luncheon, to tea, with them at parties, surrounded by them at the office, so why should she mind now?

He admitted, all the same, that this was different. The fact that Louise lived under his own roof made it different. Though why should it really? Still, the whole thing was foolish, unpermissible; but strangely revitalising. It was a long time since he had felt so vividly alive.

He didn't mean to go far. He was giving way to an attraction, letting himself be caught in a lazy, amused way. Although he felt mean to Ellen, he was allowing himself a bit of latitude. Surely after twenty years of fidelity a man . . . Well, anyway, what did it matter? The girl was going home soon. And of course as soon as Anne came home, this sort of thing must absolutely come to a stop.

Nothing could have been more innocuous than the way they spent the day, he pointed out to some invisible and inconvenient onlooker. They simply sat a long time over lunch at one restaurant and a long time over tea at another. Louise had chosen from the celebrated names he offered her.

All the same, the nearer he drew to home in the evening, the more uncomfortable he was. It musn't happen again, he told himself. He wasn't going to start deceiving Ellen, even in a mild way. He was rather silent and heavy in the train, but Louise left him to his self-reproach. She made no attempt to cajole him out of it. She let him understand that she had taken it for granted that he should spend the day with her; she would have expected it of any man. She was not the sort of woman to be without an escort.

They made no arrangement as to what they should say to Ellen. Avery couldn't bring himself to that and Louise seemed not to be concerned about it. All the same it was she who turned the enquiries.

'What did you do?' said Ellen.

Louise shrugged her shoulders.

'I went about,' she said. 'I enjoyed myself.'

'Did you get lunch?' said Ellen. 'It's rather difficult in London now. You have to be very early. . . .'

'I had plenty of food,' said Louise.

It was too uncomfortable, thought Avery. It wasn't worth it. It mustn't happen again.

CHAPTER SEVENTEEN

—◦◇◦—

But Avery didn't know his own nature, though he might have done. He was not easily roused, but once he was roused, he was almost obsessive in pursuit of his object. He should have remembered how he had followed the young Ellen, travelling with her father and aunt, through France to Switzerland, through Switzerland to Italy and back through France again, encountering her in the most unexpected places to implore her to marry him and looking, every time he turned up, more and more haggard from lack of sleep.

'It's dogged as does it,' said Ellen's father, and in that case it certainly had.

Now he was becoming obsessed again, though for a time he didn't realise it. He didn't want to find himself seriously infatuated. That would be much too inconvenient and destructive. But he kept letting himself slip a little further, sure that he could recover himself when he really wanted to.

If he didn't know himself, he knew Louise still less. But Louise knew both him and herself.

She was in her element. To have an affair on hand again was like coming to life after being dead. What excitement to be back in the game! There was nothing like it, nothing in life so breathless, so vivid, nothing that took so much ingenuity. To have all one's faculties in full play was to be truly alive, thought Louise, stretching luxuriously in her bed on these summer mornings. She knew now what she was after and she would take care not to ruin everything this time. She was older now, she told herself. She had learnt her lesson.

It was much more amusing this time when the power was all hers. Much more interesting when the heart was not involved, though Avery was certainly attractive. In a way, she was avenging herself on Paul. She was getting her own back. The conquest, the annexation of Avery was necessary to restore her confidence in herself.

As for his wife, thought Louise, hearing Ellen hurrying downstairs to make breakfast, the foolish creature didn't seem to realise that it was necessary to fight. The battle was joined and would be over before she knew there was one. But Louise had no compunction. The woman didn't deserve what she had if she couldn't keep it. Besides, why should other people always have everything and Louise Lanier nothing? It was time for a change.

Meanwhile, she played her fish. She knew all the tricks. She knew how to set up a powerful secret current between them. How to lead him on, how to evade him. How to make him angry, upset him and then soothe him. How not to be there when he expected her. As for instance, one evening when he came home, looking for her, and found she had gone to bed.

'What's the matter?' he said. 'Is she ill or something?'

'Far from it,' said Ellen. 'She looked particularly blooming.'

He went out and mooned about the garden, looking up at her window. He didn't whistle up to it, but about it. He let her hear him, in case she didn't know he'd come home.

But she gave no sign. He came to the conclusion that she was absenting herself on purpose and slammed the door of the sitting-room as he went in. How dared she treat him like this? She must go home. He would tell her so when he saw her in the morning. Then he remembered that he never saw her in the morning. He would have to wait until to-morrow night. All that time. He found relief in running her down to Ellen.

'Why should she go to bed?' he said savagely, so that Ellen looked at him.

'She ought to be helping you,' he said. 'Damn it all, does she do anything for her keep?'

'Nothing at all,' said Ellen. 'But I understood you to say that it didn't matter.'

'But she goes too far,' he said explosively. 'She gets worse.'

'I hope she exerts herself enough to teach Anne,' said Ellen. 'Or all this putting-up with her that I've had to do won't have been worth it. I wish we hadn't asked her to stay.'

'Look out. She's coming down,' he said, and unwanted excitement leaped in his veins.

She came down, cool and pale, and sat far off by the window, her smooth dark head outlined against the yellow evening light.

'I have a headache,' she said, passing her fingers lingeringly over her brow.

'I'm sorry,' said Avery, who didn't believe it.

She picked up a magazine. Ellen was darning socks. Avery read his paper.

Her scent stole across the room. He got up abruptly and went through the french windows into the darkening garden. He walked about the lawn, smoking, and Ellen was glad he had shown disapproval of Louise by going out of the room when she came into it. But, her head bent over the magazine, Louise smiled.

The tobacco plants, a cloud of white butterflies in the dark, sent out their evening fragrance. To Ellen in the sitting-room and to Avery outside the same thought occurred at the same time.

'It has just struck me,' said Ellen to Louise, dropping the mending to her lap, 'that that's what your scent is.'

'What is what my scent is?' said Louise with a deliberation Ellen sometimes considered insulting.

'The Nicotiana – the tobacco plant. Can't you smell it from the garden?'

'I smell something,' said Louise. 'Perhaps it is the same. I don't know.'

She turned the pages.

Avery, for one strange moment, felt himself enveloped in her scent. He seemed to be fighting it off, like fumes. He left the garden and escaped along the lane.

'Good evening, North,' said a neighbour, sauntering under the lamps with his dog and hoping for company.

'Good evening,' said Avery, striding on. Who it was, he didn't know.

In the sitting-room, Ellen wondered where he had got to,

and Louise was angry. It was time he came in to entertain her. She hadn't stayed upstairs and missed supper for this.

Avery wasn't coming along fast enough to please her. He was being English and slow. There was not much time left before Anne came home. After that, not only would she be about the house all the time, but Avery was far too fond of her. Louise was angry with Avery and was tempted to press matters, which would probably, she knew, be fatal at this stage.

Then Hugh came home on leave.

Hugh's parents were always glad to see him come home, but this time both of them felt positive relief. For Ellen, the moment he entered the house, the atmosphere reverted to normal. Hugh's taking it for granted that home was just as it had always been, made Ellen feel that of course it was. His young voice, his laughter, his boots on the polished floors, restored Ellen as well as the house. She was her old confident self and was brisk with Louise, demanding she should do things in the house and seeing that she did them.

For Avery, Hugh was a buffer between himself and Louise. He decided to occupy himself with his son and stave her off. The tension in the situation was relieved and Louise found herself thrust to one side.

She was so angry, she reverted to her childish habit of biting her nails until their Chinese length was so diminished that the look of them checked her. She put the bitten nails down to the account against the sluggish Avery and the superfluous Ellen and changed her tactics.

She turned her attention to Hugh.

She was all smiling glances now, and suddenly appeared very much younger. She exchanged cigarettes with him, begging him to try the French ones. Avery looked on in silent anger.

Louise tried to ingratiate herself with Ellen again. On Sunday she suggested they should have an entrée for lunch and prepared a salade de tomates, sprinkled with chives and French dressing. It looked very attractive as with a sweet simplicity she laid it before Ellen at table.

'I didn't know you could do this sort of thing,' said Ellen rather curtly. It was a bit late, she implied.

'Oh, for the soldier we must exert ourselves,' said Louise, smiling across at Hugh.

'Were you a soldier in the war, Monsieur Avery?' she asked innocently, taking her place at the table.

He had to say no, which he coldly did.

In the evenings Louise put the gramophone on and tried to teach Hugh to dance. He stumbled courteously about the lawn with her. He wasn't at the dancing stage yet, thought his mother with fond amusement.

When they sat in the warm corner outside the sitting-room windows in the evenings, Louise talked to Hugh about the state of literature in France, which, according to her, was deplorable. She knew nothing about it, but neither did her hearers. She had only to throw in the names of a few authors whose books she had seen on her father's counters: Sartre, Duhamel, Aragon – to be impressive. Avery looked at her sardonically, but she was so animated with Hugh she didn't look at him.

She followed Hugh about with noticeable admiration and Ellen was vastly relieved. This girl would vamp any male. She had tried to vamp Avery and now she was vamping Hugh. With neither husband nor son had she made any headway, thought Ellen. If she only knew, she was nothing in Hugh's line at all. He had shown his mother the photograph he kept in his pocketbook. It was the face of a young laughing girl called Margery, as unlike Louise as it was possible to be. Louise was a downright nuisance to Hugh and was almost spoiling his leave. Ellen felt she would have to say something before long, though of course it was better to leave Hugh to manage for himself.

He was evidently prepared to.

'I say, Mother,' he said one evening after supper, coming to speak to her in the kitchen. 'I'm going down to the stable. But don't tell her where I am, will you? I want to knock up some cubby-holes for Anne to come home to. I got the idea from a chap in camp. You simply make a honeycomb of wooden boxes. Anne'll love them for keeping Roma's brushes and her cleaning tackle in and the leather-soap and so on, instead of letting them lie about on the cobbles. Good idea, isn't it?'

'Very,' said Ellen warmly.

'But don't let that woman get at me, will you? Thank goodness she won't be here when I come home next. I'll go out this way, then she won't see me.'

'Be careful then. I don't know where she is.'

'She's everywhere. That's the worst of it. Bye-bye. I'm off – you come down later if you can, won't you?'

But Louise got there first.

Hugh always liked the stable. This evening, with the doors open and sunlight still pouring over the cobbles, there was a clean smell of horse, leather and straw. In his short-sleeved sports shirt and old flannel trousers, he was contented. The worst of being in the Army was that you could so rarely be alone, but here it was nice and solitary. He tried his boxes in one arrangement and then found a better. He built them up carefully, standing back to admire them, thinking of Anne's pleasure. He whistled and began to hammer cautiously. He didn't want to attract the Frenchwoman. But by and by he became so absorbed, he forgot her. He sang. He sang an old song that had just been most aptly revived.

'Margy. I'm always thinking of you, Margy . . .'

He hammered away and suddenly a shadow lay over the cobbles and Louise was there.

'Blast,' said Hugh.

'Ah, how busy you are,' fluted Louise, teetering in high heels over the cobbles towards him.

'I am,' said Hugh evenly.

'And what is it you do – hein?'

She came to lean, too close, beside him, over his boxes.

'I shouldn't stay here if I were you,' he said. 'I'm going to make an awful noise.'

He began to hammer like mad but she didn't budge. By and by he had to stop because his boxes wouldn't stand it. He stopped and sighed.

'Ah, give it up,' said Louise persuasively. 'It is so hot in here. It smells of the horse too.'

'I like it,' said Hugh curtly, more and more irritated by her presence. 'But there is no need for you to stay.'

'But I like to be with you,' cooed Louise. 'Tell me, Hugh, why are you so reserved with me? Do you not like me, Hugh?'

'I haven't thought about it,' said Hugh, not rude enough to tell the truth.

'But do think – please. You like me, Hugh, don't you?'

She clasped her two hands round his bare arm and smiled up at him invitingly. He stiffened and with his chin drawn in looked over his cheek-bones at her in acute embarrassment and distaste.

Another shadow fell over the cobbles and Avery appeared in the doorway.

'What on earth are you doing?' he said thickly.

Louise tightened her clasp on Hugh's arm, but he threw her hands off abruptly and made for the door.

'For this relief, much thanks,' he said to his father and, laughing, made for the house at the double.

Avery stood, his eyes hard on Louise, who sauntered, unperturbed, towards him.

'Well?' she said, reaching him.

'Why can't you leave him alone?' said Avery, as though it was Hugh he was thinking of. 'He's only a boy.'

Louise laughed.

'And you think I am interested in boys?' she said, mockingly.

* * *

'I knew she would make a pass at me before long,' Hugh said to his mother. 'Father was furious. I think he's telling her off. I hope he doesn't make too much of it, though. You've got to take this sort of thing in your stride. You'd be amused how much there is of it, Mother. I always thought girls were shy about that sort of thing, but Lord, no, lots of them are absolutely out for your blood. They're terrifying.'

'I think it's awful,' Ellen said. 'What does she think she's doing? What a creature . . .'

'Now don't say anything,' said Hugh. 'I wouldn't like her to think I told you. Men aren't supposed to do that sort of thing. And good Lord, what does it matter? She'll be gone when I come home next time.'

When Ellen came to discuss what had happened with Avery – there was no chance until they were in their room at night – she found him evasive. At first, she thought he must have the same idea as Hugh's, that men didn't tell tales on women. But surely that was going too far with one's wife? Hugh was their son and they were both concerned in what happened to him. But she couldn't get Avery to say anything more than: 'I think you're making too much of it. It was only fun on her part. Let Hugh look after himself.'

'Oh, I do,' protested Ellen. 'It isn't Hugh I'm thinking about. It's the kind of person Louise is. . . .'

'You're making too much of it,' said Avery again.

Ellen gave up, but she was thoughtful.

A happily married woman acquires the habit of referring everything to, discussing everything with, her husband. Even the smallest things. Like bad coal, for instance. To be able to say, sitting across the hearth from him in the evening: 'Isn't this coal *bad*?' and to hear him say, looking up from his book at the fire: 'Awful. Sheer slate,' is to have something comfortable made out of even bad coal.

A loved husband is the companion of companions, the supreme sharer, and a happy wife often sounds trivial when she is really sampling and enjoying their mutual and unique confidence. But in doing it, she largely loses her power of independent decision and action. She either brings her husband round to her way of thinking or goes over to his, and mostly she doesn't know or care which it is.

For twenty years, Ellen had been so used to acting with Avery, never without him, that she had waited for him to agree that something must be done about Louise. Suddenly, she knew that if it was to be done, she must do it herself and without telling him.

It was a momentous decision for her to come to. She didn't like making it at all. She felt she was breaking one of the countless Lilliputian bonds that bound her up with Avery.

She told herself she would wait until Hugh had gone back, but even when he had gone, she waited a little longer. She shrank from the whole distasteful business and somehow the idea of dismissing Louise made her heart beat too fast, which was nothing short of ridiculous, she told herself. She made excuses for herself by admitting that Louise had got on her nerves. It was bad to have to keep on sitting at table with a person you didn't like, to have to see her going up and down your stairs, to hear her moving about the room she called her own, pursuing her secret ends. Home hadn't been home since

Louise came into it. Slowly, slowly everything had changed. She kept rehearsing what she would say to Louise, and suddenly, after lunch one day, she said it. She felt her neck redden as she began.

'I have decided, Mademoiselle,' for some time now she had dropped the Louise. 'I've decided that it won't be necessary for Anne to do French conversation with you in the holidays. So since your affairs are settled now, I should like you to go as soon as possible, please. Shall we say at the end of next week?'

Louise wheeled round from the window. She had not expected the worm to turn like this. She was startled.

'Mais, voyons, Madame, I cannot go,' she said, waiting towards Ellen. 'It is impossible for me. My parents are at Binic,' she lied. 'Where they always go for the summer. The house is closed. Where could I go? And what should I say? They are not expecting me. It was you who asked me to stay until the end of August, Madame.'

'I know,' said Ellen. 'But I would rather you went. Things haven't turned out as I expected.'

'It is serious for me, what you say, Madame,' said Louise. 'How have I offended you?'

Ellen did not say. She only repeated: 'I should like you to go.'

'But I cannot go – not yet,' persisted Louise. 'What is it? I have the right to ask. Is it the little game I had with your – with your son?' She almost said your precious son, but managed not to. 'Surely, Madame, you see no harm in that? Truly I cannot understand the English. In France when one is

212

young, one amuses oneself. I cannot go now, Madame, unless you turn me out without anywhere to go and I don't think you will do that. I think I know you better than that, Madame.'

People are often defeated by being told they have nice natures and Ellen was defeated now. She didn't want to be, she felt no better towards Louise, but she felt she could not, as Louise said, turn her out with nowhere to go.

'Tenez, Madame,' said Louise, flicking the lengthening ash from her cigarette to the carpet. 'I do not wish to impose myself, but there is no alternative. It is only for one month. After that, you and I can part. What do you say to that, Madame?'

'I have no choice but to agree, I suppose,' said Ellen, turning away and leaving the room.

Louise looked after her with a wary expression. This was a danger signal. She must either be very careful or very bold. She must think. In the meantime, she must hide her anger at these insults and subject herself a little longer. Compressing her lips, she began to clear the table by way of a beginning.

CHAPTER EIGHTEEN

—◦◦◇◦◦—

I

The atmosphere in the sitting-room was tense on this summer evening. Avery and Louise were far apart to give an appearance of nonchalance, she in the corner of the sofa she had appropriated and he by the windows. The door had purposely been left open and the sound of Ellen's preparations for supper came distinctly from the kitchen. The two in the sitting-room were silent, looking at each other across the room.

'Listen, Avery,' said Louise in a low voice. 'Do you hear this?'

She leaned forward and tapped twice on a little table beside the sofa. 'Do you know what it means, Avery?'

He shook his head impatiently.

'It means "Je t'aime." It means "I love you." It is a signal I shall make to you when we are apart. Like this. See?' She tapped twice, quietly.

'For God's sake, don't play these games!' he said violently, under his breath. 'Dangerous, silly games – they get on my nerves. And they are not safe. Ellen will notice before long. These looks and touches . . .'

'Come along,' called Ellen coldly. 'Supper's ready.'

They sat in the sitting-room afterwards, the three of them, pretending to read. When Louise tapped out her message, unnoticed by Ellen, Avery got up abruptly and went out into the garden.

But late in the night, when Ellen slept and he lay awake because it was impossible to sleep and think of Louise in the adjoining room, he heard two distinct taps on the wall behind his head. Rigid, he listened. Surely she wouldn't dare? He must be wrong. She would never risk it. But they came again.

To the uninitiated, they might sound like water-drops, or a fly against a lampshade. But he knew what they were, and pulled the sheets over his ears.

'Damn her, damn her,' he thought violently. 'She must stop it. She must stop.'

In a moment he put his head out again to listen. The two taps came again.

He told himself he was going to put a stop to it. That was why he got out of bed and stood listening to Ellen's regular breathing, his own coming as fast as if he had been running hard. It was to put a stop to it that he went out on to the landing and found her waiting for him in the dark. She pressed herself against him.

'Avery, you've come. I love you.'

'You're mad. If Ellen wakes. It's horrible. Not here for heaven's sake.'

'Avery, I love you, I love you.'

'You'll waken Ellen yourself if you go on like this,' he whispered fiercely.

It was to stop her that he thrust her back into her own room. It was to stop her, to put an end once and for all to this hideous behaviour on his part.

* * *

It was incredible that he should sit at table in the morning and let Ellen bring his breakfast to him as usual, but he did it. He had never felt degraded before, but he felt it now. He felt a horrible desolated feeling as if he had put himself outside the pale. What pale he didn't know.

'My God, how long will it be before I can get a drink?' he thought. 'I daren't have one here. I can't get one at the station. I shan't get one before I get to London. How can I last out?'

He couldn't bring himself to kiss Ellen good-bye. He pretended to forget. She was not so eager to kiss him as she once was; she was too annoyed with his siding with Louise. She let him go without calling after him to remind him to kiss her.

Anne was coming home. Anne would save him. This disgusting madness should be put away from him then. Even Louise, with Anne in the house, wouldn't dare . . .

II

It was Wednesday afternoon and Anne was home again. The house, thought Ellen, was itself. Avery had arranged to take part of his holiday so that he could be with Anne, and the first evening when she went out on Roma, he abandoned Louise and went with her, wobbling along on the old bicycle as usual.

Louise shut herself in her room. She had spent most of her time there during the last two days and was shut in again now. Ellen breathed more freely without her.

After playing a game of squash rackets of their own invention with her father, Anne was suddenly seized by a wish for sweets from the village shop.

'Don't ask me to go with you, that's all,' said Avery. 'You've worn me out.'

'Not really,' said Anne, hugging him in case she had. 'Mummy will come with me, won't you, Mummy?'

So Ellen threw on a light coat, the belt hanging, and went happily out into the sunshine.

Half-way down the first field, she remembered she had left the letters for the post on the hall table.

'I'll run back for them,' said Anne.

'No, I'll come with you,' said Ellen. 'It's nice walking about anywhere to-day.'

'Oh, it is,' said Anne. 'Pug will love all this. Three weeks to-morrow, she comes. Isn't it marvellous?'

They turned back. They went into the garden by the side gate and strolled round the house, their steps noiseless on the grass. They arrived together at the open french windows of the sitting-room.

On the sofa was Avery with Louise.

As Ellen and Anne stood staring at them, their smiles died slowly, so that all the blood had drained away from their faces while they were still almost smiling.

The embrace endured. It should have had no witness.

Suddenly aware, Avery looked up. No one moved. The

little clock ticked. A petal fell from a rose in a vase. Her head hanging back, her mouth open, Louise opened her eyes.

It was Anne who broke the spell. She thrust her mother aside so that she could get out of the room, and with a long strangled cry of revulsion and horror, she rushed away across the lawn.

Ellen backed slowly out of the windows. She felt so sick she had to sit down on the low wall outside. The thudding of her heart oppressed her beyond everything else for the moment. The sickness cleared, leaving a cold sweat on her forehead and under her eyes. By and by she wiped her face and got up. She went into the room again.

They were standing, one at each end of the mantelpiece now. They didn't look at each other or at Ellen. Both were smoking in an effort to give themselves countenance.

'Avery,' said Ellen.

Her lips were stiff. They wouldn't make the words. She licked them and began again.

'Avery, she must go.'

Louise went quickly to Avery and put her hand in his. He dropped it.

'It was my fault,' he said.

'It's not the first time,' said Ellen. 'I know that now.'

'You must go,' she said to Louise. 'Go at once.'

Louise was beginning to recover. She had nothing at stake. In fact, the first shock over, she wasn't sorry the crisis had come. Fate had put some good cards into her hands.

'Anne saw you,' said Ellen, her accusing eyes on Avery. 'You haven't cared that I was here while you were making love to

218

this girl. In our house where we have been so happy. Where the children were born. I suppose you counted on my being blind. Well, I was blind. Because I trusted you. I would have gone on trusting you till the end, if I hadn't seen.'

Her breath drew waveringly in and out.

'You haven't minded about me, but you mind about Anne. What have you done to her?'

Avery turned abruptly and put one elbow on the mantelpiece. He went on smoking.

'You can't have it both ways, Avery,' said Ellen. 'You can't have the children and me and a woman like Louise as well. You can't have affairs and keep the love of your family too. Not unless you never let us know or see, and even then everything would be poisoned.'

'For God's sake, Ellen,' said Avery, not looking at her. 'Let me settle this. I can't do it with you here. Go away, I beg you.'

'All right,' said Ellen.

Even now, she believed he would do what was best. She trusted him to.

'I must find Anne. What shall I do for her? What will you say to Anne?' she said, going through the door without waiting for him to answer.

Her throat was parched. She went to the kitchen for a drink of water.

'He didn't deny anything,' she said, her hand on the tap.

'He didn't deny it,' she thought, reaching the kitchen garden and wondering what she had come for.

She went back to the paddock. But Roma was not there.

Anne had ridden off and it was perhaps the best thing she could do.

Ellen sat on the lowest bar of the paddock gate, propping herself uncomfortably against the bar above. Hunched over, cold in spite of the warmth of the day, she waited. She felt too sick to do anything but wait. She would be all right soon. She must be, but at the moment the thudding of her heart made her feel sick. Vaguely she wondered what was the matter with it. It had never done that before.

Anger, revulsion, hatred of Louise and above all a sense of betrayal beat in waves against the barrier of shock. They would break through before long and overwhelm her, but at present she just sat on the bar of the gate.

What got through the barrier at length was anxiety about Anne. Where was she? Never, thought Ellen, flaring into violent feeling, never would she forgive Avery for the destruction of Anne's loving innocence. She herself must face the situation when she felt less sick, but Anne couldn't and no one could do it for her. The harm done in that moment in the sitting-room would last for the rest of Anne's life.

Ellen got up from the bar and hurried across the paddock to the other gate where Anne would come in. She went down the back lane. She stood to listen for Roma's hoofs. But all she could hear was her own heart thudding still in her ears. She held her breath as if that would quieten it and listened again for Roma.

But what she heard now was the unmistakable sound of Avery's car leaving the garage. She stood incredulous. It was. It was the car. Why? She ran back into the paddock and stumbled across the rough grass to the garden. The sound of the car was diminishing into the distance. She ran to the gate. 'Avery! Avery!' she called wildly.

The car was out of sight. She stood there, the belt of her coat hanging, looking from right to left. Then she turned and went back to the house.

As soon as she went into the sitting-room she saw a sheet of paper on the table.

'Since you insist that L. must go at once, I have taken her to find a room somewhere. Not in the town here for obvious reasons. I shall be away for some time because I shall probably have to go as far as London.' Below was his big scrawled 'A.'

The first shock that afternoon had scattered Ellen's senses. The second assembled them. Her mind hard and clear, she read the note again, her lip curling.

'Since you insist . . .' He threw the blame on her that he was going with Louise. That was the sort of thing he used to do, though he hadn't done it for years.

He had gone with Louise. With the sheet of paper in her hand, Ellen rushed upstairs to his dressing-room. She saw at once that his brushes were missing. She opened his cupboards and saw he had taken his things for the night.

Her face grim, she went to Louise's room. The smell of her scent was all that was left of her. They had worked fast. Or were her cases packed ready? They must have been. Treachery was confirmed again.

'I let her take him,' she said aloud, going into her own room.

'Did I? Did I let her?'

She sat down on the edge of his bed, but got up at once as if it were tainted. Avery, who had slept here beside her all these years, Avery, her husband, her other self, to do a thing like this. She saw his face again, as it was before he knew that she and Anne were looking at him. She would never be able to forget it. He was alien, ugly. He had betrayed everything there had been between them. And for Anne to have seen . . .

She went to the window to look for Anne. The paddock was still empty, but the gate had been closed, so Anne must have come back.

She went down through the garden again. The stable door was shut, but she opened it. Anne was rubbing Roma down, her back turned. She was talking to the horse in a rapid toneless way.

'That's the way. That's a good girl. Uppa, girl.' She kept on at it.

'Anne,' said Ellen from the door. She felt she couldn't look at the child. She hardly dare speak to her. She felt plastered with shame for what Anne had seen.

'I haven't half finished,' said Anne over her shoulder. 'I shall be a long time yet. Don't wait, please.'

'Anne, come into the house . . .'

Anne shook her bright hair.

'She's gone,' said Ellen.

The brush paused.

'Has she gone?' Anne looked directly at her mother then.

'Yes,' said Ellen, her eyes fixed on Anne's face, fearing the next question.

'Where's – where is he?'

'He's – he says he's coming back later,' said Ellen, looking away.

Anne laughed shortly. It was the most painful sound her mother had ever heard.

'Don't you believe it,' said Anne. She threw the brush down on the cobbles, making Roma start, and went past her mother to the door.

Ellen put out a hand.

'Don't,' said Anne, warding her off. 'Please, Mummy.'

She walked across the lawn to the house, veered away from the sitting-room windows and went in by the back door. She went up to her room and locked herself in, locking more than the door.

Evening fell, but no one put the lights on in the house. It stood silent, doors and windows open to the soft night.

The little cat came and mewed for her supper. It made Ellen less desolate for a few minutes to kneel on the floor and feed her with bits of rabbit. The rough tongue licked her fingers with the food and Moppet purred, pleased with these attentions.

The telephone rang about nine o'clock and Ellen, her heart beating to suffocation, lifted the receiver. But it was only Mrs. Wilson asking them for coffee on Friday. It was such a long time since they had seen anything of them, she said. Ellen, trying to sound natural, said she was sorry, but they couldn't. Not this week, not just at present. Avery was so busy, she said with hideous irony. Later perhaps, she said.

Mrs. Wilson said coldly that she was sorry too and rang off. Those Norths, always so self-sufficient, always indifferent to their neighbours, never wanting anyone outside their family circle. What good were people like that in a place?

It was nearly midnight when Avery telephoned. Ellen, still in her coat, the belt still hanging, lifted the receiver.

'I'm not coming back,' he said.

'Avery, what d'you mean?' she said, her voice trembling. 'You aren't coming back to-night?'

'I'm never coming back,' he said.

'Avery!'

'I didn't want you to be waiting up,' he said. 'I'll write. I'll put things in order. In the meantime, ask John Bennett . . .'

'Avery,' cried Ellen in anguish. 'Where are you? You must come back, Avery!'

'No, Ellen. I can't,' said Avery and rang off.

He wasn't going to listen to her. He daren't.

'I've burnt my boats,' he said heavily to Louise in the hotel bedroom.

'But of course,' said Louise. 'You did that some time ago.'

Avery turned away. He was hardly concerned with her. She was there, she was inevitable. He was committed. But what he felt above everything was shame, sickening desperate shame at the thought of Anne's face. That a beloved child should have seen what she had seen that afternoon. . . . How could he ever go back?

It must have happened before, to other men, he supposed. What they did about it, he didn't know. But for him, return was impossible. He couldn't face Anne again. Ellen might in the end forgive him, but Anne never would. His life with his family was ruined. It had ended in that moment when he looked up and saw his wife and daughter in the doorway.

Though he hid under a cool manner, there was excess in Avery's nature; excess in pursuit of Ellen, in his love for Anne, in his sensual passion for Louise. He had also an excessive pride. He wasn't going back to eat humble pie for the rest of his life. Better break off, better finish, and since the cut had to come, the sooner, the cleaner, the better for them. But his preoccupation was not for Louise.

He had taken a suite at a small hotel, not, to Louise's disappointment, at one of the famous ones, where as a constant luncher and party-goer he was too well-known. Murmuring shamefacedly, he escaped into his own room now and locked the door between them.

Louise smiled. As if she cared. She much preferred to be alone. There was so much to think about. What a day! She was glad it was over, though she had come out of it far better than she expected to. In fact, now that she was getting over it, she really marvelled at her luck. Because they had been caught in the sitting-room, she had got him to come away with her far sooner than she could have hoped. It had been rather horrifying at the time, but it had got them out, it had cut him loose and that was the main thing.

Before she turned out the light, she leaned out of the bed and looked at her luggage strewn about the room. Imagine having been able to get that away too! In those few minutes! She felt a keen practical satisfaction about that.

CHAPTER NINETEEN

⟶∞◇∞⟵

'Good morning, Madam,' called Mrs. Pretty cheerfully, announcing her arrival at the back door.

'Oh, dear,' said Ellen wearily, starting up from the chair in the sitting-room, where she had spent the night. 'I'd forgotten she'd be coming this morning.'

She went to the bookshelves and pretended to be busy there so that she could keep her back turned. She felt trapped, still in her coat, her hair straggling. She smoothed it as best she could. How unbearable to have Mrs. Pretty in the house to-day.

She hadn't been able to go to bed and lie in the dark with the turmoil of her thoughts. She had to sit up with the lights on and go over and over what had happened. He'd made love to the girl in this house. He'd lived with two women at once. He'd asked his wife to leave him to settle the affair and then made off while she was away. Then he'd *telephoned* to say he was never coming back.

He had no sense of decency left. The girl had driven all sense of decency out of him. 'He must be terribly in love with her,' thought Ellen. 'He doesn't love me any more.'

She writhed at the thought that she had been such a fool. Running about the house, singing, being busy, counting on the fact that he loved her when he didn't. Making such an idiot of herself, she thought bitterly, and Louise laughing in her sleeve all the time. Perhaps they both laughed. She could believe anything of Avery now.

'How long has he been tired of me?' she asked herself.

Looking back, she had known all the time he had been taking too much notice of Louise. But she had merely thought he was being "silly." So many men were silly. What Ellen had felt when she saw him at it had been embarrassment, as if he'd got gravy on his chin at a public dinner or something like that, and she couldn't get at him to tell him about it. She hadn't been able to take it seriously. It couldn't occur to her to doubt him. She had lived in a fool's paradise all right. But she was out of it now. She saw clearly now. She would never trust anyone again after this.

Her mind caught on one point after another, tearing itself on them all.

'He used to be kind. But look what he's done to us.'

And yet he had said on the telephone, 'I didn't want you to be waiting up.' He'd just broken her heart, but he didn't want her to wait up. Ellen laughed grimly. What did he mean – he couldn't come back? She wandered about the house in the night, feeling desperate because she couldn't ask him what he meant. For the first time in twenty years she didn't know where he was.

Or was it the first time? Looking back now, she thought she saw nothing but a long trail of deceit.

Over and over again in the night, she went to listen at Anne's door. But there wasn't a sound. She daren't speak or try the handle in case the child was asleep. She profoundly hoped she was, but she doubted it. This shutting-down on Anne's part was so unlike her. Ellen reproached herself bitterly for not knowing what to do. She had always seemed to know what to do for her children. But now at the first crisis, she didn't. She was helpless. She was glad Hugh hadn't been there to see that afternoon or that would have been another thing she wouldn't have been able to deal with.

In the early morning, she put a tray outside Anne's door and knocked.

'What is it?' asked Anne in a remote voice.

'It's your breakfast, darling,' said poor Ellen, and added: 'Please eat it to help me.'

There was no answer, but later the tray was gone. Now Anne was moving about and her mother was waiting in the sitting-room, trying to think how to meet her when she came down. But Mrs. Pretty had arrived to complicate things further.

'That's where you are, Madam, is it?' said Mrs. Pretty, tracking her down. 'I couldn't find you.'

'Good morning,' said Ellen with simulated cheerfulness, keeping her back turned.

'Lovely morning again,' said Mrs. Pretty, plunging about to shake up the cushions. 'As I came up through your garden this morning, I said to myself I'd never seen anything like your flowers; lovely this year, aren't they? I always say to myself it'd be a poor world without flowers.'

'It would,' said Ellen. 'Yes.'

'What I say is you're nearer to nature with a flower than

what you are with anything else,' said Mrs. Pretty, rolling up the rugs.

'Yes,' said Ellen.

'I suppose Miss Anne was as excited as ever to get home. I haven't seen her yet, you know. Has she gone out on her horse this morning?'

'No,' said Ellen. 'She's not down yet.'

'Oh, then I'll be seeing her,' said Mrs. Pretty. 'Well, I never,' she said in rebuke, retrieving the cigarette ends thrown into the fireplace by Avery and Louise the afternoon before. 'Cigarettes the price they are and these not half-smoked. That's Mademoiselle, that is, judging by the lipstick. Just look at 'em, Madam.'

She held out a palmful and Ellen glanced, hoping Mrs. Pretty wouldn't look at her. But Mrs. Pretty was wholly taken up with the cigarettes. Her old man would welcome those ends. She hurried to pop them into her obese hand-bag and while she was gone, Ellen escaped upstairs.

In the kitchen, Mrs. Pretty leaned a contemplative fist on the table. It had just dawned upon her that there were no breakfast pots to wash up. Unless Madame had done them?

Mrs. Pretty stood in the kitchen doorway and looked into the body of the house. Funny. It was all so quiet. And yet if there had been anything up yesterday morning, Miss Beasley would have told her. Mystified, Mrs. Pretty tiptoed across the kitchen and got out her tackle with precaution. It felt as if there had been a death in the house.

Upstairs, Ellen was preparing to circumvent Mrs. Pretty's suspicions by having a shower and making up her face. As she bent to the glass, she realised for the first time that she was middle-aged.

'Was that it?' she thought. 'She is at least fifteen years younger than I am.'

Men liked youth in women. They felt entitled to it.

'Louise was right after all,' she thought. 'Unless you behave like the favourite of the harem, your husband goes off with a woman who does.

'Let him,' she thought proudly, turning from her tired face. 'Even if it had occurred to me to work at fascinating him, I couldn't have done it.

'I treated him like a partner, someone as responsible as I am for our marriage, but he walks out half-way through as if it were no more than a film show he was tired of.'

When she came out of the bathroom, Anne's door was open and Anne herself was standing at the dressing-table. Her back turned, her hair parting on the nape of her neck, she fiddled with a drawer, and there was something so forlorn in this mute invitation to her mother to come in that tears stung Ellen's eyes for the first time.

'Anne,' she said, walking in and speaking as naturally as possible. 'Mrs. Pretty is downstairs. She nearly caught me looking awful, so don't let her catch you. She's looking forward to seeing you, so we shall have to do something about it.'

'Does she know?' said Anne, and lifted such accusing eyes to her mother that Ellen almost said: 'You're not blaming *me*, are you?'

But Anne was blaming her. She was blaming and hating the whole adult world. There was nothing left, everything was

230

horrible and it was through her father that she knew it. So her eyes were accusing and when Ellen didn't answer, having forgotten under that look what the question had been, Anne repeated it.

'Does she know?'

'No,' said Ellen. 'Of course not.'

She longed to comfort and be comforted, but there was to be nothing of that sort. She knew if she tried to break down the barrier, Anne would put up another and more formidable one. She could only look helplessly and lovingly at the child.

Even Anne's looks had changed overnight. She was pale, almost plain and much older. Her mother's heart was wrung by the change in her, but all she said was: 'Would you like a bath, darling?'

'All right,' said Anne, and going to the bathroom, she locked herself in. No singing, no calling out this time: 'Mummy, do come and do my back. It's another of the things I like to come home for – for you to do my back.'

Ellen stood about on the landing.

'What do I do now?' she asked herself. 'I wait. I have to wait until he chooses to let me know what happens next.'

What was he doing this morning? How did he wake with Louise?

Ellen pressed her hand to her heart to quieten it. It had been racing madly since the afternoon before. Sometimes it squeezed itself together, paused, then shot forward again. It added to her misery. She couldn't ask the doctor about it. He would want to know if she had had a shock of some kind and she couldn't tell him what it was. She thought of ringing up her brother Henry in Manchester, but he too would have to be told what had happened and that would make it so final. It would crystallise the situation.

She wouldn't tell Hugh either. But, when Mrs. Pretty was out of the way, she would ring up John Bennett. The thought of speaking to John was like a light showing on a foggy night to let you know you weren't alone in a suddenly silent, suddenly unfamiliar world. Perhaps John would know where Avery might be.

The bolt of the bathroom door shot back and Ellen went to help Anne through her meeting with Mrs. Pretty.

'Shall I brush your hair, darling?' she said.

But Anne, who liked to have her hair brushed by her mother, shook her head.

'No. It'll do. Let's go down.'

She presented herself at the sitting-room door and stood to attention.

'Good morning, Mrs. Pretty.'

'There you are, my duck, and how are you?' said Mrs. Pretty warmly, coming to inspect her. 'Why, what have they been doing to you? You're pale. Good thing you've come home, isn't it, Madam? She wants a good rest. They push them that hard at school nowadays. It's all competition. You should see our Daphne's Jimmy. He's got a nervous break-down over trying to pass into the Grammer School. A child like that. He wakes up screaming every night about his arithmetic. It's a downright shame. Don't let your examinations get on your mind, my duck. They're not worth it. We never took no examinations, did we, Madam? And look at us.

Two happier married women you never saw, I'll be bound. Now go along to your horse and get some fresh air and a bit of colour in your face.'

Anne smiled and rushed away.

'Ah, well,' said Mrs. Pretty with a sigh. 'She's growing up.'

'I daresay she'll look better when I come on Monday,' she said later, when she was tying on her head-scarf to go home. She said it with the intention of comforting Mrs. North, who seemed in need of it. 'I should make her have a good lay down this afternoon, Madam. She's perhaps growing too fast.'

Ellen, standing about on the landing after Mrs. Pretty had gone, saw Ted Banks, the postman, getting off his bicycle at the gate. She didn't go down to meet him and ask about his garden as she usually did. She stood where she was. Perhaps the letter was from Avery. Perhaps he had written last night or very early this morning. Her heart gave one of its sickening leaps as the letter fell through the door.

But it was for Anne, a bulky letter from Pug for Anne. They wrote voluminously to each other during the holidays. Ellen was glad this had come now. It would remind Anne that, in spite of disaster at home, she still had her friend.

Standing about again, she saw Anne coming up from the paddock. As she crossed the lawn, her mother saw her lift her face and look at the house with such misery that Ellen was suddenly scorched with anger.

'I'll never forgive him. Never . . .'

A dreadful breaking-up overtook her. She felt she was going to burst into tears. But she drew a long breath and was able to smile when Anne came in.

'This letter has just come for you,' she said. 'It's from Pug.'

Anne's face lit up for a moment.

'Yes, it's from Pug,' she said, opening it. 'Sheets and sheets as usual.'

Then the light died down and she stuffed the letter into her pocket.

'Aren't you going to read it?' said her mother.

'Later,' said Anne, and they went into the dining-room to sit in something like embarrassment over lunch, Anne's eyes sliding away from her mother's in a way that deeply troubled Ellen.

Suddenly the girl looked up in her old direct way.

'Pug can't come to stay now,' she said.

'Can't she?' said Ellen. 'Does she say why?'

'No. She still thinks she's coming. But we can't have her now.'

Ellen flushed in distress.

'Oh, do have her, Anne,' she said. 'It would be much better to, and by that time it might all be different. It might be over.'

Anne leaned forward and looked at her intently.

'Over?' she said. 'It can never be over. D'you mean you would ever let Daddy come back here?'

'But, Anne,' faltered Ellen, 'it's his home. If I'd done something wrong, or if you had, we should always come home, shouldn't we?'

'It's not the same,' said Anne, white to the lips. 'He can't come back. If he ever comes back,' she said, jumping to her feet, 'I shall go away. I won't stay. I never want to see him again.'

A great sob broke from her, she rushed out of the room and up the stairs. She banged the door of her own room and locked it before Ellen could reach her.

'Anne, let me in,' begged Ellen, rattling the handle. 'Don't cut yourself off from me. Let's be together. Let's help each other . . . Anne. . . .'

But Anne sobbed on, her face buried in her bed. The storm had broken and Ellen could do nothing but stand and listen, shut out, helpless.

'Well, I hate him,' she said, turning away in the end. 'Who could forgive him for this?'

The day went by very slowly, but it carried her an immeasurable distance. She was so far now from her happy yesterday. In the middle of the afternoon, she took up the telephone to speak to John Bennett, but put it down again. If she spoke to him at the office, someone might overhear. She must wait until he was at his house in Kensington. She who had been impulsive in thought and action had to calculate now. It was six o'clock when she rang him up.

'Ellen, how nice,' the pleasure in his voice was warm. 'How are you?'

'I'm all right, thank you. Are you?' said Ellen, going through the polite exchanges. 'John,' she said abruptly. 'You haven't seen Avery to-day, I suppose?'

'No, he's on holiday of course. Has he been up to town or something?'

'He's in London, John.'

'Oh? Why?'

There was a silence.

'Is anything wrong, Ellen?'

'He went away yesterday with Louise. With the French girl,' said Ellen.

'Went away?' he said. 'With the French girl? What d'you mean?'

'Anne and I found them in the sitting-room. He's in love with her. He's gone away with her.'

There was a prolonged silence at the Kensington end.

'Ellen, are you telling me that Avery's gone off with this girl? Gone away with her?'

'Yes.'

'He went yesterday and you haven't heard from him since?' said John Bennett.

'He rang up about midnight from London.'

'He *rang up*?'

Another silence on both sides.

'Ellen, I can't believe it.' he said. 'Avery's devoted to you and the children. Gone away with the French girl? That cold-hearted creature I saw? It's one of those incredible lapses. It's an infatuation. It's temporary madness.'

'He says he's not coming back.'

'Not coming back? He'll come back all right. The fool. Where is he?'

'I don't know,' said Ellen.

'You don't know? God, if I only knew, I could get at him. London, you say?'

'The exchange said a trunk call from London. That is all I know. He rang off when I asked him where he was.'

'It's beyond me,' said John slowly. 'Avery.' There was another silence.

'I'll come to-morrow, Ellen. I can't get there in the morning, but I'll be on the train that gets in at half-past four. Can you meet me?'

'Oh, thank you, John. I need your advice. I don't know what to do for Anne. I haven't said anything to Hugh yet.'

'Don't. Wait. Avery'll be back within the next few days. Better no one should know he ever went, the fool. Half-past four to-morrow. I wish I could do something now. I'll try a few places. I'll ring round.'

'It won't be any good,' said Ellen. 'He won't have gone where he's known.'

She put the telephone down and went to wander about the garden, the lovely evening unnoticed. She came in again, tired out, and sank into her own corner of the sofa. She almost dozed, her head drooping to the cushion. But before her cheek could touch it, she moved away in horror. She could smell Louise. It was on this sofa . . . it was where they were. She went out of the room and into the dining-room, to sit there, trembling again.

She was there when Anne came down the stairs and into the room. Ellen half got up, her eyes on the child's face, wondering what to do or say that wouldn't be wrong. But Anne, making a smile with her swollen lips, reached her mother with a rush. She dropped to the floor beside the chair and, her back turned, settled there, leaning against Ellen. She reached up and took her mother's hand, putting her cheek against it, her face hidden.

'Don't let's talk about it, Mummy,' she said.

'No, darling,' said Ellen.

With the other hand, she began to stroke Anne's hair. Backwards and forwards went her gentle hand and by and by Anne's head drooped against her knee and her mother saw she was asleep.

The day had been long and bitter, there was trouble behind and before, but for this brief space in the dining-room, there was nothing but peace and love.

CHAPTER TWENTY

—∞◇∞—

In the morning, while Avery was shaving and for the time being safe, since he couldn't bolt for home with lather on his face, Louise went down the hotel staircase and out into the air to look about her.

At one end of the short quiet street the traffic of London poured in all its volume, but at the other was a square where great plane trees drooped their summer shade. There was an air of elegance and wealth about the street which was pleasing to Louise. There were a few small select shops, just opening at half-past nine on this warm morning.

Among them was a bookshop, and with a contemptuous-affectionate smile for the one at home, she crossed the street to look at it. She did it for her father. When things were going well, Louise could spare a thought now and again for her parents. Reaching the shop, she saw it sold French fashion magazines and with satisfaction went in to buy an armful.

She bought a box of dragées too from a pâtisserie, providing herself against what she feared might prove a long dull day in the suite on the first floor. Returning through the hall of the hotel, she ordered three dozen yellow roses. Avery ought to have done that, but since he had not, she would.

'What on earth are these?' he asked when they were brought up.

'Roses, mon cher,' said Louise. 'I thought they would make the room a little gayer. God knows we need something. And yellow, you see. Couleur de ménage.'

He didn't understand, of course, about yellow being the traditional colour of matrimony. But she didn't want him to. She was able to indulge in a little mockery now and again since there was no fear of being understood.

She needed relief of some sort. Avery was proving more difficult to manage than she had expected. She had tried several approaches, but the planks she put down between herself and him revealed themselves as unsafe at the first attempt to cross them. They let her down and she daren't proceed. So now she left him mostly to his silence, though this was hardly the way, she said to herself, that one expected to spend an elopement.

But she could wait, and in the meantime, the meals came up. The food was excellent. When the waiters or chamber-maids were about, she spoke French all the time. It removed her to a distance from them. They were covertly interested and referred to her on the landing as the French tart in number nineteen and Louise suspected as much. It was a repetition of what she had to put up with when she was with Paul. 'Some day,' she said to herself, 'I shall be in a position where these little people will not dare to disrespect me.'

The sitting-room was almost round, the windows were high up, the walls were pale Adam green and it was like being at the bottom of a well, thought Avery, sitting in an armchair, drinking brandy and smoking endless cigarettes.

Louise was able to get through most of the day turning over the pages of her fashion papers, but at the end of the afternoon, after tea, the papers palled and she pushed them away and sighed.

'It is melancholy here,' she said.

'I agree with you,' said Avery.

He had never suffered such hell in his life, he told himself. The awful sense of what felt like 'sin' – not sin at being with Louise, but having so harmed Anne and Ellen, a sense of being without the pale, of having lost everything, haunted him.

He turned his head and looked heavily at Louise, reliving the fateful moment.

'If only you hadn't come down just then,' he said.

'Ah,' said Louise. 'The woman tempted me?'

He deserved that, he admitted to himself, and looked ashamed. It made him more approachable and Louise took her opportunity.

'Pauvre chéri,' she said, putting out a hand to touch his.

'This room's driving me mad,' said Avery.

'Ah – and me too. I hate it,' said Louise with passion. 'We are fastened in like a pair of poultry. Oh, let's leave it, Avery. Let us go away. Let's go to Paris. To change our black ideas, let us go to Paris.'

He looked at her. He couldn't go home. He couldn't stay much longer in this damned room. He had to go somewhere. It might as well be Paris as anywhere.

'But I forgot,' said Louise, sinking back into depression. 'You have no passport.'

'I have.'

'You have?'

'At the office,' he said.

Animation rushed into her face, her hands, the very hairs of her head.

'You have your passport here? In London? Oh, Avery, let us go for it. Everyone will be gone from your bureau at this time and you have your keys. Oh, I love you for this, Avery. If you knew how je m'ennui. How tired I am of England and how I long for France. Quick! Let's go at once.'

Across the table she pulled at his hand with both hers.

'I suppose you want to go and see your parents,' he accused her, as if he would be left to himself then, he supposed.

She almost told him her parents were at Binic, but stopped herself in time.

'You forget, Avery,' she said gravely. 'I cannot go to see my parents while I am with you. They would ask questions and what could I say? They are very good people. Good Catholics. I cannot let them know what has happened. It would break their hearts.'

Avery reached for another cigarette.

'So neither of us can go home,' he said. 'Hell, what a mess we've made of everything.'

'Avery, let us get your passport and go to Paris to-morrow. It's different in Paris, you will see. Let's try Paris, Avery.'

'All right,' said Avery, without enthusiasm.

But he was willing to be carried along by hers. He was inert in his misery and there was some relief in being pushed along by someone with energy enough to do it. And perhaps, as she said, it would be better somewhere else.

He wouldn't exert himself to get his car, so they took a taxi to the Strand and got out there. They walked through the short, hot deserted streets. Everywhere seemed to smell, thought Avery. Of garbage or something rotten. At home now it was the cool of the evening and always so fresh. What were they doing? What were they thinking of him?

A little black and white cat came round a dust-bin and, arching its back, looked up at him. He bent, thinking of Moppet, and kept Louise waiting while he stroked it.

'C'est gentil, le petit chat,' she said with what sounded utter falsity to him. He knew she didn't like cats.

Still, he thought with a sigh, perhaps she said it to please him. Give her the benefit of the doubt, anyway.

They turned the corner and came to the discreet, blackened frontage of Bennett and North, Publishers.

'Tiens, this is it? ' said Louise with respect. 'An old house – quite elegant.'

He unlocked the dark-blue door and they went up to his rooms. Louise stepped about examining everything with approval. The solidity of the establishment and the rich appointments of his office made her appreciate him more. During the long day at the hotel, she had felt she couldn't stand much more of his heavy company. But his office restored his importance. The game was worth the candle after all and she must take care not to lose it by fits of petulance.

'But, Avery, you have a bath here and a bedroom,' she said, opening doors.

She came back to his desk, where he was trying to write some sort of letter to John Bennett.

'Avery, why have you a bed here?' she asked.

'What?' He looked up with impatience, without taking in what she said. So she asked again.

'Oh, because I sleep here after a late party if you must know,' he said.

'Ah, if that is only why . . .' said Louise, returning to the bedroom.

'But you have clothes here too. Your habit is here – your dress-clothes. And a valise, two valises,' she called out in a lively voice. 'Really, mon cher Avery, one would say you held yourself prepared for just such a case as ours to-day. I'll pack for you.'

He sat at his desk trying to write the letter.

'You will know by this time . . .' he wrote, and began again.

'I have been such a fool. I can't go back . . .

'Look after them.

'I don't know what I am going to do. I can't go back . . .'

It was too difficult. He couldn't do it. When Louise appeared with the suit-case, he tore the letter to shreds and put them in his pocket, so that his secretary, when she came in the morning, shouldn't know what he had attempted.

'Come on,' he said, taking the cases and his passport. 'Let's get out of here.'

Louise had almost to run to keep up with him; but she didn't mind that. He couldn't go too fast for her.

Everything was going well, she thought with elation. Life kept opening out.

Yesterday, she had no idea she would be in London to-day; this morning no idea of being in Paris to-morrow. From there she hoped to get him to La Baule. It was the season. She had always wanted to go to La Baule. It looked as if she might get there now. Besides it would do him good. He would be worth nothing at all if he went on drinking brandy all the time.

CHAPTER TWENTY-ONE

———⚬◇⚬———

At La Baule, Avery tried to write to Ellen. He couldn't even get started.

'My dear Ellen,' he tried, sitting under the sunblinds on the terrasse with an apéritif before him.

It looked so strange: 'My dear Ellen.' He had always put darling before. Never again could he say darling to her in the old sweet casual way. Whenever his thoughts turned to tenderness, he had to crush up the letter and give up for the time being.

Behind the white trellis trailed over by ivy grown in tubs, the waiter, hovering unobtrusively, knew that when the Englishman had crushed up the letter, he would call for another drink.

'Oui, Monsieur,' said the waiter and hurried off, glad of such a profitable client.

'Dear Ellen,' Avery tried in the bathroom.

The difficulty was to get alone to write. Whenever Louise came upon him, he crumpled up the letter and gave up again.

'Have you written?' Louise kept asking, and when he shook his head, she maintained a silence that was full of reproach.

Sometimes she asked him what she could do.

'I cannot let my parents know I am in France, so I cannot write at all to them. They will almost be out of their minds with anxiety.' She didn't say she had left them without news for a fortnight many a time before. 'I cannot go home. What am I going to do, Avery?'

'I don't know,' he said heavily. 'I don't know what I'm going to do myself.'

He veered from one emotion to another, all painful. Sometimes he was filled with resentful hatred of Louise. Why had she ever existed? Why had she ever come to Netherfold? She had ruined his life. She scoffed at the idea, but she *had* tempted him. If she had been a different kind of woman the incident in the sitting-room would not have happened. Of course she tempted him. He admitted that he must have been ready to fall. But no more than most men, he told himself.

It was because they had been seen. If they hadn't been seen, the affair would have petered out. As it was, he could never go back now.

When he came, as he always did, to this miserable conclusion, he turned to Louise again as his only companion. She was his fellow-sufferer. She couldn't go home either. She was cut off from her people as he was from his. He owed her something. He must make it up to her.

Also, in his deeply humiliated state of mind, Avery was very diffident. He felt no one but Louise would have him. He was quite often grateful to her for remaining with him. Especially now. At La Baule circumstances conspired to let Louise shine and to extinguish Avery still further. She was on her own ground, she spoke her own language. She managed everything. He merely stood by and paid. He had lost his importance. He wouldn't speak, except to order drinks and cigarettes, because, although it is amusing and often charming when a woman speaks a foreign language brokenly, it is ridiculous in a man, and Avery, already humiliated, wouldn't risk making a fool of himself. So he appeared to French eyes as the traditional Englishman: silent, proud, heavy and rich. And Louise appeared as what her fellow-countrymen thought of with satisfaction as 'bien française'. Wherever she was, on the beach in what seemed nothing but a big straw hat and bracelets, or at the Casino in the evening dresses she had bought in Paris, she drew all the glances.

After the first few days, during which she let him drink as much as he liked, Louise took Avery in hand. She did not openly cut his drinks down; she saw to it that he did something other than sit under the sunblinds with a glass before him. She made him swim, she made him lie in the sun and rubbed oil into his skin so that he should acquire a good tan. She sent him for walks along the edge of the sea as far as Pornichet and back. She said he was too fat. He must get his weight down, she said.

Because he wanted to be alone to think out what he should write to Ellen, he went. And when he had gone, Louise sighed with relief and herself took a brisk walk round the shops, the summer places, where Paris models and expensive cosmetics were displayed in the little cement constructions, still damp from the Breton winter. She could always enliven herself by buying something. Unlike Paul, Avery gave her plenty of money, pulling out handfuls of dirty notes and thrusting them upon her as if he wanted to get rid of them. Louise reflected grimly on the difference. With love, you don't even need butter on your bread; without it, an elaborate feast is necessary to make you come to table. She was embittered to think she should have poured out all her joy so early. But she was determined that nothing should prevent her from making the most, materially, of what came her way now.

'Ellen,' wrote Avery, sitting alone in what was called, idiotically, he thought, the 'Bois d'amour.'

He sat on sand and pine-needles in the dusky brown woods and the silence was deathly. What could he say to her?

One afternoon he fell asleep on the beach, sprawling among other practically naked bodies. When he awoke he was alone and the sand was cold. In sleep, his mind was made up. He went to his room with a grim face and wrote his letter.

In these days, Ellen no longer went half-way to the gate to meet Ted Banks the postman. She could no longer hold out an unconcerned hand for the letters, comparing gardening notes meanwhile. She didn't want Ted Banks to see she was consumed with anxiety for a letter from Avery. So she watched, hidden in the house, and when the letters fell into the box and he was gone, she ran, breathless, to see if it had come. But day after day there was nothing. She was wasted with waiting, her life was nothing now but waiting.

Yet on the morning the letter came, Ted Banks caught her outside her refuge, the house. He was early and when he arrived suddenly at the gate, propping his bicycle against it as usual, there she was in the drive, turning startled eyes towards him.

'Well, I was only saying to the missus yesterday I haven't seen you for I don't know how long,' said Ted, too busy drawing letters from the elastic band he kept them in to notice Ellen's face.

She saw at once that the letter had come. Her heart gave one of its wild plunges and, unable to speak, she held out her hand.

But Ted Banks would not be hurried. He extricated the fish bill and the Mayor's appeal for the Cancer Research Fund. Two circulars as well he drew out and then went through the rest of the post to see if there was anything else.

'How's your tomatoes?' he enquired and this was why he was being slow.

'Er – quite good,' said Ellen. A foreign stamp. Where was he? Had he gone to France with her?

'Mine are trussing up lovely,' said Ted. ''Course you have the advantage of me with your clutches. I think I'll have to treat myself to a few next year and then you'll have to look out, because I'll be beating you. There you are then. Foreign stamp this morning. Mr. North holidaying in foreign parts? Ah. I thought he must be. Not been going to the station lately. Well, it's nice weather for him, though give me Skegness. You can't beat old Skeggie for air, not if you go the world over. Well, I'll be getting on. Good morning to you. I've never had such peas in all my life as what I've had this year,' said Ted with emotion. 'Good season for peas. I daresay yours haven't been bad either?' he conceded.

'They've been very good, yes. Good morning, Ted,' said Ellen, turning into the house at last with the letter.

Her hands were so hurried she ripped the envelope across and the purple tissue lining further impeded her. She got the letter out.

After all his struggles, after all it had cost him to write, it struck her with an effect of cold brutality:

'I must ask you to divorce me, and quickly as possible. There is nothing else for it. I have written to Tom Rayner in London to act for me. You will have Roach, I suppose. There will be no difficulty and it will go through very quickly.'

Ellen looked blindly at Anne coming down the stairs. Anne, staring at the letter in her mother's hand, came slowly on. 'Is it from him?' she asked. She never said Daddy now if she could help it.

Ellen tried to thrust the letter into the pocket of her skirt.

'Why do you look like that, Mummy? Is it something awful? What does he say? You can't keep anything from me now. I know too much. What is it, Mummy?'

They stood in the morning sunlight, looking at each other, and from her mother's face Anne learned, in another lesson, that the grown-up world was not what she had thought it was, not a place of power and fulfilment, but a place of helplessness, pain and ugliness. A world not to enter. Until now, Anne had run joyfully forward, but now she was halted. She shrank back. She had learnt suspicion and distrust and most of all the fear of life that sickens the youthful heart and from which it takes so long to recover, if recover it does.

251

'What does he say, Mummy?' she asked again.

'He wants me to divorce him,' Ellen brought out at last.

Anne's face cleared and hardened.

'But why do you mind that? You were going to anyway. We don't want him. Write quickly and say yes. Do it quickly, Mummy, and then it'll be over.'

Ellen turned away, sick at heart. She went to the kitchen. Breakfast. They must have breakfast. Whatever happened, you always had breakfast.

Anne did not follow. She went into the garden, across the lawn and down the path between the apple trees. Her lips trembled. But she wouldn't cry. If she did, her mother would see at breakfast. She reached the paddock gate and leaned there, with no voice in her aching throat. But Roma lifted her head and with her own grace of welcome, a sideways toss of her head and a low whinny, came to the gate. Anne got up on to the first bar the better to lean over and clasp her round the neck; and there they stayed, girl and horse.

Roma hadn't changed. She was the same; the only one who was the same. Even her mother had changed beyond understanding. How could she possibly want him back? To want him back was to admit the hideousness. It was to say, yes, such things happen, we have to put up with them, life is like that.

Everything but Roma was changed and lost. How could she go back to school now? She had always been the envied one, the one, they said, who had everything.

It was true. Although she didn't know it, the mistresses were afraid of spoiling this charming child who had so much: brains, looks, a happy home, devoted parents who came to every school function without fail. When the parts for the school plays were being cast, although Anne was a good actress and would be a better, the chief parts were given to other, less lucky girls, in an attempt by the mistresses to level things up a little. When the names were read out, Anne felt a pang, but went on smiling and the mistresses loved her the more for it. She had so much, they said; she would soon get over it.

Anne had basked in the sunshine of her place in the school, but now everything would be different. Her parents would not come together at half-term any more and everyone would wonder why. She would never be able to talk about home now; not even to Pug. Last term she and Pug had made a covenant to tell each other everything, always, and she must break it already. She would never tell what had happened and how could she listen to Pug's confidences when she could make none of her own?

To have a secret at school is to be cut off. She knew. She'd seen unhappy girls with secrets the happy ones tried to guess, saying dramatically that perhaps the skeleton in the cupboard was a gaol-bird in the family, or a fearful scandal. Now she herself had gone over to the minority, she was cut off from the happy ones, and these were the powerful ones, the ones who won everything, the ones everybody liked. She dreaded having to go back to such a world. You had to be happy if you were going to get on. Or you had to have a friend, and how can you have a friend when you can't tell her everything?

'There's only you left,' she said to Roma.

'Anne,' called her mother from the garden. 'Will you come to breakfast?'

'I'm coming,' Anne called back.

Their voices had changed and the things they said. They spoke levelly now and kept to the point. No happy squeakings and exaggerations from Anne, no prolonged fits of laughter.

Ellen didn't wait for Anne now, as she would once have done, because she knew Anne didn't want her to. She walked across the lawn, indifferent to the neglected riot of the garden.

Signs of neglect were not so patent in the house, but they were there. Everything to do with the house seemed to have lost meaning and reason. A family is like a jigsaw puzzle. If a piece is lost, the rest no longer makes a pattern.

'He would actually marry her,' thought Ellen, reaching the breakfast table, her hand on the letter in her pocket.

He was cruel. He was callous.

'Let him go,' she thought, all at once blazing with anger.

Anger came over her nowadays in sudden red tides. She heard Anne coming and escaped into the hall to let this one subside. Her anger frightened her. Her sleeplessness, her thumping heart, the hatred, the gnawing anxiety – all frightened her. She couldn't deal with them; and she felt with bitter disgust that she ought to have been able to. All those books, all those prayers and she had got nothing from them. When everything went well for her she had been able to pray, she couldn't now. There was such urgency in her present situation that until the pressure was removed she couldn't think about God. She hadn't the patience to pray. It was a shock to her. Surely God was for these times? When earthly love failed, you should be able to draw on heavenly love. Yet she never felt less sure of it.

The old glass over the half-moon table in the hall showed that her haggard face was pale enough now to let her go to the table.

'I'll ring up Uncle John after breakfast,' she said.

Anne, eating cornflakes as if she couldn't get them down, nodded; though what Uncle John could do, she couldn't imagine. Nothing, of course. But she supposed you had to keep on telling people.

'What are you going to do to-day, darling?' asked Ellen.

'I don't know,' said Anne.

Her back was so round as she sat at the table that her mother almost told her to sit up, but stopped in time. The slightest reproof would wound and damage now. The easy interchange was all over.

'Won't you go out on Roma?' she said.

Anne shook her head and got up from the table.

'Too hot.'

She stood at the open window, looking out, then turned suddenly to her mother.

'Get a divorce, Mummy,' she said. 'And let's begin again without him. It's so awful hanging about like this. I can't bear it.'

'It's very hard,' said Ellen. 'But we must see each other through, mustn't we?'

'Mm,' said Anne, swerving away from contact. 'But don't let it go on longer than you can help, will you?'

She went upstairs to make her bed and Ellen rang up John Bennett.

'John, a letter has come at last,' she said. 'To say he wants me to divorce him.'

John Bennett did not cry out as she expected he would. He didn't exclaim that it was unthinkable, that Avery was a fool and couldn't mean it.

Instead, after a pause, he said, 'I know, Ellen. He's back. He came back yesterday.'

Ellen's heart gave another of its plunges.

'Back?' she faltered. 'At the office?'

'Yes. His holiday was up. I didn't expect him to arrive. But he did.'

'Have you – have you discussed things with him?'

'Yes,' said John gravely. 'I have. I think I'd better come and see you to-day.'

'Is he still with her?' asked Ellen.

'Yes. I'm afraid so. Yes.'

Ellen put the telephone down carefully. He meant it then? For no fault of hers that she could think of, no failure of love on her part, he would end their life together and break up their home.

CHAPTER TWENTY-TWO

⋙◇◇◇⋘

John Bennett was beginning to lose confidence in himself as mediator. He wanted with all his heart to bring Avery and Ellen together again. Because anything else was unthinkable. They had been so happy. They made such a good pair, and if John felt much more affection and admiration for Ellen, he had liked Avery; although he had always felt him to be an unknown quantity. He had always felt, he told himself, that Avery was capable of going off the rails like this. But now he had actually done it, no one was more anxious to help him on to them again. The marriage, the family, so long a source of wistful envy to John Bennett, must be saved. At first he felt sure it could be done, but now he was beginning to doubt the possibility of making either Avery or Ellen see what he called reason.

When, after his absence, Avery walked into his partner's office, John Bennett, after a moment of jaw-dropping amazement, maintained a cold silence. After all, though relieved beyond measure to see him back, he wasn't going to receive the prodigal with open arms.

But when Avery began by saying abruptly that he wanted Ellen to divorce him, John Bennett's stiff silence was shattered. He felt complete stupefaction. From his desk with its back to the window, he gaped without dignity at Avery, who stood in the middle of the room with warning in his face.

'Don't meddle in my affairs,' said his look. 'I have to come in here and let you know what I intend to do, but I'm not going further than that and don't you try to either.'

'Divorce!' breathed John Bennett. 'Divorce! You and Ellen . . . Have you gone out of your mind?' he said, leaning over his desk.

Avery looked back at him in silence.

'Don't you know how happy you've been?' said John Bennett.

A muscle worked in Avery's cheek.

'What about Anne?' said John, stabbing at random. 'I thought she meant everything to you? Will you give her up for the French girl?'

'Shut up,' said Avery savagely. 'You don't know what you're talking about. All this high-falutin' stuff – it's long past that, you fool.'

'I'm trying to help you,' said John Bennett. 'I want to help you both.'

'You can't help,' said Avery. 'It's past helping. The only thing you can do is to see Ellen through the divorce. You should be able to do that much for her.'

He wanted to taunt and sneer at his partner, because the advantage had gone over to him. Avery always had it before, better-looking, taller, easier, with a wife who hadn't left him, and children too. But now he was humiliated before this careful little man who kept telling him what he ought to do. Bringing Anne in. It was intolerable.

'Ellen's done enough for you, one way or another,' he said insultingly.

'No need to remind me,' said John Bennett. 'I don't forget it and I shall always do all I can for her and for the children you are deserting so easily.'

'You don't know what you're talking about,' said Avery. 'But have I made myself plain? This is final. I'm not going back. I've ruined myself there with them and I'm not going back to eat humble pie for the rest of my life.'

'So it's pride that makes you wreck everything, is it?'

'Call it what you like!' said Avery.

He went out of the room as abruptly as he had come in and crossed the road to the pub to get himself a double brandy. Then he went back to the hotel, to Louise. He'd had as much as he could stand for one day, he told himself.

When Avery had gone, John spent a long time in anxious thought.

'Shall I come back, Mr. Bennett?' asked his secretary.

'No. Not yet. No.'

Where had he gone wrong, he wondered? How had he made Avery so angry that he wouldn't listen to reason? Had he begun by being self-righteous and worthy? He thought he must always have seemed so to Avery, perhaps because he implied that he wasn't good enough for Ellen. But reproach and self-righteousness wouldn't do now. What would do? He didn't know, but he must find out, because so much was at stake.

He thought of them as they had been at Netherfold. Of Ellen when she came into the room sometimes and saw her family together. Her face lit up with almost childlike happiness then, as if she had found them all over again. He thought of them as they had been only last Christmas. You would have said there wasn't a happier family anywhere. Yet disaster was sitting at the table in the form of the French girl. What a queer, chancy thing life was!

Except his own. His own had always been too quiet. Marianne had burst into it, bringing variety and laughter and beauty, and had gone out, taking them with her. Quietness had fallen again. His only contact with vivid life these last years had been through the household at Netherfold, and how he had appreciated it! It wasn't only Ellen, it was the children too, and even Avery – the whole atmosphere of the place, down to the sparrows in the garden. Even those seemed happier there than anywhere else.

Yet Avery was determined to break it up.

John Bennett summoned his secretary, because he wasn't getting anywhere in his attempt to find a way out of the North trouble.

When Ellen rang up the next morning, his heart sank. He must see her, but he had no hope to carry to her, no solution to offer. She had been agitated enough when she told him about Avery's letter on the telephone. How would she take it when he told her about his talk with Avery? It was all so painful, and gentle-hearted John Bennett shrank from his part in it.

But when he reached Netherfold in the afternoon he

found that Ellen was taking everything very quietly. Too quietly, he considered. She seemed to have given up entirely.

They sat in the sitting-room, which looked queer and unlike itself in a way he couldn't account for, until he realised suddenly that there were no flowers, where once there used to be so many. He turned his head to see if it was because there were none to be had from the garden. But the borders were blousy with flowers. That was the word that occurred to him at the sight of them sprawling in all directions, full-bloom and in bud, living and dead. Nothing revealed the state of Ellen's mind and heart so clearly as the condition of her garden. She must indeed have given up, he thought, turning back to her with deep concern in his face.

'You must see Avery,' he said.

Ellen flushed painfully.

'You'll find he won't see me,' she said.

'He must,' insisted John.

'Try to make him, that's all,' said Ellen.

John made a sound of utter exasperation. He seemed to be the only one who wished to save the marriage. Of the two most closely concerned, one was determined to break it, the other resigned to having it broken. John Bennett was conscious of fatigue. It was hard work dealing with two difficult people. He hadn't expected it of Ellen, either. It seemed like a complete change of front on her part. She sounded horrified enough at the thought of divorce when she telephoned to him in the morning.

He didn't know how hard she had been thinking since then, and how mistakenly, if she had only known. She was convinced now that Avery was madly in love with Louise. After all, it does look like it when a man goes off with a woman. Ellen knew Avery's reckless abandonment to love and thought it must be the same now. Why should he leave delirious happiness to come back to a wife he no longer loved and to a daughter whose eyes he could never meet again without shame? Of course he wouldn't come back. The situation was impossible. Divorce was the only thing.

So she met John Bennett's exasperation dumbly, almost dully, and in the end he came to the conclusion that there was something baffling in the affair. He hadn't felt, yesterday, that Avery wanted a divorce for love of the French girl, and here was Ellen unaccountably letting Avery go without a struggle.

'It must have been worse than I thought. No mere going off,' he said to himself. 'It must have been something that shocked them all past mending.'

And how could he ask about that?

'I must go, Ellen,' he said heavily.

'Yes,' she said, getting up from her chair.

'Aren't I going to see Anne?' he asked.

'Yes, you are. She must come to the station with us. I don't like to leave her alone in the house much. Too quiet. The house has changed too, you see,' she said, putting out a hand to the room in a forlorn way.

She went out into the hall.

'Anne,' she called from the foot of the stairs. 'Will you come now? We must take Uncle John to the station.'

John Bennett looked up, waiting to take the child in his

arms and comfort her as best he could, or perhaps say nothing; just hug or be hugged as usual.

Her door opened and closed. She came down with a rush, coat flying, hair flying.

'Hello, Uncle John,' she said as she came. 'Are you all right? Quite well and everything?'

Her manner was jerky and casual. The change in her shocked him. She looked as if she had had a bad illness; had it still for that matter. She didn't come near him. No hugs and kisses now. He was a man, like her father. Poor John Bennett was hurt and puzzled by the look of accusation she sent him. Why him? What had he done?

'Shall I lock up, Mummy?' said Anne. 'Oh, you've done it, have you? I'll get into the car then.'

She went out of the door, tying the belt of her coat tightly at her waist, her hair falling over her face. John Bennett looked after her with concern. She was thinner and much more grown up. And Ellen looked so much older. If Avery could see these two now, surely his heart would be touched and he wouldn't be able to leave them?

'We must go if you're to catch your train, John,' said Ellen and they went out to the car.

They didn't talk much on the way. There was no small talk left and they couldn't speak of Avery with Anne silent in the back of the car. When, at the station, John Bennett prepared to get out, Ellen got out too.

'Don't bother to see me off,' he said.

'No, but I'll take you as far as the booking hall,' said Ellen.

'Are you coming too, Anne?' he said.

'I don't think I'll get out. Mummy won't be a minute,' she said. 'Good-bye, Uncle John. It has been so nice to see you,' she ended up conventionally.

'Prsh.' John Bennett made such a queer sound of hurt and exasperation at being treated to this finishing-school manner that Ellen put her arm through his as they walked away.

'Don't mind, John. She loved her father so much, you know. It's been a terrible shock to her. She's the worst of all this dreadful business. I feel I could bear it perhaps if it weren't for Anne. I don't know what to do for her. She won't let me mention him. One night she broke down and came and sat on the floor at my knee and went to sleep and I thought it was going to be all right between us. And it is, so long as I don't speak of Avery. If I do, she sheers off and won't come near me until she thinks I won't do it again.'

John Bennett sighed. He gathered his brief-case and his umbrella, without which he rarely moved, into one hand and took Ellen's with the other. He stood for a moment, feeling sad and helpless, Ellen's hand in his, and Anne looked at them from a side window with a strange watchful expression.

They parted and Ellen came back to the car.

'Are you coming in front with me, darling?' she invited.

'Oh, I'm all right here, I think,' said Anne, who once would have scrambled happily over the back of the seat to be next to her mother.

Half-way home, she asked suddenly: 'Did Uncle John divorce his wife?'

'No, he didn't divorce her.' Ellen glanced up through the driving-mirror. What was the child thinking about now? But

Anne was looking through the side window and Ellen could only see her pale straggling hair. What had happened to that lovely hair?

'I think Uncle John's always hoping she'll come back,' said Ellen.

'Oh,' said Anne. 'Is he?'

She turned her head and, through the mirror, her mother saw that her face had cleared.

In a few moments she said: 'I think I'll come in front after all,' and made one of her scrambles over the back of the seat.

'That's better,' said Ellen, and they smiled at each other.

In these dark days, there were still gleams of light. Everything is comparative and Ellen was learning to be thankful for small mercies. This one, however, did not last long.

They had supper; one of the quiet quick meals they took nowadays. Things seemed worse than ever when those two came to table, because Avery was so absent from his place, and all the fun, and the pleasure of good food, with him. Now Ellen and Anne talked a little and ate a little, with silence waiting behind them. The silence of the house was extraordinary, thought Ellen. As if something had died in it, or withdrawn from it. Not only Avery, but some invisible spirit.

They cleared away and washed-up together and then Ellen took a book into the sitting-room, but not to read, and Anne went slowly upstairs.

After a time, she came down and stood in front of her mother.

'Mummy,' she said. 'I don't want to go back to school.'

Ellen was startled. She hadn't expected this.

'But, Anne . . .' she began, a pulse beating heavily in her neck as it did at every fresh development of the situation.

'I can't go back,' said Anne. 'Let me stay with you. It'll all be so different now. Mummy, please don't make me go back. I can't sleep in that room with Pug wondering all the time what's the matter.'

'Tell her,' said Ellen. 'Tell her. She's your friend.'

'I'll never tell,' said Anne, levelling a deep, stern look at the mother who could think she ever would.

She walked to the windows and stood there while Ellen's eyes followed her in distress. Then Anne made a rush to her mother's knee.

'Oh, Mummy, let me stay here with you. Mummy, I beg you.'

'Darling, listen,' said poor Ellen, putting back the child's hair and looking into the young face exposed now in all its unhappiness. 'Listen, please, to me for a moment.'

'Mummy . . .'

'I know what you feel,' said Ellen. 'Don't think I don't know. I mind more for you than for myself. It's your first battle – come much too soon. But you should fight it, Anne. I'm not brave myself. It's all terribly hard, but we've not got to be beaten, darling.'

'Couldn't I go to another school?'

'We couldn't get you in anywhere for this term, could we? You know how difficult it is to get places in schools. And it is just this year that everything is so important for you. You must pass your exam now, because our lives are changed, Anne. I'm sure your – your father will make very good provision for you, but everything is changed. We don't know . . . I mean . . .' faltered Ellen. 'We haven't been able to think yet. There's so much to think about. We've got to plan for your future. The present is very dark, I know, but we must look to the future. We must find the sort of work you can really enjoy doing. But the one thing for the moment is to get your exam. That is the one thing we can see, isn't it?'

She spoke briskly, trying to rally Anne's courage and interest, but Anne was looking up into her mother's face, searching it, the tears drying on her own.

'Mummy,' she said. 'When you get a divorce, does it mean we have to leave this house?'

Ellen's eyes wavered. She had been afraid of these questions since Avery's letter came.

'I'm afraid we couldn't go on living here without Daddy,' she said.

'Why? Why couldn't we? He's got plenty of money. Can't he give us enough to live here? He ought to. He put us here. He's our father . . .'

'Darling, listen,' calmed Ellen. 'He will make us a big allowance, I daresay. If we take it,' she amended. 'But it would never be big enough for us to stay here. He has to live himself. With her, I suppose. They'll have to have a house too. . . .'

'Don't talk about that,' said Anne. 'But if we don't live in this house, what about Roma?'

Roma. Ellen hadn't thought about Roma. Another complication. She couldn't foresee a life where they would be able to keep Roma. She looked desperately at Anne.

'What about Roma, Mummy,' insisted Anne, shaking her mother's arm. 'You won't . . . I can't . . .' she stammered.

Ellen caught her hands.

'Anne, we can't settle everything at once. Give me time, darling. I only knew yesterday that your father wanted a divorce. I need time to think,' said Ellen distractedly.

'Mummy, please don't take Roma from me,' said Anne, looking up into her mother's face. 'Please don't, Mummy.'

Her lips trembled piteously and Ellen's eyes filled with tears.

'As if I ever would if I could help it,' she said, trying to gather the child in her arms.

But Anne threw her hands off and stood up.

'That's what it means,' she said with a sob. 'I can see it. I know. I can see. . . .'

'Oh, Anne, do be reasonable, darling,' begged Ellen, getting to her feet.

But Anne ran out of the open door, through the garden and into the paddock where Roma, grazing quietly, raised her head in welcome.

Ellen came behind, but stayed out of sight, peering through the apple trees at the child she could no longer call out to or comfort. She had been afraid that Anne would ride wildly off on Roma, but there they stood together, Anne with her arm over Roma's neck, her head low, and Roma making anxious movements, sensing that something was wrong.

To Ellen they were a touching pair. She knew what Anne felt, because she herself felt poignantly the helplessness of animals – passed on from one keeper to another, going, as they grew older, one worse every time. When this had to happen to a beloved home, or dog, or cat, it amounted, however those with no feeling for animals might scoff, to anguish.

How many times had she and Avery assured Anne that this should never happen to Roma? But now what could she do?

'Oh, God, all this is beyond me,' she said suddenly. 'Help me, and help me to help Anne. Please God, help us.'

Since that hideous afternoon she had said no prayers. Too stunned, too angry, too betrayed, she hadn't prayed. She turned back to the house, almost unaware that she had prayed now, because it had been as natural as breathing.

CHAPTER TWENTY-THREE

⋙⟨⬦⟩⋘

In the shop in the Rue des Carmes where Madame Lanier was attending to her, young Madame Devoisy was ordering cards for an evening reception.

'It will be the last for some time,' she said. Louise would have said she simpered.

'Ah, Madame, that is very wise,' said Madame Lanier, all large-bosomed agreement. 'You have your social duties, I know, but a miscarriage at this stage would be tragic, would it not?'

'Oh, Madame,' said Germaine, catching her breath.

'Alas, I shouldn't have said that,' cried Madame Lanier, getting her bulky person round the counter with remarkable speed to draw up a chair. 'How stupid I am! Sit down, Madame, I beg. Dear little Madame, sit down. I cannot sufficiently rebuke myself.'

'It's nothing,' said Germaine. 'I'm quite all right. It was just the thought. It would be dreadful if I had a miscarriage now.'

'But of course you won't,' reassured Madame Lanier.

'No, I won't,' said Germaine firmly. 'I'm perfectly well and I am so careful. Now where were we? The cards. I think a

270

plain one this time, Madame Lanier. I had deckle-edged last time.'

'You are sure you are all right?' asked Madame Lanier, dipping forward solicitously. 'A glass of wine?'

'No, no, nothing of the kind.' Young Madame Devoisy waved away both the suggestion and Madame Lanier, who returned to the other side of the counter.

They dealt with the cards.

'And your daughter is still in England?' asked Madame Devoisy, rising.

'Still in England, Madame. Her affairs are settled. I mean, between ourselves,' said Madame Lanier, dropping her voice importantly, 'she has the money. But the family is in London at present,' she went on, her voice rising, 'and frankly I think Louise is enjoying herself so much that she will stay on as long as possible.'

She laughed gaily and Madame Devoisy laughed too and said she didn't blame Louise and that brought them to the door of the shop.

A car was drawn up at the pavement and Paul Devoisy, at the wheel, was looking out anxiously for his wife.

'My husband has come to fetch me! He thinks I can't walk more than a few steps alone nowadays. Aren't men sweet when you are having a baby?' she whispered happily to Madame Lanier.

'Ah, they are, Madame. They are indeed,' said Madame Lanier. 'My husband was a veritable angel to me.'

'And yet Louise resulted,' thought Germaine. 'I hope we have a more satisfactory child than that.'

'Au revoir, dear Madame,' said Madame Lanier. 'Take care of yourself, I beg.'

'I will,' said Germaine radiantly. 'I do.'

Paul was out on the pavement to hold the car door for his wife. He bowed to Madame Lanier, who beamed upon him and withdrew to the shop.

'Ah, Henri, there you are! Just in time for me to go and look into my pans. That was young Madame Devoisy. Her pregnancy is just beginning to show. It suits her. I saw her husband. He has filled out as well.'

'What – you don't think he is pregnant too, do you?' said Monsieur Lanier, taking his place behind the counter.

'Imbecile,' said Madame Lanier fondly.

She smiled as she stirred and seasoned with her expert hand. She had enjoyed the little interchange with young Madame Devoisy and looked forward to telling Louise about it in the letter she had already half-written for the evening post. She would tell her that Monsieur Paul looked much more of a man than he used to, and his manners were wonderfully improved too. In the old days he never seemed able to meet one's eye, he was so shamefaced or shy or something, but now he was quite different. Marriage had done him good. He looked both amiable and open. In her innocence, Madame Lanier imagined this change in Paul Devoisy would give as much pleasure to Louise as it did to herself.

Soup was simmering on the stove for the evening. It would be good, she thought happily. Henri would enjoy it. Already the evenings were chilly enough for hot soup to be welcome, although Henri's nose still bore the marks of his summer holiday.

Every year, year after year, Monsieur Lanier's large nose was fiercely assaulted by the sun and the salt air of Binic. It got very red, it swelled so much that his pince-nez sat askew. They nearly always had to go to the chemist's with it. It finally peeled and was left in pink patches, but he liked it. It showed he had been to the sea, it prolonged his happy holiday. And how happy it had been this year! What delicious unbuttoned ease he had enjoyed, padding about in espadrilles and a limp cotton suit all day, sitting on the shore or collecting snails with Emilie from the hedgerows. The hotel knew him so well, they cooked for him. There had been a new chef this year and the legs of mutton were more than ever blue, bleeding and tender, which was what the Laniers liked. The pastries too had been superb. The clients sat at one long table together and the meals were ample and uproarious. Several times the Laniers had thought, separately and guiltily, that it was as well Louise was in England. Of course she would not have remained at the hotel, she would have walked out; but for them it was delightful. Madame replaced the lids of her casseroles and went to finish the letter to Louise on one corner of the dining-room table before she set it for the midday meal.

'Address to me Poste Restante,' Louise had instructed them. 'We are in London and have changed hotels twice lately, so it is best to send my letters to the post office. I shall not be home for some time yet, dear parents. There have been developments. You may have a charming surprise before long. I can't say anything yet, but don't be impatient. Trust me to do the best for myself.'

Her parents were full of interested conjecture. A girl who had already brought off a thousand pounds might bring off anything. What could it be this time? they asked each other delightedly.

'Paris is more amusing than London, of course,' wrote Louise. 'But all the same London has something and it is pleasant here.'

It was pleasanter, in fact, than she would have admitted to anyone. Certainly not to Avery. When he came home in the evenings, she let him understand, though without seeming to complain, that her days were long, empty and anxious and that it was only for his sake that she put up with them. But secretly she admitted that she hadn't enjoyed anything so much since the break with Paul.

She liked being alone all day and found plenty to do. She spent most of the morning making her toilet, while the chambermaids seethed with rage in the corridor because they couldn't get in to do the rooms.

She rarely emerged before noon. There was just time then to walk down Bond Street, Dover Street, Hill Street and round Berkeley Square for the good of her figure and to put in time until luncheon.

In the afternoon, she had appointments for her hair, her face, her hands and for fittings. She was having suits made. Whatever the defects of other English clothes, she admitted there were no suits like London suits. It was very satisfactory to buy at the best houses and she enjoyed her fittings, where her figure and her knowledgeability in the matter of cut were appreciated. The assistants treated her with respect and when she arrived her name was called before her from one to another.

'Mrs. North is here. Mrs. North for her fitting. Mrs. North in number four. Tell Mr. Dean, please. Mrs. North . . . Mrs. North . . .'

That was the name she 'took' as they say, and in this case they were right. She had taken Ellen's name without a tremor.

Between tea and dinner Louise went to the cinema if there was a French film to be seen. She found French films a relief after the naïveté of American films about heroic gunmen, so quick on the draw, and English films about heroic public-schoolmen who hardly moved their lips as they spoke and were so honourable as to be boring. The French, in Louise's opinion, were the only realists, the only ones who saw life as it was. She viewed the English in general and the North family in particular much as she viewed English films. She couldn't believe in their sentiments. They were negligible. It was only the French who felt and understood and were adult.

It would have been no good Shylock's saying to Louise, 'Hath not a Jew eyes, hath not a Jew hands,' and so on. The Jews might have, but not the sort that mattered to her. So she didn't bother about them. It was the same with the English and the Norths. The plight of the family at Netherfold did not disturb her. It didn't reach her. She wouldn't have liked to come face to face with Ellen again, but then she didn't intend to.

Meanwhile she was content to wait, and she was waiting very pleasantly. She was sure Avery would marry her, if only because he couldn't bear to be alone.

'Everything comes to him who knows how to wait,' says the proverb and for her it had been true. All she had done had been to wait and the Norths, like silly fish, had jumped out of the family bowl where they had swum together for years; one right into her net, the others to gasp their lives out somewhere else.

CHAPTER TWENTY-FOUR

——∞◊∞——

I

Avery went every day to the office. He arrived earlier than before in the mornings because he no longer came by train, and left later in the evenings because he had no train to catch. With everything breaking up around him, he clung to routine at the office. To go there every morning and leave every evening gave life an appearance of sanity. In spite of what had happened, he held to the fact that he was still earning a living, still doing something for his family and even for John Bennett, to whom in these days he hardly spoke.

He found it strangely soothing to go up the familiar staircase where the morning sunlight fell on the portrait of old Thomas Bennett, the founder of the firm. His own room was a refuge and he shut himself in with relief. He was fonder of the office than he had ever been and was working harder than he had ever worked. He was working because he liked it; he liked it better than anything that was left to him. He even went through manuscripts, glad of the distraction.

It was obvious to everyone in the office that something was wrong. The girls and the men knew that the partners avoided each other and all saw the change in Avery. At first there was a good deal of excitement and conjecture and comparing of notes; but before long most of them began to be sorry and to feel the awkwardness of the situation. John's gentleness and Avery's charm and good humour were missed. The office was not what it had been before.

One morning Avery was at his desk, painstakingly going through a manuscript. When the door opened and closed again he did not immediately look up, but remained, his glasses on his nose, his thinning crown of hair exposed as he bent over the papers. There was something touching in this view of him, but the boy who stood with his back against the door did not feel it. He was too taken up by his own violent emotions of anger and resentment. Avery looked up.

'Hugh!'

A warm rush of pleasure filled him at the sight of his son. His face lit up. He got to his feet and went round the desk. But the boy's stern face halted him. He remembered he was the prodigal father. The prodigal son could be forgiven and taken back, but not the prodigal father. No one would run to fall on *his* neck.

He stood within two yards of his son. His face changed.

'How are you, Hugh?' he said.

'All right thanks,' said the boy stiffly, as if he stood to attention. 'I haven't come to stay,' said Hugh. 'I've only come to say you must cancel the arrangements you've made for me to go to Cambridge, because I'm not going. I'm going to stay in the Army.'

'But you hate the Army.' It burst from Avery before he could stop himself.

'I'd rather stay in the Army than work here with you,' said Hugh, his eyes bright and hard.

Avery turned away as if his son had struck him in the face. He walked back to his desk and picked up an ash-tray, turning it round and round in his hands.

'Go to Cambridge, Hugh, I beg of you. Don't throw that chance away. Do something else when you've finished there if you like. Though by that time you will be older and you may understand and feel differently about me.'

'Never,' said Hugh with passion. 'D'you know the woman you're living with made passes at me? She'd make them at any man – you've left mother for a woman like that. . . .' He began to stutter in his angry distress. His face crimsoned and to his own fury his eyes filled with tears. 'You . . . you . . .' he began again.

'Hugh, don't spoil your life because I . . . because I . . . You mustn't spoil your own life, Hugh.'

'It's you who've spoilt our lives. It's you. What has Mother ever done that you should treat her like this? I've no use for you. A man who could prefer a bitch like that to Mother . . .'

His fists doubled, his teeth clenched, he looked as if he was going to strike his father.

'Hugh, I ask you one thing. Don't sign on for the Army yet. Wait. Think it over again. Go to Cambridge, I beg you.'

'I wouldn't take the money from you,' said Hugh.

279

'Mother's not going to take any money from you either. We'll manage without you.'

Avery was speechless. He stared at the boy, while Hugh glared at him, his breath coming as fast as if he had been running.

'We loved you,' said Hugh, choking at the thought of it. 'But look what you've done to us. Well, we hate you now. Anne worst of all. I'm going. And don't you dare to send me any money. If you do, I'll burn it.'

'You young fool,' said Avery. 'Hugh . . .'

The door opened and closed again. He was gone.

Avery went back to his desk. He sat there for a long time, his head in his hands. He gave himself up to his own acute misery. But after a while, he began to forget himself and think of Hugh. The boy must be stopped from doing anything so foolish as signing on for the Army.

Avery dropped his hands, which still trembled a little as he laid them flat on the forgotten manuscript, and bent over them unseeingly. What could he do for his son? Nothing, he answered himself. Nothing he could say would have any effect on Hugh. He must get somebody else to do what could be done. It must be John Bennett of course.

He intensely disliked the idea of going to John Bennett for help. But it must be done. He got up, passed both hands over his hair, walked about the room for a bit, then went across the landing to John Bennett's room.

'Hugh's been,' he said when the partners were alone. When Avery had anything to say these days, he said it abruptly.

'Yes,' said John Bennett. 'I saw him.'

'You saw him?'

Avery was unreasonably irritated that Hugh should have been in to see John Bennett.

'Did he tell you about deciding to stay in the Army then?'

'Yes, he did,' said John Bennett. 'I'm extremely concerned about it.'

Avery's irritation grew. He was the one whose business it was to be concerned about his son. No one had asked John Bennett to be concerned yet.

John Bennett rearranged the pens, the calendars, of which he always had several, the trays and other oddments on his desk. It was a way he had when he was getting ready to say something difficult.

'He doesn't want to work with you, Avery,' he brought out. 'He can't face the idea of seeing you here every day for years, after the way you've treated his mother, and I must say, I can't blame him.'

Avery flushed angrily.

'I've told you before. You don't know everything about this business. You don't know my side of it, anyway. So please spare me your opinions.'

'I'm telling you that your son doesn't want to work with you,' said John evenly.

'He told me that himself. Why do you want to repeat it?' said Avery furiously.

'Perhaps to lead up to something I want to say myself,' said John, busy with his pens again. 'The fact is, Avery,' he said, abandoning them and looking up, 'I'm not very keen on working with you myself. Don't you think it would be better all round if I bought you out of this partnership?'

There was complete silence for a moment. At the sight of Avery's face John Bennett felt suddenly and sharply sorry for what he had said. He opened his mouth to take it back. But he remembered the boy and Ellen and said nothing.

'You want me out so that you can take my son in, I suppose?' said Avery.

'Eventually, yes,' said John. 'It would save his career for him.'

'A pretty situation that would be, wouldn't it? In the publishing world. A nice confusion, eh?'

'And whose fault is that? You've asked for it, haven't you?'

'Damn it all!' Avery burst out. 'What have I done that dozens – hundreds – of men aren't doing all the time?'

'I don't know,' said John. 'Nobody has told me. All I know is you went off with the French girl and refuse to go back.'

Avery stared at him, breathing audibly.

'If you drive me out of publishing,' he said at length, 'how do you think I'm going to keep up Netherfold and maintain my family?'

'I don't think they expect anything from you,' said John carefully. 'In fact, Ellen says she won't take alimony.'

'What?' cried Avery.

'That's what she says,' murmured John Bennett uncomfortably, busy with his pens again.

He was startled to find Avery looming over him at the desk.

'That's your work,' said Avery thickly. 'You've told her not to take money from me so that she'll turn to you for help. I suppose you're going to take over my family now? Cash in on the catastrophe, eh? You're after Ellen, of course. You've been hankering after her for years.'

'Here, stop this,' said John Bennett, getting up so abruptly that he almost struck his head on Avery's chin. 'And kindly get out of here. You can't have it both ways. You've left your wife and family to look after themselves and when they do it, or somebody else tries to do it for them, you don't like it.'

'You and Ellen,' said Avery savagely. 'All this is very convenient for you, isn't it? Couldn't have turned out better, could it?'

'You drink too much,' said John Bennett. 'Don't come here breathing brandy and abuse over me any more. I've had enough of you, Avery.'

He rang the bell on his desk and walked to the door, holding it wide.

'Miss Everett,' he called. 'Will you come back now?'

II

Avery got back to the hotel while Louise was out on her morning walk. He had their rooms to himself and went through to his bedroom where he kept a bottle of brandy. He poured out a stiff drink. Then another. He was bent on getting brandy down and stood by the window, glass in hand, waiting for it to do its work. He was badly hurt, first by Hugh, then by John Bennett. They were all against him.

They knew he was down and they all combined to push him down deeper. It was a conspiracy; Ellen refusing alimony, Hugh refusing Cambridge, John refusing to continue the partnership. They were trying to punish him. They were bent on destroying him.

He poured out more brandy. They should have known, something within him cried. They should have known that he loved them, and was lost and desperate without them. For one awful moment tears gushed into his eyes, his lip shook against the glass. My God, this won't do, he thought, and hurried to drink more brandy. It would be all right soon. The brandy would see to that.

Relief began to come. Everything blurred warmly, the ache with the rest. He put the glass down and stood with the tips of his fingers to the edge of the table, looking through the open door at the rooms beyond. The oatmeal suite, he thought. Everything the colour of cold porridge. No movement. No escape. No garden, no birds singing. Damned in a private suite. And it was costing a small fortune. Still, he had to have a room of his own. He was frightened that Louise would leave him, but he didn't want to be with her. He had tried to make love to her, in case she expected it. But the memory of that awful afternoon overcame him. He felt Ellen and Anne were still there. He tried again; but it was no good.

The sitting-room door clicked open, clicked shut and Louise was there, standing in the middle of the room, examining the fit of her new suit in the glass over the fireplace. She turned this way and that, smoothing her waist and hips, looking over her shoulder at her back. Excellent.

'I need a fur tie,' she thought. 'Avery must buy me one this week. The weather is getting chilly.'

Avery, balancing by the tips of his fingers, thought she looked pretty pleased with herself. 'Why shouldn't she? She's done very well out of this,' he thought, the fog induced by the brandy lifting briefly. 'But I've got to marry her. Nothing else for it. Can't let her down too. I must stick to somebody and get somebody to stick to me. Clever girl, Louise. She'll look after me. I'm a poor fish. I need somebody. Like hell, I need somebody,' he said with a sob.

'Avery,' cried Louise, whipping round. 'What are you doing here? Why are you here at this time in the morning? And drinking again. This is too much.'

She came in swiftly and seized the bottle. She went to lock it into the sitting-room cupboard and put the key into her bag. What was he doing here? It was nearly lunch-time and she had been looking forward to a quiet meal in her special corner of the dining-room.

'Why are you here?' she asked with irritation. No need to disguise that because he was too drunk to notice. 'Why have you left the office at this time of the day?'

'I've left it for good,' he said, letting her steer him into the sitting-room and put him into an armchair.

She stared at him.

'Is it true?'

'It's true,' he said. 'I've had a hell of a morning. Hugh came. He won't go to Cambridge now.'

'Does it matter?'

'Of course it matters,' said Avery, trying to focus the face of one who could ask such a question. 'He won't go to Cambridge because he won't take the money from me. He's going to stay in the Army rather than work with me at the office.'

'So you left it?'

'I left it because John Bennett doesn't want to work with me either.'

'Then he will have to pay you a lot of money,' said Louise sharply.

'Yes, he'll have to pay,' said Avery with a sudden foolish smile. 'I'll make him pay all right.'

'Well, what does it matter then?' said Louise. 'Who wants to work in an office when there's no necessity?'

'That's one way of looking at it,' said Avery in drunken approval. 'Why work when they'll pay you not to? Except that I liked it,' he said with another unexpected sob.

'Mon Dieu, don't do that,' said Louise in distaste. 'How ugly it is. You look hideous. So foolish.'

'I beg your pardon,' said Avery, sobering. He passed both hands over his hair and wiped his face with his handkerchief.

'They're bent on punishing me,' he said. 'Ellen's threatening not to take alimony now.'

Louise laughed.

'I don't think you need worry,' she said.

'Why?'

'Everybody takes money. It's only a gesture. It means nothing.'

'What are you going to do?' said Louise sharply, in a moment.

'About the office?'

'No. About lunch. It's lunch-time. Are you coming down or not?'

'I don't want any lunch.'

'But I do,' said Louise, as if that should have occurred to him.

'You must go down, of course,' said Avery. 'I'll stay here.'

'Shall I send something up?'

He shook his head.

Louise looked round the room. He couldn't get at the brandy. But was there anything else he could drink?

'I'll go down then,' she said.

When she came back, he was sober and lunch had restored her.

'Avery, I have been thinking,' she said, coming to sit on the arm of his chair. 'If you like to work, you must work. You are a publisher. People like you. You have charm, when you are not drunk. You can open an office of your own and all the authors will come to you instead of to this Mr. Bennett. I too will work for you, Avery. When we are married, I will give receptions for the authors. We will have a very distinguished salon.'

He shook his head.

'No,' he said. 'I couldn't set up in opposition to John and Hugh. I couldn't work against them like that.'

She made a sound of utter disgust and got up from the arm of his chair.

'But you are like the hero of one of your silly English films,' she said. 'I have no more patience. What will you do then?' she said, whipping round on him. 'Think for yourself. Do something for yourself. When things go wrong, you cry, you drink brandy, you give up.'

Avery sat in gloomy silence. She went into her own room, took off the new coat and skirt, and putting on her dressing-gown, she laid herself down on her bed. She always rested in the afternoon when she had nothing else to do. She left her door open so that she could see him.

By and by, he said, thinking aloud: 'I might get Sellers and Pirbeck of New York to appoint me as their representative here. Partner really. They did once suggest such a thing. Several years ago. But I'd have to go over and see them.'

Louise sat up.

'Go to New York, Avery?' she said.

'Yes,' said Avery.

In a flash she was kneeling beside his chair, her white gown spreading over the carpet.

'New York!' she breathed. 'But how wonderful! I have always wanted to go to New York. When shall we go?'

'Any time will do for me to get away from here,' said Avery, moving restlessly. 'I don't want to be in this country when the divorce goes through.'

'No, of course you don't,' said Louise, laying her cool narrow hand on his. 'Let us go as soon as we can, dear Avery. I will go straight away to the Bureau. Will you come with me?' she asked persuasively.

'Oh, I don't know,' he said. 'I feel rather done-up really.'

'Come along. It will do you good. Go and have a bath. I once read it is physically impossible to worry in a hot bath and it is true, because I have tried it. See, I will get your bath ready and order tea up here. Then you will feel much better and we will go and book our passage – on the *Queen Elizabeth*, I hope. And we will look forward, dear Avery. Forward all the time.'

He got up, temporarily lightened. He couldn't share her enthusiasm, but at least he would be getting away, moving about.

While he was in his bath, Louise did her face again, taking off the make-up she had put on two or three hours before and putting it carefully on again. She dressed in the new suit again – these repetitious performances never tired her – and rang for tea.

New York! Better and better. The *Queen Elizabeth*. That meant more clothes. She had heard that women wore different evening dresses each night on these transatlantic trips. Never the same dress twice, and always so magnificent. The chic, she had always understood, was marvellous. Well, they should see how a Frenchwoman could look! But how busy she was going to be, she thought with delicious excitement. She would see to it that they didn't get passages too soon, because she must have time to assemble her clothes. It would never do to buy in a hurry.

What a pity Avery hadn't brought all his things away from Netherfold that day, she thought, pausing in her pacing of the sitting-room. Because he needed them and they were good things. There was no point in spending money on new ones when there was no necessity. Not for a man. It was ridiculous that Avery wouldn't write for them. But she knew she could not persuade him.

'I will write myself,' she determined as the tea came in.

'Come, Avery,' she called at the bathroom door. 'Come, mon petit. Tea is ready.'

She did her best to make everything sound very cosy and hopeful. When things were going well for her, Louise could be charming.

CHAPTER TWENTY-FIVE

❤❤❤

I

The art of letter-writing, as taught at the Pension Ste Colombe, had not included an example of a letter one could write to one's lover's wife to ask her to send the clothes he had left behind when he deserted her, and Louise spent a considerable time in wondering how to word it. It was, she admitted to herself, a difficult sort of letter.

'Madame,' she wrote at last, omitting the name of the hotel. 'Will you be good enough to send Mr. North's clothes and personal belongings to his tailors, Messrs. Peers and Vane, Savile Row, London, W.I.'

After that, she had to think again. No believe me, Madame, no distinguished sentiments, no sincerities or best wishes would do here. Finding nothing suitable in the whole range of French politenesses, she signed herself 'L. Lanier', and posted the letter with less assurance of the outcome than Ellen would have given her credit for.

In Ellen's place, she would have torn the letter up and sent the pieces to the tailors without the clothes. Louise did not think the clothes would come. But they did. The English, she marvelled, were really the most incredible people, but so much the better.

Peers and Vane sent the cases and boxes to the hotel, as instructed by her.

They arrived when Avery was with his lawyer again and Louise was able to set about unpacking them herself. In the pocket of one case she found a packet of letters, the very packet of Anne's letters she had come upon when she went through Avery's drawers the day of Anne's half-term.

'I put a seggestion in the box,' she read again on the back of one envelope.

Louise set her lips. Why had his wife put these letters in? They were a message. To lure him back, of course. Well, her little ruse should not come off. Avery should not have these letters. They would only disturb him anyway, and make him drink too much brandy. Louise felt quite justified in putting the packet into her bag to be disposed of later.

She had hardly done it when Avery came in. He stood stock still at the sight of the cases and clothes.

'Where have these come from?' he asked sharply.

Louise shrugged her shoulders.

'From where you left them.'

'How did they get here? I thought no one knew where we were?'

'They were sent to your tailors.'

Avery stared at her in silence for a moment.

'Did you write for them?' he said.

'Yes,' said Louise, putting a jacket on a hanger and carrying it to the cupboard.

There was another silence.

'How could you do a thing like that?' he said.

'But I did it,' said Louise, raising her eyebrows. 'No question of how could I. Someone had to do it and I knew you would not.'

'You were right. I should never have done it,' he said. 'But I suppose you can't understand that.'

'I never understand the English,' said Louise, calmly collecting shirts. 'You have left your wife, but you think it impossible to ask for your clothes. If that is not swallowing a camel and straining at a fly I don't know what is.'

Avery was silent again. She was right, he supposed. But poor Ellen. His face was haggard as he thought of Ellen taking his things from the drawers and cupboards in that little room at home.

'You have twenty-six shirts, mon cher,' said Louise. 'Quite a trousseau.'

II

On the twenty-second of September, in spite of her pleading and Ellen's own misgivings, Anne was to go back to school. Whether it was right or wrong to make her go, Ellen didn't know. She was sickeningly uncertain about it, as about most things in these days. Although it had not been Avery who decided everything she had never decided anything without him, and she felt now that she had lost any power of independent decision she had ever possessed. Her mind laboured back and forth over the question of Anne's return to school. Was it wise, after the shock she had suffered, to force the child into a situation she dreaded? But wouldn't it be best for her to get right away from home where everything was ruined, and be with girls of her own age and so fully occupied that she wouldn't have much time to think of what had happened? After long wavering, Ellen decided it must be best for her to go back to school.

Anne, though grimly, agreed, but on one condition. Her mother must not tell the Headmistress what had happened. Ellen blushed, caught out, because that was what she had meant to do, so that the obvious change in Anne could be understood.

'If you tell the Head, Mummy,' said Anne, white, 'I'll leave. I won't stay.'

'But, Anne,' said Ellen, 'she would understand. She'd feel nothing but sympathy.'

'I don't want sympathy,' said Anne. 'I just want nobody to know. I can't bear people to be sorry for me.'

'But people mean to be kind . . .' began Ellen, and then stopped. It struck her suddenly that she herself was just as reluctant to tell anybody, even those who must be told sooner or later. No good preaching to the child when she, an adult, shirked practising what she preached.

She had been drifting, miserably, with her own difficulties but now she must pull up and face them.

She began by giving notice to both day-women. Half the housework had disappeared with Avery and what was left she wanted to do herself. The busier she was the better.

Also, if she did as she was beginning to think she would do, she could no longer afford to pay the women.

So she nervously told Mrs. Pretty she was sorry she wouldn't need her now, and Mrs. Pretty, who had expected it, said she was sorry too and neither of them said any more.

But when Ellen said the same thing the following day to Miss Beasley, that gaunt woman turned from the sink and came out with what she had intended to say for some time.

'I'll tell you something, Madam,' she said, looking at Ellen with her red-rimmed eyes. 'Something I've never told a soul since I came to this town. I've got a husband myself.'

'A husband?' said Ellen in astonishment.

'A husband,' said Miss Beasley grimly. 'But I don't acknowledge him. It's thirty years since he paid me the same trick as what yours has just played you. I just thought I'd tell you, because I know what you're going through. But you'll get over it. You don't think so now, but you will. Look at me,' said Miss Beasley, throwing out both hands, potato in one, knife in the other, and standing proudly for inspection with her stringy neck and sparse hair. 'Look at me. I've not done so bad, have I?'

Such an appeal from such a work-worn figure took Ellen aback. It also moved her uncomfortably. She went quickly to stand beside Miss Beasley at the sink, not only to hide the tears that stung her eyes but to bear her company.

'You've done very well,' she was able to say with truth, because if Miss Beasley knew she had, she had.

'And you've got your children,' said Miss Beasley. 'I'd nobody.'

They stood together, Miss Beasley paring potatoes rapidly, Ellen watching.

'I tell you what,' said Miss Beasley, changing legs. She always stood first on one leg and then on the other. 'I shall pop in when I'm passing now and again, if you don't mind. What you want is somebody as knows what it's like. And I can give you a hand if there's any cleaning up to be done. There's bound to be. It's only to be expected.'

'Yes,' said Ellen. 'I shall be very glad to see you. You're very kind, Miss Beasley.'

'I've a fellow-feeling,' said Miss Beasley grimly.

Later that day, Ellen did another thing she had put off doing. She rang up her brother Henry in Manchester.

He was completely taken aback, not only that Avery had gone, but that she hadn't told him before.

'Why on earth didn't you tell me at once?' he asked in amazement.

'I don't know why. I couldn't, Henry. It . . .'

'But I'd have done something. I'd have gone after him.'

'It wouldn't have been any good.'

'But have you done nothing about it at all?'

'I'm going to divorce him.'

'Ellen, you can't!'

'That's what he wants.'

'But he's out of his mind at present. He'll come to his senses. Ellen, don't rush into divorce, for heaven's sake.'

'You don't understand, Henry. You don't know what – what happened.'

'I'll come,' he said. 'I'll come to-morrow, when I've finished at the hospital.'

'No, don't. Please,' said Ellen urgently. 'Not yet. You can't do anything. I'll come up and see you when Anne's gone back to school. Don't come, Henry. It's too far. You're too busy. You can't do anything and I can't say more than I've said. There are the pips going for the third time. Let's ring off, Henry.'

'I can't make you out,' he said. 'I'll ring up again to-morrow, when I've grasped all this. Good-bye, love. I can't tell you what I feel. You and Avery . . . Ellen, you can't divorce him . . .'

'Good-bye,' said Ellen.

She had meant to ask him, even over the telephone, what could be the matter with her thumping heart, but she hadn't been able to get it in. Perhaps it was as well, because then he would have insisted on coming. She didn't want him to. She didn't want to be asked any questions about what she could never tell. She would never describe what she and Anne had seen in the sitting-room that afternoon.

But the rapid thumping of her heart added to her other distresses and was another thing that must be dealt with.

After putting off from day to day, she rang up Dr. Simms and was committed to a visit. He had always been kind, he had brought her two children into the world, she was perfectly used to him, but the thought of being seen by him filled her with nervous dread. You can't hide anything from doctors. Her misery and weakness would be exposed. As soon as he listened to her heart, he would know. He knew before that. As soon as he came into the house, he knew that the rumours he had heard but refused to believe, were true. He had to wait, however, until his patient should tell him of her own accord, and she said nothing at first but that her heart was behaving strangely.

'Let me listen to it,' he said, and she held the collar of her dress down and turned her face away while he put the stethoscope to the wall of her chest. The heart told its own fast, troubled tale and the doctor listened, but his eyes were on the face of the woman he had always known as happy. What a damned shame, he thought.

'Your heart is perfectly sound, Mrs. North,' he said, taking her hand and putting her gently into a chair. 'But you have nervous tachycardia and show every sign of prolonged strain. You look as if you haven't been to sleep for weeks. Don't you think you might have consulted me before, my dear?'

'Yes,' said Ellen, with simplicity, and left it at that. 'Can you stop the thumping?'

'I can try,' said Dr. Simms. 'But can I take away the strain that causes it?'

Ellen shook her head.

'My husband has left me,' she said.

It gave her a bitter pang every time she said it; as if she cut another living bond between herself and Avery and let him be borne away. Every time she said it, it was truer. Every person she said it to pushed between her and Avery until she felt she soon wouldn't be able to see him any more. She hated to say it.

She had to say it again when she went to see the family lawyer, who believed the rumour when he heard it because, having seen so much of humanity at its worst, he could believe anything of it. All the same, he was shocked when Ellen opened the subject of divorce.

'But, Mrs. North,' he said with deep concern, 'aren't you being altogether too precipitate? Surely your husband will come to his senses and return to you? I knew his father. I've known Avery all his life. A handsome fellow like that has many temptations, but he's sound at heart . . .'

'He won't come back,' said Ellen. 'It's quite final. He wants a divorce.'

'But you know, Mrs. North,' said Mr. Roach, sitting at his desk with a roaring gas fire behind him though the morning was warm, 'we've always looked upon you and Avery as an absolutely ideal couple. Surely this isn't an irreconcilable breach? Let me see Avery.'

'It's no use,' said Ellen. 'Please do as he asks.'

Mr. Roach tried again. He tried hard, but in the end he gave up and drew a pad towards him. As he put questions and made notes, he realised that there was something behind it all that she was not disclosing. He said as much, because he not only liked as a lawyer, to get hold of the facts, but as a man he was curious by nature. She dealt with him more cursorily than he had expected.

'Adultery and desertion are sufficient grounds for divorce, aren't they?' she asked him.

'They are, yes. Yes, certainly,' said Mr. Roach.

'Then you have all the necessary evidence. How long will it take?'

Mr. Roach, piqued, altered his manner. Hitherto it had been sympathetic, now it was detached.

'A divorce nowadays is a matter of a few weeks,' he said. 'As the dates fall, it will take about six weeks for the decree nisi and another six weeks for the decree absolute. Your case will be heard in London, of course.'

'No,' said Ellen. 'I see dozens of cases are heard at Benhampton. It's only twenty miles away. I can drive over.'

'Oh, I shouldn't do it there.' Mr. Roach was shocked. His more prosperous clients always had their cases heard in London. 'It's not quite usual, you know, to have one's divorce brought up at the County Court.'

'Since it has to be heard,' said Ellen, 'it doesn't matter where. The County Court will do.'

'Very well,' said Mr. Roach with dignity. 'Please yourself, Mrs. North. I will get into touch with you in the course of the next few days. Or rather I will get young Letchworth to get into touch with you. He deals with our County Court divorces.'

'Thank you,' said Ellen.

'I'm sorry I haven't been able to induce you to change your mind, Mrs. North,' said Mr. Roach, rising. 'I think you are making a great mistake in not waiting at least six months longer for your husband to return to you.'

All these well-meaning, but uninformed people, thought Ellen, leaving him.

Now that she had cleared her own decks, she tried again to persuade Anne to let her write to the Headmistress.

'To make it easier for you, darling,' she begged.

But Anne wouldn't hear of it.

'No. She mustn't know. Why should she?'

'Because she's in charge of you. Anne, it's no good hiding the fact that this has changed you. It's changed me, hasn't it? Well, it's changed you too.'

'I'll be all right,' said Anne stubbornly. 'I won't let them see any difference in me.'

'But it will be a strain keeping it up. If somebody knew, somebody kind and wise like Miss Beldon . . .!'

'No,' said Anne.

On the morning of September twenty-second, when mother and daughter, hatted and gloved, came out of their bedrooms at the same moment, each gave the other a swift glance of relief. Ellen was startled these days to receive such an equal glance from Anne. Not the look of a child to her mother, but the level, assessing glance of one adult to another. Ellen couldn't get used to it. It made the child seem almost a stranger, and so much older.

This morning Anne's relief was that her mother, thanks to careful make-up, looked practically normal for the others to see. Ellen's relief was for Anne, because she knew the child wanted to get by without arousing comment, and because of thorough grooming, after weeks of indifference, she would do it. In her grey uniform and white blouse, she looked very brushed, washed and schoolgirlish again. She looked almost as before, but this time there were no tears, no aching smiles because it had come to the last morning at home. There was only that glance at her mother to see if she would pass muster under the eyes of the Weston girls and the Mowbrays and anybody else who might be at the station, coming in from the junction to take the school train.

301

'Ready, darling?' said Ellen.

'Yes,' said Anne.

They drove away from the house, with no backward glance from Anne. Ellen was acutely aware that Anne was steeling herself to re-enter her own world and her mother daren't say a word of encouragement, or even of love, because, mutely, Anne wouldn't let her. Since Avery's leaving, Ellen had come up against a characteristic she had not suspected in the pliant, happy child who thought everything her parents did and said was right. Whether it was strength or hardness, Ellen didn't know. But she knew so little now; about Anne, about Hugh, about herself. Louise had changed them all out of recognition.

Passing through the town, Ellen caught sight of a once-familiar green hat bearing a thin, high pheasant's feather like an aerial.

'There's Miss Daley,' she cried, slowing down. 'I haven't seen her since Christmas.'

'Don't stop,' said Anne.

At that moment, Miss Daley came to a halt on the pavement, a glad light of recognition behind her spectacles.

'She's seen us,' said Ellen.

'Don't stop,' said Anne.

'Just for a minute, darling, surely . . .'

'No,' said Anne. ' Mummy, please. We'd have to tell her. Or she knows and she'd say something. Besides, we haven't time.'

So Ellen, because Anne had enough to face already, smiled regretfully at Miss Daley and drove on. But she was sorry. She didn't even know Miss Daley's address so that she could explain.

At the station, the cheerful ticket-collector they liked was on duty.

'Well now,' he said, receiving their tickets and pushing his peaked cap to the back of his head. 'Fancy you coming along! I was only saying to Bert here this very morning as it was a long time since we'd had Mr. North rushing up at the last minute for the eight-twenty. Always at the last minute, Mr. North. Makes you miss him, does that. But perhaps he is away from home, is he?'

'Yes, he's away from home,' said Ellen, smiling, glad that people were pressing through behind her and letting her get away from the ticket-collector.

She and Anne walked through the subway in silence. They reached the platform and the Mowbray girls were there and in a moment the Westons came up with their mother and greetings and exclamations filled the air.

'Oh, Anne. Oh, Sarah. Jocelyn, you've cut your hair. Let me look. So she has. Doesn't she look different? Did you have good hols? I say, we went to France. It was marvellous. Where did you go, Anne? Oh, you never go, do you? You won't leave that nag of yours. You were having Pug to stay, weren't you? She didn't come? What was it? Why didn't she?'

As she talked with Mrs. Weston, Ellen saw Anne dealing with the difficulties that crowded up already. She smiled and met their questions. She shook her hair about and looked almost as usual.

Porters came up with the school luggage.

'Oh, why do we have to go?' groaned Christine Weston.

'I don't know why you always go on like this,' said comfortable Mrs. Weston, a daughter hanging on each arm. 'You know very well you're all happy. It's a wonderful school. I only wish I'd been at one like it.'

'I shall talk like this to my children,' said Christine. 'It's a great line.'

'You know you wouldn't miss the play this term for anything,' said her mother.

'Oh, you're right. I wouldn't,' admitted Christine, suddenly serious. 'I say, Anne, I had a letter from Jane Fairhurst last week and she says there's a rumour we're going to have boys from Overingham School to do *Much Ado* with us. I hope to heaven it isn't true. Boys!'

'Oh,' said Anne, with such recoil that everybody laughed except her mother. The play concerned these two closely; they were sure to be in it.

'Boys!' groaned Christine. 'I do like to throw myself about a bit in the plays and who can do that with boys there? Besides, I like male parts best myself. I was hoping for Benedick,' she said, strutting charmingly.

'What appalling cheek,' said her sister.

The train came in. The Westons kissed their mother. Anne kissed hers. The girls got into a compartment and reappeared at the windows; except Anne. Ellen's heart thumped unmercifully. Anne must look out and say good-bye. She mustn't go away like this – so closed up in herself.

Then further down the coach she saw Anne leaning from a window, her shining hair hanging forward under the round school hat.

'Darling,' said Ellen, hurrying up.

'Mummy,' said Anne, her lips trembling. 'You won't send Roma away without telling me, will you?'

'Anne,' said poor Ellen, straining upwards. 'How could you think I would do such a thing?'

'Oh, Mummy.'

'Darling, I'll find a way. I'll manage somehow. I'll do something, but you've got to help me, Anne.'

'I will help, Mummy. If only . . .'

'Sshh, now, sshh. Smile, darling. Trust me to do the very best I can.'

'Yes, Mummy. Let me kiss you again.'

Ellen reached up. They kissed. The train began to move.

'Write soon, Mummy. Write to-day like you used to do.'

'I will,' said Ellen.

'Good-bye, Mummy darling.'

'Good-bye . . . Good-bye . . .'

They waved until the train rounded the bend and then Ellen had to turn away to mop her eyes before she could face Mrs. Weston.

But Mrs. Weston was also mopping hers.

'Isn't it awful when they go?' she said, blowing her nose. 'But aren't we fools. They're perfectly happy when they get there. In fact, they'll be all right by the time the train passes Benhampton, I'll be bound. My husband says if we never have anything worse to cry for than the girls going back to school, we shall do very well.'

Ellen drove home, aghast at the new complication she had brought upon herself. What madness to have given Anne the idea that they would be able to keep Roma. But that piteous little face at the window at the last moment had been too much for her strength of mind. It was still too much. Because, although she saw no way of being able to keep the mare, she found herself determined to, all the same. But how? How?

She drove the car into the garage and by a series of jerks closed the heavy doors she had always left to Avery. She let herself into the house and, trying not to notice the silence, she went up to her room to take off her coat and hat. She went to the window to look at Roma, as if by sizing her up she could calculate better what to do.

In the paddock, bordered by poplars whose golden leaves glittered like tambourine coins, Roma was cropping contentedly.

'How much does it cost to keep her?' Ellen wondered. Nobody had ever worked it out.

'It depends where we live,' she thought.

So they must live where Roma could be kept cheaply. For the second time, they were committed to the country.

On John Bennett's last visit, when she and Anne were taking him to the station, he suddenly proposed that they should all go and live with him in Kensington. Ellen turned impulsively towards him, her face alight. What a solution! She longed to creep in somewhere, to 'settle' again, to shelve her difficulties, to leave them to John. And in return, how much better than any housekeeper would she manage for him. She opened her mouth to say all this, but caught sight of Anne's face in the driving mirror and did not say a word of it.

Anne was leaning forward intently, watching John Bennett and her mother with such sick distaste that Ellen almost exclaimed aloud. It rushed upon her that Anne actually suspected John Bennett of being in love with her. She remembered Anne looking like this that other time, when they took him to the station before and Anne asked about John's wife. Ellen saw that Anne was watching to see if her mother was willing to play the same game as her father, waiting for confirmation of a suspicion that all men and women were at the same thing.

Staring upwards at her daughter, Ellen drove dangerously on, with John beside her expatiating unheard on the advantages of Kensington. How on earth had the child got hold of this preposterous idea?

It must be all John's silly talk and hand-kissings. He had always pretended to adore her, and since that horrible afternoon, this had become distorted in the child's mind, with so much else.

'It's a wonderful offer, John dear,' said Ellen ringingly. 'And you are so nice to make it. It's just like you. But I don't think Anne and I could ever live away from the country, could we, darling?'

Again that look of absolute relief in the child's face. She sank back into her corner of the car, relaxed.

'No, we couldn't, Mummy,' she said. 'Not really, could we?'

She drew a long breath. Then she leaned forward until her chin pressed on John Bennett's shoulder.

'But thank you awfully, Uncle John, for asking us,' she said. She could be fond of him now that there was no danger that he and her mother would live in the same house or want to get married or fall in what was hideously called love.

'You are good, Uncle John,' she said.

It was the first warm word she had said to him and he was touchingly pleased, although they would not entertain the idea of coming to live with him, which he continued to press until the last moment for his train.

'Well, if you won't come, I shall insist on having Hugh,' he said at the car door. 'Until you are well settled elsewhere, and probably after that too.'

'Very well, John dear, and thank you, thank you,' said Ellen, kissing him, warmly. Anne leaned over and kissed him too, grateful for more than he would ever have any idea of.

To scotch at once any idea that they would go to Kensington, Ellen had said they would live in the country. Now it looked as if Roma was going to force that random statement to come true. But how, Ellen asked herself, could she find work in the country? How could she reconcile all these difficulties?

'I don't know,' she said, letting her hand drop from the window-sill and turning away.

If only there was someone to discuss it with. But even her brother, even John Bennett, both so eager to save all that could be saved, would think it shockingly unpractical to consider keeping a horse now. She remembered how amused she and Avery had been when the Roytons, having lost all their money, were offered a nice little house rent-free by some friends, but refused it because they couldn't get the grand piano in. Roma was the grand piano now and Ellen was as determined not to part with her.

She went purposefully downstairs and took bundles of papers from the desk where Avery had kept them. She spread them out over the dining-room table, then, seeing it was quarter past one, she brought a glass of milk to drink and an apple to eat while she was going through them.

Ellen, the advocate of good food, couldn't be bothered to cook for herself.

She bent over the papers and wished she was less of a duffer at figures. For twenty years she had never tried any. She had never tried to understand income-tax returns; there had been no need to since the income was practically all Avery's. She didn't even know how much the money left to her by her father provided in the way of personal income. She thought it was about three hundred pounds a year, but in these days the value must be halved. She picked up a paper and remembered that Avery had given her some shares in the hosiery company. And here was a dividend certificate. And here was something about the conversion of shares.

She pored over it. What did it mean? Had she to pay something? Or was something to be paid to her? She didn't know. Her ignorance was abysmal.

She took up the glass of milk, and while she drank she looked at the garden through the window with a sense of surfeit. There was too much of it. Everything had got so badly out of hand that she felt angry with it. It added to her feeling of fatigue, of not being able to cope with things.

It was the same with the papers on the table. There were too many of them. Avery shouldn't have left them in this state. If he had to go, he should have put them in order first. She must take them to the bank or to the lawyers.

She began to gather them up, but she laid them out again. She remembered Anne's face as the train went out – tearful, but trusting her mother to save Roma.

'I've got to sort this out for myself,' said Ellen.

She read and docketed. She puzzled, made notes, searched for other papers. She put bills together and compared what was owing with the money in the joint account she had always had with Avery.

It went dark. Rain scratched at the windows. She added a boiled egg to the belated tea, to make one meal do for two. She had joined the great army of solitary women who have boiled eggs at night, the women without men.

She was alone in the house without expectation of anyone coming into it. Weeks of this deathly evening stillness stretched before her. When the cat mewed suddenly for her supper, Ellen started.

She returned to the papers, and before she went to bed she had established the fact that she had about two hundred pounds a year of her own, if she had assessed her separate income tax correctly.

'I have two hundred a year,' she said aloud – she was already beginning to talk to herself. 'I shall work for the rest.'

Since the day Avery had asked for a divorce, she had kept it at the back of her mind that she would not take alimony. She couldn't bear the idea of being Avery's pensioner, a woman he had discarded but must still pay for. He should give an allowance to Anne, but not to her. She had two hundred a year and she would work for the rest. But where could she work where Anne and Roma could be with her?

'Sufficient unto the day,' she said, aloud again, and put the papers away.

It had grown very cold in the room. It was time for fires in the evening, but she hadn't thought of making one. She went into the kitchen, bleak and unused nowadays, and filled a hot-water bottle, hoping to get warm in bed.

In the night the silence crept upon her like a stealthy presence. She lay in fear, hearing nothing but her own heart, which, in spite of Dr. Simms's prescription, thumped as badly as ever. It would, he said, until she made peace with herself.

She turned on the lamp and reached for a book. But Avery's bed stretched beside her like a bier. She sprang suddenly out of bed and put more lights on.

'I can't bear it,' she called out, shivering in her nightgown in the middle of the room.

Her eyes fell on the electric kettle filled for early tea. It would be something to do, something to shorten the night to make tea. She switched on the kettle and got back into bed to wait for it to boil. She lay with her pillow bunched under her head in the way of those who can find no rest. The kettle began to creep gently. How often had she listened to this small, comfortable, domestic song as she waited to make morning tea and waken Avery. She pushed the memory angrily away. The fact that Avery was at this moment sleeping with Louise left her nothing to remember. What value or truth was there in any single memory of him now? He had ruined past, present and future. She daren't think about any of it.

The kettle was boiling. She got up and made tea and

suddenly the little cat was there, purring and rubbing round her bare feet.

'Hello,' said Ellen, wonderfully cheered by this arrival. 'Did you hear me? Would you like a drink too?'

She gave Moppet the saucer and got back into bed to drink tea from the cup. Moppet liked to sleep on beds, but so far Ellen had not allowed her on hers. To-night, Moppet knew there would be no opposition. The milk finished, she sprang up, kneaded a place for herself and settled down luxuriously.

Ellen was glad of her, but sleep was still out of the question. She picked up the book again. It was one Mrs. Brockington had given her, one of Evelyn Underhill's. She hadn't read it, and opened it at random now. It was just something to drive her eyes over, to keep them going until they closed.

'Selfless endurance of pain and failure,' she read. 'The destruction of one's old universe, the brave treading of deep gloomy and miserable paths – all this is as essential to the growth of man's "top-storey" as the joyous consciousness of the presence of God.'

Ellen read it again. 'The destruction of one's old universe.' Hers was destroyed. 'The selfless endurance of pain and failure.' She had to endure, but she wasn't doing it selflessly. 'The brave treading of deep gloomy and miserable paths.' She was treading them, but not bravely.

It was as if someone had spoken to her out of the silence, someone who knew, and her spirit, which had been thrashing about in resentment, anger, jealousy, self-pity, quietened itself to listen.

CHAPTER TWENTY-SIX

―――∞◇∞―――

I

Between young Madame Devoisy and middle-aged Madame Lanier there was something in the nature of friendship, though both would have been shocked to think of it as such, since both were snobbish, with a difference: Madame Devoisy looking down, Madame Lanier up. A young matron of aristocratic family was not 'friendly' with a tradesman's wife and the tradesman's wife did not expect it. But they were always glad to see each other and always had plenty to tell and to hear.

More and more frequently nowadays did Germaine say to her husband: 'Pick me up at the Librairie Lanier, will you, dear?'

'You're always there,' said Paul, but not in protest. So long as Louise was away, he didn't mind how often his wife was in the shop.

'I can wait there in comfort,' said Germaine. 'Madame Lanier understands. She's a kind woman, and really I think she is as interested in our baby as we are.'

'That's impossible,' said Paul, smiling. 'Nobody could be as interested in our baby as I am, except you.'

He was astonished by his own feelings. He had wanted
children, that was what he had married for. But never had he
expected to feel such tenderness for both mother and child.
By some mystery of marriage, his wife had become so much
part of him that he almost felt as if he were having the baby
too. He thought Germaine wonderful, so serene and smiling
through all her increasing physical discomfort. When he said
so, she kissed him and said: 'But it's worth it, silly. There's no
merit in it.'

She had put off poutings and coynesses and was a woman
now. He felt secretly humble to think he had married her
almost in condescension, comparing her unfavourably with
Louise. Louise! What undeserved luck for him that fate kept
Louise in London. He hoped she would stay there for ever.

'Ah, here is Madame Devoisy?' cried Madame Lanier one
October morning when the last leaves from the sycamore tree
at the gate of the Archevêché were scraping lightly over the
pavement. 'Good morning, dear Madame. How do you find
yourself today?'

She bustled round the counter to place a chair.

'Oh, I'm breathless,' panted Germaine, laughing.

'It is always like that towards the end, dear little Madame.
But it won't be long now, and then you will be running into the
shop just as you used to.'

'Isn't it wonderful to think I shall be bringing my baby with
me? Can I get his carriage in at the door, do you think?
Because I shall never leave him on the pavement.'

'Of course you can bring him in,' beamed Madame Lanier.
'See! The doors are double. I shall throw them wide for you.'

Germaine, smiling, pressed Madame Lanier's hand and leaned round her friend's bulk to call across the shop to Monsieur Lanier.

'Monsieur, I've brought my fountain-pen to you,' she said, taking it from her handbag and holding it aloft. 'Something's wrong. I don't know what, but you will.'

'Madame, I am at your service,' said Monsieur Lanier, coming to take the pen and carry it off to his own particular counter.

"Spécialiste du Stylo" he had written over his shop and he lived up to what he called himself. Adjusting his pince-nez he dismembered the pen with fat, agile fingers, and was at once absorbed. The women could talk unheard.

'Madame,' said Madame Lanier, leaning over the counter delightedly, 'where do you think my Louise is now?'

'I haven't an idea. Tell me.'

'New York. She has gone to New York, Madame.'

'New York!' exclaimed Germaine, with the astonishment expected of her. 'How she does travel! Has she gone with the people she lives with – North, did you say they call themselves?'

'Oh, she is with them, of course. She is quite one of the family now, you know. She says New York is wonderful, but the noise is formidable. She doesn't think they will be there long. I shall be writing to her to-day. I shall give her news of you. She always asks about you in her letters.'

'Really?' Germaine was surprised by this solicitude. 'You must thank her for me, please. Tell her I am very well and very happy, waiting eagerly for the second week in November.'

'Ah, Madame,' said Madame Lanier, pillowing her large bosom cosily on the counter. 'What a happy time this is! If only Louise could make as happy a marriage as yours or, in its humbler way, as mine!'

Germaine glanced across the shop at Monsieur Lanier, bent in such fierce concentration over the pen that all that could be seen was a mass of black hair above and beard below, divided by a pair of pince-nez. Germaine leaned towards Madame Lanier.

'Has your daughter never said anything to you about her marriage?' she asked.

'Well, strictly between ourselves,' whispered Madame Lanier, 'she had practically decided to marry André Petit when she got the news about the money the old lady had left her. She went off, as you know, to get it, and she's been there ever since. I'm afraid she has given up all idea of marrying André Petit now.'

Germaine looked puzzled.

'But she's engaged to someone in England, isn't she?'

'Mon Dieu, no,' said Madame Lanier.

'But she had a ring,' said Germaine.

'A ring!' said Madame Lanier in astonishment.

'Yes, she wore a diamond ring once when she came to our house.'

'Ah, that was the ring given to her by the old lady, Madame.'

'But she wore it on her engagement finger and when someone asked her if she was engaged she said it was a secret.'

Madame Lanier came slowly upright at the counter and gazed, open-mouthed, at Madame Devoisy.

'A secret?' she said. ' But why should she keep it secret from her parents? Engaged to someone in England? She has never spoken of anyone at all. There is no one in the family she could be engaged to. Oh, I hope if it's true, it is someone suitable and a good Catholic. But why doesn't she tell us? What is wrong with the man that she cannot be open about him? Oh, Madame, do excuse me, but I think you must be mistaken about what she said. . . .'

At that moment, Paul Devoisy appeared at the door of the shop to let his wife see that he had come with the car. Germaine called him and with a fond, possessive gesture, took his hand to draw him into the conversation.

'Paul, didn't I tell you after one of the Vente de Charité meetings that Mademoiselle Lanier had let it out that she was engaged to someone in England?'

Paul, whose policy was to deny any knowledge whatever of Louise, lifted one shoulder.

'I don't remember,' he said. 'Possibly. Why? Is the engagement announced?'

'No, no, Monsieur,' protested Madame Lanier with vehemence. 'Madame has surprised me enormously by telling me about this engagement. It is the first I have heard of it.'

'I shouldn't worry,' said Paul easily. 'My wife may have made a mistake. Perfect though she is, she sometimes does.' He smiled at Germaine and helped her out of the chair. 'I'm in a hurry, darling. I have to get back early.'

'I have not made a mistake,' said Germaine firmly. 'But don't worry, dear Madame Lanier.'

'Madame, your pen,' said Monsieur Lanier, coming to

present it with a bow. 'It is quite right now. Good day, Monsieur Paul. You are well, I hope?'

'Very, thank you, and you?'

'Monsieur Lanier, how much do I owe you?' asked Germaine.

'No charge, Madame. It was a pleasure, I assure you.'

Demurring prettily at this, Germaine was got out of the shop by her husband and for the first time Madame Lanier hurried through her farewells to be rid of her friend and customer.

'Henri,' she said, whipping round on her husband as soon as the door was closed. 'Can you imagine what Madame Devoisy has just told me? She says Louise told her last winter that she was secretly engaged to someone in England.'

Monsieur Lanier peered closely at his wife through his pince-nez. 'What?'

'She says Louise said she is secretly engaged to someone in England.'

'Mon Dieu,' he said, letting the glasses fall to the length of their black ribbon.

'But, Henri, you don't think it can be true, do you?' she asked.

'I shouldn't be at all surprised,' he said slowly. 'In fact, I think it explains everything.'

'Oh, Henri, you don't. But what is there to explain?'

'I have thought for a long time that it is very strange she doesn't come home,' he said.

'Oh, that,' said Madame Lanier, lifting her hand and letting it fall with resignation. 'She doesn't want to come home. She doesn't like it at home, papa, and we may as well admit it. But this engagement. Why doesn't she tell us? What is there to hide it for? The English are not so bad after all that one cannot admit being engaged to one. I hope he is a Catholic, Henri.'

'England is not a Catholic country,' said Monsieur Lanier gravely.

'He is not a Catholic,' said Madame Lanier. 'That's why she doesn't tell us.'

'I don't think Louise is as fervent as all that,' said her husband. 'However, she is in New York and we are here, so there is nothing for it at the moment but to go and have lunch, my dear.'

'I'll call Mademoiselle Léonie. She is in the back room this morning. Oh, Henri, I feel so agitated,' said Madame Lanier.

'I can't say I feel very tranquil myself,' he said, taking her plump arm. 'But come along. We must write at once and see if we can get our secretive daughter to disclose something of this affair.'

II

In the daytime, Louise didn't go too near the window because it made her head swim, but it was dark now and she couldn't see how high up she was. So she sat on the window-sill and looked out over the myriad lights of New York shimmering in the vast bowl of the night.

She looked at them with annoyance as if they were blazing away for nothing and so they were, so far as she was concerned. She ought to have been getting something out of this night and these lights, but she wasn't. Because Avery was drunk again.

He sprawled behind her in a chair so low that he was almost lying on the floor. He looked stupid, his shoulders thrust up over his ears. He was absolutely silent and soon he would be sick. He had this horrible habit of being sick when he had drunk too much. Louise felt a cold disgust. If he thought she was going to put up with this sort of thing, he deceived himself. She wouldn't stop his drinking yet, because if he got too sober, he mightn't marry her. But once married, he should see.

He was drinking to-night because he had botched his interview with the American publisher in the afternoon. Although it was too bad that she should have to suffer too, it served him right, thought Louise angrily. He should have done as she advised. He should have asked the American to dinner at the hotel where he could have seen her in one of her successful dresses, attracting all eyes, very soignée, very Parisian, and Avery himself, handsome in his English clothes, allowed by Louise to drink just enough to release his natural charm, but not one drop more. This Mr. Sellers would have been impressed then and would have seen that Avery was exactly the man to make contacts for him in London.

But Avery said he couldn't introduce Louise as his wife because Sellers would know she wasn't. He had seen Ellen many a time in London.

'Avery, you are stupid,' said Louise. 'What does that matter? In London, I was willing to hide with you. It was all so recent and you were known. But here, so far away, what does it matter? You must say I am your friend. In France everybody knows it is the mistresses of the ministers and other powerful men who have the influence and are seen everywhere. It is the wives, the little dowdy women, who are kept in the background there.'

Avery shook his head.

'You are stupid,' Louise told him again. 'You are ashamed of yourself, but don't behave as if you were ashamed of me, because I don't like it. I won't tolerate it, Avery.'

He wasn't ashamed of her, he muttered.

'It is because you are ashamed of yourself that everything is failing you,' said Louise. 'You must throw off this silly shame, or you will fail again here in New York.'

And he had failed, of course. His assets had been self-confidence, ability to get on with people, good looks, good humour and much charm. Where were they now? Who was going to trust this man, who looked and smelled as if he drank too much, to handle publishers and authors and agents for them? Nobody; and naturally, thought Louise angrily.

It didn't matter materially if he didn't work again. There was still plenty of money. He had told her long ago that he held the controlling interest, with his brother and sister, in the hosiery factory that had been his father's. Mr. Bennett was having to pay a considerable sum to get him out of the firm too; so there was also that, calculated Louise. And if his wife was silly enough to persist in refusing alimony, so much the better. There was plenty of money still, but if he had no work to do, no office to go to regularly, Louise would have to be too much with him. As now. He would be about all the time.

She sighed and drummed with her fingers on the window. In spite of being in New York, in spite of all her new clothes, she felt almost as bad to-night as she felt before she heard that old Mrs. North had left her the thousand pounds. That had been a great lift up, getting away with Avery had been another. Coming to New York another. But now that she was here, she was quite ready to leave it. It was enough to have been. It was really all that was necessary. It was more than Germaine had done. Germaine Devoisy was only a little provincial now compared with Louise Lanier, the despised bookseller's daughter. You might be bored in foreign places, but it made a cosmopolitan of you to have been to them.

This reflection restored her considerably. She was still living with her eyes on the Devoisys. She was always making pictures of herself as she would one day appear before them. With her rich husband in tow, she would come across them in the street or somewhere, Germaine with her pale bun of hair and the unattractive clothes of a good woman, and Louise the travelled, the finished, holding her furs up to her face. Paul could compare what he had got and what he had given up. Louise never saw further than that. She didn't try to. It was enough.

She thought about this meeting now. It was something to work and wait for. It lay ahead. It was all right. She would get to it.

And now, she decided, leaving the window-sill and stretching her hands above her head, she would answer the letter that had come from Amigny yesterday. Her father had written it, which showed how seriously they were taking the news of an engagement.

She walked over to the writing-desk and sat down. She arranged the paper, placing it precisely. Here was another letter that needed a good deal of thought, but her wits rose pleasurably to the challenge.

It really was a piece of luck that her parents had put these questions to her now. She had been wondering how to break it to them that she was going to be married and here they were, giving her an opening she never could have expected. That the engagement they had heard of had been completely fictitious didn't matter in the least.

Louise liked intrigue. She liked things to play into her hands like this, and that rather silly tale told long ago had turned up like a lucky card. She would make full use of it.

The light from the lamp shone downwards on her smooth, dark head. Her arms were bare and slender on the desk, her dress, her favourite magenta red, fitted closely over waist and bosom and spread into wide skirts as she sat. Avery was drunk; there was no one to look at her. But it really didn't matter, because she looked at herself from time to time in the mirror on the wall. She always gave as much pleasure to her own eyes as to any others. More, in fact, because she alone knew what perfect finish she had achieved.

When Avery lurched across to the room telephone to ask thickly for some seltzer-water to be sent up not a ruffle crossed Louise's brow.

'My dear parents,' her pen began to scratch. Her pens always scratched. At Netherfold, Ellen used to be astonished at them.

'There is no need for you to agitate yourselves [wrote Louise]. It is true that I am engaged and to an Englishman. But there have been difficulties and I did not want to say anything until they were over. What would have been the good of telling you about them? You could not have done anything, and for so long I have managed my own affairs, haven't I? Even now you have heard before I intended you to. I don't think it was very loyal of Madame Devoisy to make a breach of confidence. In all probability I shall be married soon after my return to London, and then, my dear parents, I shall come at once to Amigny and present my husband to you. He is charming and you will like him. But I must tell you now, dear Mamma, that we shall stay at the Hôtel de l'Ecu and not at home. There is no proper accommodation for us at home. My husband has always lived in large houses. I am sure you will agree that it is better for us to stay at the hotel. It will be less strain for you both, too.'

Her pen scratched like a mouse busily making a way through for itself. She was preparing her arrival at Amigny. Her mother would pass the news of her marriage to Germaine Devoisy. Germaine would tell Paul. He wouldn't believe it. He would think she was playing the game they had played together for years. Well, he should see. She would bring her husband with her.

'Don't be sick in here, please,' she said coldly, and getting up with a swish of her stiff silken skirts, she steered Avery into his bedroom and shut the door. She returned to the desk.

CHAPTER TWENTY-SEVEN

⟨⟩⟨⟩⟨⟩

At Mershott School, morning prayers were in progress. Miss Beldon, the Headmistress, tall, broad, fair and happy-looking, was coming to the end of the reading for the day. Below her in the hall, the girls kept as quiet as they could, though a continual shallow ripple ran over the white-bloused ranks as hair was tossed back, eyes darted up, down, sideways, slight unnecessary coughs were suppressed, smiles suppressed too. But they tried to keep still and while, with one part of her mind, Miss Beldon commended them to Almighty God, with the other part, she affectionately recognised the effort her children made to subdue their natural exuberance to the discipline of prayers.

'And there are also many other things which Jesus did, the which if they should be written, every one, I suppose that even the world itself could not contain the books that should be written,' she finished, and regretting as usual those unwritten books, she closed the Bible and looked out over the girls waiting to sing the hymn.

A shaft of sunlight picked out one young face, and Miss Beldon was startled. The girl was looking sideways and upwards with an expression of desperate unhappiness. Who was it? Surely not Anne North – looking like that? She was a gay child, full of careless happiness. But it was Anne North, almost unrecognisable from some trouble or other. At that moment, Anne turned her head and Miss Beldon hastily looked elsewhere. She knew girls didn't like to be scrutinised.

The blessing over, Miss Beldon left the rostrum and took her place at the door of the hall. She put herself there every day so that the girls, filing past, should smile and say good morning. In greeting her, Miss Beldon meant her girls to learn to greet other people. It wouldn't do to speak of it, because it had an old-fashioned sound, but they should imperceptibly acquire graciousness. A little graciousness in the streets in these hasty days would be an improvement, Miss Beldon considered.

The girls were passing her.

'Good morning, Miss Beldon. Good morning, Miss Beldon. . . .'

Miss Beldon waited for Anne North. She came up, she made a wide smile that meant nothing and hurried on, escaping. It's not that she's ill, thought Miss Beldon – she's unhappy. The hall emptied and Miss Beldon went to her own room, a pleasant place full of flowers with a bright fire and Bibby, the tabby cat, already comfortably installed on her desk.

Miss Beldon stroked him thoughtfully. How could she send for Anne North without alarming her? On what pretext? To be sent for to the Head caused a tremor in the youthful breast, Miss Beldon knew. She always had to move carefully with her girls. They would shy away at the slightest mistake on her part. Remembering her own girlhood, she knew, and was still largely baffled by, the mysterious surgings and imaginings, the fluctuations of wild happiness and despair, the light and darkness of adolescence. She carefully considered her approach to Anne North.

When the message was delivered in class that the Head wanted to see her, Anne went white, but got up from her desk and made for the door. All her fears flew to her throat. What was it? Had her father come? Or her mother? Had the Head found out? Was it the divorce? She clenched her hands and a light sweat broke out along the hair-line of her forehead.

'Come in, Anne,' called Miss Beldon. 'Sit down, dear. Isn't it a lovely morning? Look at Bibby. He does make himself comfortable, doesn't he?'

Anne smiled, her lip catching on her dry teeth. She sat down and waited, hardly breathing.

Miss Beldon's hand moved backwards and forwards over Bibby's accepting back. She was delighted to have found a pretext to send for the child.

'You were going to do conversation with a French girl during the holidays, weren't you?' she said. 'I thought I would like to hear how you got on.'

She had been pleased with her approach, but she saw at once that it was dreadfully and unaccountably the wrong one.

The girl's eyes stared into hers with horror. Her lips were white and a pulse beat wildly in her young throat.

Miss Beldon was so taken aback she couldn't speak. What had she done? What was it? She must have blundered right into the trouble. The poor, poor child . . .

The cat chose that very moment to jump off the desk and make for the window.

'All right, Bibby,' said Miss Beldon, gladly getting out of her chair and crossing the room. 'I'll open the window for you. There you are,' she said with exaggerated solicitude. 'You go out.'

She leaned out into the air herself. 'It *is* a lovely morning, Anne,' she said. She closed the window and fussed with the curtains for a moment.

Anything to give the child time to recover herself.

She went back to her desk, speaking casually.

'So you didn't do French, dear. Well, it doesn't matter as it happens. Because I've been thinking it might be as well to drop it altogether and do Latin instead for the examination.'

By this time she was seated and allowed herself to look at the girl again. The terror, or whatever it was, was subsiding. Anne was able to look back at her.

'Yes, Miss Beldon,' she said almost in a whisper.

'But you know,' said Miss Beldon lightly, 'you'll have to work hard. You've never been very serious about Latin, have you? I think you'll need extra coaching. I think I'll take you on for a bit myself, shall I? Would you like to come and do an occasional lesson in here with me and Bibby? How would that do?'

Anne managed a better smile this time.

'Thank you, Miss Beldon, I would like it.'

'We'll start on . . . let me see . . .' Miss Beldon consulted her engagement pad. 'We'll start on Thursday. Half-past ten for half an hour. I'll arrange it with your form-mistress. If that isn't Bibby wanting to come in again. What a cat! Just open the window for him, dear, will you?'

Anne in her turn was glad to go to the window to open it, shut it, stoop to pat the cat. The sweat was dry on her brow now and under her eyes the wild beatings were dying down.

'Shall I go now, Miss Beldon?' she said.

'Yes, dear, run along,' said Miss Beldon comfortably.

When the door closed, she sank back in her chair. What could have happened to make the child look like that? What was it? What could be done for her without forcing her confidence or letting it be seen that her trouble was known?

In between the comings and goings of her secretary, the knockings on her door, the arrival of first this and then that, the interviews, the incidents of her busy morning, Miss Beldon's thoughts reverted to the problem of Anne North. When morning school was over, she sent for her form-mistress.

'There's certainly something wrong,' said that young woman. 'I was coming to see you about it. She's quite changed. I don't know what's happened. She works hard, which she's never done before. She was so friendly with Phyllida Greene – Pug, you know – but now she's always off by herself. She was such a persuasive teasing sort of a child. Very lovable. I don't know what it is.'

'Something must have gone wrong at home,' said Miss Beldon.

'But her parents are so nice,' said Miss Horner. 'She brought them to see me last half-term. I should say they are an exceptionally happy family.'

'Things go wrong,' said Miss Beldon. 'Even in exceptionally happy families.'

At the end of the afternoon, she sent for the mistress in charge of the school drama.

'Miss Blackmore, I know you've been hesitating between Shirley Craven and Anne North for Beatrice,' she said. 'I wish you'd give the part to Anne, will you?'

'Certainly,' said Miss Blackmore with enthusiasm. 'I think she'll be the better choice. But you know what you said about the less favoured.'

'I know, I know,' said Miss Beldon. 'But Anne North needs to be taken out of herself in a big way. Don't tell anybody I used that reprehensible expression! After all,' said Miss Beldon, it suddenly dawning upon her, 'she was rather like a young Beatrice, wasn't she? I think it would do her good to get something of her old self back.'

Miss Blackmore smiled. What she liked about Miss Beldon was the way she *worked* for a child.

When the names of the cast for *Much Ado About Nothing* were given out in Hall, Anne blushed and dropped her head for a moment. Then she threw her hair back and smiled sideways to Pug, who stood beside her. The old interest held. In spite of everything, it was still there. Pug, so happy to be smiled at in the old way, felt surreptitiously for Anne's hand and gave it a squeeze. In the ranks, heads bobbed forwards and backwards, eyebrows signalled congratulations, smiles flashed and Anne had to smile back. She had found her place again, she felt the warmth of companionship. She was glad she had come back.

'Mummy, can you believe it? I'm Beatrice in the play,' she wrote on Sunday. '"Beatrice." What a part! The drawback is that Benedick has to be a boy from Overingham. I can't think why we have to have boys. We've never had them before. But I'm not going to bother about Benedick yet. We don't have to rehearse with the boys for weeks, thank goodness. We start reading the play to-morrow. Isn't it wonderful?'

When the letter fell through the box at Netherfold, Ellen stooped to pick it up with a sigh. Another duty letter. They had all been short and stiff since Anne went back. But when she opened this one over her solitary coffee, colour and life rushed into her face at the first line.

'Oh,' she breathed, eagerly reading. 'Oh, Anne. . . .'

Smiling, her eyes flew over the letter. Help certainly came from unexpected quarters. Someone had done exactly the right thing for the child. It hadn't been a mistake, after all, to make her go back to school.

Ellen went straight to the bookshelves and took out the Comedies. She had forgotten *Much Ado* and wanted to see at once what her young Beatrice had to say. She made more coffee and sat down with the book. She could read as long as she liked. There was nothing to do for anyone. Nobody to get off in the mornings, no bed but her own to make, no meals to think about or order. The importance had gone out of housekeeping. There were no morning conversations now over the telephone with the fishmonger or the grocer, and she had enjoyed those.

'What can you let me have to-day?' she used to say. 'I've four hungry people to feed.'

'I've got some lovely baby halibut, Madam,' said Mr. Pye, the fishmonger.

'Baby' sounded like murder of the innocents, Ellen always thought.

'Pricey, I know,' continued Mr. Pye. 'But worth it, Madam, if you'll take my advice.'

'You know I always do,' said Ellen, and they were mutually pleased with each other.

'You can have a fourteen-pound tin of custard-cream biscuits this week, Madam,' said Mr. Perkins, the grocer.

'A *tin*,' Ellen almost shrieked. 'I haven't heard of a tin of biscuits for years.'

'No more had I,' said Mr. Perkins. 'But I've just got delivery of half a dozen and I thought you might like one.'

'Indeed I would,' said Ellen fervently. 'Thank you for thinking of me.'

Ellen had liked shopping, and now it was another thing that had gone. So much, big and little, had gone with Avery. She sometimes argued with herself that it was impossible that he could have made so much difference to her daily life. But he had. She felt an immense loss. Worst of all, she felt blank at not being able to love him any more. She refused to think about him. Every time he came into her mind, she put him out.

But this morning the letter from Anne made her happy. She felt suddenly fit to go out, somewhere, anywhere, into the sun and air. She put the play down and looked round the room, wondering where to go, and was struck again by the silence of the house. Dust falling on tables and chairs, clocks ticking time away and she drifting on helpless, planless towards the divorce. She was paralysed until the divorce should be got over.

She must go out, but she must do something definite. No good wandering about the fields with her heavy thoughts. To make something for herself to do, she decided to go into the town and get some books out. No circulating library would do for Ellen, she needed the larger range of the Public Library. She hadn't been into it since Avery went, but now the thought of finding something good on the shelves woke a faint interest. She got her car out. She wouldn't be able to keep it much longer. She would be sorry to part with it, but she couldn't afford it now. After the divorce . . .

'Ellen, I beg you to take at least six hundred a year from me,' Avery had written from New York, obliged to write himself since his lawyers had failed to get her to accept alimony. 'I beg you to take it, if only to make me feel better about all this.'

He had put it in an unfortunate way. She only saw it as another piece of his old self-consideration. To make him feel better, she thought contemptuously, and tore the letter up. Besides, the postmark was enough. New York. He and Louise were enjoying themselves, first here, then there, London, Paris, La Baule, New York, while his family agonised over the breaking-up of their home and their lives.

She drove into the town now, and as she crossed the road to the Library, a woman passing in a car waved detainingly, pulled up at the pavement and got out. She was middle-aged and fancily dressed, with a hat with a veil on.

'Oh, Mrs. North, I don't suppose you know me, do you?' she said squirmingly, as if no one could possibly know her, she was so insignificant.

'No, I don't think so,' said the surprised Ellen.

'But of course I know you. By sight, that is,' said the woman, as if everybody must know anyone so important as Ellen. She was smiling with her head on one side and Ellen wished she would put it straight. 'I do hope you'll excuse me making myself known to you like this,' she said. 'But I just wanted to ask you, when you're selling your house, Mrs. North – will you give me the first refusal?'

Ellen's face stiffened.

'The house isn't for sale,' she said.

'Oh, I know, Mrs. North,' said the woman placatingly. 'Not yet. Only I just thought if I put in a word beforehand, there would be a better chance for us. I mean, everybody knows . . . I mean, I don't suppose you'll want to go on living there by yourself, will you? Yours is such a charming house, Mrs. North. I've always said to my hubby, if ever that house comes into the market, I've said, get it. And when I saw you just now, I thought it was just my opportunity. I couldn't resist getting out of the car and putting in a word for myself, Mrs. North.'

'You should have resisted,' said Ellen coldly. 'It would have been kinder of you.'

She left the woman gaping after her and went into the Library. Her heart thumped heavily again. The slightest thing set it off nowadays, and she was furious with the woman.

'My house . . . my house . . . as if I would ever let it go to a person like that,' she kept saying, walking round the

335

bookshelves without seeing anything. She knew she couldn't live at Netherfold, but it was hateful to have everybody else knowing it too. People must be standing around waiting to profit from her misfortune.

'My house . . . my dear house . . .'

She came to a sudden halt. The house was Avery's. When she was gone, he would bring Louise to it. Strangely enough this had not once occurred to Ellen. Now that it did, a deeper sense than ever of being supplanted and dispossessed came over her. She left the books and drove home.

And there, come by the second post, was a letter from her lawyers giving her the date of the court at which her divorce case would be heard.

CHAPTER TWENTY-EIGHT

——⋙◇⋘——

I

Ellen drove through the quiet country to the county town. The glow of autumn was gone, the fields were dark from the plough, the trees bare, the hedges dusky.

She had driven along this road for years with Avery. Whenever they had special shopping to do, or wanted to go to the theatre, or merely have à Saturday morning out, they had driven to Benhampton; and always, in autumn, she had made him stop at one particular place, so that she could cut dog-wood from the hedge. They both got out of the car and she with a pair of scissors she had brought for the purpose, and he with his penknife, cut long whips of dog-wood from the hedge. This was one of the times Avery showed at his most endearing. He cut carefully, choosing exactly the sort of shoots she wanted.

'Here's a good one,' he would say. 'Half a minute, I must have that one.'

'Oh, lovely,' Ellen used to say happily at his armful. 'Isn't dog-wood wonderful stuff, being dark red and delicate like that all winter in the vase in the sitting-room, and breaking out into those little painted fresh-green leaves in the spring? I'm always fascinated to think spring's lurking there all winter and will appear at exactly the right time!'

But to-day she was alone, and when, far off, she saw the dog-wood burning in the hedge, she accelerated and drove past without looking. She wondered if she would ever be able to take pleasure in things for themselves. For twenty years she had evidently taken pleasure in things so that she could use them for her husband and children, pass them on to them in the way of beauty or food or comfort. Nearly as bad as Louise, she thought grimly. Flowers, trees, the house, the garden, other people, everything had delighted her while she could look at them from the standpoint of personal happiness. Now they didn't mean anything.

She drove through the ranks of post-war, makeshift houses and bungalows that disfigured the flanks of the picturesque old town and into the heart of it. She parked her car. She had to ask her way to the Assize Court. It turned out to be almost next to the photographer's who had taken the children's photographs from babyhood upwards, and once a family group into which she had pressed even Avery. The Assize Court had been waiting darkly alongside all the time and she, unknowing, had been coming up to it through the years. Now she had to go in.

She stood outside, trying to calm her frantic heart. At last she went through the old door, into a lofty hall where there was nothing but the white walls and arched windows of the seventeenth century building. She stood in the empty silence. She thought there would have been policemen about, someone to ask, but there was nobody.

Two women came through the door, one in a red beret, the other dabbing nervously at her mouth with a handkerchief.

'Do you know where the court is?' asked Ellen.

'We have to wait in here,' said the woman in the red beret, leading the way to an inner hall.

'We sit on this bench and we wait here,' she said.

There were already five or six people, one man among women, on the bench. Ellen sat down at one end. The room had a Beggar's Opera air, with little ribbed pillars, painted white, and walls white above and panelled in black oak below. A little dock, on wheels, with wrought-iron rails round it had been pushed into a corner. It was all very toy and elegant.

'We have to wait here until we are called,' whispered the woman in the red beret, taking pity on Ellen. Ellen's heart gave its sickening beat every time the door opened.

At last young Mr. Letchworth came to fetch her and she followed him into the little court-room. There were only about a dozen people in the high-backed oak seats, polished by centuries of sittings and rubbings. In a few moments Ellen stood in a small raised place, she didn't know whether it was a dock or not. She was so blinded by the sunlight that shone directly into her eyes that she could see the judge only as something black through a haze. Above her the high white ceiling had harps and grapes in lovely relief, designed surely for happier occasions than this.

A man handed her a Bible in a benevolent off-handed way as if to say: 'Just a matter of routine. We have to do it, but no need to bother.'

The judge, a tired, kind man with his wig a little askew, looked with sympathy at the woman below him. Among the cheap women craving the court's discretion for frequent adulteries, among the men only too glad to be ridding themselves of unsatisfactory partners and also craving discretion, here was one petitioner with blind uplifted face seeking a divorce she didn't want and breaking her heart about it.

'Were you married to Avery Charles North on Tuesday, the fifth of June, 1930, at St. Thomas's Church, Mayton, and was your maiden name Ellen Pauline Denham . . .?'

It had begun.

'Avery Charles North,' called the man under the judge's chair, rising.

He waited a moment.

'No answer,' he called.

No, there was no answer. Avery was not there to save her from this, to call out that it wasn't true. Her face lifted to the judge, she made the answers. It took about ten minutes to undo what had been knitted together for twenty years.

'That's all, Mrs. North,' said young Mr. Letchworth, appearing from somewhere. 'It's over.'

She went out into the street a 'free woman' and stood on the edge of the pavement looking to left and right in bewilderment. She couldn't remember where she had left her car. That frightened her badly and she stood there, letting the traffic pour past. She felt as if she were struggling through a dense cloud of feathers in search of her memory, and it wasn't there. Such a thing had never happened to her before. The world had become suddenly strange and she was almost surprised to recognise the word 'café' on a shop front across the road. She knew she must get into somewhere and sit down until she could remember about the car. When a gap came in the traffic, she crossed the road, and went into the warmth and the strong smell of coffee that pervaded the café.

She made for an empty table in a corner and sat down with relief, as if she had been on her feet for hours. A waitress came and took a pencil out of her perm to record her order and Ellen said, 'Coffee, please.' Then remembering she hadn't had any breakfast, added, 'Cakes too, please.' She supposed that cakes were all one could get in a place like this at half-past eleven in the morning.

She sat there, not thinking, waiting for her heart to calm itself and half-way through the cup of pale coffee – for though the smell of coffee was strong in the place the coffee itself proved to be weak – she remembered where she had put the car and relief flooded warmly over her. She took a mouthful of cake, but put her fork down. It was such a dishonest cake, she thought, looking at it spilling sawdust on her plate. What a world where husbands deserted their homes and café-owners palmed off stale cakes, she thought, but dispassionately, as if she were coming round from a faint.

She asked for another cup of coffee to keep herself in countenance for sitting there so long.

'What am I?' she asked herself. 'Shorn of husband and children. What am I?'

She seemed to be so null now, without her marriage, that she tried to remember what she had been before it. She remembered an eager girl, very green, very gullible, running forward into life, with almost missionary zeal, which used to amuse Avery because it was so much at variance with her looks and her passion for dancing. She wanted to 'do something' for somebody, she said.

'But what can you do, dear little Ellen,' he said tenderly.

'I want to help prostitutes,' she had said and he had kept his face expressionless under the impact of the word and said:

'But I don't think they want to be helped.'

'I'm sure they do. I'm sure some do,' said Ellen. 'I shall go up to them and ask them.'

'I bet you don't,' said Avery.

And he had been right. One summer night when she had arranged to meet her brother in Piccadilly and by some mistake he didn't turn up, she waited alone and for a long time while women walked up and down on high heels, their eyes glinting, their mouths dark under the lights, pursuing their trade. Ellen grew more and more panic-stricken and when one of the women, almost as young as herself, asked her casually how she liked the job, Ellen rushed at a passing bus and was carried a long way in the wrong direction before she dared to get off and commit herself to the streets again to get on another.

After that, she didn't talk of helping prostitutes again but thought with passionate pity of the black people. But Africa was such a long way off and very soon Avery was turning her young face with a determined and persistent hand towards himself. He had made her think of him and had pursued her until she thought of nothing and no one else.

'No,' thought Ellen. 'I can't find any key in what I was then to what I could do now. Except that I would still like to do something for somebody as well as earn my own living. But I've got to make a home for Hugh at the week-ends and Anne in the holidays, and I must,' she thought guiltily, 'be somewhere where Roma can be too.'

How could she find a place that would fulfil all these conditions? How could she even start to look for it? She had no idea. She had never put such a question to herself before and the helplessness she felt from not being able to find an answer gave her the awful blank feeling she had had about the car.

She put her problems out of her mind and just sat there in the corner, on the papier-mâché chair, putting in time until she should recover sufficiently to drive herself home. She sat slackly, emptily, all the old fallen away and no new formulated.

All at once, claiming her attention as oddly as a twig, say, rising suddenly out of a pond, the thought of Mrs. Brockington occurred to her. Mrs. Brockington! The very name revived her. She must go at once. She picked up her bag and gloves, called to the waitress, paid her bill and hurried to her car. Driving away, she couldn't understand why, during all these awful weeks, she hadn't thought of Mrs. Brockington before.

The truth was that she hadn't been ready to think of her. In seeking Mrs. Brockington, she was seeking recovery, and she hadn't admitted, before this, any idea that she could and must recover.

The afternoon at Somerton was a time of siesta for the old
ladies, in their rooms, and when Ellen turned the iron ring on
the door and let herself into the hall, there was no one there.
Books and knitting bags guarded their owners' chairs for
them and the fire was made up so that, with a poke at tea-
time, it would blaze up warmly.

Ellen stood on the stone hearth, as she had so often stood
when she stayed in the house with the children during the war
and afterwards from time to time when Avery was in America.
She had an affection for this old house, which reasserted itself
every time she came into it. It should have been such a
pleasant place to live in, and so, materially, it was, but she
feared Mrs. Beard spoilt it by her sharp, uncertain temper.
Ellen winced to think of it; the old were so defenceless.

She was so familiar with the house that after going in
search of Mrs. Beard and not finding her, she went upstairs
and stood outside Mrs. Brockington's door to listen. Mrs.
Brockington did not lie down in the afternoons, because
once down she found it difficult to get up, but Ellen didn't
want to disturb her if she was asleep in her chair. She put her
ear to the door and by and by heard the turning of a page and
knocked.

'Come in,' called Mrs. Brockington and turned from where
she sat wrapped in shawls by the window to see who it was.

'Ellen! Why, my dear child!'

She lifted her crippled hands and put them round Ellen as
she bent to kiss her.

'Ellen, I wondered what could have happened to you . . .'

'I know. I haven't written for weeks . . . but I've been in such trouble . . .'

'Oh, what is it? Is it one of the children?' Mrs. Brockington drew back to look into Ellen's face with apprehension.

'No, it isn't that. Nobody's dead. I'll tell you.'

'Ellen, you've been ill. I can see. You're so thin.'

'No, I'm not ill. I'll tell you.'

She took some books from a chair and brought it up. She sat down and took one of Mrs. Brockington's hands in hers to rub it gently while she talked. She always did this when they were alone together, in the hope of smoothing away the pain. She was glad to do it now because somehow it made it easier to tell her tale.

It was soon told. A few words contained the loss of her husband and her home. Mrs. Brockington's frail cheek flushed and paled as she listened.

'Ellen, what a shock this is. I can't believe it.'

'I can't believe it myself,' said Ellen. 'Not even after to-day. I was so sure that I meant as much to Avery as he meant to me. And yet you see it turns out that I'm the one who hasn't mattered to him at all. I'm the one,' she repeated. 'He still loves the children. I know he could never do anything but love Anne, but he loves Hugh too, because he's given up his place at the office so that Hugh can go there. Even though Hugh won't have anything to do with him and won't let him send him to Cambridge, Avery can still put Hugh before himself. Though of course,' Ellen said wearily, 'he may not want to work now. He may want to spend all his time with

Louise. I don't know. I don't know anything about him now. I never did know anything about him.'

'Oh, Ellen, I am so sorry about it all,' said Mrs. Brockington sadly. 'With marriages and homes breaking up on all sides, I thought yours at least was safe. I thought you were so happy.'

'I was happy,' said Ellen. 'No one could have been happier. But it was an illusion.'

'No, you were really happy. You had twenty years of real happiness. It was a good allowance, wasn't it?'

'Yes, looking round on other people's lives I suppose it was,' admitted Ellen.

They were silent together. During Ellen's tale, the old woman saw or thought she saw that it was the child, Anne, who was keeping her parents apart. But she said nothing. It was too late. The divorce had happened. She wouldn't throw Ellen into worse agitation and confusion by saying that Avery might not have wanted it at all.

'What shall I do?' said Ellen. 'What shall I do now?'

'You must go forward,' said Mrs. Brockington. 'You must go on with love and courage, Ellen, and trust to God to carry you forward through your life.'

'I haven't your faith,' said Ellen. 'I have the start of faith, but I never seem to grow in it.'

'I think,' said Mrs. Brockington, considering this, 'I think the way to grow in faith is to behave as if all God's promises are true, and miraculously, you find that they are.'

Ellen still looked bleak and unhappy.

'My dear, dear Ellen,' said the old woman. 'I know you

think all happiness is over for you. I once thought so too. But I tell you that sitting here in this overcrowded room, my husband, my sons, and my home gone, I am often so happy, so companioned by what I humbly but boldly *know* to be the Spirit of God Himself that I could burst out singing. And I often do.'

Mrs. Brockington leaned back in her chair and smiled radiantly at Ellen, and Ellen began to smile in response. This was what she needed to hear. This promise. Warmth and hope stole into her heart. She went on stroking Mrs. Brockington's hands.

'And in the meantime,' said Mrs. Brockington, 'don't go back to-night. Stay here with me, so that we can think out something practical. I can lend you everything you need.'

Ellen considered this. There was nothing for her to go home for.

'Except my little cat,' she said. 'And she's very sensible. She'll go to William if I'm not there to feed her.'

'Then it's settled,' said Mrs. Brockington and at that moment the gong went for tea.

'Switch off the radiator, will you, dear?' said Mrs. Brockington. 'And hand me my lace shawl. I don't go down in this woollen one. How nice it is to have you to wait on me.'

As Ellen went slowly down the staircase with Mrs. Brockington on her arm, she felt new and strange. She was without all her advantages and privileges now, and the world seemed different for that. But of course the old ladies clustered round the fire didn't know it and greeted her as usual with cries of welcome and surprise. How was she, they asked. How were the children? How was her husband? And why hadn't she been to see them this summer? While Ellen was answering or eluding their questions, a day-woman brought in the teapots, white for China, brown for Indian, and put them on the round table to the left of the fire. In a moment, Mrs. Beard came in, bringing a cake she had made herself in spite of being in a bad temper all day.

'Well, I never,' she cried at the sight of Ellen. 'How did *you* get in? What a stranger you are! All summer you've never been near us . . .'

Her sharp eyes were so arrested by Ellen's face that she forgot what she was saying, but recovering herself, turned to the table and began to cut up the cake with a quick, capable hand.

'You like China, don't you, Mrs. North?' she said, pouring out one cup and leaving the old ladies to fend for themselves as usual. She brought Ellen's tea to her and took another sharp look at her.

'What's gone wrong here?' she wondered.

Aloud she said: 'You're never going to drive all that way back to-night, are you? I should think you'd better stay here.'

'Mrs. Brockington's just suggested the same thing,' said Ellen. 'And I would like to stay if you can do with me.'

'We can do with you all right,' said Mrs. Beard. 'But I must go and catch Phœbe before she goes, or I'll have the bed to make up myself. All the staff sleep out here, you know. If you'll come round to the office any time between after tea and six o'clock, say, I'll take you up.'

'What a lovely cake, Mrs. Beard,' said old Mrs. Fish ingratiatingly and Mrs. Beard snapped her eyes at her and went out.

III

When Ellen went to the room Mrs. Beard called the office, Mrs. Beard wasn't there, but on the top of the desk lay the county evening newspaper and the first thing Ellen saw, looking down, was: "Local Decree" and her own name. She was standing with the paper in her hand when Mrs. Beard came in.

'I knew something was wrong as soon as I saw you,' said Mrs. Beard. 'Now I know what it is and I'm sorry. You're the last person I'd ever have thought it would happen to. Sit down. Will you have a whisky and soda? It'd do you good. Smoke?' said Mrs. Beard, offering a packet of cigarettes.

'I don't smoke and I don't drink,' said Ellen. 'Though I've often wished lately I did both.'

'Well, it's never too late,' said Mrs. Beard, lighting a cigarette from the one she had just finished. 'The worst of it is once you've started, you can't stop. Drink's nothing to me, but smoking's my ruin. I've always got a cigarette in my mouth. I spend pounds a week on them and I've got an awful cough. Do you know I cough up *squares* of phlegm,' said Mrs. Beard, looking deeply at Ellen. 'However,' said Mrs. Beard, waving smoke aside, 'to go back to you. What are you going to do with yourself now?'

'I don't know,' said Ellen.

'Is the house yours?' asked Mrs. Beard in a practical way.

'No,' said Ellen.

'What alimony are you getting?'

'None.'

'None?' said Mrs. Beard, astounded. 'None,' she repeated. 'How on earth's that? Did you do something you didn't ought to?'

Ellen shook her head. 'I won't take alimony,' she said.

'You won't take alimony?' repeated Mrs. Beard incredulously, and stared at this phenomenon before her. 'You won't take alimony? Have you gone off your rocker?'

Ellen sat and let herself be stared at.

'D'you know how hard money is to come by for women like us?' said Mrs. Beard. 'We're not the new sort of women, with University degrees in Economics, like those women who speak on the Radio nowadays, girls who can do anything. We're ordinary women, who married too young to get a training, and we've spent the best years of our lives keeping house for our husbands. Not that we didn't enjoy it, but now you're out on your ear like me at over forty. My husband died and didn't leave me a cent, so I had to work. But yours is living and he's bound by law to provide for you.'

'Why should he?' murmured Ellen.

'Why should he?' said Mrs. Beard indignantly. 'Because he took the best years of your life, and your youth and looks. . . .'

'Don't speak as if I had been a sort of kept woman,' said Ellen. 'Where there's no more love, I couldn't take money. Besides, I'm too young to be anybody's pensioner. I have two hundred a year of my own. I'll work for the rest.'

'What at?' said Mrs. Beard.

'Well, like you, I can only do something connected with housekeeping. I'd like, eventually, to do a job like yours. How did you start?'

Mrs. Beard lit another cigarette from the one she had just finished and threw the stub with a practised hand into the fire. She looked thoughtfully at Ellen, sniffing once or twice.

'If you're serious, medea,' she said, 'there's a job here right now, waiting for you.'

'What d'you mean – here?' said Ellen, leaning forward in instant interest. 'What job?'

'Assistant to me, of course,' said Mrs. Beard. 'I've been trying to get somebody for months, but of course nobody'll come. It's too damned quiet, but you like the place. You may be the answer to prayer, medea. I'm going off my rocker, I can tell you, with all I have to do. From your point of view, it's a good idea too, it seems to me. You can have your daughter here in the holidays. You'll be learning the ropes. I know I've got a bad temper, but you'll just have to put up with it. I might be worse. What do you say to it? Four pounds a week and your keep.'

'I say yes,' said Ellen without hesitation. 'I'll come like a shot if you think the committee or whatever it is will have me.'

'I know they will,' said Mrs. Beard calmly. 'They do whatever I say. They've got enough sense for that.'

'Oh – wait,' said Ellen, ' I've got one condition. Don't laugh – but I must bring our horse too and my little cat.'

'Horse?' said Mrs. Beard. 'What an expense.'

'It's Anne's horse. Her father will pay for keep and all that.'

'Well, I've no objection,' said Mrs. Beard. 'There's plenty of grass about here, and the old stables are empty. There's everything, if you come to think of it, isn't there?'

'There really seems to be,' breathed Ellen.

'But don't get the idea that it's all beer and skittles for all that,' counselled Mrs. Beard. 'You won't like getting up at seven o'clock in the morning. . . .'

'I've done it for years,' said Ellen.

'And being at my beck and call,' continued Mrs. Beard firmly. 'And the old dears will drive you dotty. At least they do me. First one's in bed, then another's in bed. They're always losing things and pestering me about them. They've all got fads and fancies. The last one that came, Mrs. Hadfield, hid butter in her room till you could smell it on the landing; you know what it's like – like sick, isn't it?' said Mrs. Beard with one of her startling similes. 'I told her, I said, next time you get any butter sent you, for God's sake bring it to the table and get it eaten up before it stinks the place out. Well, when are you going to start?'

'As soon as I've cleared up my things at – at Netherfold,' said Ellen, who had been going to say 'home.' 'I must divide up the things. But is the job really definite?' she asked incredulously.

'Well, we'll clinch it,' said Mrs. Beard, reaching for the telephone. 'I'll put a call through to the Chairman of the Trust at once. When I work, I work fast,' she said, dialling the exchange.

Ellen kept her eyes on Mrs. Beard. She was both excited and bewildered. It had all been so quick. Was she actually on the verge of getting her first job?

Mrs. Beard asked for a London number.

'Of course, he may be out,' she said, the telephone to her ear. Even waiting for a call, she had to smoke, and manœuvred with one hand to get a cigarette out of the packet into her mouth. She had hardly lit it before the call came through.

'Quick work,' she remarked. 'Is Mr. Somers in? The hotel speaking.'

She nodded to Ellen and waited again. She was enjoying herself, being very much the Manageress.

'That you, Mr. Somers? Mrs. Beard speaking. No, everything's quite all right, thanks. But I've got a chance of an assistant and I want your permission to take it. Well, you know what I do here. It's too much for me. Yes, well, that's very nice of you. I'm glad I'm appreciated,' said Mrs. Beard, with a wink offside to Ellen. 'It's a Mrs. North I want to engage. She's stayed here as a guest many a time. I know her very well. She's a nice type of person.' Mrs Beard held the receiver to her bosom and turned to Ellen. 'How old are you?' she said.

'Forty-three,' stammered Ellen.

Mrs. Beard put the telephone back to her ear.

'She's forty-three, but active. She's had a bit of bad luck. She's giving her home up. Her husband went off with a French girl. Man in good position too. She's just divorced him. Well, I'll write fully to-morrow. I just wanted to clinch the matter at once, you understand me. We fixed the salary when

I sent the advertisement in, didn't we? You all right, Mr. Somers? No coughs or colds or anything like that?'

Ellen leaned urgently over the desk.

'Ask him about the horse,' she whispered. 'The *horse*.'

'Oh, Mr. Somers,' Mrs. Beard called out. 'Mrs. North wants to know if she can bring her daughter's horse? It can go in the park, I suppose, can't it? You've no objection? Good. Goodbye, Mr. Somers, take care of yourself.'

'Nice old man,' she said, putting the telephone down and turning round with satisfaction to Ellen. 'What's the matter?' she said sharply.

Ellen changed her face quickly.

'Nothing,' she said.

'You want to come, don't you?' asked Mrs. Beard suspiciously.

'Indeed I do,' said Ellen, rallying. It had been a shock to hear herself – her precious self – described as a nice type of person whose husband had gone off with a French girl. Forty-three, but active.

She wanted to laugh, to rush off and tell Avery and laugh till she cried. But, holding on to the back of the chair, she suddenly had such a shattering vision of herself, as she was, not as she fancied herself, that all impulse to laugh left her. That she should have thought the description funny showed the extent of her vanity and self-importance. She admitted, in all soberness, that it was a perfectly proper description.

'What did you want to look like that for?' asked Mrs. Beard. 'You looked as if you had seen a ghost.'

'Far from it. Just the opposite,' said Ellen. 'But never mind. I've had rather a bad day, you know.'

'You have, medea,' agreed Mrs. Beard. 'I should go and have a good lay down before dinner. We'll talk to-morrow. Number seventeen, I've put you in, next to your friend, old Mrs. B. It'll be nice for you being here with her, won't it? And nice for her, too. She can't do up her back hair so well now, and you'll be able to pop in and help her. I think you and me will get on all right,' said Mrs. Beard expansively. 'And there's prospects here for you, you know. Oh, there's prospects. I shan't stop much longer. I'm fed up with the place. I am really.'

'You've been saying that for a long time,' said Ellen.

'Yes, but I've meant it,' said Mrs. Beard. 'Nobody believes me, but I've meant it. But what chance have I had of going to look at other places? I've been tied hand and foot here. There was a good advert in the paper only this morning. See,' said Mrs. Beard, opening a drawer in the desk and bringing out a folded newspaper. '"Manageress wanted. Small select hotel Brighton, etc. . . ." Brighton! Just my cup of tea. But there'll be others, and when you come, I'll be able to leave you in charge and pop off and have a look at them for myself. Then when I find something decent, I'll take myself off and leave you to it. How's that?' She laughed heartily and lit another cigarette. 'But go and have a lay down. You look as if you're dropping on your feet.'

'No, let me help you. I'd like to.'

'No, thank you,' said Mrs. Beard firmly. 'I couldn't do with you about. The evening women will be arriving in a minute, if they're not here already. So make yourself scarce, please, and go and be a guest as long as you can. I only wish I could.'

Ellen went, not to lie down but to find Mrs. Brockington, who was in her room, making her necessarily slow and difficult preparations for dinner.

'You're nearly finished,' said Ellen, self-reproachfully. 'And I meant to do everything for you to-night, but you'll never guess what I've been doing. I've been getting myself hired to come here, actually here, as assistant to Mrs. Beard. I'm coming as soon as I get my things cleared up at home. Yes, and I get four pounds a week and my keep and I can bring Roma and Moppet. Anne can be here during the holidays and Hugh at the week-ends as often as he can come, as guests of course. All my immediate problems have been solved by Mrs. Beard at one swoop.'

'Now isn't that queer?' breathed Mrs. Brockington. 'I've been thinking of just that very thing, as I've been dressing. It's just what I was going to suggest to you. The only trouble was that I wondered how you'd manage to work with Mrs. Beard. She'll be difficult, I'm afraid, Ellen dear.'

'I daresay she will. But I shall have to be easy, that's all. And you know, I like her. She may have a bad temper, but she's got a warm heart. At any rate, she's put new life into me to-night. Let me do your hair.'

'Thank you, dear, if you will. Just put that little dressing-cape over my shoulders. It will be wonderful for me to have you here, Ellen. It'll be like having a daughter at last. You don't think you'll be too buried, do you? After all, you're still young, I don't know that you ought to spend your time with a lot of old women. You may want to marry again some day, you know.'

Ellen drew a sharp breath and shook her head.

'I was married once and for all,' she said. 'Do I put these little combs here? Have I got them right?'

'They're very nice, thank you, dear. Well, come here until you are healed up,' went on Mrs. Brockington. 'It sounds an excellent arrangement, if only you can stand Mrs. Beard. We badly need someone like you here. Someone with a sweet temper like yours to stand between her and us. It will make a great difference to us all. And how lovely to have a young girl bringing life into the house in the holidays and Hugh at the week-ends. Of course you'll have no privacy; everybody will take such a violent interest in every detail of your life. I wear black velvet ribbon round my neck at night, dear. Can you put it on for me?'

As Ellen adjusted the ribbon she remembered with a stab that Louise used to do just this for old Mrs. North. What was Louise doing now? Celebrating with Avery, in all probability. She didn't even know where they were.

'I've thought of something else too,' said Mrs. Brockington, handing up a cameo brooch to be pinned on. 'When you've sorted out your own things, I'm sure Mr. Somers will let you store them here. There are so many outbuildings in excellent condition. The old laundry, for instance.'

There was something fruitful about this scheme, thought Ellen later. It kept budding and branching all the time. In a few moments, Mrs. Brockington and Ellen had passed beyond the mere storing of furniture in the old laundry into its possible conversion into a small self-contained house for her and the children.

'But they'll never let me have it,' said Ellen. 'It's too good to be true.'

'I think Mr. Somers will be only too delighted to have it done, at your expense, of course, and you say you can afford it, don't you? Think how it will add to the assets of the place. Of course, he'll let you have it done. He's an old friend of mine. I'll write to him myself. It would solve so many of your difficulties. You'd have a home . . . Oh, Ellen!' she broke off in distress.

For Ellen had put her hands over her face. She stood there, weeping into them, while old Mrs. Brockington struggled up from her chair and put her arms round her.

'It's nothing really,' wept Ellen.

'Was it something I said?' said Mrs. Brockington. 'I'm so clumsy, babbling on like that.'

'It's nothing but relief,' said Ellen, going to her bag in search of her handkerchief. 'It's the relief, that's all,' she said, drying her eyes. 'After this morning. This morning there was nothing, and now there is something, after all.'

The gong went.

'Oh, what a sight I've made of myself,' said Ellen. 'And they'll all have read the evening paper by now and they'll think I'm crying for that.'

'Bathe your eyes with cold water, quickly, dear. And here's some witch-hazel and some cotton wool. You'll be all right in a moment. Put plenty of powder on,' said Mrs. Brockington, as anxious to get Ellen's face right as Ellen was herself.

Red-eyed but smiling, Ellen kissed her old friend.

'You're such a comfort to me,' she said, and they went down together.

In the dining-room, where the shutters were closed against the night and the lamps on the tables lit under rosy shades, the old ladies waited to be served. They had read the paper, but Ellen couldn't have come into gentler company. There was no avid curiosity, no malicious speculation, no self-congratulation that such a thing couldn't happen to them, as there might have been among younger women. These women were old, time had softened them, they had learnt something from loss, helplessness, loneliness; they knew that almost anything can happen to anybody. They were kinder than when they were young.

So they tried, without a word, to show Ellen they were glad to have her there; and were almost proud that she should seek refuge among them on this bad day in her life.

CHAPTER TWENTY-NINE

—◇◇◇—

I

When Ellen drove in at the gates of Netherfold the following afternoon, she was astonished to see the front door fly open and Hugh appear on the steps. He stood staring at the car as if he couldn't move for a moment; then reached it in a bound and pulled the door open.

'Mother! Mother, I thought . . . Oh, Mother!'

Before Ellen could get properly out of the car, he threw his arms round her.

'Oh, Mother, I didn't know what had happened to you. What a fool I am. I thought the divorce had been too much . . . and when you weren't here . . .'

'But, Hugh,' said Ellen, 'I'd no idea you would come home. I never thought . . .'

'I got leave. I came last night. I got in through the box-room window. Oh, thank heaven you're all right.'

He dropped his arms and smiled into her face.

'What a night I've had. I didn't go to bed. I was just going to ring up the police. Oh, Mother, come in. Come and tell me where you've been.'

'I'm so sorry,' said Ellen contritely, letting herself be taken into the house. 'If I'd only thought you might come home, but I never dreamed of it. I've only been to Somerton.'

'Oh, Mother,' he laughed ruefully. 'What a fool I was. But it's his doing,' he finished, suddenly sobering. 'We're frightened at anything now. After what he's done, we feel anything might happen.'

'It's my fault,' said Ellen. 'I should have thought that you might come home.'

'It's my fault, really,' said Hugh. 'I didn't ask for leave until the last minute. I couldn't bring myself to say why I wanted it. But I got it out in the end.'

'Let's have some tea, darling,' said Ellen. 'You need it.'

'Tea!' said Hugh. 'Tea won't do. I'm ravenous all at once.'

'Dear, dear,' said Ellen, fussing about in her old house-wifely style. 'In five minutes you shall have an omelet, bacon, coffee and goodness knows what.'

'Take your hat off first.'

'Here you are then. And my coat. Now let me get to my pans. Get a plate, so that it can be warming. Oh, how glad I am to see you.'

She was full of the happy surprise of having a strong young son to come and concern himself for her. Somehow it had not occurred to her to expect it. That she should do things for him she took for granted, but that he should now be able to do them for her astonished and warmed her. Funny, she thought, one day the tide turns. Children rely on their parents for years and all at once parents find themselves relying on their children.

'I've so much to discuss with you, Hugh,' she said, loosening the edges of the omelet with the palette-knife.

'You look much better than I expected, Mother. Did you get through all right?'

'It was pretty bad,' said Ellen. 'But it's over. Put the kettle on for my tea, will you? Haven't you eaten a thing, Hugh?'

'I had two eggs last night. I thought you'd be coming in any minute. It wasn't until about eleven o'clock that I began to be anxious in earnest. Oh, Mother,' he hugged her again so suddenly that she almost upset the milk pan. 'You must never let anything happen to you.'

He couldn't do enough for her. He made her sit down, even putting a wholly unnecessary foot-stool under her feet, while he washed up. He kept smiling at her. His relief was so great that it dissolved all adult reserve. He showed plainly his love for his mother, and that did her good. It was what she needed.

They talked unceasingly. Hugh liked the idea of going to Somerton and was enthusiastic in his plans for making a house out of the old laundry, but he didn't like to think of his mother's being assistant-manageress to Mrs. Beard or indeed to anybody at all.

'You'll be like Miss Daley,' he said, as if that was unthinkable. 'Mother, you can't.'

'I'm going to,' said Ellen firmly. 'I'm needed there, and much as I love you and Anne, I can't sit about doing nothing but wait for you to come home. So don't say any more about it, and let's get on with all the arrangements we have to make. Isn't it splendid about Roma?'

His face lightened.

'Grand. Anne must have Roma. She can't lose everything at one blow. And Moppet will like Somerton, won't you, bad little cat? She can have as many kittens as she likes there. There'll be room for them all. How did Mrs. Beard take the idea of the laundry-house? I suppose you told her.'

'Goodness yes. I asked her advice at once. If she'd been opposed to it, it would have been absolutely off. But she was quite willing, so long as we have a bell and a telephone put through from the house. There'd better be a door through too, I think, don't you?'

'Mmm,' said Hugh in a business-like way. 'It might be as well. What a good thing you furnished Anne's bedroom and mine as presents for us last year. We can take all our own stuff with us now. Otherwise, I suppose we'd have had to leave it behind.'

Ellen looked bleak for a moment. Everything had to be calculated, she supposed. She had the miserable task of dividing her things from Avery's, of splitting the home from top to bottom. But she would do it alone. The children shouldn't see the dismemberment.

'We shall do very well, Mother,' said Hugh. 'We'll manage without him. He shall see. At least, he shan't see. We'll never even let him know where we are.'

'No,' said Ellen, but a strange pang pierced her.

II

When Hugh had gone back, Ellen began the task of division. She sent for lawyer and valuer and grimly did the thing properly. She went through everything with them, even table-napkins and teaspoons; they drew up lists of what was Avery's and what was hers. Hers were much the longer. Most of the furniture for Netherfold had come from her father's house after his death. It would now furnish the old laundry almost completely.

The lists had to be submitted to Avery for his agreement. She told the lawyer to send them to him through the bank.

'I don't want to know where he is,' she said. 'And once I have left this house, he is not to know where I am.'

The break he had asked for should be clean and final. If she was to make a new life, she could not afford, emotionally, to be disturbed by news of Avery and Louise.

She strained towards this new start now like someone coming to the end of a long, exhausting run. But there were still several weeks to go before she could leave Netherfold and it was sad and enervating to have to stay in a once beloved home that was dying on her hands. That was what it was like. All incoming and outgoing tide of movement that once flowed through the house had ceased. The tradesmen's vans stood no longer at the gate. No cheerful cry of 'Fish' or 'Baker' sounded at the back door. One bottle of milk stood solitary on the step where once there had been whole companies. The telephone never rang. Nobody came to the door; even the charity-collectors passed her by, perhaps because they were too embarrassed to face her, or because they didn't like to ask her for money in case she couldn't spare it now.

She imagined what a sensation she must be making in the lane, but she didn't meet her neighbours. Her husband and children had been enough for her in the old days, so she had not made any real friends. All that people round about had got from her had been a smile and a wave from the car as she sped past, and they got that still. But nobody came to see her. Nobody knew her well enough to come.

Except Miss Beasley, who had not forgotten her promise to help with the clearing up. She firmly refused payment, but Ellen made her take so much in kind that Miss Beasley protested.

'I'm doing too well out of this,' she said. 'I wanted to help you and now you're not letting me have the satisfaction.'

'You're not only helping me,' said Ellen. 'But you're taking things off my hands that I don't know what to do with.'

So having put it on that basis, they continued with the sorting and the packing and the work of destruction, of which there seemed to be as much, Ellen thought, as there had been when old Mrs. North died.

'If Louise hadn't come back then,' she thought, 'I shouldn't have been doing this now.'

One morning, what she had been waiting for arrived, a casual intimation that her decree had been made absolute.

'No one need worry about getting a divorce in these days,' she said grimly. 'It's as easy as pie. Just in time for Christmas too. Avery and Louise will be pleased.'

One morning later, the bell rang, and when Ellen opened the door there stood Miss Daley, still wearing the hat with the pheasant's feather, her face puckered in distress, clasping a newspaper in her hand.

'Oh, dear Miss Daley,' cried Ellen, warmly drawing her in.

'How glad I am to see you. I have so wanted to know where you were. Come into the kitchen with me. I'm just having some coffee and you must have some too.'

'I came straight away,' said Miss Daley in a strangled voice. 'I changed my day off. I didn't know a thing about it, till I saw this paper this morning. I never heard a single thing. I suppose it's with me being at Adlington now. It's six miles out, you know, and I don't go to the chapel any more. And my people don't take the local paper. But this morning when I opened this daily picture paper, I felt quite ill, Mrs. Avery. I just told them I'd have to come at once. I didn't even know if I'd find you here.'

'Sit down,' said Ellen, putting her into a chair. 'What's so new to you is months old to me, you know. I've got over the worst. See, here's a cup of coffee. You were so good to come. I can't tell you how glad I am to see you. But what is it in the paper?' asked Ellen, suddenly realising that there must be something fresh, and in a London paper too. 'What is it?' she said sharply.

'Haven't you seen it?' faltered Miss Daley, witholding the paper. 'Oh, dear. I don't want to be the one to bring you more nasty news.'

'What is it?' asked Ellen, her heart beginning to hammer. 'Let me see what it is. Give me the paper.'

'Well, he's married her. There's a photo of them. See.'

On the middle pages, with pictures of a cat, a storm at sea, a murderer, was a photograph of Avery, unmistakably Avery, coming down the steps of a registrar's office with Louise, smiling in a fur coat and orchids. Underneath, it read:

'Publisher's Bride. Mr. Avery North, of Bennett and North, publishers in the Strand, from whom his former wife recently obtained a divorce, after his marriage yesterday to Mademoiselle Louise Lanier. The honeymoon will be spent in France, the bride's native country.'

He had lost no time. He had married her as soon as he could. Ellen put the paper down and turned away. The look on her face was too much for Miss Daley. She wept, putting her hands up under her glasses to hide her tears.

'It's awful,' she wept, shaking her head until the pheasant's feather rocked like the mast of a foundering ship. 'Breaking up a family like yours. I never saw a married couple as happy as you and him.'

'Don't cry for me, Daley dear,' said Ellen. 'It's over now, you know. I'm getting used to it. It was only the sight of him . . .'

'What did you let her into your house for?' asked Miss Daley, dropping her hands and looking at Ellen with wet unspectacled eyes. 'You're no match for such as her. You brought her in and let her see your house and your husband and all you'd got, and she thought she'd have them, and she set herself to get them and she's got them. See what a mess you're in now. Lost everything through a perfect stranger. What're you going to do with yourself, love? Where're you going to?'

'I've made a very good arrangement,' said Ellen, glad to turn the conversation. 'We're all going to Somerton Manor, even the horse and the cat, and I'm going to be assistant-manageress.'

'You're never going to work?' said Miss Daley in a shocked voice.

'I am,' said Ellen. 'I want to. I'm looking forward to it.'

'Well,' said Miss Daley, taking off her glasses to breathe on them and rub them up. 'You were always very capable. I daresay it won't be much harder than running your own home. With this difference,' she said weightily, 'it was your own home and you were your own mistress. I suppose,' she said, putting her glasses on and looking at Ellen with diffidence, 'there wouldn't be room for me there?'

'You!' cried Ellen, her face lighting up with pleased surprise. 'You! Oh, I'm sure there's room. They're so hard up for staff they don't know which way to turn. But do you want a place? Don't you like where you are?'

'Well, I can't keep myself on what they give me,' said Miss Daley. 'They're very nice people, but they can't pay more than thirty shillings a week. It's not their fault, but I can't manage. It takes a week's money to get my shoes soled and heeled, Mrs. Avery. I've never been so shabby in my life and I've never been able to afford a holiday since you saw me last. The Minister could only give me a pound a week, so I had to leave there, leave the chapel and everything. I thought I'd manage on thirty shillings, but I can't. I daresay your hotel would pay me two pounds, wouldn't they?'

'Three. Quite three, I should say,' said Ellen.

'Wouldn't I be in clover?' said Miss Daley. 'If I could come with you, I'd be that happy. I've always been fond of you, Mrs. Avery, and there's nothing I'd like better than to be where you are.'

'I'm going to take a leaf out of Mrs. Beard's book,' said Ellen, making for the hall. 'I'm going to ring her up at once.'

'Make some more coffee,' she called, waiting for Mrs. Beard, 'that must be stone cold.'

Mrs. Beard was more business-like than old Mr. Somers had been. She wanted to see Miss Daley before she would do more.

'Wait a minute, Mrs. Beard,' said Ellen. 'Miss Daley,' she called. 'Didn't you say it was your day off?'

'Yes,' said Miss Daley, appearing in the hall. 'I've got till the five-o'clock bus to-night.'

'We'll come over straight away, Mrs. Beard,' said Ellen. 'We might as well get this settled.'

'Well,' breathed Miss Daley.

Ellen drove across the county to Somerton. There had been a stiff frost in the night. The summer straws dangling still from the hedges, caught from the wagons as they went by, were frozen waterfalls. Vivid scarlet hips flashed suddenly out of the frosted scene. Miss Daley and Ellen exclaimed at the white, smoky beauty of the distances, with a tree standing like a ghost in a field here and there.

When they went into the hall at Somerton, the old ladies turned from the fire with cries of welcome for Ellen. They knew now that she was coming to live among them and were sure that things would be better. They knew they had a champion in her.

Miss Daley stood diffidently apart until the greetings should be over. Good intentions gushed strongly within her as she looked on. If she got to this place, how she would serve them all. She saw herself ministering to the old ladies and looking after Mrs. Avery on the sly.

'It'd be a good thing for her to have me about,' thought Miss Daley, 'because I know what she's been and what she's come from. She thinks it's going to be easy to work for her living, but she doesn't know what it's like. I'll be here to keep the worst off her, if I get this place.'

Clasping her handbag, Miss Daley felt strong and full of power to help everybody. She put up a fervent prayer that she would get satisfactorily through the interview with Mrs. Beard, who from all accounts was a bit of a tartar.

Ellen took Miss Daley to Mrs. Beard in the office. She left them together and went upstairs to Mrs. Brockington.

She meant to tell her friend that Avery was married to Louise, but she couldn't get it out. She couldn't say anything. She knew her tongue was tied because, in spite of all the proofs he had given of it, she couldn't bear anyone else to know, she couldn't bear to know herself, that he finally preferred Louise to her. Some time she must tell Mrs. Brockington. But not to-day. It was too new. She must get used to it herself first.

She chattered to Mrs. Brockington about Miss Daley and about her plans for removal to Somerton. Then she said she must go down and see what was happening, because they must start on the return journey to Newington.

'Take this book on Albert Schweitzer with you,' said Mrs. Brockington. 'I think he must be the greatest man of our time. A modern saint. Do read it.'

'I will,' said Ellen. 'Your books help me. Very often when

I've been at the end of my courage, I've opened one of your books and found exactly what I needed. Good-bye, darling, I'll soon be here for good now.'

'Well, we've fixed things up,' announced Mrs. Beard from her desk. 'Thanks for bringing her over, Mrs. North. I shan't know myself with all the help I'm getting. P'r'aps my temper'll improve. We'll be able to put up a notice on the main road: 'Open to Non-Residents.' I've always wanted to do it, to bring a bit of variety into the place, but of course it's been out of the question. But it isn't now. I'll keep the two of you busy all right.'

'We shan't mind, shall we, Miss Daley?' said Ellen.

'Oooh, no, Mrs. Avery. I'm looking forward ever so much to coming. It's lovely here,' said Miss Daley, red in the face with excitement and the heat of the office. 'I'll go back and give my notice now. Never a nice job, is it? But I'll get it over straight off and then I'll have nothing to do but look forward.'

'Oh, by the way, medea. There's something that will interest you,' said Mrs. Beard, flipping a letter across to Ellen and lighting another cigarette. 'The old gentleman gives his consent to the conversion of the old laundry on condition he approves the plans. You're to live there rent free, which is natural, seeing you'll've paid for the alterations. You pay for your own lighting and heating, you get all the meals you want in the hotel free of charge and your children have to pay for theirs at the usual rates. It all seems pretty O.K to me.'

'It sounds splendid,' said Ellen. 'I'll go straight ahead and get an architect to it.'

The atmosphere in the office was one of mutual satisfaction, only ended by the appearance of Jim at the door to say the coal had come, but they hadn't brought any coke for the boiler.

'Blast,' said Mrs. Beard, making for the door, followed by Miss Daley's rounded eyes. 'Let me get at that man. He'll damwell go back for it. Good-bye, you two. Get here as soon as you can. I need you.'

Miss Daley sang most of the way back. It was rather like being boxed in with a loudspeaker, but Ellen didn't mind; she was glad Miss Daley was happy. She smiled once or twice at some particularly soaring whoops to think what agonies of suppressed laughter Anne would have gone through once, and would again, she hoped. She felt sure there would be many musical renderings for the old ladies in the future.

Things were working out better for Anne than her mother had dared to hope. She was rehearsing with Benedick, a boy called Julian from Overingham School, and she actually liked him. He began by being 'not so bad as I expected' and went on to being 'Quite nice really.' Then she wrote frankly 'I like Julian.' In her last letter she had said: 'I've told Julian and Pug about having to leave home and going to Somerton. I was so glad about Roma that I had to tell them. It was so lovely.'

Ellen had shed tears of relief over this letter. She was grateful to this unknown boy who, because Anne could like him, was redeeming, in some measure, the whole of his sex. Ellen had little conscious knowledge of psychology or its terms, but she knew the revulsion that any crude manifestation of sex brings to a young girl. It falls like a black frost on the hidden buds of natural love, so that there is no flowering. Nothing but disgust and fear. She didn't expect Anne, at sixteen, to fall in love with this boy, but she didn't shrink from him. She liked him enough to give him her confidence, and Ellen was grateful to him.

It was only when Ellen had seen Miss Daley to her bus, driven home and locked herself into the house for the night, that she came back to the kitchen table, where the picture paper still lay face upwards. All day long, driving through the winter scene, talking to Miss Daley, Mrs. Brockington, and Mrs. Beard, a picture of Avery and Louise had been fixed in her mind, eternally coming down the steps from their wedding. Now that no one was watching her, she took the paper in both hands and stared at it for a long time. She thought Avery looked awful, both ill and dissipated. He was scowling, presumably at the camera. He had always hated being photographed. Louise looked extremely pleased with herself, as well she might.

Ellen burnt the paper in the kitchen fire, giving herself no chance to brood over it again. She made tea for herself and opened the book on Albert Schweitzer. She deliberately put herself in touch with greatness. She read first with determination and then with absorption.

* * *

At Mershott School that same morning, young Miss Blackmore, who was producing the play, sought Miss Beldon in her room.

'I know you think I take regrettable papers,' she said, laying one before her Headmistress. 'But I like pictures and sometimes they're quite useful. This explains everything, doesn't it?'

Miss Beldon bent over the photograph of Avery and Louise and her face was grave.

'Poor child. Poor Anne. And her poor mother. They seemed so happy always. A Frenchwoman. Good gracious, I think it must be the girl who was going to coach Anne during the summer. So I did blunder on the trouble after all. Oh, dear,' grieved Miss Beldon. 'I wish Mrs. North had felt able to tell me. But Anne is better, isn't she?'

'Much better,' said Miss Blackmore. 'Being Beatrice in the play has done a great deal for her. She's absolutely delicious in the part. And the boy's so good too. They're an enchanting pair. I love the boy – long leggy creature with floppy fair hair and a skin like a girl's. Of course you've seen him. But not as Benedick. We're going to be good this year. You'll see.'

Miss Beldon smiled and gave back the picture paper.

'So long as this hasn't done too much damage to the child,' she said. 'I hope she doesn't see that photograph.'

Her hope was realised. Anne didn't see it.

* * *

In London, Louise cut out the photograph, removed everything from the print except "Publisher's Bride" and enclosed it in a letter to her parents.

'Here I am with my husband after our civil marriage yesterday. It is a good photograph of me, isn't it? You haven't seen Avery yet, but within the next few days you will. I haven't booked a room at the Hôtel de l'Ecu, but if there isn't one there when we arrive we shall go to the Hôtel de la Gare or the Baudoin. I shall come alone to see you first, because after all this time there is so much to say. Then Avery will join us. You must both come to dinner, the first night, at the hotel. We will have a celebration with champagne, Papa! So don't make any preparations, Mama. You can't, because you don't know the day or the hour! But expect us. I am coming. Madame North is coming!'

She felt that by throwing in the name 'North' like that, they could be absorbing it. She didn't think she had ever mentioned Avery's Christian name to them, but if she had it didn't matter. All English names were strange to them and it would be easy enough to gloss that over.

She expected questions, but she felt she could meet them without trouble. Her parents were kind and good, but not very sharp, she considered. She had deceived them for years, she could do it again. In all probability for the last time. There would be no need for subterfuge after this.

CHAPTER THIRTY

$\Longleftrightarrow\Diamond\Longleftrightarrow$

The hour of noon was striking from all the churches in Amigny as the station taxi-cab crossed the bridge over the river and Louise let down the window to Listen to them. There was the Cathedral, there was S. Jacques, there was the Hôtel de Ville. She knew them all. But it was cold, so she put the window up again and drew her fur coat closer. She and Avery had arrived by the night ferry in Paris that morning and had take the first train to Amigny; she was eager to get home.

Avery sat back in his corner, scarcely glancing at the scene. This visit was something he had to get through. It was another thing he had brought upon himself. Since that awful afternoon in July he had gone floundering on like a drunken man. He had, he admitted, been drunk most of the time. But the marriage ceremony with Louise had brought him up short. It was like a bucket of cold water thrown over him. He was appalled by what he had done. He was committed to being with her now and he couldn't bear it. For the present, he was just something in tow. He was the foreign husband who had to stand about to be looked at, unable to say an intelligible word to her parents or anybody else. Not that he had anything to say. What had he to do with these people? He folded his arms with a gesture of endurance and sighed.

Louise was craning forward to look out of the window. She had never felt such interest and satisfaction in coming back to her native place before. It might look exactly the same, a little grey town all spires and trees, but she was different. Louise Lanier, the daughter of the bookseller in the Rue des Carmes, was coming back with a rich husband and a social position as good as any Devoisy's. She knew what a sensation she would make. Such a fur coat as hers, such pearls had not been seen in Amigny before, because the women who could afford to buy such things didn't dress like that. They were dowdy with true provincial and Catholic dowdiness. Germaine Devoisy, for instance, was probably wearing beige woollen dresses this winter; or bottle green.

'Pass slowly down the Rue Goujon,' she said to the driver. 'I wish to show my husband something.'

It wasn't that. She wanted to look at Paul's house from her new point of vantage, to look at it in triumph. But as the taxi-cab approached the house, she saw that the big doors were open and the sight of a perambulator in the courtyard filled her with jealous rage. Not that she wanted Paul's son, but that Paul should have him was intolerable; and Germaine would be giving herself such idiotic maternal airs.

The cards announcing the birth of this child had been printed at the shop, and Madame Lanier, thinking to please, had sent one to Louise: 'Monsieur et Madame Paul Devoisy ont la joie de vous faire part de la naissance de leur fils Hubert' was printed on the little buff-coloured card. Louise had torn it up with vicious fingers. It was so small that there wasn't much to tear, which enraged her further. The child must be more than a month old now. She would have exulted to hear that he was puny or ailing or something. Perhaps she would hear. Perhaps her mother would have something of that sort to tell her.

The taxi crossed the cathedral square and drew up before the Hôtel de l'Ecu. This hotel had always appeared as the epitome of luxury to Louise as a child and now she was going to stay in it. The porter came out, respectful in striped waistcoat. She saw at once that it was young Adolphe Bertier, whose mother kept the pâtisserie in the Rue des Carmes, but he didn't recognise her.

'Have you a double room with a private bathroom disengaged?' she asked.

'No rooms with private bathroom, Madame.'

'No, I suppose it is too much to expect in a place like this,' said Louise. 'Have you one of those large rooms overlooking the square? One with two balconies?'

'Yes, Madame, the best of those is free,' said young Bertier, surprised she should know of them.

'I will have it. Do get out of the taxi, Avery,' she said testily in English.

She went into the hall of the hotel, which was warm after the cold air outside and impregnated with the delicious smell of escalopes de veau or something of the sort. Ah, the good smells of France, she thought. No food ever smells like ours.

The occupants of the bureau, Monsieur Bernard and his

daughter in glasses, who had been at school with Louise, were startled by the elegance advancing towards them.

'Ah, Madeleine, good morning,' said Louise graciously. 'How are you?'

'Madame?' stammered the astonished Madeleine. 'Oh, is it possible?'

She whipped off her glasses to look.

'Louise, is it you? It can't be!'

'Yes, it is I. I have brought my husband. He is English. He speaks no French, or not enough to mention, so I can't present him to you. I have just arrived from London after my marriage. I want to stay here and go quietly to my parents by myself first. I want to prepare them a little, as you will understand. I hear the best room on the first floor is free. I will have it.'

'With pleasure, Madame,' said Monsieur Bernard, taking a key from a hook. 'Good morning, Monsieur. May I felicitate you on your marriage? You do us honour by coming to our humble hotel.'

Avery smiled and bowed as was expected of him and followed Louise into the lift, which shuddered upwards to the first floor. The hotel proprietor opened the door of his best room and Louise walked in.

'Ah,' she said with satisfaction.

She was inside this room now, instead of outside, crossing the square on her way from school, looking up at the strangers on the balcony, lucky people who could afford to stay at the Ecu and be waited on, and go away to Paris or other places afterwards.

The room was big, with long windows reflected in a huge arched glass over the fireplace. The parquet shone like honey, the beds had plump yellow eiderdowns, there were two fringed armchairs.

'Don't you think this is very nice, Avery?' she said, putting her arm through his for the benefit of Monsieur Bernard. She mustn't forget they were just married.

'I'd rather have a room to myself,' said Avery.

'Ah, but you can't,' said Louise, sure that Monsieur Bernard could not understand English as spoken by Avery, who barely moved his lips. 'You must remember,' she said in an aside, 'that this is our honeymoon.'

'That is all, Monsieur Bernard,' she said, dismissing him. 'We will come down to lunch almost at once, but first I must telephone to my parents to let them know we have arrived.'

'Very good, Madame,' said the hotel proprietor. 'The telephone box is downstairs.'

Avery went to the basin to wash. His eyes were full of the grit of the French train. Louise was at the window.

'Haven't you even glanced at the Cathedral?' she said, looking at its ancient façade across the square.

'I saw it as we arrived,' said Avery.

'So it is not worth looking at again?' said Louise, turning from the window.

He showed no interest in the place where she was born, or in anything that concerned her. When he was sober, he was indifferent, and when he was drunk, he was repulsive.

'And *I* am waiting to wash *my* hands,' she said haughtily, as if, like Louise XIV, she must never wait for anything.

'You should have taken single rooms,' said Avery. 'Then you could have had a basin to yourself.'

'You will keep up appearances here if you never keep them up anywhere else,' she said fiercely. 'This is my native place. We went through that farce of a marriage so that I could come back to it. Remember that.'

'Right you are. But I hope it will only be for a few days.'

'That remains to be seen. You have kept me away for many months. You can at least allow me a week or two now, I should hope.'

'I can leave you here,' said Avery, pleased with the sudden idea. 'Business can call me back to England.'

'Perhaps. But not yet,' said Louise. 'I am going down to telephone to my parents now. You can wait for me in the hall. Since you can't speak French you can't go into the dining-room to see that we get a good table as another man would do, so you must wait until I do it for you.'

She hurried down the short flight of stairs with a smile of anticipation. She was quite looking forward to the exclamations that would greet her over the telephone in a moment. Dear things! It would give them so much pleasure to know that she had arrived.

She got the number and heard the telephone ring on the desk in the shop.

'Allô, allô?' said Mademoiselle Léonie.

'Give me Monsieur Lanier, please,' said Louise, to spare herself any sensation on the part of Mademoiselle Léonie, who had always bored her.

'What name, please?'

'Give me Monsieur Lanier,' repeated Louise.

'Very good,' said Mademoiselle Léonie and called: 'Monsieur! Someone wants you on the telephone. She won't give her name.'

Louise waited, smiling. After all, this was quite a moment. 'Allô, allô?' said her father's voice.

'Papa.'

There was a silence. The excitement must be too much for him. He actually couldn't speak.

'Papa! Are you there, Papa? You haven't collapsed, have you?'

'No, Louise. I am here,' he said. 'When did you arrive?'

'Half an hour ago. We are at the Ecu. I shall be with you the moment we've had déjeuner. I shall come by myself, as I said, so don't worry about any preparation. Don't let Mama dress up or anything. Is Mama there? Shall I speak to her?'

'She is in the kitchen,' said her father.

'Oh, then don't bring her to the telephone. It would take too long, she is sure to be excited. I must go in to déjeuner. My husband is waiting. Embrace Mama for me. I embrace you too, dear Papa. In about half an hour's time, then. Good-bye.'

She smiled as she left the box. She had never spoken to her father over the telephone before, so hadn't known how unnatural he sounded. Poor darling, fancy not being used to the instrument after all these years!

She beckoned to Avery in the hall and together they went into the dining-room. Their entry made quite a stir among the clients, mostly men, industrialists who came every day. With an eye for an attractive woman, they observed Louise with admiration and were amazed when the whisper, started by Monsieur Bernard, went round that she was the daughter of Lanier who kept the bookshop in the Rue des Carmes. Several of them recollected then that they should know her, and tried to catch her eye so that they could salute her. But she wouldn't let them. They wouldn't look at her in the old days; they shouldn't have the chance now.

But she felt the flattery of their glances, and chattering in English to Avery, which impressed them the more, she made an excellent lunch. She sent for the hotel proprietor to tell him that it was the best meal that had been served to her in the last eight months, though much of that time, she added smilingly, had been spent in the best hotels in London and New York.

'We French are the only people who know how to eat,' she told him and he was charmed.

'My parents will dine with us here to-night,' she said. 'Please see that there is plenty of champagne.'

He was more charmed than ever.

By the time she was smoking a cigarette over her coffee, the industrialists were wondering why on earth they hadn't noticed her when she lived in the town, why they had let her slip through their fingers, why they had let an Englishman get her. She was wasted on him to all appearances; a sulky-looking fellow, pouring brandy down his throat with his coffee. How could he appreciate such a flower of French femininity?

Louise stood up and Monsieur Bernard hurried forward to help her on with the fur coat she had thrown over the back of the chair. She hadn't left it in her room. It was too valuable to risk, also she felt it should be seen. Monsieur Bernard told his daughter afterwards that never, in all his experience, had he such a soft, light fur coat in his hands.

'She has done very well for herself,' he said, and wondered why his daughter should be so plain and short-sighted, and, in spite of a substantial dowry, unmarried.

'Avery, you must come with me as far as the cathedral,' said Louise. 'Then I can show you where the Librairie is. You can go into the cathedral and I will come and fetch you later. I shan't be long. Only about a quarter of an hour.'

Avery demurred, but she insisted that he should start out with her. If she left him in the hotel, he would drink more brandy and be unable to make an appearance at all. She took him firmly by the arm and piloted him to the cathedral.

'Now, look down that street there. You see the white sign with the blue lettering? That is my father's bookshop. I shall soon be back for you. There is plenty for you to look at in here.'

She pushed open the padded leather door and saw him inside. In France she treated him as if he were slightly deficient mentally.

She walked quickly across the square, looking about her with smiling interest. After all, it was good to come home. She passed the Pharmacie Petit, even catching sight of André measuring something in a beaker. She laughed and hugged her fur coat tighter. A priest passed on the other side of the street. She thought it was the Abbé Champery, but would not look to see. She didn't want to meet any of the cathedral clergy. She passed the Pâtisserie Bertier, with its delicious chocolate truffles, ticketed 'Spécialité de la Maison' in the window. She must buy some of those on her way back to the hotel.

Here she was! Here was the old familiar door that went 'ping' when she pushed it open. Her father was standing in the middle of the shop, waiting for her.

'Papa,' she cried and stood for a second so that he could take in her rich elegance. Then she moved swiftly to embrace him. She never kissed anybody, because of her lip-rouge, but she pressed her cheek, first one and then the other, to his.

'Papa!' she said. 'I'm so glad to see you. Where is Mama? Mama!' she called out, hurrying through to the house. 'Mama! I'm here. Where are you?'

Her mother stood in the passage, her face convulsed, a handkerchief pressed to her lips.

'Mama, what in God's name is the matter with you? Are you ill?' said Louise, coming to a halt.

Madame Lanier shook her head and burst into tears.

'What's the matter?' said Louise sharply. 'What is it?'

'Come in here, Louise,' said her father, leading the way into the dining-room. 'And explain something to us. If you can.'

Louise followed him. On the table, already cleared, were two photographs: one the snapshot she had given them after her first visit to England, the other the newspaper cutting of herself and Avery after their marriage. Louise stood, looking down at them.

'What's the matter?' she said.

Her father stood beside her.

'This man, your husband,' he said, laying a shaking forefinger on the newspaper cutting, 'is the man here, is he not?' He pointed to the family group in the snapshot. 'He was then the husband of that woman. Is that not so?'

Louise stood very still, thinking rapidly. She had been caught off her guard. Madame Lanier stifled a choking sob behind her.

'Why do you call him your husband?' said her father.

'He is my husband,' said Louise.

'Last year he was her husband. Did you seduce him from his wife then? Did you break up this family who had been so good to you?'

'He fell in love with me,' said Louise harshly.

'It was a vile thing to do,' said her father ringingly. 'I am bitterly ashamed of you.'

'You know nothing,' said Louise, wrapping her coat round her and walking to the stove. 'What do you know of the world? These things happen.'

'Since he married you, he must have been divorced from her,' said her father, confronting her with terrible sternness.

'He was divorced. Yes,' said Louise. Since they asked for it, they should have it.

'He was divorced because of you?'

'Yes, if you like to put it that way.' She shrugged one shoulder.

'But you are a Catholic,' said her father. 'The Catholic Church does not recognise divorce. Therefore you are not married to him.'

'Bah,' said Louise. 'I am not a Catholic. Life destroyed my faith long ago.'

Her father took off his pince-nez and wiped them. They were steamed over by the sweat of his emotion.

'You mean *your* life destroyed your faith,' he said.

'Oh, Henri,' sobbed Madame Lanier. 'Don't say such hard things to her. She is our daughter, our only child.'

'I regret the fact,' he said. 'She has behaved abominably. She is excommunicated. She has cut herself off from her Church and her family.'

'Oh, don't talk such rubbish,' blazed Louise suddenly. 'You are fifty years behind the times. You are stupid. You have always been stupid. What have you ever done for me? What have you ever known of me? Look at me!'

She threw out her arms to let them see her in her beautiful clothes, with all her finish.

'Do I look like the daughter of a provincial shopkeeper? Why didn't you do something better for me? If you hadn't kept a shop, Paul Devoisy would have married me. It was because of you,' she cried loudly, 'that he left me and married Germaine Brouet. Because of you, do you hear? Because of you!'

There was a dead silence in the room except for a faint ringing of an old lustre set off by the shrillness of Louise's voice.

Madame Lanier had let fall her hands from her face and was staring at her daughter in slow horror. Monsieur Lanier drew a long breath and stood rigid.

'Paul Devoisy,' said Madame Lanier in a whisper. 'It can't be true.'

'It is true,' said Louise, lifting her chin at them.

'Paul Devoisy,' repeated her mother.

'Yes, Paul Devoisy. He was in love with me for years and I with him. But what did you know about that? I suffered horribly when he married Germaine Brouet,' said Louise. 'But what did you know about that either? My parents,' she said with scorn.

'Oh, Henri,' said Madame Lanier, going to her husband. 'Help me. I have never known my own child. Paul Devoisy . . .'

Monsieur Lanier put his arm round his wife.

'It is nothing we have done, Emilie,' he said. ' It is her own sin. She was always an unnatural child, cold, thankless, selfish, but we had no idea – we were too innocent – to dream that she was depraved as well. She has deceived us very thoroughly.'

'Thank you,' said Louise shortly, from the stove.

'We shall not receive this man you call your husband,' said her father. 'You are our daughter. We can't get away from that. If you leave him, you are at liberty to come home. But never, so long as you remain with him, shall you come under this roof.'

His wife grasped his coat, aghast. But she made no protest.

'Very well,' said Louise, her eyes black in her white face. 'As you wish. It doesn't matter to me. What pleasure do you think I can find in this place? What makes you think I should ever want to come back?'

She walked to the table and picked up her bag.

'I will leave you,' she said. 'Not many parents would be willing to give up a daughter for such silly ideas. You should move with the times, my dear Papa, or you will be left behind. In fact, you are left behind, aren't you? By me. Good-bye.'

She walked past them and through the door into the shop. Mademoiselle Léonie, who had just come back from lunch, gave a cry of surprise.

'Oh, Mademoiselle Louise . . .'

'Get out of my way,' said Louise through her teeth. 'Let me get out of here.'

She wrenched the door open, left it wide and went up the street. She was so angry she could hardly walk. To be rejected by her parents, who had always been under her thumb! How dare they? As if she cared. They flattered themselves. Well, they had upset themselves far more than they had upset her, and serve them right too.

Where was she? What was she supposed to be doing, she wondered, coming to a halt in the street. She remembered she had to go to the cathedral in search of the husband she had brought to show off. She was angry with him too, because she couldn't use him now. She was like a furious wasp ready to sting wherever she could.

* * *

In the cathedral, Avery had been sitting for what seemed a long time on a rush-bottomed chair. All time was long to him nowadays, unless he could lose count of it in brandy. With a heavy eye, he looked about the ancient, immensely high interior. It was gaunt, dusty and very untidy with vigorously disarranged chairs. On the altars were artificial flowers and long white-painted tubes, very chipped, with little dips in the tops to simulate candles. Better not put anything on the altars at all than that sort of thing, he thought. The whole place lacked the cared-for appearance of an English cathedral. But it was used. Far off at the high altar something was going on; he didn't know what. Priests and servers stepped about and knelt and bowed. There was a continuous nasal chant.

Avery watched men and women come in, kneel, light tapers before images, go out again. What did all this mean to them? Obviously something. He envied them. If he could believe that saying prayers would help him out of the mess he had made of his life, he would say them.

There wasn't a single place in his mind he could let his thoughts rest on. He couldn't bear to think of Anne. Not only could he never see her again, but he couldn't even allow himself to think of her. Shame was the most destructive emotion of them all. He thought he could have borne anything but shame.

He could think of Ellen. He thought almost all the time of her. She was the only one who could have understood what he felt and suffered; and he was cut off from her and could never see her again either.

He'd no work. He never talked to anyone. He never saw his friends. If he even met his old train companions, Weston and Holmes, he'd have to travel in a different compartment.

He'd no home. He had the house, but to live there with Louise was unthinkable. He must go back and put it up for sale, but he would get away again as soon as possible.

And then what?

In desperation, he knelt down and put his hands over his face.

'God, help me,' he said. 'I can't help myself.'

Louise found him like that. She sank to her knees beside him for the sake of appearances and said in a fierce whisper:

'Come out of here. We're leaving. We're going back to Paris at once.'

He turned his tired face and red-rimmed eyes towards her.

'What?' he said.

'Come out,' she said, getting up and clattering over the stone floor in her high heels.

'What's happened?' he said when they were outside.

'My parents won't receive you,' she said, hurrying across the square. 'They know you were divorced, so in their eyes we are not married. They know I was the co-respondent. They had it all worked out before I got there. So they have finished with me. I have no home now. No parents. You see what you have done for me.'

Avery looked grim and said nothing. In the cathedral he had had some hope of being able to leave her. If she had settled at home, he could have done it.

Louise was consumed with anger. She had been humiliated. She was to be humiliated again. What could she say at the hotel? How countermand the dinner for four with plenty of champagne? To arrive in triumph and depart in shameful hurry – that was a nice thing to happen to a bride, a returned daughter.

She was blazing with anger as she reached the opposite side of the square with Avery, and suddenly, in front of her, was Paul Devoisy with his wife, pushing a perambulator.

Louise stood stock still on the pavement, staring at Paul as he stared at her. She was the first to recover. She was exultant at this most unexpected chance.

She half-turned and put out a hand to draw Avery to her side. She cast an amused glance over Germaine, shapeless still from childbirth and, as she had foreseen, wearing beige with a dowdy hat on her great bun of hair.

'How nice to see you, Paul,' said Louise. 'May I present my husband, Avery North? He is English, but you speak the language well, as I remember. So you can both say "How d'you do" to each other.'

The men murmured stiffly.

'My husband will be interested to meet yours, Madame,' said Louise. 'Paul was my first love, weren't you, Paul? No need to deny it.' She lifted a hand, laughing. 'My husband knows all about it, naturally. But we had some good times together, hadn't we, Paul?'

Paul Devoisy stood rigid, his hand on the perambulator handle. His wife beside him was white to the lips.

'And this is your son,' said Louise, graciously, moving to look under the hood.

Germaine darted forward and drew up the covers so that she shouldn't see him. Glaring at Louise, she protected him as from the evil eye.

'You must be very satisfied with your son, Paul,' said Louise. 'That is what you married for, isn't it? Well, good-bye. My husband and I are on our way back to Paris. Good-bye, Madame.'

She bowed, wrapped her magnificent coat around her and went into the hotel.

The two on the pavement stood where they were. Then Germaine let out a long wavering breath and bent over the perambulator handle as if she was going to faint. Instantly, Paul put his arm round her.

'Lean on me, Germaine. Let me get you home.'

She straightened up immediately and threw him off.

'Don't dare to touch me,' she flashed. 'You liar. I shall never forgive you. Never. Over and over again, you told me you never knew her. I shall never believe another word you say. You hideous liar!'

'Germaine – what could I do but lie? It was all over. Darling, you're ill. Let me take you home quickly.'

'Don't touch me. Don't dare to come with me. Go away. Go anywhere. I don't want to see you again.'

She rushed away, jolting the perambulator roughly up and down the kerbs, straining at it, pursuing such a reckless course that Paul, coming behind, was frightened. She would hurt herself. She wasn't strong yet. She would be ill.

When they reached their own courtyard, she tore the covers off to take the baby out of the perambulator.

'At least let me carry him in for you,' Paul implored her. 'You might hurt him. You might let him fall.'

'And that's all you care about. You only married me to get him, didn't you?' said Germaine breathlessly. Her looks terrified him now. Her lips were blue.

'Germaine, don't make yourself ill.'

'What would that matter to you?' she said, picking up the child. 'Go away. I don't want to see you again. If you come home to-night, you can sleep in the yellow room. You're not

393

coming near us again. This is my baby. I'll bring him up to know what a liar his father is. I'll tell him. He shall know.'

She went up the steps to the house-door and pulled at the bell. As she waited for it to be answered, she had to lean against the door-post with her eyes closed. In a moment she was admitted, and while the man-servant stared incredulously, she slammed the door in her husband's face.

He stood on the steps for some time, then he got into his car and drove back to the quarries.

* * *

At the Hôtel de l'Ecu, the smart luggage was being piled into a taxi-cab.

'I regret, Monsieur Bernard,' Louise had said, 'my husband has been called back to England on business. There was a letter at my parents', you understand. I am so sorry, We will pay for the room for the night, of course. The dinner with champagne we must postpone. But we shall probably be back very soon!'

Tipping lavishly, she got into the taxi and was driven away; across the square and over the bridge again. The only satisfaction she had got out of the visit had been the encounter with Paul and Germaine Devoisy. She had at least brought that off. But even that hadn't been the triumph she planned. He wasn't the Paul she had so desperately missed. He had gone soft and domestic. His eyes had been for the effect the meeting was having on his dowdy wife and not for Louise's beauty and the memories of their love-affair. She felt bleak and empty; there would be nothing of Paul in her life from now on. You couldn't eat your heart out for a man pushing a perambulator.

The short winter afternoon was over when the Paris train drew out. Louise watched the handful of lights which was the town lose themselves in the darkness. It was unlikely that she would ever come back to Amigny. Her parents would no doubt forgive her. They would want to see her again. But she wouldn't forget the scene that day; monstrous and stupid as it had been. She knew she would punish them far more than herself in refusing to see them.

But she was bitter. Paul with his domesticity, her parents with their piety, Avery with his remorse or whatever it was – all of them were obsessed with something other than Louise. Once she had come first with these people, and she ought to come first still. She hadn't done anything to change them, she told herself. But she would look elsewhere. Where, she didn't know yet. But she would do something for herself, never fear.

CHAPTER THIRTY-ONE

—◦◇◦—

When Paul Devoisy went home to dinner that night, he found the table laid for himself alone. Madame, he was told, would not be coming down. The baby was fretful. She had ordered a fire in the room and would have some soup sent up. She did not wish to be disturbed.

After his solitary meal, Paul went up to listen outside the room he had shared, until now, with his wife. He tried the door; it was locked. He could hear the small, continual whimper of the baby and wondered anxiously what was the matter with him. He had always been so good. They had not had a single disturbed night with him since he had come home from the clinic with his mother.

Germaine was evidently walking about the room with him, trying to soothe him. But it sounded as if she was crying herself. She sang softly to him.

'À côté de ta mère, fais ton petit do-do. Sans savoir que ton père. . . .'

The baby fretted. Paul was wretched, listening. If only she would let him in. He was good with the baby.

'Germaine,' he said, at the crack of the door.

Silence fell in the room.

'Germaine, let me in to help you with him. Please.'

She came to say from her side of the door: 'Go away. You've done enough to us for one day. Don't you understand that to upset me upsets him? Leave us alone to get quiet as best we can.'

Paul went down and spent a miserable evening in the salon. He held a book, but let it drop every few moments to wonder what Germaine was doing and what he could do to bring her round. He shouldn't have lied about Louise. To Germaine, who was so truthful, it would seem a denial of their trust in each other. He should have told her every-thing at once. But Louise was too near at the time, she kept appearing and reappearing. He had to lie about her, or so he thought, and after the first lie, he had to keep on lying.

But what trouble it had brought. Germaine was not strong enough to be upset like this. He felt he had harmed her, destroyed her faith in him and fallen from her good opinion, which had, of course, been impossibly high, but which had made him proud all the same.

The log fire fell into grey ash. He was too taken up with anxiety and self-reproach to think of putting more wood on. The room grew cold. He roused himself about midnight and went upstairs.

He listened at the door of the room where his wife and son were and was relieved to hear nothing. The baby must have settled at last. He went to the yellow room and got into the large bed he had never slept in before. It was comfortable enough, but it was a long time before he fell asleep.

He woke suddenly. The baby was screaming. He sprang out of bed and seized his dressing-gown. She must open that door now. It was serious.

But the door was already open and she was calling: 'Paul! Come quickly. Paul!'

'What is it? What's the matter with him?'

'I don't know, I don't know.'

The baby was violently sick. Then he seemed to collapse, his eyes rolling up, in a way that terrified his parents.

'Give him to me,' said Paul. 'While you put your dressing-gown on. You're shivering. Then I'll ring up the doctor.'

'Don't move him. Put my dressing-gown round me. Go and telephone at once. Oh, Blessed Virgin, don't let anything happen to him! Run, Paul.'

It seemed to take a long time to waken the doctor, but when he answered at last, he said he would come at once. He had only a couple of streets to cross. Paul set the front door open and ran upstairs to tell Germaine he was coming.

She was standing where he left her, her dressing-gown fallen to the floor, and from her face he saw that, in the few minutes he had been away, the baby was worse.

'What is it?' he asked sharply.

'I don't know. Don't touch him.'

Paul picked up the dressing-gown and wrapped it round her. He held it in place with his arms and together they lived through an age of fear and aching love, not moving, their eyes straining for a sign of life in their child.

The front door closed, the doctor came quickly up the stairs and into the room. He lifted the baby's eyelid, then listened to the heart without a word.

'Is he – breathing?' Germaine said with difficulty.

'Yes,' said the doctor. ' Just.'

He opened his case.

'I'm going to give him an injection. What have you been doing to him? He's completely exhausted and at his age he can't stand that. Has he been sick for long?'

'He vomited up his last two feeds,' said Germaine.

'And he's had violent diarrhoea, I suppose? Do you realise that this is a very young baby and that you can't play tricks with his stomach like that? You ought to have sent for me at once,' said the doctor severely.

Germaine stood until the injection had been made. Then she swayed on her feet.

'Paul, take him . . . I feel faint . . .'

The doctor swiftly took the baby.

'Get her into bed, Paul. Cover her warmly. She's cold. What's that in that flask? Hot milk? Excellent. You see that tube of tablets on the top of my case? Crush one up and give it to her in the milk. And then go down and telephone to the clinic and ask if Sister Monica can come at once. For the next two or three days. Your wife must rest. What has she been doing to upset herself and her milk like this?'

'It's my fault,' said Paul.

'Then you ought to be ashamed of yourself,' said Doctor Lemaire.

'I am,' said Paul.

'Well, go down and get through to the clinic. If Sister Monica can't come, get Sister Marie-des-Anges, and then get your car out and go and fetch her. Germaine, don't worry any more. The child'll be all right.'

Within the hour, the house was quiet. The doctor was gone, the fire made up and Sister Monica installed with the baby, now sleeping. Germaine, as ordered by the doctor, had removed to the yellow room with Paul. In the big bed, he held her close in his arms to warm her. She still had fits of shivering, as much from nervous tension as from chill. In spite of all he could do, she would not stop talking.

'I hated her, Paul,' she said. 'I was terribly jealous. She's so much more attractive than I am. You must have loved her.'

He thought of denying this to comfort her. But there had been too much dishonesty. There must be nothing but the truth between them now.

'Yes, I loved her in the only way I was capable of then,' he said.

'But you do love me now, don't you?'

'You know I love you,' he said, tightening his arms. 'I've never loved anyone as I love you. You're my wife, you're part of me. You know that.'

'Yes, I do really,' she admitted, her wet cheek against his.

She was quiet for a moment, then she began again.

'You think he'll be all right, don't you? You think he'll be better in the morning?'

'The doctor was quite confident he would.'

'Ever since he was born, he's been so good. He's come on so well. I should never forgive myself if he had a set-back now because of me.'

'Because of me, you mean,' said Paul. 'It's given me a bad fright,' he said, in a moment. 'I didn't expect that old affair to rear up out of the past and make you and the baby ill.'

'But isn't it queer,' said Germaine thoughtfully, 'how everything is somehow *connected*?'

'It is,' said Paul gravely.

There was more connected than he knew. He didn't feel he had treated Louise badly in any way. Affairs of that sort were a commonplace. They all had to end. She seemed to have done very well for herself. What he reproached himself with was that he had lied to his wife. It had provoked a scene that might have killed his son. He thanked God that he had escaped such a terrible punishment for what he thought of as a very venial sin.

He had never heard of the Norths, far away in England. He would have been amazed at the suggestion that he, at such a distance, could have had anything to do with the breaking-up of that family. He had no idea that it was, in great measure, because of him that the man he had seen on the pavement in front of the Hôtel de l'Ecu that afternoon had lost everything he cared about.

CHAPTER THIRTY-TWO

Christmas was over. It went off very well. Ellen herself felt far better than she expected to. She was like a shipwrecked mariner who, though he has no hope of going home any more, is nevertheless humbly grateful to find himself on land at all.

Anne had arrived at Somerton two days before Christmas. To her mother's anxious eyes, she seemed older and quieter, but very different from the unhappy girl who had gone back to school in September. The fact that Roma was there to welcome her seemed almost to make up for everything. Christmas, Anne felt, was going to be good after all, and at once set about the decoration of the house. It was something she felt she ought to do for the old ladies, but it turned out to be a great satisfaction to herself.

'Such scope here,' she said from the top of an immensely tall pair of steps, watched by an admiring and exclamatory group below.

Hugh came on leave and plunged at once into carpentry in the old laundry. Anne joined him. Ellen was amazed by their enthusiasm for their new home. As if it could ever be anything but a makeshift little place after Netherfold. But to them it was an adventure. It was theirs, they felt responsible for it. They felt responsible for their mother too. She must be looked after. She must be protected from 'him'.

Ellen was touched by their new care for her, but she was, all the same, secretly appalled by the ruthlessness with which they had cut Avery out of their lives. She was glad they had been able to do it, she was relieved, but she was also appalled.

Hugh's leave was soon over, but Anne had still ten days of holiday left. Her mother noticed that she talked quite easily about going back to school now. No silences and aching smiles now, and again Ellen's feelings were mixed. She was glad, but rather wistful too.

It was the middle of January now, a fine cold Wednesday morning. Ellen, who had half an hour off before serving lunch, came out of the porch in her old coat, the belt hanging, to cut sprigs of winter jasmine for the tables. Jasmine was all there was at present; soon there would be winter aconites and snowdrops, floods of gold and white under the trees; then daffodils, then primroses and violets – as Anne said, such lots of everything. In the intervals of cutting the jasmine, Ellen looked speculatively at the unused orangery. As soon as she could she must do something there. What plants and flowers for the house she could grow! Without her being aware of it, the interest and pleasure of life, of sheer living, was beginning to reassert itself in her.

From where she was, she could see Anne cantering about the park on Roma. As she came through the hall, she had seen the old ladies collected at the windows on that side of the house to watch.

The little cat, who knew mysteriously when Ellen was in the garden, appeared beside her. Moppet had settled sufficiently at Somerton by this time to clatter her nut, brought from Netherfold, about the hall in the evenings, affording as much sport to the old ladies as to herself. She had been an imperious little creature enough before she came to Somerton, but now she had a larger court. She was never without a knee to sit upon, all knitting being laid aside to accommodate her.

When a car drove suddenly into the gravel sweep, Ellen kept her back turned for a moment to run, in her mind's eye, over the contents of the larder. She was responsible for lunch to-day and she hadn't expected outsiders. The newly-erected board on the main road must be responsible for these arrivals, she supposed. She must go in and fill up more pastry cases quickly and put those two soups together to make a mine-strone. With grated cheese served separately. Having decided this, she turned to greet the man and woman who had left their car and were walking towards her.

Avery and Louise stood within two yards of her. Avery. She only saw Avery. All she thought of was to get away from him. She backed into the porch and started to close the door. Then she flung it wide open and went to him.

'Go away,' she said vehemently. 'Go at once. How dare you come here?'

'Ellen,' he stammered. 'Ellen, I'd no idea you were here.'

'You must have known,' she said roughly.

'I didn't know. You must believe me,' he insisted. 'Ellen . . .'

'Why did you come then?' said Ellen challengingly.

'I had to go to Netherfold about the sale. We hadn't had anything to eat this morning. We saw the board. That's all. I didn't think anybody would recognise me here – I've only been once. That's how it was. You must believe me, Ellen.'

She stared at him, her heart hammering. He was so changed, thin, haggard. She swallowed visibly and said again, but without the vehemence: 'You must go. Anne mustn't see you. She's there.' She put out a hand blindly in the direction of the park.

Avery looked, then stepped quickly back out of sight.

'She mustn't see me,' he said.

But he tried to see her. He stood there, craning to see her, and just then she cantered across his view, laughing, her bright hair flying. He turned back to Ellen with his eyes full of tears.

'Is she all right?' he said.

'She seems to be,' said Ellen, speaking to him reluctantly. 'But it will be all undone if she sees you now.'

'Yes,' said Avery. 'I must go.'

But he didn't go. He stepped back out of Anne's sight and said humbly from a distance, 'Are you staying here, Ellen?'

'I live here,' she said. 'I work here.'

Miss Daley, coming to find Ellen, appeared suddenly in the doorway. She gasped at the incredible situation, and without being seen by either Ellen or Avery, withdrew into the porch again. The little cat who had bolted in when the car arrived now came out and made an ecstatic discovery of Avery. She rubbed round his ankles, looking up into his face and waiting to be picked up. But he didn't notice her either. His eyes were intent on Ellen.

'Avery,' said Louise sharply, 'this is all very well, but I'm hungry. This is an hotel and I demand to be served. Your former wife must keep away from the dining-room if she doesn't wish to see us. I'm going in.'

She moved towards the house, but Avery turned swiftly.

'If you go in there,' he said, 'you'll get away as best you can, because I shall drive off and leave you.'

Ellen stared at him in amazement. This wasn't the voice of a lover. It was the voice of cold dislike. As Louise walked haughtily back to the car, Ellen said in spite of herself: 'Aren't you happy then?'

Avery laughed shortly.

'Happy? I'm wretched. How could I be anything else – away from you all?'

They stared at each other, he compelling her to realise his desperate situation, she aghast and bewildered.

'Avery,' called Louise from the car. 'You said you were going. So let us go.'

'Ellen, come here where Anne can't see us,' pleaded Avery. 'For five minutes, Ellen. Then I'll go and you need never see me again.'

She went with reluctance. There had been too much already. 'Not again – not more,' she protested mutely.

The little cat galloped happily after them into the walk between the yew hedges.

'I wish you hadn't come,' said Ellen in a strangled voice. 'I could have managed. I was managing. But if you're unhappy, that makes something else to be borne. Though why it should, I don't know,' she said, hardening herself against him.

'Oh, Ellen,' he said. 'What a mess I've made of everything.'

'You have. Why did you marry her if you didn't love her? But I suppose you did love her when you married her.'

'Of course I didn't,' said Avery harshly. 'But I couldn't come back home, could I? I never can come home, so long as Anne's there.'

'No, you can't,' said Ellen sternly. 'Anne's life must be kept clear at all costs – to me or to you.'

'I know,' said Avery with all his heart. 'But will you try not to hate me, darling? Can you ever forgive me, do you think?'

This was too much for Ellen. A great swollen wave of misery engulfed her. She felt blindly for her handkerchief.

'Oh, I wish you hadn't come. I could have managed if I hadn't seen you. Now I see you I find I don't hate you at all. . . .'

'Oh, Ellen . . . if you knew what it means to me to hear you say that. To think I haven't damaged you all beyond repair . . . it's just like you, the dearest truest . . .' he said incoherently.

'Why did you rush into marrying her?' wept Ellen. 'We're divorced now. Why did you do it?'

'She had to go home,' said Avery. 'She had to be able to go back to her parents. But they wouldn't have her when she got there. They're strict Catholics and they say she isn't married. I never saw them and now I don't know what to do about her. I can't live with her. It's impossible. I don't like her. But that is my problem. I must work out my own salvation. But I'll be better now I've seen you. I'll pull up now. I'm going to try to get some sort of a job in father's factory. You'll keep in touch with me, won't you, darling? And try to meet me sometimes and tell me how you're going on and everything. Is Anne really all right? I can look at her from here. She can't see me.'

The little cat, tired of being unnoticed, chose this moment to make a sudden spring at him. He was obliged to gather her up and let her sit on his arm with her paws on his shoulder as she used to do. He stroked her almost violently to keep himself in countenance and smiled apologetically at Ellen for this demonstration of affection on Moppet's part.

Ellen found the situation unbearably poignant – Avery so close to her, looking through the hedge at Anne because he mustn't be seen by her, and the cat the only one to welcome him.

In the car, Louise, furious at being kept waiting, and for such a reason, was doing up her face in a savage sort of way, pressing her lips together to put lipstick on, putting powder on and taking it off again, brushing her eyelashes upwards.

Round the edge of the door in the stone porch, a pair of glasses kept appearing and disappearing. Miss Daley wasn't spying on the two in the double hedge, she was looking at Louise. Somebody ought to go and tell her off, Miss Daley considered. She oughtn't to be let get away with it. Somebody ought to avenge Mrs. Avery.

'There's nobody to do it but me,' said Miss Daley. 'I've had it in for her for a long time. I'm going.'

She emerged from the porch and marched over the gravel to the car. Louise, intent on the glass in her compact, didn't see her until Miss Daley thrust her face in at the open window beside her.

'Good morning,' said Miss Daley, with heavy sarcasm.

Louise was startled. She looked as if she couldn't believe her eyes.

'What are you doing here?' she said harshly, powder-puff suspended.

'What are you doing here is more to the point,' said Miss Daley. 'Pushing in, upsetting Mrs. Avery again after it's nearly broken her heart leaving her home, which you've stolen from her same as you've stolen her husband. You don't know what shame is,' said Miss Daley breathlessly, getting as much said as she could. 'You wormed yourself in at The Cedars and got money left you, and you repay the old lady by smashing up her son's life. Because it's as plain as a pikestaff he doesn't want you,' said Miss Daley, pointing to the hedge. 'But you're getting as much out of him as you can, poshing yourself up in fur coats and pearl necklaces . . .'

'What's going on here?' called an angry voice from the steps. 'Where is everybody? It's not my job to dish-up and serve to-day that I know of. I've just come down to find the pies on the burn . . .'

'Oh, Mrs. Beard,' cried Miss Daley, skittering over the gravel. 'Just a minute. Hush, do! See!'

'Who is it?' said Mrs. Beard, all interest. 'Who's that?' She looked round Miss Daley at Louise in the car.

'It's the co-respondent,' said Miss Daley, and Louise heard her. 'It's the woman that stole Mrs. Avery's husband.'

'Well, I never,' said Mrs. Beard, advancing for a closer

view. 'She looks like it. She may have got him to marry her, but she looks a tart still. You can take my word for it, because I've seen plenty.'

Louise flung open the car door and got swiftly out.

'Avery!' she called out. 'Avery! These women insult me. *Avery!*'

He came quickly. Not to protect her who was more than able to protect herself, but to prevent her from attracting Anne's attention. He thrust her back unceremoniously into the car.

'Be quiet,' he said sternly, and got in himself.

He started the engine, and in turning the car round, brought it up beside Ellen.

'Ellen,' he said. 'I have to go, but what a difference you have made to me, darling . . .'

Louise, white with anger, leaned forward and pressed her finger on the horn.

Avery struck her hand away, and with a last look at Ellen, swept swiftly round the gravel and out of the gates.

'What a bitch,' said Mrs. Beard. 'Still, he asked for it, poor chap.'

Ellen stood stiffly, her lips pressed together, her eyes brimming with tears.

'It's a bit thick,' said Mrs. Beard. 'Now she's got this to get over, as if she hadn't enough. Don't come in yet, medea. Me and Miss Daley will serve up. You don't want to look as if anything's wrong when Anne comes in. I'll keep the gong back a few minutes. Walk about inside the hedge for a bit.'

Ellen turned and went back under the yews.

'That was a trap,' said Louise furiously as they drove away. 'You went there on purpose.'

'You know very well I didn't want to go there,' said Avery. 'It was you who insisted when you saw the board.'

'You are quite capable of pretending you didn't want to go.'

'I wouldn't trouble to pretend,' he said coldly.

'You troubled to pretend to your wife for weeks on end,' said Louise. 'You weren't so particular then.'

He wasn't listening to her. For him, her barb was drawn. Ellen had forgiven him. His children never would, he knew; but Ellen had forgiven him. In those few moments, she had given him hope and purpose. He would redeem himself. He could, now that he had something to work for. She was the harmony of his life. What a disordered existence he had led without her. If it took years – and it would, until Anne had settled in a life of her own – he would wait and hope to get back to Ellen.

Louise, seeing him smile as he drove, clenched her teeth. She hated him. She could have beaten him with her fists. He had let his wife insult her by never once looking at her. She might not have been there, the way that woman had treated her. Then he allowed those two servants to add their insults, then he had insulted her himself by calling his wife "darling" and crying over her.

She hated him. She wanted to burst out and tell him so, she wanted to abuse him and tell him that he bored her, that the English bored her, England bored her. She wanted to tell him that she was going back to Paris, to get a flat there, to live in France, but not with him. He would have to compensate her. She had lost her home and her parents because of him. He would have to keep her for the rest of her life. But she clenched her teeth and said nothing. To hear that she would leave him was precisely what he wanted. So he shouldn't hear. The whole business must be carefully manœuvred, so that she could get out of it with the greatest advantage to herself. She could divorce him any time she wished for refusal to co-habit. But she would bide her own time. A nice thing for him to be divorced twice!

So sitting beside him in silence on the way to London, she smiled too; though differently.

* * *

At Somerton the gong went. Ellen went to the ha-ha dividing the garden from the park to wave her handkerchief to Anne, who was sauntering on Roma down by the stream and out of hearing. Ellen held the handkerchief aloft and the wind dried the tears out of it. She felt very tired. The painfully achieved repairs to her life were all broken down. A great rush of love and compassion had swept them away. Now she must start again and it all seemed chaotic and impossible. For years to come, she would be torn between Avery and the children. She must never let them know that he was waiting for them to go so that he could come back. At the thought that they might ever get an inkling of that she winced with pain. Strangely enough, it seemed, at this moment, as if it would take more courage to live knowing that Avery wanted to come back than it would have taken to live with no hope of it.

But she had learnt something from those last lonely weeks at Netherfold. She had learnt to wait for the changes and the help that life brings. Life is like the sea, sometimes you are in the trough of the wave, sometimes on the crest. When you are in the trough, you wait for the crest, and always, trough or crest, a mysterious tide bears you forward to an unseen, but certain shore.

In the meantime, the first thing to be done was to go in and take over her work from Mrs. Beard. Anne had seen the handkerchief at last and waved in reply.

Ellen hurried into the house to the downstairs cloakroom to remove the traces of tears as best she could with her powder-puff. In a moment, Anne burst in, all freshness and breathlessness.

'You've got here very quickly,' said her mother.

'Well, first I ran,' said Anne, pulling off her riding boots. 'Then I jumped the ha-ha.'

'Anne, you didn't!' cried Ellen in astonishment. 'It's so wide and deep.'

'Doesn't matter,' said Anne, laughing with pleasure at her triumphant leap. 'I knew I'd get across.'

Ellen smiled. But this youthful confidence was catching. Already she was being lifted by the swell of the mysterious sea. Creeping into her heart was the realisation that, although she could not be with him, Avery was restored to her.

Persephone Books publishes the following titles: